A SAGA OF LIFE AND ROMANCE IN AN ENGLISH VILLAGE

Beatrice Emily Beisley

? Pen name of Stella's brother (Loader)
his mother's maiden name?

MINERVA PRESS
MONTREUX LONDON WASHINGTON

A SAGA OF LIFE AND ROMANCE IN AN ENGLISH VILLAGE

ISBN 1 85863 563 2

First published 1996 by
MINERVA PRESS
1 Cromwell Place,
London SW7 2JE

Printed in Great Britain by
B.W.D. Ltd., Northolt, Middlesex.

A SAGA OF LIFE AND ROMANCE IN AN ENGLISH VILLAGE

All characters in this book are fictional, and any resemblance to any person, living or dead, is purely coincidental.

I wish to record my grateful thanks to Margaret Loder; for without her prodigious help, the book could not have been submitted.

I dedicate this book to all women wherever they may be.

Chapter 1

Tillingthorpe was a village set in the vale of the White Horse in the county of Berkshire.

It had, like all English villages, evolved in its local disposition, moulded by the feudal manorial system instigated by the Saxons.

The Enclosure of Land Act 1803 had ensured that it would be forever encapsulated in an environment exceedingly fertile and beautiful; its hedgerows thick with dog roses in July, its meadow land dappled with lady-smocks, cowslips, ox-eye daisies, all appearing with magical regularity in the season appointed by Mother Nature.

The woodlands, spinneys, and copses, were illuminated by the heavenly blue of masses of bluebells, their perfume attracting a veritable invasion of bumble-bees, honey bees, hoverflies, and many other winged insects, all industriously probing the bell-like flowers where nature told them an inexhaustible supply of nectar awaited their tiny, searching, harvesting tongues.

Tillingthorpe was of mixed types of architecture. Some typical Cotswold houses of grey stone with shingle tiles - the others of Berkshire brick, flint and thatch - clustered round the Norman church.

The village had a population of four hundred souls. Many of the families had inevitably intermarried producing the usual crop of weakly and mentally retarded children. The church register recorded centuries of Bakers, Wilsons, Chapmans, Clarkes, Whites, names the vicar was often required to inscribe in his scholarly hand on baptismal certificates, church records of marriages, and, sadly, deaths.

The forbears of these stalwart yeomen and rustic craftsmen were the bowmen who fought with Edward III at Crecy in 1346, with Edward at Poitiers in 1356, with Henry V at Agincourt in 1415 and the present generation of these remarkable - but not rare - Englishmen had recently fought in the most terrible, the most horrendous conflict known since the human race was created – the great war of 1914–1918.

In the local pub they met in long winter evenings bonded into a silent comradeship, which only men who have suffered the unspeakable horrors of trench warfare would fully comprehend. The games of dominoes and crib were conducted in almost complete silence, their thoughts flickered like the flames in the fire which blazed in the large grate prompting their imagination to see again the men who had never returned but would never be forgotten.

A printed notice on the wall at the side of the bar, announced that whist drives and other social activities would be organised immediately to raise money to defray the cost of erecting a War Memorial; design to be decided at a parish meeting.

Strong opinions had already revealed a divergence of views throughout the village. Some (including the vicar, the Reverend Sebastian Erasmus Copplethwaite M.A. (Oxon.)), favoured a stained glass window. Others stated a strong preference for a statue of a private soldier leaning on reversed arms in the military ceremonial attitude of mourning.

The more ambitious inhabitants clamoured for nothing less than the building of a Memorial Hall, which, as they pointed out would be of great service to the coming generations and might even provide a source of revenue, which was a cue to inform their doubting audience that this income could be utilised for the acquisition and equipping of a football field, a long desired requirement of the village school.

Others favoured a simple vertical stone cross surmounted by a steel sword on north and south faces; the whole edifice to stand on a substantial stone plinth bearing the names of the fifty men who left their homes never to return. This was the design favoured by the survivors and was, incidentally, the least costly.

However, all were agreed that the matter should now be regarded as of great urgency; after all, it was now two years since the signing of the armistice on November 11th 1918.

A committee was duly appointed to expedite all decisions to ensure completion. The meeting then dispersed to continue their vociferous arguments in The Beldrake Arms known to all as The Red Lion, because the arms portrayed a lion rampant on a white field.

The Red Lion appeared to be an elongated structure with a massive porch; in reality, further investigation revealed two wings extending from the south wall and including stabling for five horses. The east wing comprised a dairy with further bedrooms above. The west wing housed a spacious harness room where the air was redolent with the pleasing smell of leather. Above was a rat-proof grain store.

This enclosure was entered by a massive stone and brick archway which pierced the west wing. The whole area was cobbled by large flints garnered from some unknown beach.

The interior of the inn was a maze of passages and alcoves with so many cupboards that one was almost overwhelmed with a burning curiosity to discover what was hidden in their dark capacious interiors.

Glass cases mounted high under the ceiling sported a diverse collection of weasels, otters, even that rarity a pine marten; a sinister looking pike and various birds, a corncrake, a woodcock, all incarcerated in their lonely crystal chambers. A large tawny owl, with a watchful, feline, unblinking stare, gazed down upon the comings and goings into the Bar Parlour; the only bird endowed with the eyes of an animal.

In the public bar, the only adornment was a large painting over the mantelpiece of the greatest racing filly of all time, Pretty Polly. She ran in twenty-two races and was unbeaten in twenty-one of them.

A fox mask, mounted over the door giving access to the public bar, its lips drawn back to reveal its formidable array of fangs, was, according to popular legend, killed on the cobbled apron in front of the porch in 1804.

One high-backed pine settle was placed at right angles to the fire; a small table, black with age, polished and preserved by the spillings from countless mugs of ale, was ensconced in a recess to the right of the bar. A right-angled oak bench seat in the corner and a window seat completed the furnishings.

At the back of the bar a row of oak barrels rested on the trestles and good English ale gushed from their wooden taps when requested, to quench the thirst of men who toiled ten hours a day in the fields and longer in harvest time. Men like Amos Hollingsworth, the stockman, Dick Lee and Chalky White, ploughmen, together with the two carters, Joe Johnson and Will Cox. These sturdy yeomen were but the nucleus of families whose ancestors had tilled this land three hundred years ago.

Then there was the wheelwright, Bert Wilson, and Timber Woods, the joiner, whose duties also included coffin maker and undertaker. Bill Copeland, the blacksmith, perhaps the most interesting and humorous of them all, had served throughout the war as a farrier sergeant in the Royal Engineers. When he unbuckled his thick leather apron and draped it over his anvil at the end of the day his steps would unerringly take him directly to The Red Lion.

Joshua Humphrey, the landlord, knew exactly what time Bill would arrive to slake his thirst and always had two pots ready to draw two foaming pints of ale immediately Bill's bulky form cast its shadow on the flags through the open door. Bill, with equal alacrity, would put down fourpence for the two pints of beer. Raising one of the mugs he would drain it without pausing for breath, feeling his whole body soaking up the fluid as sand in the desert soaks up a precious water spillage.

Joshua was the fourth generation of Humphreys to keep The Red Lion. He walked with a pronounced limp, having sustained a severe shrapnel wound in his right leg at Passchendaele. His great-grandfather, grandfather, and father had always served in the military; indeed, his great-grandfather, Samuel, had lost an arm at Waterloo having sustained a bone-shattering wound inflicted by a ball from a Frenchman's musket. When these gruesome and agonising operations were performed by the so-called surgeons, often recruited from barbers, the only anaesthetic was a leather pad for the victim to bite on, accompanied by a stiff ration of rum.

His grandfather, Herbert, had survived the Crimean War and had emerged comparatively unscathed, apart from a Russian sabre slash which had left a livid eight inch scar running vertically down his back from his shoulder - luckily - parallel to his spine.

His father, Thomas Humphrey, had fought in South Africa in both the Zulu and Boer Wars and lived to tell his children of his exploits in many blood curdling clashes with magnificent black warriors who fought their battles with a deadly long bladed spear known as an *assegai* and a club with a spherical knob named a *knobkerrie*.

He would speak of the epic battle of Rorkes Drift, where B Company of the 2/24th Regiments of Foot (which later became the South Wales Borderers Regiment and the Warwickshire Regiment) covered themselves in glory in the bloody hand to hand fighting and won eleven VCs. Their names and exploits will be recorded in letters of gold in the annals of history.

The Zulus also fought heroically in stubborn defence of their homeland; qualities in their character hitherto unknown and therefore unappreciated, emerged after the battle; the qualities of gallantry and magnanimity.

Now to Joshua Humphrey who had served in the Royal Berkshire Regiment, whose epic march from Kabul to Kandahar is commemorated by a magnificent memorial in the Forbury Gardens, Reading. Joshua continued the family tradition of inn-keeping.

Apart from the blacksmith, the wheelwright and the joiner, there was also a village shop, where one could buy goods of such variety that only by frequent visits to the store could one learn what was really available. The shop was also a meeting place for the village wives, who flitted in and out like a colony of bees.

"AUNT HAZEL'S FATHER - MAJOR MORLEY TOOK PART IN THIS MARCH

These frequent gatherings were presided over by the elderly Mrs. Howkins, the proprietor, who – being slightly deaf – would cock her head to one side in a curious bird-like mannerism to catch every detail of the spicy exchanges she could sense in the muted voices of the small cluster of women, only two of whom would be there to make a purchase.

The village wives would often gather in the shop mid-morning to gossip and exchange notes about their respective husbands and Mrs. Howkins could scent a scandal as hounds scent the pungent, acrid odour of a fox.

Mrs. Howkins had always insisted vehemently that only she knew the true identity of the father of Kate Farrel's illegitimate son, Timothy, who was an indentured apprentice to Timber Woods, who had the responsibility of ensuring that Timothy would – in seven years time – be respected as a fully skilled journeyman tradesman.

There was a great deal of conjecture concerning Timothy's real father; many of the inhabitants of Tillingthorpe were of the opinion that a certain Peregrine Albert Rudolf Devereaux, son of the Very Reverend Paul Archibald Yule Devereaux, Esquire, B.A. D.D. (Cantab.) who was the incumbent of the richly endowed living of St. Mary's church in the prosperous town of Wantage.

So strong and widespread were these insinuations that the Reverend gentleman inserted in *The Wantage Clarion* a notice, informing all people known to be perpetuating these libellous and scurrilous rumours, that they would be pursued with the full rigour of the law.

In spite of these dire threats, discussion was discreetly continued in the sheltered gatherings in Tillingthorpe. After all, Kate Farrel was a very comely girl with a cloud of auburn hair cascading down in soft waves over her elegant shoulders; she was also highly intelligent and quite artistic. She worked in a high class milliners shop in Sheep Street, Wantage.

Although Timothy had been born in Abingdon poor law infirmary, expensive flowers had been sent to Kate with a card with the letter P on it. When the curious nurses questioned her as to the identity of the sender, Kate first smiled and pleaded ignorance.

Information concerning these events filtered back to Tillingthorpe by word of mouth, where further mysteries concerning Kates son awaited a solution.

Kate was born in the village and had attended the local school until she was fourteen years old. Her father was the village cobbler, having learned his trade in the army. He was also an ambitious man who was well aware that he could treble his earnings if he set up shop in Abingdon. This ambition was eventually achieved. His old cottage was now occupied by Ted Turner the young cowman at Home Farm.

This digression does not, I fear, solve the two remaining mysteries that, up to the present, were still unexplained. For example, why was Kate immediately rehoused in Cock-a-Dobbie cottage, belonging to the Church? 'Cock-a-Dobbie' is an ancient Saxon expression meaning 'Where Fairies Dwell'. Lastly, who paid the five golden sovereigns to Timber Woods to defray the legal article fees?

Kate, revelling in the exasperation and intense curiosity of her neighbours, would only respond to their persistent enquiries with a radiant smile and say, "My Tim has good blood in his veins." Such response only served to inflame their insatiable desire to know who really was Timothy's father. It was like putting a torch to a dry straw rick.

Martha Howkins had been widowed in the Boer War and left with two little boys, and having lost the support of her husband, faced up to her desperate situation with the courage and fortitude displayed by women of that era. She was sternly resolute in her determination that her small brood would never go hungry nor unshod. She was – fortunately – in good health and physically capable of doing field work, of which there was an abundance. Mangold pulling, potato picking, hoeing, singling; all this was extremely laborious work. Martha, while preoccupied with these wearisome activities, gave thought to the day when her ageing body would no longer cope with the long hours and the assault on her female physique.

Her son Amos, now fourteen, had joined the Royal Navy. George, the elder by a year and a half, had left home to join the Grenadier Guards as a drummer boy. Although she missed them about the home (they were good boys) and felt terribly the dreadful heartache she concealed from the world so stoically, she decided to open a village store to compete with the shop in the neighbouring village of Copthorpe. She also intended to apply to the postmaster in Wantage to allow her to designate a small part of her shop as a post office.

Her cottage was the largest in the village, having been, originally, the house of the head gamekeeper on the Beldrake estate. Gamekeepers normally had large families, most of whom would be absorbed by the estate as gamekeepers, foresters, ploughmen or carters. The daughters would enter the Big House - as the mansion was called - as parlour maids who would, one day, become cooks or housekeepers with enormous responsibilities.

The room at the front of Martha's cottage was approximately fifteen feet long and ten feet wide. A second-hand counter was obtained from the joiner who agreed to deliver it and install it for twenty-five shillings. Martha had now received approval to take on the postal duties and a man would be sent over to instruct her. The salary would be twenty seven shillings and sixpence per week and would be reviewed every two years.

Since her sons had left home and were no longer a drain on her meagre resources she had saved one hundred pounds, more than sufficient to build up a stock that she knew from experience would command a ready sale.

Martha could now relinquish the punishing field work and remain snug in her own home never again to endure the cruel exposure of bad weather. Her post office salary would keep her in food and the cash taken in the shop would clothe her and allow for stock replacement.

The residue would provide for the day when she would become old and infirm.

After four years of hard but congenial work, Martha was a prosperous shop keeper and her prosperity had been further enhanced by a substantial weekly order from the Big House collected by one of the grooms in a pony and trap. The cook at Highfield Farm also placed a regular order for such requirements as flour, salt, pepper, nutmegs, cinnamon, bottles of sauce, rice, tapioca, mustard, and so on.

The years passed and a new crop of children played in the school playground; the little girls with their skipping ropes chanted rhythmic rhymes that their mothers and grandmothers had chanted long years ago. The boys played football and became so engrossed in games of marbles or tic-tac that they were afflicted with a sudden loss of hearing and ignored the hand bell rung so vigorously by the youthful monitor. Only the stentorian authoritarian bellowing of the headmaster could browbeat them into a submissive return to their irksome studies.

It was now March in the year 1930 and the hedgerows were spattered with that unfailing herald of spring, the blackthorn.

A great air of sadness was perceived among the older folk in the village. The sad news that Caleb, the shepherd, had been found dead in his small hut high on the downs. The tragic event had been made known, firstly to Joshua at The Red Lion, who would, in due course, inform other men regarded as the village elders, who would in turn inform the womenfolk.

Caleb was one of the few shepherds to continue wearing the traditional smock. Forty-five years ago, when he had become betrothed to Rose, the pretty, comely dairy maid, she had already purchased a bale of linen, sufficient to make her beloved Caleb three smocks neatly pleated in the traditional Berkshire pattern; the women of every county stitching their own unique design. Two were for daily use and one for special occasions, like going to Church on Sunday, attending christenings and the like, but the most important festival would be the Michaelmas Fair in Abingdon, where, once a year, he would enjoy several mugs of ale in The Horse and Groom talking to other down land shepherds, whom he only met twice a year, once at the Fair and again at the sale of lambs in the spring.

The bailiff at Home Farm gave orders to John Waring, the carter, to prepare the best haywain for Caleb's funeral. John Waring scrubbed the wain with a stiff yard broom; he then spread fresh ivy and newly cut reeds like a carpet on the floor timbers of the hay cart; black ribbons were fastened to the brow band of the bridle which the selected shire horse would wear.

The vicar, the Reverend Sebastian Erasmus Copplethwaite had already called on Caleb's widow to convey the condolences of the parish to her family and to select hymns. Funerals, in those days, were solemn and sombre ceremonies and anything less than three hymns would be regarded as disrespectful to the deceased.

Their first choice was 'We plough the fields and scatter'. The second, Caleb's favourite, 'All things bright and beautiful' and lastly 'The Lord is my shepherd'.

Caleb had died suddenly of heart failure; he was seventy years of age and his passing was as he would have wished; in the midst of his beloved flock. It was thought that the shepherd was making his customary evening check on the lambing ewes.

His much lamented death had occurred on Monday evening; his funeral would, therefore, take place three days later on the Thursday. On the appointed day, at least two hundred people turned out to make their own sad farewells to one of their own, whom they had always loved and respected for his kindness and wisdom; only men who live in close daily contact with the miracles of nature acquire this profound knowledge. Only when asked did the old shepherd give others the benefit of his many hours, nay, years of contemplation of the frail human race and its many weaknesses with all its perpetual problems.

Caleb firmly believed in God, Heaven and an After Life. He did not need the Parson to convince him there was a place called Heaven.

When Caleb sat down at midday under the lee of a grassy bank he would gaze down into the valley where the smoke from the cottage was scattered into puffs of cotton wool by the fish tailing wind. When his keen appetite had been satisfied by the chunk of cheese and crusty freshly baked bread, followed by a generous wedge of home-made fruit cake, all washed down by a flagon of cold sweet tea, the old shepherd would allow his memories to dominate his thoughts. He would recall the days when he was courting and saving every penny for his marriage. He would call to mind vividly the harvests of hay and corn when friends and neighbours would respond to the cry to get it in before the storm broke.

Now Caleb, the shepherd, was lying in his coffin awaiting the final call from the greatest of all shepherds.

Timber Woods, the village carpenter and joiner, was distantly related to the old man through his wife and was determined to provide Caleb with a coffin fit for a king. He carefully selected nicely grained well-seasoned planks of elm; nothing better than elm wood to keep old Caleb warm and dry.

When the casket was completed and finished with several applications of beeswax, Timber set about preparing a brass plate. He did not have proper engraving tools so ingeniously sharpened a small round file and with remarkable skill etched the following inscription, in neat copperplate writing on the bevelled plate.

HERE LIE THE MORTAL REMAINS OF

CALEB MARTINDALE

FAITHFUL HUSBAND, KIND FATHER

AND THE

GREATEST SHEPHERD BUT ONE.

Timber wanted to ensure that when the Resurrection came, God would be shown the plate and give Caleb a place on the right hand of his throne.

The day of the funeral was very cold with the wind veering to the north-west. The cortège assembled outside Caleb's home; the coffin would be borne by his two sons and four grandsons.

The perfectly marked shire horse, Monarch, with his four white socks and the typical white blaze down his forehead, stood perfectly still as though he knew of the need to be on his best behaviour. Black ribbons had been plaited into his thick mane; he too must show that he, would pay his respects to the passing of a much-loved man.

The pall bearers emerged from the cottage bearing the elm coffin.

The small group clustered at the garden gate were silent and motionless, overcome by the awe that funerals engender.

The coffin slid easily and silently on to the green layer; Caleb's smock was neatly folded lengthways and placed on the polished elm coffin. On top of this was carefully placed his shepherd's crook. It was a Berkshire crook, unlike the open ram's horn crooks of Westmoreland. Caleb's crook was beautifully fashioned from steel by a blacksmith and very narrow in the throat to enable the shepherd to capture or restrain the sheep by either fore or hind leg.

Caleb and his border collie, Nell, were together twenty-four hours a day. At night she slept in a basket at the foot of the old man's bed. When Nell was younger she had saved Caleb from a dangerous bull by sinking her teeth into its nose giving Caleb time to get away.

After the coffin had been placed on the hay cart, Nell leapt up and lay side by side with it. Monarch responded to a touch on the bridle and moved majestically forward to begin the short journey to the Church.

On arrival at the Lych Gate Caleb's sons and grandsons gently slid the massive elm coffin from the haywain and carefully placed it on the mortuary stone, which had been placed there centuries ago for this very purpose.

Caleb was a giant of a man standing over six feet tall with broad shoulders. He must have weighed at least fifteen and a half stone, but the pall bearers were very strong men, cast in the mould of the man they had come to bury.

While the crowd of mourners made their way into the church, the bearers drank the traditional pot of ale before raising the coffin to their sturdy shoulders; then, lead by the vicar, the cortege made its way to the church porch where the sexton awaited.

This sad and solemn procession was followed by Caleb's dog, Nell. Nell bore no resemblance to the mongrel, mud-stained farm dogs, so common in that area. No! Nell was a true border collie, her mother being a pedigree Welsh springer spaniel and her father a pure bred English collie - Nell was a very handsome dog being perfectly marked. Her back and flanks were a beautiful golden colour. Her perfect white ruff cloaked her shoulders and extended on to her chest to ripple in creamy white down her chest making her forelegs all white but she had only white socks on her back legs.

Her matronly rump was surmounted by a magnificent plumy tail with a splash of sooty black on the gold. It was terminated by a gleaming white tip, so precisely marked that one could easily imagine it had been painted on. Her wise brown eyes were set in a well-shaped head and were surrounded by symmetrical brown patches smutched with sooty black. A white line divided these patches and opened out to a pure white muzzle terminating in black, moist, nostrils.

In her fourteen years of life Nell had produced twenty puppies which Caleb, grudgingly, had sold to other shepherds when they were three months old. Nell's uncanny skills with sheep were famed throughout the whole county of Berkshire and consequently there was never any shortage of buyers, eager to give Caleb one gold sovereign (a week's wages) to acquire one of Nell's progeny.

All these twenty sovereigns had been carefully put away by Caleb Martindale in a small leather bag secured at the top with a leather thong and at this very moment nestled in the depths of Caleb's clothes chest, a large wooden box, where the overpowering reek of moth balls protected his best suit and best smock from marauding moths.

This small cache of gold would ensure that his beloved Rose, his help-meet would be kept in warm clothing and be well shod for the rest of her life.

This, then, was the dog which had played such a significant part in her master's long life. All this qualified Nell to be among the chief mourners assembled that day to make their final farewells to this man who forged a noble link with their honest stalwart forbears, many of whom lay in that very churchyard; their names carved on many of the leaning grave-stones by masons long gone.

Dear patient reader, I fear I have allowed my pen to run away with me, but we must make haste and return to the Church.

When the coffin had been placed on the trestles in front of the altar rail, Nell lay down at the feet of Caleb's widow, Rose, her head resting on her forepaws.

After the usual address, exalting the finer virtues of the deceased, followed by a prayer, followed by the two hymns, the organ played the opening bars of the twenty-third psalm and the congregation broke lustily into 'The Lord is my shepherd'.

At these words Nell lifted her head and stared intently at the coffin for a full minute – she then rose to her feet and left the Church.

This strange behaviour did not escape Rose's notice but she never once referred to it.

Nell continued down the path to where Monarch was tethered, crunching crushed oats from a nosebag. Nell sprang up on to the layer of reeds and ivy and settled down to await her mistress.

Monarch blew through his nostrils as horses do when suddenly startled by the unexpected.

Caleb had now been lowered into his final resting place; a tiny posy of primroses and violets lay on the brass plate so neatly inscribed by Timber Woods. It was Rose's last expression of love and grief for the husband who now lay so snugly in his impressive elm coffin. She was not shocked by the depth of the grave for she was well aware that space had to be left for the day when she and Caleb would be re-united. That day, according to Mrs. Copeland and Mrs. Howkins, would not be long delayed.

Rose's sons, after all was over, lifted Caleb's widow up on to the buck board of the hay wain and took her back to her cottage, aptly named The Haven. Nell, still lying on the reeds, leapt down and followed them into the cottage. She drank thirstily from her bowl of water but ignored a tempting dish of food.

That night Rose opened the back door to allow Nell to attend to call of nature. She did not return; and Rose instinctively knew where she had gone.

Nell made her way to the churchyard and located Caleb's grave in the south-east corner of the church, where in daylight, one could see across the valley up on to the downs where Caleb Martindale and his dog Nell had spent so many happy years working together in snow, rain and sunshine. Nell sniffed around the grave, gave a subdued whine, then trotted down the path, leapt over the Lych Gate and followed the track, she knew so well, up on to the downs to Caleb's hut. The door was kept closed by a large stone which Nell easily rolled aside.

The hut contained a rough-hewn chair, hurricane lamp, matches, four candles, a can of oil and a tin box where Caleb kept a ball of string, a knife, two clay pipes, plus a plug of dark strong tobacco. A pile of sacks were neatly folded to give Nell somewhere to rest when they sheltered from the rain. Nell stepped on to her resting place, curled up, and died.

The next morning, Caleb's widow rose at her customary hour of six a.m. Throwing a thick woollen shawl over her head and shoulders she walked down to her son's cottage and requested him to prepare a sack of straw, take a spade and go up to Caleb's hut where he would find Nell lying on a pile of sacks; he was instructed to bury her high up on Glebe Down.

Caleb's two sons, William and Harold Martindale regarded their late father with respect and covert affection; they were still feeling the awful and peculiar sense of loss that always afflicts the bereaved.

These very explicit directions at such an early hour startled William, but over many years, he had become acquainted with his mother's remarkable powers of intuition and to question her orders would be unthinkable. After he had had his breakfast, William proceeded to carry out his mother's bidding.

Twenty minutes later, he made his ascent to Glebe Down and pondering this second grievous task in two days, William entered the hut where his father had spent so many hours of his life and saw Nell lying on the pile of sacks his mother had so accurately described. But how could she possibly have known?

William selected a spot sheltered by the grassy bank where his father would sit and smoke a pipe of tobacco while he ruminated on the changes in the only way of life he had ever known; for example, the raucous stinking tractors which threatened to render the noble shire horses - which had served man so faithfully for so many centuries in peace and war - extinct.

While Caleb was preoccupied with these daily cogitations, Nell would lie very close, occasionally looking up into the old man's face. She was anxious to get back to work; to enjoy the excitement of herding sheep. Caleb never whistled commands to Nell; it simply was not necessary. He would merely point with the staff of his crook and she would know exactly what he wanted her to do.

Proceeding to the foot of the bank William dug a deep hole, placed the sack of straw in the bottom, fetched the body of Nell and gently lowered her into the grave. Afterwards William and his brother, Harold, ordered the village stone mason, Eli Marriot, to lay a protective flag stone on the grave bearing the legend:

HERE LIES CALEB MARTINDALE'S

SHEEP DOG 'Nell'

FAITHFUL UNTO DEATH.

1916 - 1930

A large flock of sheep is not only an exceedingly valuable property, but needs the constant attention of a highly competent shepherd. For two days they had been merely overlooked by the hedger and ditcher, Daniel Hubbard. Septimus Reeve, bailiff to the Beldrakes who owned the flock and the grazing rights, realised the urgency of the new appointment and duly offered the post to Nathanael Martindale, the twenty-four year old grandson of Caleb; he was married to Emma and had a three year old son and was therefore, regarded as a responsible and reliable young man who would continue the family tradition of shepherding. This also pleased the young Viscount Beldrake, who was anxious to continue the policy established by his late father who regarded his servants with considerable benevolence and was always delighted when a father was followed by a son in his chosen trade.

Nine months had elapsed since the old shepherd's death and his widow, Rose, appeared to have little interest in life, not even a visit from her great-grandson, James, whom she adored, could bring a smile to her wan face or a twinkle to her fading eyes. In the evenings, spent alone in her cottage, she would doze off, invariably dreaming of her beloved Caleb, allowing the fire to go unreplenished and the room to become unbearably cold.

Early one morning, when William made his customary check on his mother's welfare he found that she had died – one assumes peacefully in her sleep. The doctor wrote 'Death from natural causes' on her death certificate and in brackets 'Hypothermia.'

Rose had resolutely resisted all attempts by her two sons to get her to live with each of them in turn, but when they became more persuasive she would, very solemnly, say that if she left her home Caleb might stop his evening visits as he would not like the strange house.

Three weeks before Christmas another funeral cortège carried Rose down the aisle of St. Botolph's church and after the service re-united her with Caleb, as the ladies of the village had so confidently predicted in the preceding month of March.

A month later, her grandson moved from his cottage in the centre of the village into The Haven which lay adjacent to the track which led up to the downs.

The Haven had a large garden where Caleb had grown all the vegetables they would need. Rose grew flowers and tended the single bramley apple tree, two Victoria plum trees and a massive white hart cherry tree. All these trees had one thing in common, each was encircled at its base by a broad band of forget-me-nots; each side of the front door a phalanx of hollyhocks stood tall, like sentries guarding a sanctuary. In the corner of the hawthorn hedge, which enclosed the property, a carpet of strong, sweet-smelling lily of the valley flourished, glowing in its garb of virginal white.

This exquisite setting, redolent with nostalgia and ancient Berkshire history, would now be the home of Caleb's grandson Nathanael, and he would doubtless strive to follow the standards of honour and honesty his grandfather had lived by.

Chapter 2

Three years had come and gone in Tillingthorpe and strange events were about to unfold.

Martha Howkins had - in some indefinable way - given signs of being deeply preoccupied with some matter in which she and she alone would be engrossed. No one could really put their finger on a reason for Martha's sudden change of manner. Mrs. Copeland, the blacksmith's wife, had already expressed her gravest concerns to Mrs. Wilson, the wheelwright's spouse and was worried that Martha was becoming weak in the head. Both agreed that it might be Martha's age and if this should be the case what would happen to the business, especially the post office. Their curiosity reached a fever pitch when Joshua Humphrey's wife visited Martha's post office at eight a.m. to find her entry forbidden by a sign conveying the blunt message 'CLOSED'. This was hitherto unheard of, and when this intelligence became public knowledge in The Red Lion that evening, the village buzzed and hummed like an angry colony of bees.

One week prior to these mysterious and exasperating developments, Martha Howkins had received a long, buff-coloured envelope containing a letter from Messrs. Bramwell, Bramwell, Sons & Partners, who were described in the heading of the thick heavily embossed paper as Attorneys at Law and Commissioners for Oaths, of Knightsbridge, London.

Martha's hands trembled as she read the official looking enclosure wondering how such grand, important people could have known of a poor ageing shopkeeper in an obscure Berkshire village. She read on, almost overwhelmed by the attention of these lordly lawyers to a humble God-fearing woman such as she, and almost fainted when she saw the words, 'One Thousand, Five Hundred Pounds' and in brackets the numerals (£1,500). In those days, £1,500 was a colossal amount of money.

The letter proceeded in its pompous tone to inform Martha that this sum would be paid to her in exchange for the tenancy. The shop, like all the other properties in Tillingthorpe, belonged to the Beldrakes and was rented by Martha for a weekly rental of three shillings. The £1,000 was for the tenancy and the £500 for stock and goodwill. The letter continued to warn Martha that the transaction must be treated as absolutely confidential and under no circumstances must any third party be privy to the arrangement until negotiations had been completed.

Martha's hands were still trembling; the mere thought of all that money had almost caused her to faint, impelling her to reach up to a small wooden cupboard where her groping hands sought a bottle of Dr. Mackenzie's Smelling Salts. The sharp ammonia vapours, scented with lavender water, restored Martha's reeling emotions sufficiently to allow her to prepare that universal panacea for all kinds of shocks, great and small: a cup of tea.

Martha sat in her wooden armchair long into the night, pondering when and how she should respond to this nerve-shattering letter and the proposal set out with such breath-taking candour.

At the hour of midnight precisely, confirmed by the measured sonorous chimes of her grandfather clock, Martha heard a voice, a voice that in some strange inexplicable way, appeared to echo simultaneously through her confused mind and heart. It said, "Go to the vicar!"

For many years afterwards, Martha insisted that it was the voice of God. Only good could emerge from such faith: for this experience implanted in her mind an unshakeable belief in the Almighty.

The following morning, Thursday, Martha despatched a brief note to the Reverend Sebastian Erasmus Copplethwaite requesting a visit without delay to advise her on matters of extreme urgency which would affect her whole life. The note was placed in the grubby hand of Richard, a village boy of ten years, with Martha's vehement exhortations to run to the vicar and insist that the note be handed to the vicar at once. Twopence was pressed into the urchin's palm to spur him on this most important errand.

At twelve noon, when Martha closed for lunch, the vicar knocked on the door. She hastily admitted him, pausing to glance furtively up and down the road. She then ushered him into the parlour. Without further ado, Martha placed the letter in his hands and said,

"I would like you to read this, sir, and give me your candid opinion."

The Reverend Copplethwaite perused the letter with intense deliberation; he was patently flabbergasted by its contents. Until this moment, he had remained standing but he suddenly sat down on Martha's armchair, the better to compose his thoughts, in order to make a meticulously sound judgement from a comfortable support. Martha awaited his pontifications with some apprehension.

The vicar had now recovered from his astonishment and could focus his astute, scholarly mind on the problem which was Martha's and now his.

He was a keenly observant man and he had perceived that Martha's hitherto unblemished record of attendance at church was no longer free from lapses; he had also noted that her vocal contribution to the hymn singing was noticeably less fervent. Her hands revealed that arthritis had set into her swollen knuckles. Then there was the uncertainty created by her two sons, Amos and George, who had not been home for over two years; in view of the fact they could lose their lives in the service of king and country they must, therefore, be ruled out as either moral or material support for their mother.

The Reverend Sebastian Erasmus Copplethwaite gazed into the fire as he grappled with Martha's dilemma. After a long and tormenting silence, the vicar turned to Martha and uttered his simple, lucid and reasoned judgement:

"Martha you must accept this exceedingly generous offer." Martha's lungs exuded a great gasp of relief; all the anxiety, the tension, the heart searching had disappeared as a blast of air sweeps away the mist that hangs over the downs encapsulating the sheep and saturating their heavy fleece.

The vicar enquired where she would live after the shop and post office were in a stranger's hand. Martha replied,

"My widowed sister in Oxford would allow me to live with her. I think I should pay her a visit and discuss it." The vicar approved of this precaution.

After this momentous solution to her problems Martha offered the vicar tea and biscuits and while they faced each other across the table she told the Reverend Sebastian Erasmus Copplethwaite how she had received a divine instruction and direction to consult him about her complex troubles. He nodded and agreed wholeheartedly that God is always there to help the sinner in his hour of travail. Before he departed he offered to write to Messrs. Bramwell, Bramwell, Sons & Partners on Martha's behalf to accept their offer. A kindness she gratefully accepted.

That evening Martha wrote to the carrier, Albert Dodson, who plied his operations linking a chain of villages. He drove a large van drawn by a pair of dappled grey Welsh cobs. Albert would - on request - carry heavy parcels, go shopping for provisions, deliver messages, and pick up items bought at auction. On occasion, he could be persuaded to take as many as three passengers. Any one wishing to avail themselves of this facility would have to be prepared to rise very early and even to wait, sometimes in the rain.

Martha wrote to Albert Dodson and arranged to meet him on the main road at the Tillingthorpe turning. The day arrived which Martha had anticipated with suppressed excitement. It would be quite an adventure for her to go to Witney, where she would get the bus to Oxford.

It was three years since Martha had seen her sister Mabel, who had been widowed in the Great War, but as the meagre war pension was insufficient to maintain her, she had worked as a seamstress in a large store in the city of Oxford. She resided in a small narrow street off St. Giles.

Martha alighted from Albert's van, arranging to meet him the next morning for the return journey.

After an evening animatedly describing the mysterious letter with its implications of financial independence, Martha asked her sister if she would be prepared to accept her into her home as a paying guest. Mabel, unhesitatingly, acquiesced; she was childless and therefore lonely and Martha's presence would bring great and welcome financial and social advantages. Mabel would certainly feel the reassuring comfort of the added security that her sister would bring.

Martha, greatly elated by the successful outcome of her visit, returned to Tillingthorpe fully confident that all her fears were no longer a threat and that her future looked very rosy.

The next morning, another letter arrived from the London lawyers; this one was more bulky than the first one and contained an intimidating large blue document. A letter enclosed requested Martha attend a local solicitor's chambers where she would be required to sign, in the presence of a witness, the deed of sale, relinquishing the business to their client, a Miss Isobel Patricia Langthorne, who was expected to arrive at Tilbury docks the next day. Miss Langthorne would be available to add her signature to the deed three days later. This formality would seal the negotiations, and a cheque for £1,500, made payable to Martha Howkins, would be forwarded.

The Reverend Copplethwaite, in the meantime, had suddenly realised that the Beldrakes, who owned the property, had not been consulted. Feeling a trifle embarrassed by this oversight, that was not only an act of discourteous presumption, but also of dubious legal implications, he decided that this appalling oversight must be dealt with, without procrastination. He rang the estate steward's office and was told that the lawyers Messrs. Bramwell, Bramwell, Sons & Partners had been in constant communication with Viscount Beldrake, who fully approved of the transaction. The vicar replaced the telephone earpiece on its fork shaped bracket somewhat bemused by this enlightenment.

Why, he pondered, had the London lawyers consulted the Beldrakes? As a paragon of discretion he sensed that he had inadvertently stumbled on a secret that only the Beldrakes, the lawyers and Miss Isobel Patricia Langthorne shared. The answer to this tantalising enigma would be denied him for several years to come. He concluded that Martha should be left in blissful ignorance of this mysterious knowledge.

On the Thursday afternoon at approximately three o'clock, Mrs. Copeland visited Martha's shop on the pretext of buying half a pound of Cheddar cheese. Her pointed probing thin nose scented that Martha's recent furtive behaviour was concealing affairs that she should know about.

Her innate cunning curiosity dictated that any direct questioning would cause Martha to resentfully clam up and, if prodded too deeply, meet any such personal queries with a sharp rebuff. No! This was not the way to unearth the juicy secret that she was certain Martha was concealing.

"Did you enjoy your holiday?" the blacksmith's wife enquired, at the same moment feigning a disinterested manner by closely scrutinising a card bearing pencils with a rubber at one end, retained by small elastic loops. Mrs. Copeland continued her verbal encircling, as a questing fox prowls round a hen coop, to trap Martha into making an unguarded admission. But Martha appeared not to notice, in her obvious pre-occupation with more pressing thoughts. Then, out of the blue, Mrs. Copeland got her reward. "I am selling my shop!" Martha blurted out as though in a trance.

"Selling the shop?" repeated the blacksmith's wife, reeling back from this totally unexpected, shocking revelation.

"Yes," said Martha, "but not a word to anyone mind. I've been sworn to secrecy. I've sold it to a lady from India."

Mrs. Copeland's heart was palpitating so violently that she decided that this was more than flesh and blood could stand. She beat a hasty retreat, muttering that she must go and prepare her husband's tea.

She returned home to the forge, where her husband and some helpers were about to engage in the tricky operation of lowering a red hot steel tyre on to a wagon wheel. Once the tyre was lowered carefully over the wheel, the helpers would move in with buckets of water to quench and contract the steel tyre on to the wooden rim of the wheel. At this very crucial moment the blacksmith's wife – unable to deny herself the glory of being the first to discover Martha's closely guarded secret – moved close to her husband's side and whispered in his ear her tit-bit of forbidden knowledge.

The astounded smith exploded in a tirade of obscenities, so loud and so fierce, that the startled helpers allowed the hot tyre to escape from the firm grips of their tongs and fall on the wheel. The smith's rage was contagious and evoked a sympathetic stream of profanity from the helpers, like some fiendish anvil chorus.

That evening Bill Copeland wended his way to The Red Lion almost from force of habit than to quench his insatiable thirst. After all, the very nature of the blacksmith's trade caused floods of perspiration to flow copiously from his brow, chest and back, causing severe dehydration; Bill would have been intensely bemused by such scientific terminology. "No," he would have said, "He was sweating like a pig."

Joshua noted the expression on Bill's face; black as a thunder-cloud he would have said. He silently placed the usual two pots of ale on the bar. Bill downed his first pot of ale, not with his customary breath-taking gulps, but rather like a man plagued by some dark secret that no-one could share.

In fact he was still brooding over the terrible and disastrous events triggered by his wife's startling revelations during the most delicate manoeuvrings of the red-hot steel wagon tyre.

Joshua tactfully left Bill to his own reverie and assumed a comfortable stance on folded arms with elbows firmly planted on the counter the better to observe a game of solo whist, in which Chalky White, Joe Johnson, Will Cox and Bert Wilson were all actively engaged. The game was now about to be concluded with Bert Wilson, the wheelwright, being in debt to his fellows, to the tune of one shilling, having failed by one trick to fulfil his attempt to 'go abundance'.

In the diversion created by all this excitement at the table in the alcove, the blacksmith beckoned to Joshua and leaning close to Joshua's ear said, "Now don't let this go any further, but Martha Howkins has sold her shop to a black lady." Joshua removed his pipe from his mouth and stared at the blacksmith in stark disbelief. He knew, as a business man himself, that this earth shattering news was just not possible, for he was well aware that Martha's shop and cottage belonged to the estate and could not be sold. Joshua gave the smith a long quizzical look and perceiving the angry glint in his eye decided that this was not the time nor place to argue with Bill concerning the authenticity of the secret the smith had imparted to him a few moments ago.

That night, over his supper of cheese and pickle rounded off with a chunk of his wife's delectable bread pudding, followed by a mug of cocoa, he unburdened himself of the secret to his wife Hilda. Hilda would – the next morning – see to it that the secret became public knowledge and although Joshua knew, only too well, of his wife's inability to be discreet, he did not wish to transgress the smith's trust which he valued most highly.

The morning after these secret exchanges occurred Martha was exceedingly puzzled by the crowd of village women who occupied the spacious area in front of the counter. They appeared to shout their vociferous inquisitive queries all at once, causing Martha considerable annoyance and embarrassment. Martha was a woman of strong character; she had to be, having no husband or family to turn to for additional support, moral or practical.

City dwellers immersed in their self-centred insular mode of living would scoff and sneer at all these details of life in an isolated village. 'Piffling', 'Trivial', would be their scathing comments but at the same time they would succumb to pangs of envy when contemplating the peaceful and tranquil way of life in an idyllic environment. Indeed, some of them – the more affluent – would buy the homes of these humble people when opportunities were presented.

They do not know that the integral communal spirit is a relic of turbulent times when their unity was essential for survival. While living their own separate family lives, they would unhesitatingly rally to the aid of any who might need their help, like ants pouring from their tiny citadel to deploy their armies in defence. When someone died, they were all involved and felt genuine sorrow for the bereaved, even though their participation might be limited to drawn curtains and removal of caps when the funeral procession passed. A major catastrophe, such as a thatched roof ablaze, would bring them hot foot to form human chains passing buckets of water with incredible speed, while others hooked the blazing bundles of straw from the conflagration.

Thus, when Martha's secret became public knowledge, they were profoundly sorry that someone who had played such an intimate and important role in their lives was about to leave their midst, perhaps forever. Once they had been made fully cognisant with the facts of the rumours while congregated in Martha's shop, their resentment swiftly evaporated as the early morning dew yields to the rising sun.

During the briefing in Martha's shop of her eager inquisitors, she thought it an opportune moment to warn them that the shop would be closed for two days to allow the new incumbent to settle in.

Martha had arranged for the removal men to call one day following a telephone message.

Chapter 3

One week passed when the Reverend Sebastian Erasmus Copplethwaite called to tell Martha that the new postmistress would like to take possession on Monday, April 20th, if convenient, but added that she would like to meet Martha before she departed and suggested she should remove all her furniture on the Monday and stay the night with them. They would take her to her sister Mabel's house in Oxford in their car the ensuing day. She was urged to accept these arrangements by the vicar who offered to phone the lawyers, Messrs. Bramwell, Bramwell, Sons & Partners to finalise this last link in the chain of remarkable events which would culminate in Martha's departure from Tillingthorpe where she had been born, married, given birth to two sons, and sadly widowed.

Martha was now financially comfortably off. The £1,500 had been augmented by another £1,000 which Martha had saved over the preceding eight years and had wisely invested, due to the good offices of the vicar who made sure that she was competently advised by accompanying her on her visit to his good friend, the bank manager.

The vicar and Martha now awaited, a trifle apprehensively, and with much curiosity, the arrival of the new tenant. Apprehension from Martha who wondered how the residents of Tillingthorpe would react to a black lady in their midst, because foreigners were a tiny minority in England and anyone from such an exotic country and nation as India was virtually unknown. At least 60% of the population had never seen a person with a black skin.

The vicar's burning curiosity was about to be alleviated, but only partly. As a gentleman the Reverend Copplethwaite would never indulge in any vulgar display of personal emotion; his curiosity was well concealed behind his impassive countenance.

The appointed day and hour arrived and Martha trembled with a fear that any simple country woman would feel at the awareness of the responsibility implied in her personal reception this day of a person who might not be welcome in the Tillingthorpe community. It was common knowledge that strangers who took up residence in any English village were not welcomed. Frequently they were victims of open hostility, although it must be said that with the passage of time this unfriendly attitude would diminish and they would be fully accepted by the village folk. Even people who came from a nearby village would not be immune.

A large pantechnicon now appeared, approaching Martha's cottage; it stopped opposite a woman weeding her front garden and a few words were exchanged, the woman pointing directly towards the vicar and Martha. What the expectant couple could not see was a Morris Cowley Saloon car following the van, driven by a young woman. The large van halted, the driver opened his window and called to Martha, "Are you Mrs. Howkins?" Receiving confirmation that she was the very same, he alighted from the cab and disappeared behind the vehicle, accompanied by his mate, to unlock the large doors and prepare to unload his cargo. While this brief distraction was in progress, the young lady driver of the car stepped briskly towards the vicar and Martha, introducing herself as Isobel Langthorne.

The vicar's self-control was momentarily breached, betrayed by the unguarded gleam of astonishment in his piercing blue eyes. Eyes which had quelled many an obstreperous curate who had, impertinently, requested an opportunity to conduct Evening Service. Such insolence was always crushed with an irresistible glare and an abruptly turned back. This silent admonishment would be pursued at dinner that evening by a terse reminder from the Reverend Sebastian Erasmus Copplethwaite that in spite of the curate's recent award of a B.A. in Divinity he was still very inexperienced in matters parochial. These rebukes were, unfailingly, effective in the suppression of any repeat of such rebellious thoughts or suggestions.

Martha was staring at Miss Isobel Langthorne with the fixed stare of a woman who simply could not cope with the evidence of her own eyes. This lady was white not black. Isobel took Martha's hand, gave her a radiant smile, and said, "Aren't you going to make us a cup of tea?" This homely request was sufficient to break the spell which held Martha so firmly in its grip. Martha recovered her composure, curtsied to this patently very genteel lady and led the way into the shop where Martha had generously bequeathed a tea service to her successor which was laid out on the counter with a tempting home-made cherry cake on a plate. The milk, contained in a small tin can with a lid and carrying handle, was suspended in the dark cold water of the well, to prevent it going sour, which Martha departed to retrieve.

During this mild commotion, Isobel's mother joined her daughter and the vicar and was duly introduced. The vicar enlightened them concerning his presence and the events of the previous week, hoped that they would soon settle into village life and, when convenient, would honour him with their presence at dinner. The two ladies assured him that they would look forward to such an occasion and thanked him, most warmly, for his courteous and warm welcome to his parish.

Martha was now preparing the cups of tea as the young lady desired. They all sat down on chairs hastily brought from the van; the vicar took advantage of this distraction to make a detailed study of the two ladies.

Isobel was wearing a neatly tailored costume of Donegal tweed, the collar of a cotton shirt blouse was turned back over the collar and lapels of her jacket. Her tiny waist was accentuated by a broad suede leather belt. Isobel was about five feet ten inches tall, her dark brown eyes looked almost black in the dim light of the cottage; her dark, lustrous hair fell to her slender shoulders in soft waves. The flawless complexion of her face was enhanced by the contrast of her beautiful hair.

The vicar, surreptitiously contemplating the beauty of this mysterious new-comer to Tillingthorpe, observed - strictly to himself of course - that she was the most exquisitely lovely creature he had ever encountered.

Her mother was about five feet eight inches tall with nut brown hair, now displaying thin streaks of grey. She also had dark brown eyes; her face and eyes, to the vicar's worldly wise gaze told him that here was a woman who had - perhaps - very recently suffered profound and protracted grief; a human and poignant experience that had tested her levels of moral fibre to the very boundaries of her physical and mental tolerance.

It was now discovered, by the removal men, that most of the furniture could not be manoeuvred through the narrow cottage door. The women selected three beds, two wash-stands, four arm-chairs and a small Pembroke table as a dining table. Martha had left a long narrow kitchen table of pine; the top was two inches thick and scrubbed white. The removal men were instructed to return the surplus furniture from whence it had come; in the depository in Oxford.

The next day, after they had taken Martha to her new home in Oxford, they said, "Goodbye," with a promise to fetch her for a weekend after they had settled in.

In the evening, when they were alone in their new abode and exchanging intimate thoughts, they both confessed to feeling terribly despondent after they had made a cursory inspection of their compact quarters. Nothing could be in sharper contrast to their previous life in the regal and colourful splendour as the wife and daughter of a colonel in the Bengal Lancers.

Isobel had received a first class education in England followed by two years at a French finishing school, all at colossal expense. When the two years at the French academy for young ladies had expired, her father had persuaded his sister, Cynthia Langthorne, to escort his precious daughter on the long journey to India, where she was eagerly awaited by her doting parents.

The voyage passed without incident. On arrival in the sub-continent they stayed at a hotel in Bombay to rest before embarking on the exhausting, enervating train journey. On the third day at the hotel, a soldier of her father's regiment appeared and announced that he would be their escort and bodyguard to ensure their safe arrival at the colonel's house.

He was armed with a scimitar, a service pistol and a three foot stave. He also produced three first class train tickets, purchased on the orders of the colonel. The two ladies were advised that the train would depart in one hour on the hour and he would supervise the transfer of their luggage from the hotel to the train. Their arrival at Calcutta concluded a journey that Isobel would never forget; the smells, the noise, the gorgeous colours of the women's saris and the vast awesome panoramas viewed through the carriage window. To a bird, the long train crawling across the endless plains must have looked like a giant centipede.

The colonel's car, with an orderly in the driving seat, was waiting near the station entrance. From the open windows of the car, Mrs. Langthorne anxiously scanned the seething crowd of people for the long awaited glimpse of her daughter.

The flailing stave – wielded with breath-taking dexterity – heralded the presence of the formidable escort who was busily engaged in cutting a path, through the close packed crowd, to allow the memsahibs to proceed unhindered by this motley gathering which included people of many races. Some of the fiercer hill tribesmen, all carrying rifles, glared resentfully, but the regimental badge of the Bengal Lancers, displayed so proudly on Akbar's turban, deterred any liberties that they may have been contemplating.

The two ladies were followed by a porter with their luggage. He would be handsomely rewarded with one rupee. His was a responsible task, because not only did he have to transport the cases from the train to the car but, in addition, fight off the thieving hands of those who, exploiting the concealment provided by many bodies squeezed tightly together, would swiftly snatch one or more of the cases, which they knew would contain many articles, that would bring a generous profit when offered for sale in the bazaar.

Akbar rewarded the porter with one rupee and climbed into the vacant seat adjacent to the driver, after ensuring that the ladies were comfortably and safely ensconced in the rear seats.

The colonel, Isobel's father, had changed from his grand uniform into a sports jacket and cavalry twill trousers, his feet encased in buckskin chukka boots supplied by Alan Macafee of Dover Street, London. He stood at the top of a flight of stone steps beneath an archway, awaiting his daughter's arrival.

When he saw the car sweeping into the courtyard he ran down the steps, opened the car door, helped Isobel out and enveloped her in the affectionate embrace of a father who has been parted from a beloved daughter for far too long.

The colonel's wife greeted her daughter and sister-in-law with delight and relief; any mother would heave a deep sigh of relief to greet a beautiful daughter who had arrived safely after a journey of so many thousands of miles by train and sea.

It was not Isobel's first experience of the vast, awe-inspiring land where every day a never ending pageant paraded before the eyes of those who took the trouble to behold.

Isobel had been taken to India when she was six years old and could recall a daily life that closely resembled all the excitement of adventures of Marco Polo. She was surrounded by servants who adored her and devoted their lives to the fulfilment of her slightest wish. She in turn loved them all with a little girl's trusting innocence. Isobel had an English tutor who gave her two hours of instruction in the three Rs every morning and at her mother's insistence she received instruction in music on the magnificent Bechstein piano installed in her mother's drawing room. Her mother was well aware that a working familiarity with classical composers, coupled with a high level of competence on the piano, was not only an essential part of a young well-bred lady's cultural aura, but a valuable social asset.

This constant fairy tale existence came to an abrupt end when Isobel returned to England accompanied by her mother to complete her education. Isobel's name had been recorded at a famous public school for young ladies when she was three, and now at fourteen years of age, she regarded the prospect with nervous apprehension as she recalled the horror stories of young girls who had survived the rigorous, spartan regimes that were regarded as the hallmark of the very best of academic establishments devoted solely to the training of young ladies in their formative years.

Isobel faced up to the ensuing two years when she would suffer many minor and humiliating indignities, all considered by the redoubtable and highly qualified teachers, to be an essential part of the character-building processes that all young ladies of quality must submit to. The two years passed – thankfully Isobel thought – swiftly and were punctuated by frequent and prolonged vacations with holidays spent with kind relations who endeavoured to compensate her for the cold baths, crowded dormitories and stodgy meals served in a communal dining hall, presided over by the headmistress and her minions at the top table, which was located on an elevated stage strategically sited to permit maximum field of view over the sea of white girlish faces.

A massive cameo brooch was pinned at her throat and pince-nez spectacles peeped from a special pocket in her blouse; these were standard equipment for all headmistresses. When these glasses were clamped firmly on to the bridge of her nose, in front of her piercing blue eyes, the most recalcitrant pupil would quail before this onslaught on her very soul.

When girls were sent to the head to be disciplined by Tabitha Gertrude Rollenson-Talbot, they were instructed to knock with the antique brass knocker and wait for the peremptory summons to "Enter". The brass knocker was cast in the mould of a thatched cottage. When the knocker was elevated, the interior furnishings would be revealed. In their adult life, many of the girls would recall this novelty with nostalgia.

Isobel eventually turned her back on this experience with not one tiny pang of regret and after a brief holiday with her aunt, departed for Paris to complete the process – prescribed by her elders – which would turn her into a well-balanced, self-assured young woman.

Madame Dupont's Academy for Young Gentlewomen was housed in a small château, five miles from Paris, and was luxuriously appointed and stood in verdant meadows, surrounded on three sides by a loop formed by the river Seine.

The curriculum consisted of deportment, physical training, music, embroidery and art. Much emphasis was placed on equitation, both side saddle and astride. Each morning, the girls would assemble in the château's private riding school to be instructed in the noble art of horsemanship by an ex-cavalry officer of the French army. The French are famous as exponents of elegant and highly skilled equitation. This subject together with the music tutorials were strong favourites of Isobel.

The girls were also encouraged to have a friendly relationship with all the servants in the house, which ensured a fluency in French language spoken with the correct accent.

The two years at Madame Dupont's Academy passed quickly because they were so happy and now Isobel looked forward to the day when she would be reunited with her mother and father.

Her arrival in India has already been described and we must now rejoin Isobel if we are to share her exciting life that now unfolds.

To say that Isobel's life was idyllic would be incongruous. Idyllic is an adjective only applicable to the incomparable landscape of England, with its lush meadows grazed by shorthorn cattle, its meandering rivers flanked by reeds and tall bullrushes with their chestnut coloured seed heads swaying in the breeze. All this aquatic growth was home to moorhens, voles and water rats, who, in the deep, dense greenery, felt safe in their complete concealment. Sometimes, a vixen, with four hungry cubs to feed, would use this same cover to stalk an unsuspecting mallard after an unfruitful nocturnal expedition.

England, with its miles of hawthorn hedgerows used, on occasion, by thrushes, blackbirds and numerous smaller birds as nesting sites. Sometimes, honeysuckle would use this thick, thorny, fragrant barrier to support its clusters of curious sweet-scented flowers.

The great mansions with their ornamental lakes covered with aquatic carpets of water lily pads, where the beautiful white flowers would close up and dip their heads under water until the rising sun persuaded them to rise and show their lovely white and yellow faces to an expectant world. Green and blue dragonflies zoomed, dipped and hovered over these cool green islands. England with its historic manors, its mellow rambling rectories, its ancient churches, its towering cathedrals erected by powerful kings to the glory of God. Its massive ancient and historic castles, some of them erected a thousand years ago, still broodingly waiting to repel the invader.

Put all these things together and that, to a proud Englishman, would be idyllic.

Isobel's daily life was, as the colonel's daughter, of considerable privilege. It was a never ending round of riding, tennis, parties, polo club balls and visiting friends or a visit to the bazaar, escorted by Akbar, who had now been appointed permanent escort and bodyguard.

When Isobel had been home for about six weeks, her nineteenth birthday was only about two weeks away. Her parents had already decided to arrange a dance in their daughter's honour. It would also create opportunities for Isobel to meet other young sons and daughters of senior officers in the Bengal's and also Skinner's Light Horse regiment who were stationed nearby. Skinner's wore a similar uniform to the Bengal's, the only major difference being that their three-quarter skirted tunic was dark green.

Isobel and her companions awaited this momentous celebration with excitement tinged with impatience. All preparations were made by the servants who, when questioned by Isobel, would only give one of those exasperating wait-and-see smiles.

The private ballroom was a scene of feverish and enthusiastic activity. Climbing roses were trained up the walls between the windows which extended from floor to ceiling. At one end of the room was a stage where the Royal Artillery Regimental Band would play. At the other end, a buffet where drinks and cold refreshments would be served by footmen, who would be in blue three-quarter length tunics, white cotton jodhpurs, soft leather slippers and white gloves to complete their attire. All wore a light blue turban.

Colonel Langthorne was a man of athletic physique, exactly six feet in height. When he was dressed in full ceremonial uniform, about to go on parade, he was a giant of a man. The thigh boots with their substantial heels, plus his turban, enhanced his stature by another fourteen inches, making him appear well over seven feet tall.

Like all men in his position he was a strict disciplinarian but also a man of cheerful disposition with, apparently, not a care in the world. He lived for his wife, daughter and the Regiment. He regarded himself as a lucky, happy and fulfilled man.

The great day had now arrived and Isobel awoke to the strains of 'Happy Birthday To You' played by the Regimental Band. Isobel swiftly showered and dressed in her riding clothes, descending to the breakfast room where her parents waited to greet their daughter on this most important day. At the side of her plate, she found two small parcels. One, from her parents, contained a gold Rolex wristwatch; the other a gold replica of the Bengal Lancers badge, mounted with sapphires, rubies and diamonds. Every man in the regiment had contributed, from the lowest trooper, with his few annas, to the Adjutant's substantial cheque.

Isobel went to the courtyard in front of the house to await the groom who would bring the ex-polo pony which she usually rode. She heard the clip-clop of hooves and looking towards the entrance, saw the groom leading, not her pony, but a magnificent light dapple grey pony. It was a thoroughbred Arab mare. As it drew near, Isobel's eyes widened with surprise and delight. The pony's unique colouring set off its silver mane and tail.

The young woman was spellbound by this wonderful and generous present from her father's closest friend, the elderly and fabulously rich Maharajah of Bahadra.

She moved towards the pony and caressed its proud arched neck and looked into its large vice-free eyes. The brow band of the bridle was studded with turquoise, the saddle was a typical Arab saddle, with a high arched pommel and a high rectangular cantle. It was covered in claret-coloured quilted velvet. The pommel and cantle were decorated with highly polished brass domed upholsterer's nails. The stirrups were fitted with toe guards to prevent the rider being dragged should she be unseated.

Isobel was so enchanted by the sheer beauty of her present that she decided not to ride, but to spend the time in the stable feasting her eyes on this perfect specimen of an Arab horse; running her hands over its satin coat and rewarding it with sugar lumps.

Isobel spent the rest of the day receiving her younger friends who had also brought presents. A lovely papier-mâché handkerchief box decorated with flowers and butterflies, a large Indian silk scarf printed with lotus flowers and an elephant carved from a block of ebony with real ivory tusks.

Feeling tired in the heat of the day and with the inevitable headache caused by so much excitement, Isobel retired to her room to sleep, in order to be dewy fresh for the ball.

She was roused by her maid, who would prepare her for what promised to be the happiest night of her life yet where she would, unknowingly, encounter an evil man who would destroy her small family and indeed her life.

Her mother entered the room bearing a jewel-case containing a tiara which she thought Isobel would like to wear on this very special night. To her surprise, Isobel rejected the suggestion as she had already chosen a butterfly clip, inlaid with sapphires, emeralds and rubies, which she had requested the maid to arrange in her dark hair. Isobel was a girl of simple tastes and had already decided that her only adornment would be her parent's gift: the wristwatch, the regiment's present, the Bengal Lancers' brooch and the butterfly in her hair.

Isobel's ball gown was made from pale cream satin – it had a scoop-type neckline encircled with a narrow, double thickness hem – the bodice was tight fitting, revealing the twin domes of her burgeoning symmetrical breasts. The skirt was given a gentle fullness over the hips, which accentuated her slim waist. The sleeves extended to midway between her elbow and wrist, gently ballooning out above the inch-wide, double-thickness cuff, which was embroidered in silk with a motif of pink rosebuds. Twelve inches above the hemline - which reached to the floor - swags of pink rosebuds were thickly embroidered. The pale cream satin caused her lovely complexion to glow and her dark eyes to look more lustrous. An elliptical fragment of black velvet was secured to the back of her regimental brooch to make it more conspicuous.

The young officers from the regiment had invited all the officers of their neighbours, Skinner's Light Horse. They surrounded Isobel in a protective wall of scarlet and green. All vied with each other to keep Isobel amused and entertained; her radiance and peals of laughter testified to the success of their combined efforts. Every man present fell in love with Isobel that night.

At frequent intervals, Isobel glanced round the room to locate her father and mother and when their eyes met, they smiled reassuringly at each other.

Her father now approached, he begged the young gentlemen to forgive his intrusion and requested a moment's privacy to introduce a special guest.

"Isobel, allow me to present His Highness Prince Sabridin Abdul Suliman." Isobel regarded this guest coolly and did not like what she saw.

He was richly dressed: his expensive attire proclaimed him a man of great wealth and influence. His eyes, set in a pock-marked face, appeared to be floating in oil. So unlike the lustrous eyes of his fellow countrymen.

"He is an old friend of mine," her father said.

The Prince was wearing a maroon three-quarter length tunic of the finest silk, which partly covered his doeskin jodhpurs, from which his soft satin slippers protruded. Isobel noted that he wore the old-fashioned type where the pointed toe was curled back over the instep; a fashion now eschewed by many of the Princes. Sabridin wore a white turban adorned with a large five pointed diamond star.

Her father's guest bowed low over Isobel's extended hand and she was thankful that kissing of hands was not part of oriental formality.

Prince Sabridin had been educated at Harrow and thus spoke perfect English. He addressed Isobel with the words,

"I wish you happiness this day and do most sincerely hope that Allah will bless you with many more happy birthdays and that your flawless beauty will not fade with the passing years."

He then slid his hand into an inside pocket of his tunic and produced a small jewel case which he proffered with the English, "Many happy returns of the day." Then with another low bow he said, "I hope you will be pleased to accept my humble gift, Memsahib, as my personal tribute to the beautiful daughter of my good friend, the colonel."

Isobel thanked him and replied, "May I open it now?"

"Please do," responded the cunning rascal. She pressed the tiny catch opening the small case to expose a heavy gold ring with one enormous ruby retained in its setting with opposing tiny gold tiger claws. Isobel gasped at the sheer unadorned beauty of this finest of Burma rubies, for no other stones supported this flawless gem. It was as large in diameter as an old English sixpence. The facets so cunningly cut illuminated the heart of the ruby like the last glowing ember of a dying fire.

Isobel looked the Prince straight in the eye and said, "I hardly know what to say; 'thank you' sounds so inadequate."

"Your happiness is reward enough," he replied. Turning to her father he said, "Perhaps you will honour me with a visit to my simple dwelling and of course that invitation includes your lovely daughter."

Isobel returned to her happy band who were watching these events with disgust etched on every glowing boyish face. One of the company, a subaltern named Graham MacDonald, looked at the departing Sabridin and commented dryly, "If that gentleman laid on the ground side by side with a cobra, it would be difficult to know which was which."

Isobel interjected and said, "I, too, found his presence repulsive."

She then showed them the ruby. Lieutenant Gibson whistled and said, "That stone must be worth every penny of £30,000!"

Isobel turned pale and gasped, "I can't accept it, I must give it back."

"Please do not be so indiscreet; it would deeply offend the old villain and when in India, it is not good to have enemies."

At that moment, the Maharajah of Bahadra appeared, this prompted Isobel to break away from her youthful escort and walk swiftly to the old gentleman impulsively throwing her arms around his neck and kissing him on the cheek. "Thank you a million times, Your Highness, for the most beautiful, the most wonderful present I have ever received in my whole life."

The old man was deeply touched as he felt her young body pressed closely to his in an expression of utter innocence and trust. The Maharajah enfolded her in his arms, smoothed her hair as one would a little girl, and murmured,
"I am so glad you like her. What will you call her?" he enquired.

Isobel thought for a few seconds and then said,
"I will call her Bahadra."

"You have chosen well," the old man said, "Bahadra means place of the lily pools."

"Oh! How enchanting!" cried Isobel, "and how appropriate."

The next day, she rode her prized gift for the first time and revelled in the admiring looks of all the many onlookers.

The colonel's daughter continued her never-ending days of delight amidst the many people who adored her; the servants were her good friends and were treated as such, a relationship which stimulated their unswerving loyalty to their young mistress.

One morning, she encountered her father as he left the parade square on his way to his office. Isobel looked up into his face and reminded him of the invitation of Prince Sabridin, extended on the night of the ball, immediately after presenting her with that magnificent ring.

"Come with me child, I have something to tell you about him."

She sat down in a high, straight-backed chair and gazed at the colonel in anticipation.

"Sabridin is not really a prince by birth, but he is extremely wealthy and wields considerable influence in the bazaars whence he gathers much vital intelligence, which is regarded by the political agents as absolutely crucial to the security of the province. For this reason he was made welcome in the homes of senior officers."

Her father proceeded to tell his daughter that it was strongly rumoured that he had murdered his father to obtain money to build up his business empires in Calcutta and Bombay. His father had two shops in the bazaar from where he sold small gold trinkets, blankets, shawls, cooking pots and pans and various other commodities. The political agents had long suspected that these two shops were merely a facade which concealed the evil and nefarious practice of dealing arms, drugs and slave trading. No hard evidence had ever been obtained to the regret of the agents, against the cunning old villain.

Sabridin, his son, had stumbled on his father's enormous cache of many thousands of rupees. This discovery signed the old rogue's death warrant, for his equally evil son was obsessed with ambition and would be totally ruthless in its fulfilment. He arranged for an accomplice to administer a drug, which would induce a massive and fatal heart attack in his father.

Sabridin was known to be an employer of child slave labour whom he made work twelve hour days. Many of these children had been snatched from villages a thousand miles away. The evil Sabridin had extensive factories turning out vast quantities of high quality textiles for export. He also had two smaller factories, one engaged in silk production and one other manufacturing exquisite Indian rugs for export to America, Paris, and many other cities all over the world.

In the meantime Sabridin had found it expedient to visit Jaipur to complete the arrangements of further business enterprises and to establish an alibi. During this absence, his father had died and had been - to Sabridin's great relief - cremated.

Isobel had listened to this catalogue of villainy wide-eyed with horror and when her father had concluded, she noted a look of acute anxiety tinged with fear. The colonel then swore his daughter to absolute secrecy, as in the enlightenment he had revealed information to Isobel known only to the political agents.

"I shall return his gift at once!" ejaculated Isobel.

"No. No, please do not engage in anything so indiscreet! Asiatics are exceedingly sensitive to snubs which they regard as insults never to be forgiven."

Isobel noticed the alarm etched on her father's handsome face and promised to be polite to this horrible man should she ever encounter him socially. Many years afterwards, Isobel would recall this conversation, for it held the key to her father's inexplicable violent and tragic death.

As she made her exit from her father's office, he exhorted her to never disclose this conversation, not even to her mother. Isobel gave this assurance and promised to put it from her mind.

Isobel, in her youthful resilience, soon relegated this incident to the innermost recesses of her mind and pursued her daily happy round with all the tireless energy so typical of young girls who have not a care in the world. Isobel loved to stroll in the gardens at night gazing up into the enormous blue-black dome of the sky where God had strewn billions of glittering jewel-like stars.

Colonel Langthorne also appeared to thoroughly enjoy his life as an officer in the famous Bengal Lancers and all the allied pleasures that go with that life; polo, pig-sticking and the thrill of the tiger shoot.

His wife enjoyed her privileged life and had many good friends, both Indian and army. She visited and saw many magnificent palaces and went on escorted trips into the spectacular countryside where she saw sights that would linger in her memory for ever. The wonderful display of English roses which flourish in India are a delight in themselves. The verdant plains with their exotic flowers, shrubs and trees. The mountains mantled with rhododendrons, almost up to the snow line, provided a panorama of heart-stopping beauty. Isobel's mother was most certainly not neglected and never, never bored.

Isobel sometimes wondered if she would wake up and discover that it was all a dream, conjured up by the romantic stories that she had read during her school holidays. The very next day, she would awaken to the realisation that it was indeed all very real.

Every morning, Isobel rode her adored pony, Bahadra, accompanied by Akbar who would ride five yards behind, only spurring his own mount forward when admiring crowds impeded his charge's progress. The mere threat of the long baton, carried in a tubular scabbard attached to Akbar's saddle, was sufficient to open a path for Isobel's pony.

The endless preoccupation was with riding, tennis, sightseeing, visiting friends – of which there were many – and watching her father's regiment on parade, a sight which always made her heart swell with pride, for was she not part of it, a real life daughter of the regiment? Sometimes Isobel would join the recruits in the covered riding school under the critical eye of Major Irving, chief instructor in equitation to the Indian Cavalry Brigade.

Military riding rotundas were constructed by laying pine boughs on the concrete floor, this was followed by a thick layer of birch twigs, then this foundation was built up with regular additional layers of peat. This flooring was kind to both horse and rider.

Isobel glowed with good health and happiness, stimulated by this perpetual, colourful, exciting adventure, which, every day, painted a new canvas of this vast, mysterious, beautiful and sometimes menacing country. Surely no country in the world has witnessed so much savagery, so much blood spillage, so much fiendish cruelty and so much splendour.

Chapter 4

In the month of September, a perverse and cruel fate was lurking and waiting as a Bengal tiger awaits its prey, ready to destroy with primitive ferocity and speed.

Thursday was always reserved for polo club meetings, presided over by Colonel Langthorne. On this awful occasion, the colonel called in to kiss his wife and daughter: a gesture contrary to his normal practice.

"I will be home at about nine o'clock after the committee have adjourned the meeting, as usual." he said. At nine-thirty, the colonel had not returned, but at nine forty-five, his failure to appear aroused a deep apprehension tinged with a terrifying sense of foreboding.

At nine-fifty, Mrs. Langthorne rang for her footman and requested him to look for the colonel, as he had not returned home at the time he had specified and she was a trifle anxious, in case some harm had befallen him.

The servant went to the bar in the officer's mess where he was confident that the colonel would be having a drink with his brother officers. After enquiring of the whereabouts of the colonel, it was suggested he might be in his office. The servant was about to discover that fate had already struck with the destructive, explosive, searing power of a thunderbolt on the unsuspecting victims.

He knocked on the massive teak door to await the summons to enter. His deferential tapping did not elicit the anticipated order to enter. The footman knocked again, much harder, which reflected the anxiety transmitted to him. Again there was only a barren silence. The servant opened the door very, very slowly and peered through.

His eyes dilated in horror at what he perceived: the colonel was slumped over his desk, his head lying in a dark pool of blood, his service pistol had slid under a chair against the right hand wall, hurled there by the last convulsive reflex action his master would ever make.

The footman, very wisely, departed in great and urgent haste to inform the regimental surgeon, Captain Wagstaffe. Captain Wagstaffe turned pale after hearing this shocking news and ordered the servant to say nothing about the matter until he himself had investigated the scene of this fearful tragedy.

The captain entered the colonel's office, observing the awful scene as reported to him. He stepped close to the body, made a cursory check for any sign of life in his colonel's inert body. Finding none, he called the chaplain on the office phone and awaited his arrival. In the meantime, he made a thorough inspection of the room, taking care not to touch anything, although he and many others had left fingerprints in the course of their many duty calls.

The chaplain arrived, said a prayer over the body, and then discussed with the captain the choice of person to perform the unenviable task of conveying the grim world shattering tidings to the colonel's wife and daughter. That was a duty that anyone could be forgiven for refusing to carry out. It was swiftly decided that the chaplain, by virtue of his calling, would be most suitable for this harrowing task.

The colonel's wife was now frantic with worry, because the servant she had originally despatched had not returned.

As far as the servant was concerned, this was not surprising. He shrank from the confrontation with Mrs. Langthorne which would force him to disclose the dreadful knowledge that he had so recently acquired. Indian servants were touchingly loyal and would do everything in their power to shield their masters and mistresses from harm, be it physical or otherwise.

The chaplain was now knocking on the door; he was invited to enter.

Mrs. Langthorne became deathly pale, her womanly intuition told her what she had feared; something terrible had occurred. Isobel was also present. The priest glanced anxiously from one pale apprehensive face to the other. He requested them to sit.

He then addressed them in as firm tones as he could muster:
"The colonel – your husband – has been the victim of a shooting incident. I have to tell you that his wounds were fatal." The chaplain uttered that final word as though it had been dredged from the depths of his soul.

Mrs. Langthorne received this fearful, mind-shattering news with the magnificent self-control that only well-bred English women display when a catastrophe of the first magnitude descends upon them, or in a life-threatening situation. The priest glanced at Isobel who was sitting rigidly erect in a chair and had the appearance of a woman who had been turned to stone.

He moved towards her to offer words of comfort but suddenly and swiftly Isobel leapt from her chair and retreated to her room where she threw herself on the bed and collapsed in a deluge of tears.

Her mother, left alone with the chaplain, enquired of him further details of the horrendous discovery. He related how the footman had made the initial discovery but wisely called the doctor who, in turn, had summoned him to the ghastly and tragic sight that met his eyes on entering the colonel's office. She listened intently, visualising a macabre picture which would be indelibly etched on her memory for ever.

Throwing a large silk Indian shawl over her shoulders she commanded the chaplain, "Take me to him."

They entered the grim mortuary in silence. The colonel lay on a marble slab, still wearing his mess dress. Apart from a small wound to the side of his head he looked as he had always looked, a handsome officer of the Bengal Lancers. To the amazement of the chaplain, no tears were shed that night.

Funerals in India were always arranged with what was – to the uninitiated – undue haste, but there was a reason.

The Adjutant had already given instructions for a funeral which would accord full military ceremonial to the deceased and much respected Colonel Langthorne D.S.O., M.C.

The next day, Mrs. Langthorne rang the colonel of the Royal Corps of Signals requesting the use of a motorcycle despatch rider to convey the tragic news of the colonel's death to the Maharajah of Bahadra. This was an urgent and important mission as her husband and the Maharajah had been very close, almost like brothers.

They had first become acquainted when the colonel was at the Royal Military Academy, Sandhurst and the young prince was attending the Staff College, Camberley. Although the Maharajah was five years the colonel's senior - fifty-six - they shared the same interests and enjoyed a comradeship going back over thirty years.

The despatch rider - a sergeant - was instructed to warn the steward that the letter contained tragic news and that the Maharajah must not be left alone when he read the contents. These orders were carried out strictly to the letter. The journey of fifty miles was soon completed.

The Maharajah was seated in his garden beneath a canopy reading a copy of *The Times*. A small table stood nearby with a glass jug of iced lemonade placed on it - a glass tumbler stood adjacent to the jug. The Maharajah, recognising Mrs. Langthorne's writing opened the letter. The servant hovered discreetly in the background.

The old prince read the letter, rose to his feet and emitting a hoarse cry, fell across the table, knocking the jug and glass over with a tremendous crash, alerting the servant who rushed to his master's aid.

A doctor was sent for and transported the prince's Rolls Royce at great speed amidst a cloud of dust. The doctor immediately certified that the Maharajah had succumbed to a cerebral haemorrhage, induced by a sudden and powerful surge in his blood pressure motivated by shock. Fate had decreed that these two fine men should not be parted by the death of one of them.

Meanwhile, arrangements for the colonel's funeral were now complete. A gun carriage had been provided by the Royal Horse Artillery and outriders would wear their full dress uniforms. The colonel's charger, with his thigh boots reversed in the stirrups, was led by his personal groom immediately to the rear of the gun carriage.

The next day, a cloud of mournful sadness hung over the barracks as a thunder-cloud threatens a mountain peak.

The colonel's widow and daughter hid their tumultuous emotions beneath their black veils. They rode in the colonel's staff car, the very same vehicle which they had used on that exciting day, almost a year previously, when Isobel had rejoined her parents.

A major and a captain rode on one side of the gun carriage. On the opposite side, the escort consisted of first and second lieutenants, their swords carried at the slope. Behind, a company of dismounted lancers formed into columns of three, their drawn sabres tucked beneath their left arms with the left hand grasping the hilt, the curved end pointing downwards. Four riflemen and three trumpeters followed the column.

The service conducted in the garrison church was an impressive and colourful spectacle. The colonel's sword and many decorations were laid on the heavy mahogany coffin, supported on a bier, draped with a saddle cloth bearing the insignia of the Bengal Lancers.

A brass plate on the coffin testified that it contained:

THE LAST MORTAL REMAINS OF

COLONEL GILES HAROLD ALBERT LANGTHORNE.

D.S.O., M.C.

1879 – 1930.

The trumpeters and the firing party followed the procession to the graveside. The colonel's widow and daughter took up the traditional position at his head. The rest of the mourners - and there were many - spread themselves round the neatly cut grave.

Up to this moment, the two ladies had concealed their grief with admirable self-control and dignity, but when the chaplain reached the point about 'man born of woman', Isobel sobbed audibly. Her mother moved closer, putting a protective arm round her waist.

The trumpeters stepped smartly forward to sound the 'Last Post', as the chaplain engaged in the symbolic sprinkling of earth on the casket. The firing party then fired three volleys over the open grave; 'Reveille' concluded the final ceremony.

The troops formed up behind the band and marched back to barracks to a lively march in two/four time.

Chapter 5

At the inquest the air of mystery deepened. Evidence was given that testified to the colonel's soundness of mind; others stated that he was a very happy family man without a care in the world who was greatly respected in the regiment. Further enquiries failed to uncover any financial worries; indeed, this investigation revealed his bank account showed a deposit of twenty thousand pounds. Why would Colonel Giles Langthorne take his own life when he had everything to live for? The coroner, whose duty it was to analyse the evidence, concluded that he could only record an open verdict.

This terrifying and mysterious tragedy would be discussed in the officer's mess for years to come and these discussions were even more animated when it became apparent that the death of the colonel and his bosom friend the Maharajah were purely coincidental and unconnected.

A terrible dilemma now faced Mrs. Langthorne and her daughter. The fraternal and protective life of the regiment would, for them, now come to an abrupt end. Something had to be done and swiftly. Mrs. Langthorne decided to invoke the advice of the Adjutant, Major Mackenzie, who made the following comments. It would be unwise for them to remain in India, as the country was very unstable and a widow and daughter would be very vulnerable. The army, with its machine-like precision, would demand their evacuation of the house to provide quarters for the new colonel. The widow would not receive a pension: he suggested, therefore, that the £20,000 should be invested to give her a small annual income. The regiment would, he felt sure, donate two thousand pounds from the benevolent fund. The government would pay all the costs of their return to England.

Mrs. Langthorne thanked him gratefully for his generous and practical advice and asked for time to discuss this very serious predicament with her daughter.

Isobel had spent many hours in her room wondering why vindictive fate had chosen their small honourable family for this destructive visitation. One day, lying on her bed, she realised that her mother needed her support. It was as though some indefinable power had torn aside a black curtain of stultifying indecision. She now accepted that her beloved father was gone forever and that if they were to survive in a harsh world, she must brace herself to summon all her inherent courage and coolness.

Isobel decided to go for a ride on her Arab pony, an exercise that would stimulate her brain and might provide answers to their numerous problems. An hour later she returned, with her confidence much enhanced and an idea which she firmly believed would at least provide them with a home and a modest living. Isobel was well aware of the pitfalls that they would face together.

Without changing from her riding clothes, she ran to find her mother, who was astonished at the transformation in her daughter's appearance and general demeanour; a trifle shocked also so soon after the funeral, now a week ago. Isobel blurted out her idea, which was regarded by her mother as ludicrous in the extreme, but Isobel was a very shrewd girl - far more astute than her mother had ever realised. Her father had often spoken of his cousins, the Beldrakes of Berkshire, and their five thousand acre estate. Isobel's plan was to write and ask for their help in acquiring a village post office.

This enquiry elicited a warm response, with the promise that they would make all the arrangements. This development pleased Isobel immensely.

She had observed the lifestyle of the Indian traders and their obvious prosperity, and believed that the idea could be developed extensively once she had established a business foundation. The idea was to bear fruit beyond her wildest dreams in the years to come. Isobel knew that the solution to their precarious existence would be only in her ability to be independent of employers.

There remained one other major problem for her and it was a strictly personal matter. Her Arab pony, Bahadra. Again she turned to the adjutant for help. She made an appointment to meet him in his office and without further ado, asked if he would care for the pony until such time as she could afford to send for her. It would be a man with a heart of stone who could deny Isobel any favour - large or small.

The adjutant smiled as he listened to her pleadings and replied, "Leave it with me and before you depart I will have worked something out."

Isobel had now convinced her mother that her scheme was worth consideration. It had one important advantage: they would be together.

Two weeks had now elapsed since the colonel's mysterious death and Major Mackenzie was standing in to cover the colonel's duties. The major was a man who was endowed, by nature, with very keen powers of observation and his long army experience had made it even sharper. He sat down in the very chair occupied by the colonel the night he took his life. He noted that a desk calendar had one date clearly marked with a red ring round it - the twentieth of September. The major believed that in some indefinable way this date had, not only an important significance to the colonel, but, some unexplained connection with his death. It would be another eighteen months before his suspicions were confirmed.

He meticulously studied Colonel Langthorne's desk diary but finding no leads there, visited Mrs. Langthorne to seek access to her husband's private diary, locked in a drawer in his dressing room. Looking through it he found the same date circled in red ink. He told Mrs. Langthorne of his belief that this date had an unknown link with her late husband's death. She assured him that she had no information to impart about what might or might not happen on the day indicated - September the twentieth.

The major departed and felt intense chagrin that neither diary had disgorged one tiny clue. This date was to haunt Major Mackenzie for many years to come, a secret he never shared. Mrs. Langthorne never disclosed this conversation to Isobel.

The furniture in the house belonged to the army, only the porcelain and silver belonged to Mrs. Langthorne. Packers were invited into the house to pack one large crate and several cabin trunks.

Mrs. Langthorne had inherited a large quantity of antique furniture from her parents, in fact, more than they could ever need. On the death of her father, she had been bequeathed the contents of a fifteen room rectory. This was now in store in Oxford.

Their passage on the liner, 'Star Of India', had been booked for January the fifteenth. The heart-numbing wrench of saying goodbye to their hundreds of friends was drawing ever nearer and both mother and daughter anticipated the final day with dread.

The regiment had thoughtfully arranged a social evening, to which all the guests from Isobel's birthday party would be invited. The two ladies were now able to present brave faces to the world without embarrassment and were resigned to turning their backs on a country and people they had grown to love.

The social evening was most certainly not a mournful interlude of tearful embraces; more like the sadness one feels when saying goodbye to a much loved friend on a railway platform.

A group photograph of all commissioned and non-commissioned officers including the late Colonel Langthorne, and signed by them all on the wide white mount surrounding the picture was presented to the colonel's widow.

The young subalterns assured Isobel that she would be sorely missed by them all and promised to call on her when they returned to England for their three month leave entitlement after two years. Isobel assured them she would look forward to that day.

One more painful duty had to be performed; a visit to the military cemetery to bid farewell to an adored father and husband. The visit was concluded with one last lingering caress of his headstone and a photograph taken to provide a pictorial record of the colonel's last resting place.

On the fifth of January, they left the cantonment to begin the long journey back to England. They would be escorted to Bombay by two off duty subalterns, with the ever faithful Akbar in attendance. The two young officers said their farewells to Isobel and her mother, who would spend one night at the hotel keeping Akbar to supervise the stowage of their possessions on the ship 'Star Of India'.

The next morning, they made their way to the docks, escorted by the servant. After all formalities had been completed, they said goodbye to Akbar, after Mrs. Langthorne had rewarded him with ten pounds, for which he was deeply grateful and very surprised by such generosity.

After a voyage of approximately six weeks, they arrived in Tilbury docks, London, where they were met by the Beldrake's lawyer who escorted them to a modest but comfortable hotel. Before leaving, he informed the ladies that he would collect them the next day and take them to the chambers to sign the necessary documents completing the transfer of Martha's business.

Chapter 6

As the reader is aware, the Langthornes have now taken possession and are striving to come to terms with this drastic change of environment.

They were - as they confessed to each other - depressed by the dark, gloomy interior of the cottage and thankful that they had arranged the two day closure which would, at least, give them an opportunity to steel themselves for the trials which would test their resolve to the very limits of human endurance.

The next morning, they decided that the kitchen would be their nerve centre and the very first stimulus of that nerve would come from the excellent and spotless cooking range, where Martha had cooked scores and scores of roast beef and Yorkshire pudding dinners.

Inside and to the right of the back door, there was a wood store stacked to the ceiling with cut and split wood, suitable for the range, because Martha had shrewdly guessed the new incumbent would not be physically capable of doing this vital domestic chore.

Isobel promptly lit the fire and waited for the kettle to boil; as she sat there, she drew strength from the warmth and morale lifting comfort that a glowing, crackling fire always brings. She explored the comprehensive stock of provisions in the shop and selected cereals, bacon, and eggs which really were fresh. Reaching up to the many pots and pans hanging from stout hooks in the ceiling, Isobel selected a frying pan, washed it, and proceeded to cook a real English breakfast. Making a cup of tea, she took one up to her mother who commented on the appetising odour emanating from downstairs. A few minutes later, Isobel was joined by her mother and together they made a hearty breakfast of bacon, eggs, fried bread and tomatoes, followed by toast - real toast made by impaling the slice of bread on the toasting fork, hanging at the side of the range, and presenting it to the glowing embers of the fire until each slice became a rich, golden brown which was then coated with butter followed by a generous spread of marmalade. Isobel and her mother declared, in unison, how much they had enjoyed the meal and how surprised they were by their keen appetites.

The warmth and the glowing fire had infused new strength into them and they felt that their plight was not as dark and hopeless as they had thought on the previous night, also their eyes were adjusting to the dark interior of the cottage which, on inspection, became more appealing by the hour.

The next day was the day appointed for Isobel's instruction in the postal department and a certain Mr. Pringle would be calling to instruct her in the mysterious and important duties of one of His Majestys postmasters or mistresses.

Mr. Pringle wore glasses with round, thick pebble lenses, which made the eyes assume an owl-like appearance, which in turn was accentuated by his black hair line terminating in a V-shape, three inches above the bridge of his nose. This gentleman was a typical civil servant of the old school and the black shoe-button pupils of his eyes would visibly gleam when he spotted a minute error made by a careless and hapless subordinate.

Isobel was amused by Mr. Pringle's archaic habit of wearing spats, but she would soon observe that he also had another equally old fashioned but less pleasant habit; the taking of snuff.

When her mentor arrived at nine o'clock and saw Isobel, he was obviously astonished by the sight of this beautiful young lady with the unmistakable aura of aristocracy. Such was his discomfiture, he appeared to lose some of his air of officialdom which never failed to intimidate applicants for appointment to the important status of postmaster or mistress in the service of His Majesty, King George the Fifth, for was he not a servant of this very august person?

In spite of these confidence-boosting thoughts, his ill-fitting grey suit seemed to hang on the frame of Archibald Pringle like the cladding of a scarecrow in a cornfield. His scrawny turkey-like neck protruded from his celluloid collar – only requiring the labour saving application of a damp cloth – like the neck of some grotesque phoenix rising from the baggy folds of his shabby suit.

Mr. Pringle felt that a timely pinch of snuff would restore his violently disturbed equilibrium. He produced a small black box and inserting a practised thumb and forefinger extracted a tiny amount of the dark brown powder which he inhaled with a noisy and disgusting sniff; then, with the trumpeting noise of an elephant, he vigorously blew his nose in a large, red spotted handkerchief, which was then wielded with dextrous flicks to remove the flecks of snuff from the lapels of his putty coloured beltless raincoat.

"Now, young lady, will you kindly inform your mother that I am in great haste to catch the Oxford bus and would be obliged if she will present herself for the necessary instruction which is the purpose of my visit?"

Isobel replied, "It is not my mother who has made the application, it is me!"

This was more than flesh and blood could cope with. "You?" he cried, with the painful anguish of a man who has been stung by a hornet.

"Yes!" Isobel replied. The soothing opiate of the snuff which had restored him to his normal unctuous self had now faded, and what was worse, this young woman displayed no sign of the humility he had come to expect from applicants who sought elevation to one of the highest realms of the civil service.

He thought that she should be made aware of certain facts concerning his own exalted status in the Postal Service. He informed Isobel that he was the postmaster of the principal post office in Cowley, with responsibility for an annual turnover in excess of one hundred thousand pounds. Furthermore, he was the son-in-law of the senior postmaster in the city of Oxford. He peered at Isobel with his round eyes to assess the impact of this impressive catalogue of the ramifications of the obvious power he exerted – or might exert – in the service.

Isobel looked duly impressed and said, “How interesting.”

This response appeared to have smoothed some, at least, of Mr. Pringle’s ruffled feathers. Then, producing a large silver watch, connected and secured to his waistcoat by an equally heavy silver chain with links the shape of a ship’s anchor chain, he said,

“I have only one hour left to instruct you, so please indicate which part of your shop will be allocated to the postal service.”

Isobel led him to the back of the counter with a few shelves for forms and a cash drawer, with its wooden hemispherical compartments for coins and rectangular sections for notes. He showed Isobel that postal order numbers were recorded on a chart and must be carefully ticked off as issued over the counter. She was shown the simple system for her personal accounting and form filling. Mr. Pringle then reached into his briefcase and drew out several rubber stamps, which he insisted must be kept in a secure place at all times. Several bundles of official looking forms were taken from the bag and deposited on the shelves.

“These,” Mr. Pringle said, “are Road Fund Licence Application forms, but I imagine that you will not be requiring many of these in Tillingthorpe. Here are forms for Dog Licences and Wireless. These are very important and are intended for notification of outbreaks of swine fever, anthrax, foot and mouth disease and rabies. All these forms must be submitted in triplicate, signed by a veterinary surgeon, police constable, and, in some cases, by a magistrate.”

Archibald Pringle then added, in his most pompous manner, gazing into Isobel’s incredulous eyes, “If I had my way, there would be another form for outbreaks of bubonic plague.”

Isobel was quite alarmed by this frightening prospect and said, “Do you really and truly believe this is a possibility?”

Mr. Pringle nodded sagely and said, “Not only do I believe it to be a possibility, but some time ago I wrote to the Postmaster General in the House of Commons in the hope that he would be equally concerned about this loophole in the form filling duties of the Civil Service."

To Mr. Pringle, form filling was the necessary oil on the government machine and was not to be neglected.

Isobel realised that Mr. Pringle - in spite of his objectionable habits - could be a useful ally in the coming months and looking into his face, said, "If you would like to take some refreshments, I could run you back to Cowley in the car, this would save you the worry about time, and of course, I would like you to meet my mother."

Mr. Pringle consulted his large silver watch once more and said, "I must confess, I would like a refreshing cup of tea and as you have so kindly offered to take me back, I will have time."

Isobel ushered him into the kitchen apologising for the spartan furnishings, due to the inability of the furniture men to manoeuvre their large furniture through the small doors of the cottage.

She made a pot of tea and laid out a variety of biscuits, while her mother engaged the attention of their guest.

"Does your wife assist you in the business?" asked Mrs. Langthorne, tentatively. Mr. Pringle gulped in astonishment that anyone could be so unenlightened that they could refer to the post office as a business.

"My dear lady," he replied, in a patronising tone of voice, "the Post Office is second only to the armed forces as an organisation of national importance." He stirred his tea and stared gloomily into space then added, "I fear my wife does not enjoy the best of health."

The ladies murmured their condolences as he went on to explain that his wife, Mrs. Pringle, had suffered a severe nervous breakdown when her Pekinese dog, Toto, was killed some years ago. It had all happened because a stupid, dilatory postman had failed to close the rear gate and the dog, as dogs will, went into the road and sadly came to an untimely end beneath the wheels of a brewer's dray.

Unfortunately, leaving gates open was not a dismissible offence and he had to report that the man who had caused Mrs. Pringle so much grief was still in the service.

Accepting his second cup of tea and engaging in the lengthy stirring process, which not only served to dissolve the very last grain of sugar but also stimulated his powers of recall, he then added more cheerfully that his wife, Mrs. Pringle, was able to visit Toto every Friday afternoon. Observing the puzzled look in the eyes of his listeners, he explained that Toto had been buried in a dog cemetery, two miles from Cowley, on the Reading road; Mrs. Pringle was thus able to place fresh flowers on the grave every week.

Once again a close examination of the watch reminded him it was time to return to his own office to reassume the reins of power. Rising from his chair he graciously thanked them for their hospitality and said, "If you have any difficulties please ring this number - 47284 - which will connect you to my office between the hours of eight in the morning and seven in the evening."

As the trio passed out through the shop, Mr. Pringle turned to Isobel and said, "Oh, by the way, workmen will be calling to fix a brass trellis grille to the counter. It is in the regulations and does ensure that the public do not get too close when being served."

After a forty mile drive, they arrived at the large sprawling estate of Cowley, and under Mr. Pringle's directions, drew up outside a very impressive post office, both ladies expressing their admiration of such an important and imposing office. Mr. Pringle interpreted these comments as envy and informed Isobel magnanimously that it was highly conceivable that - with his recommendation - she could aspire to these dizzy heights in the service as she gained more experience. As he alighted from the car he said, "I will be sending you a copy of the Official Secrets Act which you must sign in the presence of a witness." Then, turning away, he entered his very own ivory tower.

Isobel and her mother returned to Tillingthorpe to make preparations for the next day - opening day - and wondered what the future held in store for them both. They anticipated that there would be a period of inactivity until the inhabitants had made the momentous decision to accept the newcomers. This would not be an easy decision for them to make, for the two ladies were not only strangers, but had come from a foreign land many thousands of miles from England. The following day, all such conjectures were to be proved quite false.

At ten o'clock, five of the village wives, headed and marshalled by the blacksmith's wife, entered the shop. Isobel greeted them with a smile and awaited their requests. Five pairs of quizzing eyes were focused upon Isobel as various emotions flickered on their countenances as the shadows from the sun in a cloud-ridden sky moved slowly across the downs. The feelings, so revealed, were surprise at the colour of Isobel's skin - white not black - also at her flawless beauty and all felt a strong urge to curtsey to this aristocratic presence.

Isobel repeated her question; "Can I help you ladies?" That scored a bullseye. They were not addressed as women, they were obviously regarded as her equals: ladies.

Mrs. Copeland stepped forward and said, "I would like three pounds of self-raising flour, a quarter of Brooke Bond tea, and half a pound of butter."

The butter was stacked on a cold, marble slab, presented to Martha Howkins by Eli Marriot, the village mason. The packets of Brooke Bond tea were on a shelf at Isobel's back - so far so good - but the MacDougals flour presented her with her very first problem. Where did old Martha store the flour? This was a first class opportunity to enlist the aid of Mrs. Copeland's knowledge, experience and seniority. "Oh, dear!" Isobel exclaimed, "I omitted to check with Martha concerning the storage of perishables. Are you able to help me, please?" The blacksmith's wife flushed with satisfaction as this extraordinary person appealed to her for help and in so doing recognised her status as the respected wife of one of Tillingthorpe's leading tradesmen. Mrs. Copeland stepped even closer to the counter and pointed to a deep close fitting drawer, lined with zinc, to keep out any mice that had escaped the break-back traps scattered throughout the cottage by the previous owner. "Thank you so much. You know,

I will have to rely on you ladies to help me over the difficulties I shall encounter in my settling in process, not only in the shop but as a newcomer to the Tillingthorpe community."

This was a potent diplomatic master stroke, ensuring that all five customers would become powerful allies in breaking down the prejudices and barriers that both Isobel and her mother would face.

It was now the turn of the joiner's wife, Mrs. Woods, to step forward and make known her requirements, at the same time suppressing a strong impulse to curtsey.

"Half a pound of streaky bacon, a bottle of H.P. sauce, and two pounds of sugar, if you please." The order of sauce and the sugar was soon disposed of, but the bacon, well that was a very different kettle of fish. It would involve considerable mechanical knowledge and expertise to operate the antediluvian bacon slicer. Isobel was visibly alarmed at the prospect of operating this fearsome and complicated machine. She made a rapid decision to call for help from the customer. Mrs. Woods was not unacquainted with the machinery in her husband's workshop and responded with alacrity to this second appeal for help in the space of a few minutes. Raising the counter flap, she at Isobel's behest, demonstrated the simple skills of slicing bacon. Isobel, once again, murmured her appreciation of this very practical assistance, although Isobel was painfully aware that she would need further instruction before she could handle this monster with the same aplomb as Mrs. Woods.

Now it was the turn of the publican's wife, Hilda Humphrey's, who it must be said, relished this opportunity to demonstrate her superior knowledge and experience when it came to showing a respectful and deferential manner to the quality. Mrs. Humphrey had been in service at the Big House as a parlour maid before she had married Joshua and was, therefore, well instructed in master and servant relationships. It must be recorded that Hilda was still an attractive woman and when she was courting years ago, Joshua was regarded as a very lucky man. She stepped forward – and gave a little curtsey – that would teach her ignorant companions how to treat a gentlewoman.

"A packet of Garibaldi biscuits, a pot of Colman's mustard and a pound of Cheddar cheese, if you please, ma'am, and would you like me to show you how to use the cheese wire?" Hilda knew instinctively that no gentlewoman would know how to cut wedges of cheese. Isobel accepted this third offer of help warmly and realised these kind folk were not only providing valuable instruction but cementing a most desirable customer goodwill.

Now Mrs. Wilson, the wheelwright's wife, placed her modest order.

"I want a quarter of Lyon's tea, a packet of table salt and a packet of cornflour." This presented no problems for Isobel and she was now feeling more at ease with the customers. Mrs. Wilson gave her a friendly smile as she felt inside her purse and selected the right amount of cash.

Last, but by no means the least, the mason's wife prepared to make her purchase. She did not object to being last, as this waiting time gave her an opportunity to make a surreptitious appraisal of this young lady who had displaced Martha as their new postmistress. She liked what she saw and afterwards said as much to her companions as they made their way home. The consensus of opinion was that Isobel would – in spite of being a lady born and bred – be well-received in Tillingthorpe as the successor to the more familiar Martha.

The afternoon was equally busy and time flew as no problems reared their ugly heads. At the end of the day, Isobel counted the takings and was very surprised by the final check of twelve pounds, eleven shillings and threepence. That was really encouraging and augured well for the fortunes of the new young proprietor of Tillingthorpe Post Office.

Soon Isobel was to be confronted with a new and totally unexpected dilemma that would be generated, paradoxically, by the increased trade both in the shop and in the post office.

The elusive prospect of winning a vast fortune by the simple method of inscribing eight crosses on a piece of paper, known as a football coupon, created an almost insatiable demand for postal orders and stamps every Thursday. Isobel was yet to learn that she would be paid commission on the sale of postal orders.

A phone call from Mr. Pringle informed her that she would now be responsible for the payment of old age pensions due to the forty-two elderly denizens of Tillingthorpe. This new duty would be very time consuming and Isobel knew if matters were to be kept under control, immediate action must be initiated.

That night, Isobel discussed this unforeseen problem with her mother, emphasising the urgency of what could be a threat to their slender financial resources. It was concluded that help must be obtained forthwith, but where and how could they find someone who would possess the necessary attributes of intelligence and honesty? The latter virtue was of paramount importance.

The lifeline to all the parishioners and a fount of wisdom and discretion needed to be consulted if any hope of a solution was to be found with the minimum of delay. That latter-day Solomon was, no less, the Reverend Sebastian Erasmus Copplethwaite D.D. M.A. (Oxon.). Isobel rang this mentor and solver of all humanities, trials, spiritual and temporal, to request an appointment with this scholarly man of the cloth.

The Reverend Sebastian Erasmus Copplethwaite was delighted that Isobel had decided to seek his advice so quickly and her soft feminine voice on the phone was music to his ears, for that same voice heralded an advent of further communication.

It must be made plain that the vicar of St. Botolph's church was no social climber; vicars were often the social superiors of the incumbent lord of the manor who sponsored the living. It had long been a tradition that the younger sons of many aristocratic families would enter the Church, even the youngest sons of dukes, thus many vicars were entitled to append the prefix the honourable Reverend, etc., to their names.

Truth be told, the vicar was consumed with a burning curiosity to discover the connection between the Langthornes and the Beldrakes. The Reverend was confident that in the fullness of time, he would find the solution to this most baffling and irritating mystery. After all, the church had centuries of experience extracting the truth from heretics and believers alike. As the acquaintance ripened, he would, with consummate timing together with the cunning conspiratorial skills of a medieval cardinal, unearth the information which he longed to possess.

Isobel's call for help presented the opportune moment for the vicar to reiterate his invitation for Isobel and her mother to come for dinner at eight in the evening on Wednesday. He regretted that this was the only evening available, as on Thursday he had an appointment with the bishop. Friday was always devoted to visiting the elderly and the sick in the parish, leaving Saturday for conferring with the organist and choir master and finally for refining his sermon to be delivered to his faithful flock on Sunday.

The Reverend Copplethwaite had been a widower for many years and the demise of his beloved wife, Rosemary, in the early years of his appointment, had imposed serious doubts concerning the holy intentions of the Almighty. The son that he had yearned for, to follow his footsteps to Eton and Magdalen College, Oxford, had been denied him. His bitterness, directed at a cruel fate, was exacerbated by the bishop, who imposing on his tragic loneliness, placed unwanted curates in his spacious rectory where so many rooms, all richly furnished, echoed to rare footsteps impinging on the wide elm boards. Another objection was the presence of his latest and detested pupil in matters theological; Andrew Joseph Gilbert, D.D. (Oxon.). It would not be easy to discipline a young man, so new to the ministry and so full of his own importance, in the presence of Miss Isobel Langthorne.

The vicar decided that after dinner, when his charming guest and her mother needed to confer with him concerning their as yet unspecified problem, he would sternly request the despised curate to retire, as the ladies had come to discuss matters unconnected with the Church, of a very confidential nature. The vicar concluded that this bumptious, arrogant young man must not be permitted to be present when his guests arrived, so after a moment's thought, he hatched a scheme to circumvent any risk of such a disaster.

He rang for the parlour maid to inform the curate that his presence was required immediately in his study. While she departed to convey this imperious command, the vicar penned a letter to his friend, the vicar of St. Mary's, Copthorne, a village six miles distant. The young curate appeared; he was a handsome young man with a devilish twinkle in his blue eyes, and of athletic physique. Not like a man of the cloth at all; more like the captain of a university rugby football team. The parlour maid, the house maid and the cook all adored him, and for this very reason the vicar had, on several occasions, found it necessary to admonish Andrew Joseph Gilbert for undue and unseemly familiarity with the servants. These admonishments were sometimes delivered with a warning that unless such familiarities ceased forthwith they would be followed by an adverse monthly progress report to the bishop. All these homilies had little effect on the curate, who had frequently asserted he accepted these irritating curbs as hazards of the job.

However, it was now six forty-five and the curate was about to be sent into temporary exile to the neighbouring parish to deliver an important missive to the Reverend Felix Chambers.

"Shall I take the car?" the thorn in the flesh of the vicar enquired.

"Certainly not," was the tart reply, "You may take my bicycle."

The vicar's guests would arrive about seven thirty and allow his reverence to receive them with the dignified decorum their social status demanded. It was now seven thirty and Isobel and her mother, at that precise moment, were two hundred yards from the entrance into the rectory drive. The Reverend Copplethwaite, standing at the heavy church-type door, awaited their arrival. He had already checked with the cook and was assured that dinner would be served punctually at eight. Within a few minutes the car appeared and the vicar stepped forward to assist the older lady to alight.

"So glad you could come," he said, "I have been looking forward to your visit all week." He led the way into the spacious entrance where the parlour maid took their coats.

He then proceeded from the hall into the sitting room, the late Mrs. Copplethwaite's personal domain, accordingly furnished and decorated with impeccable taste. On each side of the Victorian tiled fireplace, in the alcoves, two bookcases hugged the wall from floor to ceiling. They contained many of the great classics – Jane Austen, the Brontë sisters, Alexandre Dumas, Victor Hugo's *Les Miserables*, Homer's *Iliad*, Chaucer's *Canterbury Tales* and works by George Eliot, the famous Victorian female novelist.

An enormous settee was strategically placed in front of the fire; two large armchairs were to the right and left, all covered in floral patterned chintz. An exquisite Queen Anne writing bureau stood adjacent to a Pembroke table which supported two valuable Chinese pot pourri vases.

The longest wall in the room, opposite the fireplace, was completely covered by a massive mahogany and glass cabinet displaying many examples of Crown Derby and Staffordshire pottery. In the centre a remarkable display of work by Josiah Wedgwood completed this collection of rare and precious porcelain.

To the right of the door giving access to the dining room, a tall bay window looked out on to an orchard. To the left of this door stood a fine Sheraton tallboy.

Above the fireplace there was a head and shoulders portrait of the Reverend Sebastian Erasmus Copplethwaite in his Master of Arts academic gown and mortar board. Other spaces were filled with Mrs. Copplethwaite's watercolours of local cottages and landscapes.

The Vicar poured three fine vintage dry sherries as an aperitif while saying, "Please do make yourselves comfortable." Isobel and her mother accepted this cue to sit down on the settee and remarked on the pretty tiling of the fireplace. While sipping their sherry, the vicar made small talk, "Are you settling in your new quarters?" he enquired.

"Yes, we did feel a trifle depressed at first, but we are now feeling a lot more cheerful and the village folk have been so helpful." Mrs. Langthorne responded.

Turning to Isobel he said, "What of you, Miss Langthorne, do you think you will be happy in Tillingthorpe?"

"Oh yes, I think the countryside is so lovely and when I get my pony, I am truly looking forward to exploring the local area."

The vicar seized on this remark knowing that this seemingly innocuous reference to a pony could be a significant pointer to other intelligence. "Pony?" he repeated.

"Yes, I have a thoroughbred Arab pony, but sadly, circumstances forced me to leave her in India."

Circumstances, the vicar mused, I wonder what those particular circumstances were. Being a skilled and wily tactician this was definitely a matter to be left to another time, another place.

"I hunt with the Berkshire you know and have a couple of hunters in my stable. If you ever feel you would like to ride you are welcome to use them." Isobel declined saying she would not be able to cope with a mount as large and as powerful as a hunter.

The sound of the dinner gong signalled the end of this conversation and led by the vicar, they filed into the dining room.

This room was panelled in oak. The ceiling was beautifully decorated by an oval painting in the centre of Miriam finding Moses in the bulrushes. Four small, circular paintings depicted the heads of saints. The room was about thirty feet long and twenty-five feet wide. The fireplace, constructed of marble and about eight feet long, had a heavy marble mantelpiece supported by angels. Above the fireplace and sculpted in chalk were the arms of one of the more noble past bishops of Oxford. A shield displayed the arms of the city of Oxford, supported by a Talbot and a stag with a bishop's mitre as a crest. The walls supported various oil paintings, one of the 'High' in Oxford, one of the Isis attributed to Herring Senior, and one of the White Horse at Uffington by William Lovel. Mention must be included of the fine moulded frieze under the ceiling, depicting the fruits of the earth, corn sheaves, bunches of grapes, apples, and so on.

But now we are hungry and must join the Reverend and his guests in this magnificent room. They had barely sat down when the door was thrust open and the curate, muttering his apologies, appeared.

"I do apologise, sir, I was delayed by the vicar of Copthorne, who insisted on an immediate reply to your letter." The Reverend Copplethwaite, now seated in that throne of authority at the head of the table, graciously excused this lapse. He knew exactly why the Reverend Felix Chambers had insisted on penning a response by return.

The vicar airily introduced his guests to the curate, who had now turned a deep cherry red and was apparently having trouble with his breathing as he stared at the ladies as though in the spell of some hypnotic trance. All his ebullient self-assured, 'What have we here then' attitude appeared to have drained out of his feet, as bath water makes its gurgling exit down a plug hole.

Isobel looked straight into his face and murmured a polite, "How do you do." Mr. Gilbert, the curate, was in a daze; why did the supporters of the mantelpiece keep changing places and why, for goodness sake, was there a curious vibrating under his feet?

The vicar, observing this extraordinary behaviour said testily, "Sit down, man. I shall speak to you later."

The curate was to discover that his allies, the cook and two maids, had betrayed him. They had told him that his vicar had invited two ladies to dinner, and as the curate lacked opportunities to become acquainted with members of the opposite sex of appropriate social status he presented a highly receptive ear to this inside information, which made his hopes soar like a lark. When they told him it was the new owner of the village shop and her daughter, his joyful hopes plummeted to earth like a shot pheasant. An image flashed into his brain of a buxom middle aged woman with rosy cheeks and a daughter fifteen years of age with plaits down to her waist. When he, subsequently, saw these ladies in the flesh he was quite unprepared for the paralysis which engulfed him in the dining room.

Isobel endeavoured to engage the young cleric who sat opposite in conversation, without any semblance of an animated reaction. The old vicar was amused by the young man's discomfiture and apparent preoccupation with his own thoughts. Such a change from his asinine comments, such as, "With the greatest respect, sir, may I suggest that your sermons should be shortened to allow more singing of hymns or psalms." Or, even worse: "I think if the rood screen were to be removed it would permit the service to become more public, more open as it were." This last suggestion was regarded by the vicar as downright heresy, as this was the very first act of vandalism perpetrated by other priests whenever they infiltrated Church of England parishes. No, the Reverend Copplethwaite was more than satisfied with his companions at dinner this night.

The vicar was a real Englishman, and his table was well-served by his present staff every day with a varying menu of steak and kidney pies, steak and kidney puddings, roast beef with horseradish sauce and Yorkshire pudding, rabbit stew, roast pork with apple sauce, all followed by real puddings, not sweets, jam roly-poly, rhubarb tart, plum pies. Not this French trash of two lettuce leaves and four shrimps with mayonnaise, or frog's legs, or, even more revolting, pickled snails. An English parson needed something very substantial in his belly if he rode to hounds, and expected to serve his parishioners in matters of baptisms, funerals and putting the fear of God into the hearts of so many sinners. He explained that hounds first hunted fox in Berkshire under the mastership of John Loder, Rector of Hinton Waldrist and lord of the manors of Hinton and Longworth, 1760 to 1805.

Dinner over, the vicar excused himself and his guests, by informing the curate that the ladies had come to discuss confidential matters to which no third person must be privy. They were matters of non-parochial substance. As he led the guests into his study, he threw this parting shot over his shoulder to the curate. "I hope you will use this opportunity to further your theological studies which you have somewhat neglected of late?"

The study was lined with books, a double mahogany desk dominated the room. Numerous photographs of groups of young men in college blazers were scattered around the study. A large, very beautiful portrait in a silver frame, of his late wife, Rosemary, was placed near his blotter, to permit him to raise his eyes to look adoringly at her.

When he saw his guests comfortably seated, he rang for the maid to bring in the coffee. Turning his attention to the ladies, he said, "Now, how can I be of service to you?" Isobel then explained the sudden and unexpected surge in demands on both the post office and shop, and how she and her mother had decided that - in spite of their limited income - no option was available to them, but the engagement of someone to operate the shop while Isobel coped with the post office. Having made this decision, they were then confronted with yet another problem: how, as total strangers with only a vague knowledge of the people in Tillingthorpe, could they recruit a young person who was both intelligent and honest?

"Well," he replied, "This is not the most difficult situation to which I have been asked to find an answer to, in my parochial duties, and I can, therefore, give you an assurance that I am very confident that when I call upon you in two or three days hence I will be in a position to nominate a candidate who will surely meet all your specified requirements."

The vicar then skilfully turned the conversation to his opening gambit, which he hoped, would lead him to the connection between the Beldrakes and the Langthornes.

"I understand you came to Tillingthorpe from India."

"Yes," Mrs. Langthorne confirmed, "Two very different environments, I fear."

"My brother, Viscount Copplethwaite spent three years there," he said. "He was a colonel in the 17/21st. Lancers. That was many years ago, of course, and he has been retired these many years."

The two ladies looked at each other, a trifle surprised by this double revelation: first that he came from a landed, titled family and second that he was not unacquainted with both the army and the country they had so recently left. Then the vicar adroitly changed the theme of the conversation by informing them he had been the youngest son in a family of seven including his parents. "Four boys and a girl!" he stated laconically.

Isobel and her mother thanked the vicar for his kind hospitality and added, "When you can find time, we would love you to take tea with us. Do say you will come." said Isobel.

The vicar expressed his pleasure at receiving this rare opportunity to enjoy the companionship and conversation of refined and educated gentlewomen. Then his face momentarily clouded with sadness, glancing towards the photograph of his late wife, he said,

"You know my wife was a very cultured woman and I miss her very much. In fact, when she was taken from me, I had grave doubts concerning the compassion and pity that we have all been taught to expect from God."

Mrs. Langthorne interjected, "I know exactly what you mean."

The Reverend Sebastian Erasmus Copplethwaite escorted his new found friends to the car, thanking them profusely for the visit and hoping that it would not be long before they honoured him with another equally enjoyable evening.

Chapter 7

The next day the groom came from the Big House for the very substantial order that was placed every week and Isobel needed her mother's help to cope with this and the other order from Home Farm. It was a hectic day and both were relieved when Saturday midday closing time arrived.

Sunday morning brought another surprise, Viscount Beldrake appeared, to discover for himself how his relations were adjusting to this drastic change of lifestyle and environment. He looked at Isobel with open admiration; he was only twenty-six years of age and still a bachelor. It was, therefore, quite natural that at that moment he should feel a sharp pang of regret at the close blood relationship she enjoyed with him.

Turning to Mrs. Langthorne, whom he rightly addressed as aunt, he invited her to offer any suggestions which would enable him, as landlord, to make practical and structural alterations which would improve their quality of life. After a brief consultation, they all made a thorough inspection of the property. It was decided that the cool, spacious larder, with its shallow lead-lined curing trough and large hooks in the overhead beams, should be cleaned, whitewashed and fitted with marble slabs. No one was aware that beneath this larder was a secret chamber; much would later be revealed concerning its history.

The three adjacent rooms, including the present wood store, would be knocked into one long room to form a kitchen, which would be fitted with an Aga cooker. The existing kitchen, as used by Martha, would be converted to a sitting room. The cooking range would be removed and the massive inglenook fireplace restored. The back and front doors should be replaced with wide, arched church-type doors to permit at least some of their large furniture to be brought in.

Turning to his aunt, the young gentleman said, "You cannot possibly remain here while all this disruption is in progress, so I insist that you move into the Dower House until such alterations are complete; you can still operate the business and return at the end of the day to the peace and quiet that I offer." Mrs. Langthorne and her daughter unhesitatingly accepted this generous offer. As the Viscount made towards the car, Isobel suddenly remembered the Official Secrets Form and requested her kinsman witness her signature; he readily complied with Isobel's request.

An army of workmen and tradesmen descended upon the cottage and all worked like beavers to transform the building as speedily as possible. The head gardener then appeared with two under gardeners to lay a lawn, and plant shrubs, roses and flowering trees.

When the old range was removed, it necessitated the stripping of some crude wooden panelling which enclosed the cooker, extending to the ceiling. This exposed an enormous open fire, six feet deep and five feet high; it was eight feet long with an oak beam, twelve inches by twelve inches, and twelve feet long. The original fire basket was still in place. Bench seats were fixed to the right and left walls.

On either side of the inglenook, two wooden doors, carved with oak leaves, were flush with the wall: about fourteen inches by fourteen inches. In the right hand cupboard there were three Waterford glass goblets with green shamrock leaves in the bottom, a tobacco jar and a broken clay pipe.

The young and excited apprentice peered into the darkness of the left-hand cupboard: his keen young eyes spotted a small hole in the back wooden panel. He reached in and, placing his finger in the small orifice, pulled. To his astonishment, this tiny door opened and revealed an even darker cavity, which his eyes could not penetrate. Amid great excitement a torch was sent for and the beam, piercing the womb-like darkness, rebounded in a thousand sparkling, twinkling, flashing facets of light. The boy was now trembling with apprehension, in case some hidden malevolent creature mounted guard over the treasure. Urged on by his comrades he thrust his arm to its fullest extent into the cavity and gingerly withdrew what resembled a large baking tin overflowing with jewels and necklaces.

They were now afraid to touch it and summoned Isobel from the post office to see the secret hoard which they had wrested from the bowels of the old inglenook. Isobel's eyes dilated with wonder at this momentous discovery.

"We must summon the police at once!" she cried. "It must be stolen property, therefore no one must touch it." Isobel rang the Oxford police, who informed her that they would treat the call as an emergency and would be there in half an hour.

They arrived and were escorted to the hoard of gems. The detective sergeant said, "It must have been there for a great number of years as no robberies of this magnitude have been reported for at least fifty years. It could, possibly, be deemed treasure trove. We will have to convene a coroner's court at once; in the meantime, I will list the items in the presence of you all before taking the whole lot into police custody." He addressed himself to Isobel saying, "We will keep you informed."

When the baking tin containing the hoard was removed by the detective sergeant, all present gasped at the dazzling array of glittering splendour. The police then commenced the cataloguing, with all the meticulous, ponderous thoroughness of the law; reminding all witnesses that they might be called upon to give evidence in a coroner's court and such grave responsibilities were not to be taken lightly.

ONE MASSIVE GOLD CRUCIFIX.
TWO EMERALD AND RUBY PENDANTS.
THREE DIAMOND AND SAPPHIRE PENDANTS.
ONE RUBY AND SAPPHIRE PENDANT WITH LARGE PEAR-SHAPED PEARL DROPPER.
THREE DIAMOND AND EMERALD NECKLACES WITH MATCHING EARRINGS.
TWENTY GOLD LOCKETS STUDDED WITH DIAMONDS.
FOUR MAGNIFICENT DIAMOND, RUBY AND SAPPHIRE COLLARS.
TWENTY HEAVY GOLD BROOCHES.
ONE SAPPHIRE COLLAR SUPPORTING A SPECTACULAR OPAL, SET IN GOLD.
TWENTY GOLD BRACELETS.

FOUR PAIRS OF GENTLEMAN'S SILVER SHOE BUCKLES, SET WITH EMERALDS.
FIVE PEARL COLLARS.
SIX PEARL NECKLACES OF LARGE PEARLS WITH DIAMOND CLASPS.
FIFTY ASSORTED RINGS – LADIES AND GENTS.
A MAGNIFICENT DUCAL CORONET SET WITH RUBIES, SAPPHIRES, EMERALDS AND DIAMONDS.

The assembled onlookers; workmen, and Isobel and her mother, were all engrossed in one universal thought: who would be declared the ultimate owner of this exceedingly valuable hoard? The finder, Isobel and her mother, or the owner of the cottage, Viscount Beldrake.

After the listing of all these precious articles, the detective turned to the stunned onlookers and said, "Now, do you all agree that I have made an accurate inventory of the entire contents of this tin?" All quietly agreed that this was so. Again, the detective sergeant reminded all and sundry that they might be called to reaffirm this corroboration on oath.

That night, in The Red Lion, Joshua was so busy drawing pots of ale that he engaged in the unprecedented act of calling his wife, Hilda, to assist him in the bar. This time, The Red Lion bore an even stronger resemblance to a bee hive, where the bees' tranquil and industrious preoccupation with their timeless activities had been brought to a halt by an invasion of wasps.

Some of the younger patrons became so heated in their vehement opinions as to who was the rightful owner of the jewels, that their belligerence had to be quelled by the vast looming presence of the blacksmith towering over them. This impromptu self-appointed jury decided that one half should go to the young apprentice who found it, one quarter to the postmistress, Isobel, with the remainder to be divided between the rest of the village.

Some were so confident that this would happen, that they were telling each other how they intended to spend their allotted portion.

Isobel and her mother had already informed the police that the property was owned by Viscount Beldrake and did they not agree that the viscount should be made cognisant with all the facts surrounding the discovery? The detective agreed that this was absolutely imperative and furthermore that he would permit Viscount Beldrake to examine the jewels.

While this sensational discovery excluded all other topics of conversation, in every nook and cranny of Tillingthorpe, the vicar, who had already learned of the location of the hoard, was already engaged in his personal researches into local history. He soon unearthed what he believed to be the answer to the identity of the man who had hidden the loot many years ago. The vicar read in a book in his library that a certain Robert Noakes was hanged for highway robbery on the gibbet, which stood on Mortimer common in south Berkshire. His elder brother, Daniel Noakes, had been head keeper to the Beldrakes and had lived in the cottage, now the post office.

Up until 1810, Robert Noakes had gathered a rich harvest from travellers on the Oxford to Bath road. He appeared to have an uncanny knowledge or warning of when the Red Coats were waiting in ambush for him and never once rode into the trap, where he would have come to a violent and ignominious end. Several times he had been pursued to the outskirts of both Copthorne and Tillingthorpe where he appeared to vanish from the face of the earth. When he was finally captured, one mystery was never solved: the total disappearance of his horse, which had carried him to his secret refuge on so many hard-pressed pursuits. The horse was a half-blood light chestnut gelding with one white sock on his off foreleg. Robert Noakes was once heard to comment that he could never love any woman with the same devotion as he loved his horse.

The vicar was certain that this was the man who had hidden the jewels in the inglenook nearly a hundred years ago. The vicar continued his probing into the lives of Robert and now Daniel Noakes. The church register revealed the tragic record of Daniel's death at the hands of a gang of poachers in November, 1832. The vicar was soon to learn of other facts which supported his suspicions that the two brothers may have been accomplices in crime.

The large garden was bounded on one side by a stone wall, the other two sides, comprising a right angle, consisted of a hawthorn hedge. The stone wall was built on to the house and was pierced by a solid wooden gate, five feet high. This wall was smothered by a rambling rose and the part adjacent to the gate was cloaked in a blanket of dark green ivy. Close examination of this wall, which protruded twenty feet from the house, revealed that it was considerably thicker than the other section which continued to enclose the garden on one side.

The gardeners sent from the Big House to tidy up and plant the badly overgrown half an acre of garden, turned their attention to the unsightly growth of ivy. It soon yielded to their bill hooks and to their astonishment exposed another wooden door. The door appeared to be strongly secured by a large staple-shaped steel handle and only by accident did they discover the clever secret bolt action. When the handle was lifted, the top swivelled, withdrawing the concealed bolt permitting the door to be opened.

The passage between the double wall was stone-flagged and gave access to yet another door which opened easily. A flight of stone steps ran down from this door and the workmen, with beating hearts and mounting curiosity, descended into the room beneath the larder. A crude wooden bed with a straw mattress and a pile of grubby blankets was placed against the wall. On the opposite wall stood a fireplace with a wide, tapering chimney breast; if one looked up the chimney, one could discern foot and hand holds, formed by the simple expedient of omitting bricks during its construction.

A narrow ladder was brought and a volunteer ascended the chimney. He shouted, "There is another door here."

"Where does it go?" came the cry in unison from the less daring souls clustered below.

Many years ago, before this door was fitted, it was laid flat on the ground and painted; while the paint was still wet, soot was shovelled on to it making it quite invisible to anyone who might look up the chimney.

Urged on by his friends, waiting excitedly below, the young workman crawled through the small hatch door. He discovered that, as he suspected, it gave access to the vast roof space to which there was no other entrance.

"I'm coming down," he called, and two of his mates hastened to man the ladder. When he set foot on the hearth he said, "It leads into the roof area." Two of his comrades, whose imaginations were still fired by the discovery of the treasure which had lurked all those years in the inglenook, insisted on climbing the chimney into the roof in case their colleague had failed to locate other treasures.

All, wishing to make an impression on the lovely Isobel, rushed into the house to inform her of their latest uncovering of the secrets of the old village shop. Isobel was as excited and as curious as the workmen and promised to share their discovery as soon as her waiting customer had been served. A few minutes later, Isobel appeared in their midst and amidst much jostling for position, they showed her the secret passage which led to the chamber. As they all stood in the underground chamber, the excitement shining in Isobel's dark eyes was all the reward they could wish for.

That night, all the workmen assembled in The Red Lion to savour to the full the envy of lesser people who were acutely disappointed that the revelations did not refer to further discoveries of treasure. Joshua was quite stunned by this second discovery which filled his bar and threatened to exhaust his stocks of ale. Joshua turned quite pale at the thought of such a disastrous state of affairs and would regard this as a personal disgrace, as never in the history of The Red Lion had a landlord 'run dry'.

The Reverend Copplethwaite had now found what he considered an excellent solution to the problem they had put to him on that never to be forgotten night when the Langthorne's came to dinner. He was also keen to tell them about his research into the lives of the Noakes brothers and his consequent belief that they had hidden the cache of jewels in the inglenook fireplace. He picked up the phone on his desk and called Isobel to enquire if it would be convenient for him to call one evening, after closing time, as he had good news for them. Isobel advised him that they were now living at the Dower House on the Beldrake estate and they would, therefore, be able to entertain him to dinner. This news was music to the vicar's ears.

"I will arrive promptly at seven-thirty, if that will be suitable." Isobel assured him that he would be very welcome. The vicar replaced the earpiece and pondered this fresh development where the Beldrakes had reared their obtrusive head.

"Patience, old chap, will bring the answer to the riddle which has plagued you for so long," he murmured to himself.

While all the excitement held the inhabitants in its thrall, Mr. Pringle had received the Official Secrets Act Form, signed by Isobel and witnessed by, what appeared to be, a Viscount Beldrake. Mr. Pringle, being unable to accept the evidence of his own eyes, opened the drawer in his desk and extracted a large round magnifying glass and peering intently through it was able to confirm that the witness was indeed a titled gentleman. Mr. Pringle ruminated upon a postmistress; no, a sub-postmistress, who had friends among the landed gentry. Instinct warned him that he must tread warily and any future dealings with the sub-postmistress of Tillingthorpe must be conducted with the utmost caution. The Viscount, would doubtless have friends in high places, even in the House of Commons, and quite possibly the House of Lords. These conjectures made him feel quite ill and very vulnerable.

He decided that this was one of life's tormenting trials sent to plague conscientious senior postmasters. He would grasp the nettle firmly. Then, writing in his desk diary he recorded that on the eighth of April he would visit the Tillingthorpe Post Office with the authority vested in him by that august personage the Postmaster General of all England.

At the specified date, he would call at the Tillingthorpe Post Office, but he must take care not to expose the fear that the Viscount's signature had instilled in him. For example, he must avoid making concessions or granting favours beyond Isobel's official entitlements, for that would arouse suspicions in Miss Langthorne's pretty head. He concluded that this matter was not of an urgent nature and could thus await his personal convenience.

The vicar was awaiting, with a pleasant sense of anticipation, his dinner appointment at the Dower House. The next evening the Langthorne's were waiting in the drawing room - with the absence of servants - Isobel would receive the reverend gentleman at the open door, take his hat and coat and lead him into the drawing room where Mrs. Langthorne would entertain him while Isobel prepared to serve the meal.

Chapter 8

The Dower House although the size of a small manor house, was richly appointed. Portraits of the Beldrakes ancestors and beautiful tapestries graced the walls, while precious porcelain and ornaments were scattered on the several tables, cabinets and pedestals.

One of the kitchen maids from the Big House had volunteered to assist Isobel in the preparation of the dinner. A cutlet of salmon was chosen as the first course, accompanied by a medium quality German white wine. This was to be followed by roast pheasant, courtesy of the head keeper, served with mushrooms, tomatoes, sauté potatoes and bread sauce. The selected wine would be an inexpensive vintage Bordeaux claret. To complete the meal, chocolate mousse was served.

After dinner they all retired to the drawing room where the vicar became more mellow with a large brandy and an excellent, fragrant cigar. The ladies indulged in a Benedictine liqueur. At her mother's prompting, Isobel played Chopin, Brahms and Mozart on the Broadwood grand piano.

The Reverend Sebastian Erasmus Copplethwaite positively glowed with utter satisfaction and pleasure. Indeed, he could not recall an occasion, since his wife's death, when he had felt so much enjoyment. It had not escaped his shrewd observing eyes that Mrs. Langthorne was still a very attractive woman and would grace, nay improve, the environment of any rectory in the diocese. He was convinced that this night, the friendship between church and post office had been much enhanced.

He now consulted his gold hunter pocket watch, with a dial displaying all the phases of the moon, together with the day and date. "Dear me, ladies," he exclaimed, "How swiftly the time has passed, I must not impose on your hospitality a minute longer than it takes me to offer my solution to the personal problem you consulted me about on the night you honoured me with your presence at my home. I will tell you about my choice of an assistant to you in your business."

Ted Turner's daughter was one of the brightest pupils at Tillingthorpe School and had won a scholarship to Witney grammar school. Sadly, she did not enjoy the fruits of her diligent studies because her parents could not afford the various expenses of uniform, sports equipment and books, etc. The headmaster of the village school kept her on as a pupil teacher until she reached the age of sixteen years, when with great reluctance, he had to dispense with her services. Her name was Jane Sarah Turner. He had approached both her and her parents, who were delighted with this opportunity for their daughter, which would also supplement the slender family income and provide Jane with pocket money.

The Langthornes listened attentively and when the vicar had finished, they accepted this solution to their dilemma with alacrity and thanked him most profusely for his very practical help.

"Now I really must tear myself away from the charming company of your good selves, but before I depart I must extract a promise from you both, that in the immediate future you will honour me with your presence at dinner to relate the result of my personal researches which I am very certain will convince you of the identity of the persons involved in secreting the loot discovered in your cottage."

Isobel's eyes glowed with anticipation at the mere thought of such exciting and startling discoveries. Even Mrs. Langthorne expressed her wish to be enlightened concerning the thrilling facts which had emerged from the vicar's researches.

"Would the very next evening be too early?" he queried.

"Oh, most certainly not!" Isobel replied. "I simply cannot wait a single minute longer than necessary."

"Wouldn't it be marvellous to be able to visualise this rogue, for that is what the police believe he is." The vicar said his goodbyes, saying how much he looked forward to their pending visit and promising to present Jane to them in the morning at eleven o'clock.

The next day at eleven o'clock as arranged, the vicar appeared with Jane, introducing her to the Langthornes, who took to her as ducks take to water. They offered Jane two pounds ten shillings a week with a white coat provided free and refreshments at ten-thirty each morning in the kitchen.

Jane was approaching her seventeenth birthday; a slim, attractive girl with fair hair and blue eyes and of happy disposition. Her sudden recruitment into the Langthorne household would change her life profoundly, because fate had decreed that her happy, bustling life with the Langthornes would eventually lead her to a young man who would, ultimately, make her his bride-to-be, joined in holy matrimony as man and wife by the Reverend Sebastian Erasmus Copplethwaite, D.D. M.A. (Oxon.). That happy day must be left in the store of life's unexpected surprises of good fortune. It was agreed that Jane would report for her new duties at nine o'clock on Monday. The vicar also took his departure, reminding the ladies that he would await their arrival at seven thirty that evening.

Isobel was all agog with the anticipated disclosures as to the identity of the man who had hidden the jewels in the inglenook fireplace. That evening, both ladies said how fortunate they were to enjoy the friendship of such a kind, scholarly and cultured man.

Chapter 9

It was time to go and it would be ungrateful and discourteous to keep the vicar waiting, although it was now the end of April and the evenings were balmy. A few minutes later, the vicar greeted them at the door and the delight on the gentleman's face was plain for all to see. They entered the drawing room where, this time, the curate sitting in one of the fireside chairs, was reading an old edition of *The Wide World Magazine*. He rose to his feet as the guests entered and bowed.

Mrs. Langthorne looked at this young man, the bane of the vicar's life, and thought how incongruous he looked in his drab charcoal grey suit and dog collar. In spite of that, he reminded her of the young subalterns in her husband's regiment and she suspected that he might be happier in army life than as a servant of the Church.

"How long have you been in Tillingthorpe?" she politely enquired.

"One year precisely," he replied. Isobel seized this opportunity to make an appraisal of this young man who had been so subdued and silent during dinner on their previous visit.

The dinner gong signalled the end of any further observations and they trooped into the dining room, where the curate was relieved to see that the angel supporters of the mantelpiece, unlike that last disastrous, humiliating occasion, were perfectly still. The dinner proceeded with small talk, which permitted Mrs. Langthorne to probe gently and tactfully into the curate's background.

"Do you," she asked, "have any brothers or sisters?"

"I have one brother at Oxford studying medicine and an elder sister who is sister tutor at Bartholomew's Hospital, London." Mrs. Langthorne waited, in the hope that this patently unhappy young man would contribute to the desultory conversation. Isobel then stepped into the breach to engage the curate, in the hope that he would become a little more extrovert and subscribe more of himself. The vicar surveyed these efforts of the ladies to stimulate his young assistant with sardonic amusement, as the contrast in the curate's arrogant, boisterous behaviour was so marked.

"Did you enjoy your three years at college?" she enquired.

"I used to row for my college," he said. "Regrettably, I never succeeded in my trials for the Varsity Eight, but competition is very keen and only the heaviest and most skilful are chosen."

The vicar, feeling in a magnanimous mood, said to his guests, "My curate secured a first class honours degree at Oxford and his father was a distinguished surgeon at Guy's Hospital, London. Mr. Gilbert does tend to 'hide his light under a bushel' but credit must be given - as in his case - where it is so handsomely due." The curate acknowledged this rare bestowal of praise and smiled at Isobel, who was now beginning to feel a trifle sorry for this brow-beaten young man.

"We would like you to come to tea one Saturday afternoon. Would you come?" His eyes lit up and his face appeared to be bathed in a holy light.

"I would love to come," he responded.

"This coming Saturday at three, then," Isobel suggested.

The vicar signalled the end of dinner and rose to his feet. Turning to Mr. Gilbert, he said, "I will be in my study for the remainder of the evening with my guests and on no account am I to be disturbed." The curate nodded.

In the study, the vicar said, "Since my dear wife passed away, it has been my custom to sit here in a quiet reverie while enjoying a glass of brandy and a good cigar. Would you be offended if I enjoyed my brandy and cigar while I relate to you the result of my researches into our local history which I believe will reveal the identity of the man, who not only hid the jewels, but who also stole them from law abiding citizens who were travelling on the turnpike from Oxford to Bath in the stage coaches which ran a regular service?"

The vicar then produced his volume of *The History of the County of Berkshire* and opened the tome to a bookmark which he had placed at the appropriate page. He showed Mrs. Langthorne and Isobel the reference to the highwayman, Robert Noakes, hanged on the gibbet on Mortimer Common in the year 1810.

He drew their attention to the fact that his brother was head keeper to the Beldrakes and lived in the house now occupied by Isobel and her mother. The vicar then expounded his personal opinion that the brothers were comrades in these heinous and capital offences. He was very confident that Robert could not have hidden his cache of gems without the full knowledge and acquiescence of his brother Daniel. The ladies were awe-struck by this saga of violent crime associated with not only the village, but the very place in which they were living.

Suddenly, Isobel remembered the vicar had not seen the secret room beneath the larder and exhorted him to come and inspect the chamber with its cunningly concealed escape hatch. The vicar considered that these three significant pieces of evidence were conclusive proof of his own theory. The vicar continued, musingly, "If what we all suspect is true, it could affect the coroner's verdict at the forthcoming inquest." He decided it would be prudent to take legal advice and said as much to his guests. "Yes, I shall call at my solicitors, Beadle, Beadle and Sons at their chambers in the High, Oxford." They parted that night with feelings of tense excitement, the vicar promising to keep them informed, Isobel reminding him to come and see the sinister chamber uncovered by the workmen.

Thanking them for a rare and pleasant evening they said, "*Au revoir.*"

That night, lying sleepless with excitement, Isobel was not frightened by the vicar's discourse about the highwayman as she allowed her girlish, romantic imagination to run riot.

A poem by Alfred Noyes was one of her favourite works; it was called 'The Highwayman'. He was deeply in love with the innkeeper's daughter, Bess. He would ride up beneath her window and standing on his saddle would tap softly on her casement with his whip until she rose from her bed and came to greet him.

Isobel fell into a fitful sleep, and what was that tapping on her window? She saw him in her dreams.

He'd a French cocked-hat on his forehead,
A bunch of lace at his chin.
A coat of the claret velvet and breeches of brown
doeskin.
They fitted with never a wrinkle.
His boots were up to the thigh.
And he rode with a jewelled twinkle,
His pistol butts a-twinkle,
His rapier hilt a-twinkle,
Under the jewelled sky.

Isobel woke with a start to the sound of tapping on her bedroom door. Her mother called, "We have overslept and must make haste to prepare." Isobel leapt out of bed, and hastily dressing, splashed her face with cool water which immediately revived her. She ran downstairs into the kitchen and made tea. They scrambled into the car and drove to the post office where they unlocked the door with only a few minutes to spare. It was Saturday and they closed promptly at one, so it would not be too hard on them.

Isobel remembered that the curate was unaware they had taken up temporary residence in the Dower House and asked her mother to phone the Rectory to rectify this omission. At three-thirty, on the dot, the curate arrived at the Dower House; he leaned his bicycle against the wall and grasping the cast iron knob of the bell, gave it a double tug. He was dismayed by the thunderous clanging reverberating through the vast hall. Isobel, guessing that Mr. Gilbert had arrived, hurried to the door. "So pleased you could come," she greeted him, "We have been looking forward to your visit."

She led him into the beautiful drawing room, where he felt somewhat overawed by the grandeur of the chamber and the splendour which surrounded him. Isobel conducted him to a large rectangular window which provided extensive views over the park and sat beside him on a cushioned window seat. "Is this your first visit to the Dower House?" she enquired of Mr. Gilbert.

"I am afraid so: such grand places do not come within the orbit of my humble parochial obligations, but thanks to you, I have been granted a glimpse of 'how the other half lives'."

Isobel was wearing a kilted skirt of hunting Stuart tartan with a pure silk shirt blouse open at her throat, revealing a small heart-shaped locket on a gold chain. It contained tiny photographs of both her parents. Her feet were encased in flat-heeled plain black leather shoes with a small rectangular silver buckle. Isobel wore fine black woollen stockings.

Picking up a cashmere cardigan she turned to the curate saying, "Shall we walk in the garden?" Mr. Gilbert's heart not only soared like a lark, but sang like one. The pleasure of walking in any garden with this vision of loveliness was given to very, very few men and an added bonus was the absence of the vicar with his frequent acerbic interjections. "You must excuse my mother's absence – she is resting and will join us for tea."

In that idyllic environment, the curate became more relaxed and confided to Isobel that he harboured grave doubts concerning his future in the church and had, at times, in the solitude of his bachelor quarters contemplated resignation and a change of vocation. A change of horses in mid-stream as it were. His mother however – the daughter of a bishop – was anxious for him to remain with his present commitment. Isobel gave a sympathetic ear to these outpourings and told him he reminded her of the young subalterns in her father's regiment.

His eyes lit up as he embarked on another outburst of soul baring. "Do you know, I always wanted to make a career in the army but reluctantly, I yielded to parental pressure." As an afterthought, he added, "They do give me an allowance of seven hundred pounds a year."

Danger signals were sounding in Isobel's head as she realised they were straying on to dangerous ground. She laid her hand gently on his arm, saying, "Do excuse my digression, but there is something I must ask you, something quite exciting. Have you heard about the secret room discovered by the workmen?"

"I have heard vague reports about the hoard of jewels, but none of that which you refer to."

"When you have time, do come to our house and I will show you myself." The curate promised to give her a ring to check when it would be convenient.

At this moment, Mrs. Langthorne appeared, greeted Mr. Gilbert warmly and informed them that she had prepared tea. Isobel and her mother were pleased to perceive that Mr. Gilbert had changed from his normal funereal clerical attire into a well-cut sports jacket and grey flannel trousers. The trio then entered the house and adjourned to the drawing room where tea had been laid out on a snow white lace tablecloth on a small table. It consisted of salmon sandwiches, lettuce and tomatoes from the kitchen garden, mayonnaise and thin brown bread and butter, followed by jam sponge provided by the Beldrake's cook.

With the two ladies all to himself and the absence of the vicar's acid wit, the young man positively glowed, his cornflower blue eyes sparkled and his dark hair gleamed like the sheen on a swallow's wings.

Mrs. Langthorne then turned her maternal attention to the young Mr. Gilbert. "Have you any hobbies?"

"Oh, yes," he replied. "I fish - only coarse fishing, you understand, as I could never afford the astronomical fees demanded for even one day to fish in trout and salmon rivers. I am also a member of my old college Rifle Club."

"What college would that be?" Isobel interjected.

"Jesus – what else?" He replied with a broad grin.

The time passed all too quickly and at six o'clock, the curate announced, despondently, he would have to return to the rectory. "Why don't you take Mr. Gilbert back in the car?" Isobel's mother suggested.

"What a good idea!" Isobel agreed. "We can put your cycle in the boot." The two young people set off in the car and chattered animatedly during the short journey of two miles.

That night, at dinner, the vicar flashed surreptitious, suspicious glances at his dining companion. He had never seen him display such consideration, such deference; he even engaged in intelligent conversation. That had never been known in the one year he had resided at the rectory. The vicar on occasion, had confided that, to him, it seemed more like ten years. It was futile to pray that the bishop would soon find him a living, because he might be replaced with someone who was even more of a know-all and possibly more arrogant. The reverend dismissed these forebodings to ponder this remarkable change in his curate's demeanour. The more engrossed he became, the more baffling this mysterious transformation appeared.

The wily old fox decided that he must approach this perplexing state of affairs with extreme stealth if he was to find a logical answer. "Did I see you entering the church this afternoon with the mason?" he queried nonchalantly.

"No, sir, I went for a cycle ride. I took your bicycle: I hope you do not object?" A long pause. Round one to the curate.

"Are you aware that Jane Sarah Turner, the cowman's daughter, is about to start work in Tillingthorpe village shop as an assistant to the Langthornes?" Again the curate was forced to confess that he was in total ignorance of any such developments.

There followed an even longer silence before the vicar would launch, for now, his final sally. "I have been informed that extensive alterations are being effected in the post office and there are rumours, circulating round the village, that all this costly work has been carried out on the express orders of Viscount Beldrake. Had the curate been privy to such rumours?"

The curate, well aware of the reason for the vicar's subtle probing, felt that it was now his turn to indulge in subterfuge.

"Really, sir, you surprise me, I had no idea such rumours were rife." This riposte was delivered with just the right amount of astonishment. The vicar decided the matter must not be pursued, as he wished to avoid the arousal of his curate's suspicions. He would lay and bait other traps in the fullness of time. The most aggravating aspect of this enigma was Mr. Gilbert's obvious happiness. That was most decidedly not normal.

Chapter 10

All the alterations had now been completed and after thanking the Viscount for his generosity and hospitality, Mrs. Langthorne and Isobel moved back into the post office. In spite of the excellent improvements in their living quarters, they could not suppress a sharp pang of regret that the grandeur of the Dower House would no longer be their home.

Jane Turner, their new assistant, brightened their lives as a sunbeam pierces rain clouds. She had an impish sense of humour and Isobel's frequent gusts of laughter convinced her mother that Jane would be a great asset to them and to the business.

Tillingthorpe, like all villages, was slowly but surely increasing its population which meant more trade for shop and post office. Takings were increasing at a steady but constant rate. One hundred pounds a day was quite common; on a five and half day week, that pushed the takings to nearly five hundred and fifty pounds. Isobel's salary had been reviewed, enhancing the original twenty seven shillings and sixpence to three pounds. Commission increased this sum to four pounds. Isobel and her mother now felt more content and more secure.

Their frequent excursions into the beautiful surrounding countryside made them realise how lucky they were to have turned disaster into a decisive victory. They made weekly visits to the historic city of Oxford, where they were enchanted by the scholastic seat of learning, all saturated in noble English history. Isobel loved to take coffee in the numerous small cafés where the undergraduates would congregate to discuss the merits and eccentricities of their respective tutors.

Times were looking rosy for the two ladies and Mrs. Langthorne was secretly relieved that she had supported her daughter in what she at first regarded as an outrageous and ludicrous idea. She shuddered to think what might have happened had Isobel been at the mercy of an unsympathetic employer. However, they were now self-supporting and financially sound.

One morning, the vicar called to inspect the secret chamber beneath the larder. Isobel showed him the solid wooden door giving entry to the secret passage between the double wall. They descended the flight of stone steps into the chamber, where, if the vicar's assumptions were correct, the famous highwayman, Robert Noakes, hid from the pursuing Red Coats. The vicar was profoundly impressed, especially when Isobel pointed to the secret hatch in the chimney. "My, my, what ingenuity - how clever," he murmured. Isobel returned to her duties as postmistress of Tillingthorpe while the vicar took tea with her mother in the kitchen.

It was now the month of May and all around the air was laden with the almond-like perfume of the hawthorn which clothed every hedgerow in a creamy white mantle. The woods and copse on the Beldrake estate were adorned with the blue mist of a sea of bluebells.

On a lovely Tuesday morning, Isobel was humming the Brahms lullaby while checking her supply of wireless licence forms, with her back to the door. Jane was in the kitchen where she was enjoying her break and by the sounds emanating from there, amusing her mother. Isobel was aware that someone had entered; she turned around and was immediately transfixed as she stared into the eyes of a man, who did not look through the brass screen as all her other customers did, but over it. He was a giant. Isobel continued to stare into this creature's wide-set grey eyes, not the blue-grey eyes so many people record on passport applications, no, these were dark slate grey eyes, like the mottled grey on a pigeon's wings. They gazed upon the world with a steady challenging look of curiosity. These were the eyes of a man who would definitely not 'lose his head when all about him were losing theirs'. Isobel, not having the gift of second sight was not aware that she was held in thrall by the presence of a man who would, one day, become her lawful wedded husband. He was Lance Robert Howard-Coleman, Esquire of Cornwall Court, Oxford.

He repeated his request, "Could you direct me to the estate office on the Beldrake estate."

"Do forgive me," Isobel replied, "I was so astounded by your height that I did not hear you the first time."

"I am so sorry if I startled you," he said. Lance appeared to her girlish gaze to be eight feet tall.

He was dressed in a grey open-necked shirt with a navy blue cravat with white polka dots. He wore a corduroy jacket with grey fustian trousers. His feet were encased in brown veldskoens. He had removed his tweed cap, exposing his thick straight dark hair.

"Do excuse me but I have never seen a man so tall." He smiled as she stood at his side directing him to the Beldrake estate.

Isobel was intrigued by this handsome stranger and at the first opportunity would establish his identity. After they had closed for the night, Isobel spoke to her mother about this God-like giant who had deigned to visit earth. Mrs. Langthorne detected that her daughter was more than interested in this unknown gentleman.

Subsequent enquiries addressed to their friend the vicar, who, hitherto had never failed to find an answer to the riddles they had presented to him, found him for the first time nonplussed and completely baffled by this latest enigma. As Isobel looked hard into his face, willing him to name this man who had preoccupied her thoughts since that never-to-be-forgotten May morning when she had turned to see the giant gazing straight into her eyes over the brass grille. The vicar stared back at Isobel with a blank expression that signalled that he had no knowledge of this gentleman and was quite certain that he did not reside in his parish.

Isobel decided that she might never see her giant again and strived, without a great deal of success, to put him from her mind; then she grasped the consolation that one man would certainly know and that man was Stan Peacock, the postman, who called every morning to deliver her small private bag.

The next day, before Stan could complete his dash-in-dash-out manoeuvre, Isobel intercepted him to enquire if he knew of a man who stood eight feet tall with grey eyes and dark hair. Stan gazed into space, thought long and hard and uttered the disappointing response,

"No, Miss, no, definitely not." But seeing her pretty face cloud over, he said,

"I will make enquiries; I can't promise anything mind, but I will try." There was still hope fluttering in Isobel's breast and with the resilience of youth she switched her mind to other matters.

The takings continued to increase, prompting Isobel to conceive another madcap idea. When they made their weekly trip to Oxford, Isobel insisted on visiting a different café each time. Mrs. Langthorne noted that on all these visits, her daughter was unusually alert and keenly observant of all the activity around her. She was not aware that her daughter was making a shrewd assessment of the commercial and economic potential of these establishments. That night, before retiring to bed, Isobel presented yet another impetuous and startling idea. A coffee tavern modelled on the eighteenth century coffee shops in London. Her mother promised to give the matter her most earnest attention.

'Everything in the garden was lovely' at Tillingthorpe Post Office. The deep wounds inflicted by their own very personal tragedy were beginning to heal until one day, right out of the blue, they had a phone call from a young subaltern of Colonel Langthorne's regiment. Isobel called her mother, amid great excitement, at hearing the familiar voice of Lieutenant Billingham. He was in great haste and would be very brief. When would it be convenient to call upon them. "I have a message for you from the adjutant, Major Mackenzie, but would prefer not to talk on the phone." Swiftly conferring, the ladies nominated May the thirtieth which fell on a Sunday, in one week's time.

They awaited this reunion with mixed feelings. Sadness, because this young man had been so intimately involved in their lives at the time of the tragedy. Joy, because he was also a link with some of the happiest times of their lives.

Chapter 11

Life in the village pursued its uneventful course; the five ladies who were her very first customers still came for their ritual gossip. They were not now so solemn; Jane would not allow them to be. She was a natural mimic and kept them constantly amused with her impersonations of the vicar and certain village inhabitants who had incurred their mutual displeasure. Isobel would often join them and, in particular, noted that the customers tended to increase their purchases when humoured by her new assistant, whom both Isobel and her mother regarded as a treasure.

One morning, Mrs. Langthorne invited Mrs. Copeland, Mrs. Woods, Mrs. Marriot, Mrs. Humphrey and Mrs. Wilson to come and inspect the extensive alterations to the cottage. Glancing at each other in silent appreciation of this rare chance to learn more of the newcomers to Tillingthorpe, for that was how they would be regarded for at least five years, they all trooped into the new kitchen with its oil burning Aga cooker, with its four capacious ovens and gleaming in its black vitreous enamel finish. The visitors to this holy of holies were quite overawed by this cooking range, the like of which they had never seen in all their born days.

They were then conducted into the new sitting room and shown the small cupboard with its secret compartment where the hoard of jewels had been hidden. There were lots of 'Oohs' and 'Ahs' and 'Well I never' ejaculations as they all peered into the depths of the dark interior, only turning away to scrutinise the transformation of old Martha's kitchen.

"Do you think we could go and see the secret room?" enquired Mrs. Copeland.

"By all means!" Mrs. Langthorne replied. Then picking up an electric torch, she said, "Please follow me." The excitement among the ladies was building up to fever pitch. She showed them the solid wooden door giving entrance to the recently discovered passage between the walls and led them through the second door down the stone steps into the secret chamber. Some shuddered as though they sensed some evil presence and when Mrs. Langthorne invited them to stand on the hearth and look up to the cleverly disguised hatch, their curiosity was completely satiated.

All the ladies would save their adventure until they and their husbands had had their supper when they could relate these remarkable events with the maximum dramatic impact. That is all except the blacksmith's wife, Mrs. Copeland, who could recall her husband's explosive reaction to the disclosure of another secret. Indeed could any woman ever forget that day? She decided it called for a very subtle gambit like: "You'll never believe what I saw today, Bill. I was in the shop this morning with other wives when Mrs. Langthorne appeared and invited us into the back, etc., etc." Yes, that would be the ploy. Some men of his age had been known to drop dead or at least have an apoplectic fit and she didn't want to lose him; after all, he had, as she had often remarked, taken the best years of her life. Then there was his pension to consider; if he died before he had paid sufficient stamps, she would not receive a widow's pension. It did not bear thinking about. She must be very careful.

The last time she had shared a precious secret with Bill he had been like a bear with a sore head and would not speak to her; not even when she tempted him with his favourite meal; herrings soused in vinegar, followed by bread and butter pudding. If the blacksmith died prematurely, that would be a selfish act so typical of men.

On Sunday morning, Isobel and her mother awoke in an atmosphere of tension, anticipation and excitement. All these emotions appeared to have fused into one solidified threat to their powers of self-control. Almost a lingering heartache, too painful to bear. It would conjure up, so vividly, images of the father's mysterious and tragic death, the awful overbearing sadness that they had felt when forced to turn their backs on a land and a way of life which they had loved so deeply and the fear of insecurity that awaited them in England. They must now look forward to a happier life unclouded by these mournful reminiscences.

It was imperative that the reunion with the young subaltern should not take place in an aura of doom and gloom. They would prepare to entertain this old friend who would be as excited as they were and would have much to tell and little time to tell it. There would be fond messages from old friends in and out of the regiment. He would tell them who occupied their old house and the name of the new colonel. That would be poignant news indeed.

The women bustled about in an endeavour to stifle their tumultuous thoughts. The arrival of a large Armstrong Siddely limousine outside their door caused their hearts to palpitate with eagerness to welcome this youthful but highly regarded link with their past lives. Isobel threw her arms around Richard and kissed him on the cheek, Mrs. Langthorne, although equally delighted to see him, was a little more restrained, more dignified in her greeting. They retired outside to sit on the lawn where they would enjoy maximum privacy.

Firstly he informed Isobel that her Arab pony was in fine fettle and should arrive in about three months time in the care of Akbar who would remain with her for the whole period of quarantine.

A reproduction full length oil painting of Colonel Langthorne in the full dress of the Bengal's would arrive. They would, no doubt, recall the original which had hung on the wall in the officer's mess. The same artist had been commissioned to ensure an accurate portrayal of the colonel.

Major Mackenzie had been appointed in his place and the choice was popular in the officer's mess. He then produced a letter from this officer addressed to Mrs. Langthorne, marked 'Private and Confidential'.

"Now you must be the first to know of my forthcoming marriage to Lady Lydia Templeton, daughter of the Earl of Beckindale."

"Wedding?" the ladies echoed.

"Yes – and you will both receive invitations in due course."

"I have to tell you, with some regret, that I have resigned my commission in the regiment and will take up an appointment in my future father-in-law's bank. In four years time, when I'm thirty, I hope to stand for Parliament in Steeple Aston, a constituency not very far from here."

They now adjourned to the house for tea and further assuaging of the ladies insatiable desire for more and yet more news of India. After tea the young man had exhausted all the news and messages of goodwill and rose to take his leave. As they passed through the new wide front door, "Wait!" he exclaimed, "I have another very, very, important message. I am asked to invite you both to take tea with my relations where I am staying at present. In fact that is not my car, it belongs to my father!"

"When would you like to come? I must know now." Isobel and her mother quickly conferred and decided that the tenth of June, on Saturday, would be very suitable as Jane could take over the shop and post office in the morning leaving them free to be picked up at two in the afternoon.

The young man departed saying, "Don't worry, I've told them much about you and the fact that you are my very good friends will ensure a warm welcome."

The lives of Isobel and her mother were becoming more interesting and more exciting day by day. But life will never become immobile and Mrs. Langthorne and Isobel had sufficient strength of character to realise that their own lives must keep pace with this progress.

Isobel had now discussed her latest brain child with her mother, who, caught up with the tide of her daughter's enthusiasm, agreed to visit an estate agent to invoke his aid in finding suitable premises. A decision was made to seek the advice of accountants and auditors to learn the hard economic realities of such a venture. Isobel planned to establish her coffee shop in the High to cater not for undergraduates, but for the many mature professional people whose chambers were concentrated in that area. She wanted university dons, solicitors, accountants, surveyors and estate agents.

On the Friday preceding their Saturday visit, they received a phone call from the estate agent informing them that a highly suitable premises had been discovered and awaited their inspection; they were warned that the lease would not be cheap as it was situated in a building which comprised part of a bequest to Christchurch College. It was, nevertheless, an ideal property in an ideal situation and the agent advised immediate negotiations if it was to be secured. He added that it was a prime choice and that it would lend itself perfectly to the project they had proposed. He would await their further instructions.

Chapter 12

The great day arrived and Isobel and her mother wondered what new adventure awaited them. Lieutenant Richard Bellingham arrived at the appointed hour in the Armstrong Siddely; having explained that his open sports car would not be suitable for the dignified transport of his two old friends, the Howards had insisted that his companions on the hour long journey should enjoy a modicum of comfort. During this hour, their young friend bombarded them with queries about their own experiences and struggles to rebuild their shattered lives and who had dreamed up the superb idea of the village store and post office? This led them to tell him about the hoard of jewels which the vicar assured them must be the ill-gotten gains of the highwayman, Robert Noakes. He listened intently as they described the secret hiding place. The young man was still young enough to be intrigued by these stories of highwayman's loot and secret chambers.

"Gosh!" he exclaimed, "I would love to see it!"

"Oh, you must see it when you make your next visit." Isobel replied. "I should love to show you and tell you how it was all discovered."

As Richard turned off the main road on to a narrow minor road, he said, "In a few more minutes we should be there."

"Are they relatives of yours, Richard?" Isobel enquired.

"Yes, in a way, because they adopted me when I was three years old and brought me up. I was at Eton with their son."

He turned the car and drove through the tall wrought iron gates surmounted with the arms of the Howard family. The house was named Cornwall Court because it had once been owned by the Duchy of Cornwall. It had been given to an ancestor of the family by the Black Prince in appreciation of services rendered, financial and military. The two mile long drive ran through a magnificent avenue of horse chestnut trees, all in full bloom. With their erect floral clusters they resembled enormous and gigantic green chandeliers.

The two ladies felt butterflies in their tummies, wondering who resided in such regal and grand remoteness. However, their young driver did not appear to be over-awed, nor abashed by it; but half turning his head said, "You will like my family; they are lovely people." The car had now entered the final stretch and was descending into a shallow valley with a river flowing through it.

When they saw the house, the ladies gasped audibly at the sheer size and extent of it. The house was gabled and built of grey stone blocks with leaded lattice windows. It was, in short, a typical Cotswold mansion; it had obviously crouched, in this sylvan setting, for several centuries. "Richard," Isobel exclaimed, "We are totally overwhelmed by this enormous house."

"Oh, please don't be," he replied, "My family are very down to earth and you'll love them, I'll warrant. Especially Lance!" He grinned. Then as an afterthought added, "Lance is my adoptive brother. We grew up together, went to the same Prep School and left Eton at the same time. He went to Magdalen College, Oxford and I, as you are aware, entered Sandhurst."

They were now alighting at the massive entrance and was she in the grip of some delusion or was that her giant standing with hand outstretched to assist her mother? It was he; her cheeks were scarlet. She clutched at her mother's arm for support to prevent her knees buckling as the giant smiled down at her saying, "So, we meet again."

"What?" stuttered Richard. "Do you mean to say you two have met before?"

"Yes, we have met before!" Lance replied.

"Where?" Richard demanded.

Lance looked at Isobel, winked and said,

"Ah! That would be telling." Richard was exceedingly nonplussed and a trifle exasperated as he saw his long planned surprise introduction of beauty and the beast fail with all the anti-climax of a damp squib at a fireworks display.

All entered the house where Mrs. Hannah Howard, with her two daughters, Margaret and Christal, were waiting to welcome Mrs. Langthorne and her daughter, Isobel. Richard had told them so much about the background of all their respective lives in India and had described Isobel and her mother so accurately that when he formally introduced them, the Howards felt that they were meeting old friends after a long absence. The two Howard girls quickly detached Isobel and her mother from the reception, took their coats and showed them where they could refresh themselves.

Isobel turned to her mother and said, "Now do you believe me about the giant?"

Her mother smiled indulgently and replied, "Yes, I do, but remember your father was almost as tall and even appeared taller than your giant when dressed for parade."

When they emerged from the bathroom, they espied a maid waiting at a discreet distance to conduct them to the drawing room where the family were awaiting. All that Richard had said about their hosts being down to earth people was a very fair assessment of this contented genteel family. Richard appeared to look, well, somehow different to the young subaltern of the Bengal's they had come to know and love. When they were all seated at table, Richard, who was placed between Mrs. Langthorne and her daughter, turned to Isobel and said,

"Isobel, old girl, I do hope you won't think me lacking in discretion but I told my family about that old villain, Sabridin, and the ring he gave you for your nineteenth birthday."

"Oh, yes," the Howard girls exclaimed in unison, "How romantic, we would love to see it."

"If you will accompany my mother and me when we return home, I will gladly show it to you." Isobel assured them.

"I hope you are not planning to make your visit too brief?" Mrs. Howard interjected.

"I fear we must not tarry too long as we have to open for business promptly at nine in the morning."

Now it was time for the giant, who had up to this moment preferred to remain silent, to improve on this idea by saying, "Would it not be a better idea if Mrs. Langthorne and Isobel made another visit and stayed for the weekend?" The giant was not going to allow this beautiful butterfly, who had so unexpectedly flitted into his life, to flit away into the great unknown.

One day when she was prepared to settle, he would have his net poised to descend gently over her outstretched wings, and to make her his captive. If that plan was to have the remotest chance of success he must have more opportunities to be present when she alighted to refresh herself with life's nectar.

Isobel looked at her mother with pleading eyes, willing her to accept this kind invitation. "Thank you," Mrs. Langthorne responded, "You are very kind and if you are all quite sure you will not find our presence too intrusive, we would be delighted to accept. I will confess, since we left India, Isobel has had no social life whatever, and it will be good for her."

After the meal was over the two Howard girls whisked Isobel away to see their own special quarters which comprised the whole of the smaller wing of the house. Their own bedrooms, their own sitting rooms and their private music room, with two Broadwood pianos where they would play duets. Christal was a very talented artist, as the many watercolours scattered round the house testified. She was fortunate in having her own studio with large north-facing windows which would provide the canvas with the soft northern light that all true artists feel to be essential.

Mrs. Langthorne and her daughter said their goodbyes to the Howards, thanking them for their hospitality and remarking on the extraordinary coincidence that Richard should be their mutual friend. Mrs. Howard rejoined, "Oh, yes. He is our adopted son. We took him when he was three years old."

Richard was anxious to be off and gave an impatient toot on the horn. The girls called, "See you soon, and don't forget to bring the ring." Isobel assured them she would not forget. The giant reminded Mrs. Langthorne that when they came for the weekend he would fetch them, as he was longing to see where the jewels had been hidden and the secret chamber where the highwayman took refuge from the Red Coats.

Richard drove swiftly and unable to contain his curiosity a moment longer, called to Isobel, who was sitting on the back seat with her mother, "Where did you and Lance meet? I must know; after all, you both spoiled the big surprise that I had planned so long ago."

Isobel, sensing Richard's disappointment, told him of the morning that Lance came into her post office to ask the way to the Beldrakes estate office.

"Well, well," he murmured, "So that was it."

When they parted at the front door of their house, Isobel held Richard's hand and kissed his cheek, saying, "Don't be too despondent; if it wasn't for you, we would never have become acquainted with your lovely family."

Richard seized these crumbs of comfort, muttering, "That's true, very true." After all he had accomplished his plan to bring his brother, Lance, and Isobel together, and savouring this thought felt a little less defeated.

Chapter 13

The first post on the Monday brought two important letters. One from the Oxford city police informing them that the court had reached a verdict - not treasure trove - because it had been found inside a privately owned building; the jewels would be deemed to be the property of the owners, the Beldrakes. The following day, Isobel had a phone call from the Viscount, requesting that they visit him at their very earliest convenience, as he wished to discuss these most recent developments with Mrs. Langthorne and her daughter. The Saturday was selected, as it was early closing and any discussions could be conducted at a leisurely pace, but unknown to them, these would also be brief.

They arrived at the Big House at and were shown into the library by the butler. The Viscount rose to his feet, kissed his aunt, shook hands with Isobel and enquired if all was well with them. Mrs. Langthorne answered in the affirmative and added,

"Yes, thanks to your exceedingly generous help which has transformed our lives. While it is in our minds, Isobel and I have made a decision that if acceptable - we would like to recompense you for the considerable financial outlay that you incurred in the structural alterations and renovations which, as I said, have improved the quality of our lives in many ways. We, therefore, propose a repayment of ten pounds a month until such time as it takes to dispose of the debt. May I also add that we both most sincerely hope that you will not feel this proposal as an affront to your kindness."

The Viscount laughed, hugged his aunt and said, "If that is what you desire, please go ahead, but I do most solemnly assure you that you need feel neither embarrassment nor obligation. After all, you are my aunt and if one cannot help one's relations, who can one help?" Mother and daughter smiled at each other as this obstacle had been safely cleared.

The young Viscount rang for the butler and requested that tea for his guests and himself should be served. He sat down at the ornate regency table where he had been examining the jewels, now contained in a large steel deed box, and handed them the letter he had received from the Oxford city police clarifying the coroner's verdict. He awaited their comments which surprised him.

"What a relief. We are so glad as we have been extremely worried at the prospect of such a grave responsibility."

The butler served tea as the Viscount propounded his plan: his mother, sister, his aunt and Isobel would be permitted to select two articles from the hoard. The heavy gold crucifix, which must have been the property of some unknown ecclesiastic, should be returned to the church by presenting it to the Reverend Copplethwaite. The remaining articles should be offered for sale at the London house of Sotheby's; the proceeds to be spent on the erection of a village hall, to be known as Tillingthorpe War Memorial Hall. "Oh, I almost forgot - two hundred pounds to be paid to the young apprentice and one hundred pounds each to his mates, and four hundred pounds to Martha Howkins." The Viscount then concluded with, "Only if you both agree, of course." Isobel and her mother expressed their admiration and full approval of this ingenious idea to spread the benefits of any funds raised at the sale throughout the whole village.

Once this proposal became public knowledge, Joshua Humphrey, at The Red Lion, would, yet again, be packed out with customers who, primed with the heady strength of Joshua's ale, would become more irate, more argumentative and all with their own very personal plans for the sharing of the treasure. Some of the older inhabitants were of the opinion that Martha, who had after all lived in the post office for many years, should be given the lion's share of the spoils. The younger members, who were already succumbing to the powers of Joshua's ale and thinking in terms of motorcycles, howled down this suggestion, as it would reduce the amount each would receive. "That would not be acceptable to anybody," they cried belligerently. One youth, standing in the corner, had the temerity to suggest that all the money should be given to the orphanage in Witney. This daft idea only served to inflame and enrage the heaving, swaying crowd. When the cry went up, "He's from Copthorne, he's a bloody foreigner!" He was jostled so forcibly that he was squeezed out of the bar into the passage as a pip is squeezed out of a lemon. They all agreed that he must be a nutter and resumed their squabble concerning the apportioning of the money; after all fair's fair and they only wanted their rights.

The news had leaked out that the treasure was worth over a million pounds, causing their ambitions to soar to unexpected heights. Some were now saying openly that they did not want a motorbike but intended to buy an M.G. Midget sports car. The thought of one million pounds to be shared out seemed to increase their thirst, and once again, Joshua had to call on his wife to assist him in keeping pace with the insatiable demands of what, he was now convinced, was an invasion of madmen. Their vociferous arguments finally came to an end when Joshua called time and all vacated The Red Lion to stand in little groups as the word had now increased the value to two million pounds.

Quietness now descended upon Tillingthorpe and Joshua could have his supper in peace, wearily telling his wife that he was beginning to wonder if public life was worth the candle.

But there were two letters for the Langthornes. The second, from the estate agent in Oxford, confirmed the offer of an eminently suitable premises in the High and enclosed a photograph of a large rectangular room, forty feet long and twenty-five feet wide. Isobel had already made an appointment for her and her mother to view on Saturday at two, which meant the post office, but not the shop, would close at eleven.

They arrived at the agent's office in the High at one forty-five, and were immediately taken to the property. The suggested room was over a shop which hired and occasionally sold academic gowns, college blazers, school and college ties, cravats and white sports flannels. The room was approached by a staircase leading up from a private entrance. When Isobel saw it, she instinctively knew that it was absolutely perfect for the project which she had in mind.

There was also an important facility, not mentioned by the agent; a kitchen. The large landing at the head of the stairs also accommodated a toilet and large wash hand basin. This was not only desirable but downright essential. “The room,” the agent was saying, “was, many years ago, the headquarters of the Oxford Antiquarian Society but, over the years, membership had increased and they had, therefore, moved to much larger premises.”

Isobel was enchanted with the room which was panelled in oak. A plaster frieze married the panelling to the ceiling and displayed the arms of every college in full heraldic colours. In the centre of the ornate plaster ceiling, the arms of the city were encompassed in a large circular moulding which matched the pattern of the frieze, incorporating tiny masks of the kings, queens and bishops who were the benefactors of the various colleges.

Isobel stared into space; she could see the whole thing, the high backed settles with a small canopy which would infer a cosy privacy to her scholarly customers. The settles would face each other across an oak table. The seats would be upholstered in a tapestry patterned fabric and each pair of settles would be illuminated by wall-mounted, antique finish, candle lights. The bow window looking down on the High was partly stained glass and gave the room an atmosphere of tranquillity. She was brought out of her reverie by the agent’s voice declaring that the kitchen would have to be gutted at considerable expense. He urged them to seek a lot of professional advice from an architect, the bank and a solicitor.

The financial and legal implications were immense, and only a daring and entrepreneurial personality would be able to cope with a venture of this magnitude. They accepted his offer to obtain estimates gratefully and he promised to keep them fully informed of all ensuing developments, but added the warning that once the availability of this chamber became known, he would come under pressure from the Antiquarian Society to act. Isobel and her mother returned to Tillingthorpe and resolved to discuss the plan in detail when they had the necessary data, which they would commit to paper to facilitate a factual picture of their subsequent deliberations.

While all these stimulating events filled Isobel’s head, day and sometimes night, Mr. Pringle lurked in his office like some denizen of a cave in the darkest depths of the ocean, contemplating the necessity of a tour of inspection to that far flung office in Tillingthorpe, a small cog in a vast and important civil service machine. He had conceded that Isobel was an intelligent young woman and decided that he would regard this inexperienced person, with friends in high places, as his protégée, to be groomed for a more exalted career in 'the service' than her present role. He was only ten years away from retirement and the possibility could not be discounted that she might - with his tutelage - even take over the vacancy his retirement would create at that pulsating nerve centre, Cowley Post Office.

He knew that his eventual relinquishing of power would - quite naturally - send seismic shock waves through 'the service' and he would, doubtless, be fobbed off with an M.B.E. when all his superiors expected Mr. Pringle to become Sir Archibald Pringle. That, sadly, was the unfairness of life.

He jerked himself out of these depressing ruminations and rang Tillingthorpe Post Office. Isobel took up the phone and said, "Hello."

"Pringle here," a voice responded.

"Oh! Hello, Mr. Pringle, how are you?"

"Very well," came the voice of officialdom.

"And Mrs. Pringle?" Isobel enquired.

"As well as can be expected of a woman who is still in a state of shock."

"Yes," Isobel said sympathetically "I am so sorry." Then to change the subject, went on, "When are you coming to see us again, Mr. Pringle?'

This was more to the postmaster's liking. "Would Tuesday be convenient?" Isobel confirmed that Tuesday would be very suitable. "Before I ring off, do you need any more forms? We've had a run on Wireless and Dog Licence application forms."

Isobel laid the phone down to make a swift check. She picked up the phone, "Are you there, Mr. Pringle?"

"I'm here," he replied.

"I am getting rather low on Gun Licence application forms," she exclaimed.

Ah! that was music to the ears of the postmaster of Cowley. "Right, I'll bring a few over," he responded, with a ring of satisfaction in his voice.

"What time can we expect you?"

"About ten in the morning. Will that be alright with you?" Isobel confirmed that would be quite convenient. That concluded the superior's communication.

On Tuesday, Mr. Pringle arrived and Isobel could sense that there was something indefinably different about him. Then, looking down, she realised that Mr. Pringle had relinquished the sartorial practice of wearing spats. Isobel would never know the reason for Mr. Pringle's abandonment of these accessories, which he fondly believed enhanced his air of dignity and officialdom. The truth was that he had received a hurtful letter from head office urging all senior postmasters, whose duties included supervising and instructing new and junior members of 'the service' to assume a mode of attire more in keeping with the twentieth century, and the wearing of spats was henceforth to be actively discouraged. Mr. Pringle would never, ever divulge the contents of this directive, which struck a mortal blow at the very heart of his authority. No! Wild horses would not drag it from him and if this became public knowledge it could trigger a wave of insubordination.

Isobel took the replenishing stock of forms from him, placed them in the rack and said, "Do come through, Mr. Pringle, my mother is about to make tea."

Mr. Pringle looked around, with an owl-like expression, and said, "My word, you have made alterations."

"Yes," Mrs. Langthorne replied, "Our landlord has been very kind to us and I am sure you will agree that it is a great improvement on the old kitchen you saw on your previous visit."

"It certainly is," he remarked.

"Did you read about the discovery of the hidden treasure in *The Oxford Herald*?" she enquired.

"Oh, yes," he responded, with just a hint of excitement in his voice. "I had intended to give you a ring but pressure of work – quarterly accounts you know, drove it from my mind!"

Isobel had returned to her post office duties and this devotion to duty had not escaped the approving observation of Mr. Pringle's all-seeing eyes.

Mrs. Langthorne had risen from her chair and displayed the interior of the small cupboard with the secret door in the back. "Will this treasure be awarded to you and your daughter?"

"Oh, no!" exclaimed Mrs. Langthorne, "It has already been declared not to be treasure trove and has been handed to the owner of this property by order of the coroner."

"May I enquire the identity of your landlord?"

"Viscount Beldrake; this house is part of the estate."

Mr. Pringle breathed a silent sigh of relief. If the residents of Tillingthorpe Post Office suddenly became affluent, it could be an embarrassment, not only to him, but to his immediate superior, the postmaster of Oxford: his father-in-law. "Please do not judge me rudely inquisitive, but did this same gentleman witness your daughter's signature on the official secrets form?"

"That's right," Mrs. Langthorne affirmed. Mr. Pringle stared down at the tiny vortex in his tea cup as he digested this vital disclosure. So they were not related. What a relief!

He consulted his watch saying, "My, my, how time has flown. I shall be just in time to get the eleven-fifteen bus to Oxford. I will make a quick check with the postmistress, no, sub-postmistress, then I really must go." Having satisfied himself that Isobel wanted no further supplies or advice, he departed. He regarded his visit as extremely fruitful.

Chapter 14

The following Saturday, Isobel and her mother would be collected by Lance Howard-Coleman. The postman, Sam Evans, could never understand why Lance was addressed as Howard-Coleman when his parents were plain Mr. and Mrs. Howard. Toffee-nosed that's what it was; all people with double-barrelled names were snobs. They imagined ordinary folk were impressed; not him, not Sam Evans. He was shop steward in his local branch of the Workmen's Union and a regular reader of the Daily Worker. He had even started to read Karl Marx and was thinking about a correspondence course in economics. After all he was always referred to by his mates – with great respect – as 'Educated Evans', and he must live up to his name.

At quarterly Union meetings, Sam always impressed the spell-bound audience with his oratory when he stunned them with terms like 'not negotiable' or 'contrary to the constitution' and his favourite quotation from Karl Marx: 'Each according to his needs'. He always had a standing ovation when concluding his speech with the clarion call: 'Workers of the world unite'.

A merciful fate had decreed that Sam should be kept in total ignorance of the real reason for this double-barrelled name, as such enlightenment could be dangerous for middle-aged men of belligerent disposition. Sudden and severe aggravation had, on more than one occasion, been known to provoke fatal seizures.

When Lance was sixteen years of age, his grandmother, Eliza Coleman, anxious to perpetuate the name of Coleman, now in danger of extinction, had bequeathed him twenty thousand pounds, to be invested until he attained the age of twenty-four years, on condition that he incorporated the name of Coleman with Howard and promised to pass the name to his children. Isobel could not know at present, that she would, ultimately, be instrumental in consolidating this process.

At two, Lance arrived to collect Mrs. Langthorne and her daughter. Isobel met him at the door with a warning to mind his head and ushered him into the sitting room. Lance sat down and said, "So this is where the jewels were found. I insist that you tell me every tiny detail of this extraordinary exposure of local history." Isobel showed him the twin cupboards and the secret panel in the back. Lance peered into the dark interior saying, "Well, well and to think that the jewels were lying in there undiscovered for so many years."

Isobel closed the door and said, "Now you must come and inspect the secret room." She led him to the concealed gate into the passage between the two walls. Lance was fascinated by the ingenious bolt mechanism and followed Isobel to the inner door and the stone steps where they descended into the chamber. Isobel could detect the excitement in Lance's reaction, but when she indicated the escape hatch up the chimney he was truly amazed and full of admiration for the ingenuity of the people who put it there. She explained about the deliberate coating of soot and the foot and hand holds created by leaving out bricks at intervals.

Lance turned to Isobel and said, "Do you know I would not have missed this for anything and I will never, ever forget this experience. I could almost feel the presence of Robert Noakes."

Isobel shivered and said, "Let us return to mother, it's so creepy."

They came back into the light and Lance, looking round, exclaimed, "What a delightful spot this is, it is so tranquil and green; quite idyllic."

"Sometime you must come to tea and we can sit in the garden and talk." Isobel retorted.

"I should love that," Lance replied, "and I will hold you to that promise." They returned to the house, where Mrs. Langthorne awaited them.

"Well, what did you think of it all, Lance?" she enquired.

"Fascinating, truly remarkable and quite intriguing." They picked up their small cases and adjourned to the car.

All this recent activity, together with these comings and goings of strangers to the post office, had been observed and noted by several inhabitants of Tillingthorpe and would, doubtless, be discussed with the usual exaggerations by the villagers who could not abide mysteries.

Isobel was wearing her Donegal tweed suit and a silk blouse with a Peter Pan collar. Her butterfly brooch was pinned to the lapel of her jacket. Mrs. Langthorne wore a lilac coloured suit, a pale green blouse and a rope of pearls, a present from her husband.

Lance suddenly stopped the car, turned to Isobel, and enquired if she had the ring, she assured him that she had. "Thank Heavens for that!" he ejaculated, "My sisters impressed on me I must not allow you to forget as they are curious about it."

Mention of the ring reminded them both that Isobel's birthday had come and gone without mention, because both had mutually decided not to arouse painful memories.

Lance kept up a running commentary all the way and appeared to know every village, and many of the inhabitants, some of whom waved to him. When they were getting near to the estate, Lance informed them that during their first visit, his father had been away on business, but this time they would meet him. Mrs. Langthorne murmured, "It would be a pleasure to meet the head of your lovely family." Cornwall Court loomed even larger than the last visit but, Isobel mused, giants needed a big house to live in.

This time, only the girls were there to receive them. After a brief greeting, the girls seized their small cases and cried, "Follow us." After passing through endless corridors and rooms they came to a pair of large double mahogany doors. Margaret Howard threw them open to reveal an enormous room, forty feet by thirty feet. Two modern beds were placed at each end. The walls were hung with tapestries and many fine pictures, mostly landscapes by famous artists. At each end there were twin fireplaces. They were constructed of green marble, each mantelpiece supported large mirrors in gilt frames.

They extended to the full width of the mantelpiece and were five feet high. The large rectangular windows yielded a spectacular view across the valley.

Margaret showed them the spacious bathroom. They had never seen such opulence in their lives, not even in the palaces of the Indian princes they had visited so often. Then Margaret showed them another smaller bathroom, which, she assured them, was for their exclusive use. Then returning to the bedroom she opened a small corner window and pointed to another wing of the house directly opposite, saying, "That's our suite of rooms, so we are not far away from you. One last thing: tea will be served at four, so when you are ready, just press the bell at the side of the fireplace and Sarah will come to collect you."

The staff at Cornwall Court were all addressed by their Christian names and were regarded and treated as members of the family. The staff of two footmen, two housemaids, a cook and two kitchen maids were presided over by Granville, the butler, who had been with the family since he was a boy of fourteen years.

He had served with his master through the war as batman in the Grenadier Guards. He was now forty-four years of age and had become somewhat portly. His face was pale and expressionless, just a trifle mournful. He would have been a valuable asset to any undertaker and indeed had once been offered the post of head pall-bearer by an Oxford undertaker who was of the opinion that these rare qualities were going to shameful waste in domestic service. Granville was the only member of the domestic staff to be addressed by his surname. When Mr. Howard tactfully suggested he fall into line with the other members of staff, Granville obstinately refused, saying that he did not approve of such familiarity between servants and masters. It was not conducive to the appropriate levels of discipline. This mode of address, between master and loyal retainer, did not extend to servants of lesser status. Cooks and butlers were, of course, of equal rank.

The cook, Mrs. Pike, had once related to the other servants - amid hoots of laughter - that when Mr. Granville's predecessor and mentor retired, at the age of seventy-two years, he had bequeathed to his pupil a secret formula for the curing of squeaky boots. Hence the howls of derision; until the cook had drawn their attention to the disastrous impact such an eventuality would have on the dignified and authoritative demeanour of the important men who had devoted their lives in the service of many aristocratic families. All agreed that it did not bear thinking about.

It was a tradition that butlers always sat at the head of the table in the servant's hall, but Granville insisted on his meals being served at a table placed in a small room off the butler's pantry. He had served his apprenticeship under the stern eye of Mr. Simpson, who had been butler to the Howards for fifty years.

When Granville, aided by the two footmen, served dinner at eight, he was always immaculately turned out in morning trousers, a tail jacket, a wing collar, and a black and white check tie, tied with a large Windsor knot. White gloves completed his attire. He was truly a majestic figure and his knowledge of wines was encyclopaedic. He regarded the serving of wine at table as the equal of the ritual of Holy Communion in church.

Isobel and her mother lay on their respective beds for half an hour to refresh themselves. At three they rose, bathed and dressed for tea. They both decided to wear linen suits; Mrs. Langthorne's was beige in colour and Isobel's white. Isobel's was more elaborate with a bolero which had been embroidered all round the edges with daisy-like flowers. In the centre of the flowers, semi-precious stones had been secured. Her waist was encircled with a narrow belt similarly embroidered. The whole ensemble had been made specially for her when they lived in India.

At three forty-five they rang for the maid to escort them to the drawing room. Sarah quickly appeared. "Are you Sarah?" Mrs. Langthorne asked.

"The very same, ma'am," the maid admitted.

"You are going to guide us to the drawing room, I believe?"

"That's right."

"We are so relieved, as we feared that we might get hopelessly lost in this great house."

"When I first came here, five years ago, I often got lost," Sarah confessed, "but then we had a lot more servants and all I had to do was keep walking until I saw someone." By a system of short cuts, the maid soon delivered them to their destination. A knock on the door elicited an instant response of, "Come in, Sarah."

There appeared to be two giants awaiting them; one with twinkly blue eyes and grey hair, the other smiling boldly at her, she knew already. Mrs. Howard introduced Mrs. Langthorne and then Isobel gazed up into Mr. Howard's countenance with the wide eyed wonder of a little girl. "My, my, you are pretty," this giant said as he took her hand. "Now, you come and sit with me and watch my son's eyes turn green with envy." Isobel dutifully sat with him on a long chesterfield settee smiling at Lance.

"My son has told me all about the highwayman's loot and the secret chamber." Isobel informed him of the workmen's excitement when the young apprentice found the secret door in the back of the cupboard and revealed all the jewels. Then the discovery of the concealed door leading to the secret passage by the gardeners, and lastly the hidden chamber with its cunningly contrived escape hatch. The grey-haired giant's eyes never left the young girl's face and an observer would never know if the giant was enthralled by the story of secret rooms and highwayman's loot or enchanted by this young girl's incredible beauty.

The secret of Isobel's charm was that she was – like a little girl – blissfully unaware of her beauty and unworldly innocence. Little girls will stare a man straight in the eyes and if they are sure that he is not evil, they will not care if he is handsome or ugly, rich or poor.

The arrival of the maid with tea signalled the end of this little tête-à-tête and as they took tea the table hummed with mundane small talk, much of the conversation directed at Richard's forthcoming wedding; the girls demanding Richard divulge all the closely guarded details of the bride's wedding dress and how many bridesmaids, etc. Richard said that all of this intelligence was most definitely not in his possession.

Then the girls turned their attention to Isobel and demanded to know if she had brought the ring; not disclosing that they had already dragged confirmation from their brother. Isobel groped in her soft leather handbag and produced the small case containing the ruby ring given to her by the evil Sabridin Abdul Suliman. All present gasped when Isobel removed the ring and handed it to Mrs. Howard for inspection. Mrs. Howard was struck by the size of the stone and its vivid purity of colour. Isobel drew her attention to the tiny glow in the heart of the ruby. "Oh, yes," Mrs. Howard exclaimed. "I do see what you mean. How very, very strange," she murmured.

Christal clamoured to be next to examine this ring with such a romantic story behind it. "May I try it on?" she enquired of Isobel.

"Certainly," was the response. "Please do."

Christal slipped it over her engagement finger saying, "It's truly most impressive."

Then it was Margaret's turn to scrutinise this remarkable gift, prompting the question, "When is your birthday, Isobel?" Isobel informed them that it was May 20th.

Richard quietly engrossed in his recollections of that never to be forgotten party in India when that villain, Sabridin, presented the ring to his colonel's daughter. "Do you remember, old girl, how you wanted to give it back and how we dissuaded you from such action, warning you that a rejection of the gift could be dangerous?"

"Dangerous?" the sisters enquired.

"Yes," Richard explained. "It would have been dangerous in the extreme. Dangerous, because India is a volatile country and dangers to the white population are always present. Had Isobel refused to accept the ring, Sabridin would have been deeply offended and humiliated. He would have reciprocated with an abiding hatred for the rest of his life. In India we rule with a mixture of firmness and diplomacy but, having said that, it is a wonderful place for a young English officer to serve. I shall miss the regiment and I shall also miss India.'

"Why did Isobel wish to return the ring?" Mrs. Howard desired to know.

"I learned from Richard and his brother officers that Sabridin was a man of evil repute."

It was now the turn of the menfolk to pass an opinion. Mr. Howard examined the ring more closely saying, "It must be exceedingly valuable; have you a strong safe in your post office?"

"No." Isobel told him, "Although Mr. Pringle has hinted that when the takings reach a certain figure, a safe will be installed without cost to ourselves."

"Well, young lady, I think you should deposit this obviously historic piece - because that is what I believe it is - in our safe."

Isobel looked at her mother who thanked him for his offer and said to her daughter, "I think that is a splendid idea."

Richard, once again, informed all present that, in his assessment, it was worth every penny of thirty thousand pounds. One very good reason for keeping it in a secure safe place.

Lastly, during Lance's examination of the ring, Isobel announced, that if she ever learned that Sabridin was dead, she would send it to Sotheby's of London to be sold to the highest bidder and the proceeds to be donated to form the basis of a trust fund to help needy Indian troopers and their families. Lance looked across at Isobel with a curious look of admiration. Not only was this young lady stunningly attractive, but she was also generous of spirit. To the young gentleman, this was a most satisfactory insight into the personality of the woman he intended, one day, to marry. Lance had fallen in love with Isobel that day when their eyes met over the brass screen provided by her benefactor, Mr. Pringle.

Had they not been brought together by Richard's matchmaking machinations, he had resolved to pursue his natural motivations - boy meets girl - without allowing too much grass to grow under his feet; because he regarded that unforgettable meeting of twin souls as the herald of a more profound and closer relationship, perhaps the most significant and important event of his whole life. The more Lance saw of this girl, the more impressed he became. Although he had been meticulously careful to mask these reflections of his innermost thoughts, his mother was fully aware of her son's day dreams and hoped, with all her heart, that she would, one day, welcome this charming creature into her family as a daughter-in-law.

The maid removed the tea tray and during this momentary diversion Mr. Howard said, "If you come with me and bring your ring we will lock it away." Taking her hand he led her along vast corridors lined with family portraits, through countless rooms packed with priceless antiques, into his study. He pulled on one section of a bookcase which opened like a huge door to expose the door of a safe. After selecting the combination of numbers and letters, the door swung open.

Mr. Howard invited Isobel to place her ring in a small steel drawer. Then, reaching into the dark recesses he drew out a large jewel case. When open, it revealed a magnificent coronet encrusted with diamonds. "Look at me, Isobel; stand up straight." When she complied with these demands, he carefully lowered the coronet on to her head. "Perfect!" he pronounced, "Perfect. It could have been made for you." Leading her to a mirror he exhorted Isobel to look. She looked and gasped at the reflection of this magnificent, scintillating crown, for that is how it appeared to her, and furthermore, for a few exciting moments, she was a queen. She came back to reality when she heard the words,

"If ever you get married, Isobel, I shall insist that you wear it on your wedding day!" Isobel blushed and Lance's father noted this unmasking of a dormant emotion with much satisfaction. He already harboured fervent hopes that this lovely young woman would, one day, become his son's bride.

Closing the safe door he walked over to his desk by the window, picked up a photograph and said, "I think you know these young rascals." Isobel looked at the silver frame in his hand containing a photograph of two Eton boys with the twin gate towers in the background.

"No," Isobel retorted.

"That's my son on the left."

"But he has fair hair," she interjected.

"Yes, that's right; all the Howards are born blond but their hair goes dark as they mature."

"The other boy, is he Richard?"

"Yes," Mr. Howard confirmed. "Richard was my cousins son, but when his parents were murdered by tribesmen in India, we adopted him and consequently Richard and Lance are very close; more like brothers, and we love them both equally."

"How old were they when this photograph was taken?"

"About seventeen, I think." Isobel thanked him for showing her the photo and the coronet.

"That was a real thrill," she told him. "Now I must dress for dinner, but first I have to find my mother."

She met her mother as she emerged from the drawing room. She informed Isobel that the girls had arranged for them, accompanied by Richard and Lance, to walk up to the woods on the crest of the hill to hear the nightingales, who returned every year to nest in the dense thicket on the edge. Isobel was delighted with the idea, as she had never heard this legendary small brown bird in full song. They would all leave the house at nine in the evening which would give them time to change and not to delay Mrs. Langthorne and her daughter's return to Tillingthorpe.

Isobel chose a peacock blue dress to wear at dinner. It had a tight fitting bodice which exposed her shoulders; the skirt had a slight fullness to give shape to its severity of line. Her only jewellery was her small gold locket and, of course, her gold Rolex wristwatch; her nineteenth birthday present. Her three-quarter length sleeves displayed the watch, of which she was very proud. Her mother wore a black gown relieved only by a diamond brooch of a running horse with plumed tail outstretched.

Lance, Richard and Mr. Howard rose to their feet. Lance's serious expression and watchful eyes indicated that he was almost overawed by the striking presence of this young lady. Richard, who derived great satisfaction from the obvious success of his matchmaking proclivities savoured to the full this most recent confirmation - which had not escaped his keen eyes - of the undoubted triumph of his long laid plans to bring his adoptive brother and Isobel together, in what he was sure, would be a life long partnership.

Dinner passed with the usual light-hearted chatter kept flowing by Richard's sparkling and witty tales of army life. The girls, Isobel, Lance and Richard requested to be excused in order to change into more suitable clothing for the walk to the woods to hear the nightingales.

On the way, Richard skilfully led the way with the two girls, Margaret and her sister, Christal, leaving Lance and Isobel to follow. Lance was very conscious of Isobel's close proximity and the bean flower perfume that she always used.

When she had lived in India she had worn a slight touch of attar of roses, never the more sophisticated musky perfumes which were quite abhorrent to her.

Anyone who has stood downwind of a field of beans in full flower will never forget that so intensely English, haunting fragrance, till the day they die. It was distilled by an old family firm of seedsmen. It was Bees or Carters who sold it by mail order.

Lance questioned Isobel about the post office and her reasons for taking it. Her escort listened intently as she related their tragically changed circumstances and their need to earn a living, and how she had observed the prosperity of the Indian merchants. Isobel added that the post office was only a stepping stone to further ventures and then described her plans in Oxford. Lance had already been fully briefed by Richard so these revelations were not as startling as they might have been.

They were now very close to the thicket and could plainly hear the subdued twittering that precede the full throated liquid cascading burst of song made more magical by the velvet darkness of the night. They spread their rugs on the sward and listened with awe to the nightingales now in full voice. Isobel looked up into Lance's grey eyes and said, "That is the most beautiful sound I have ever heard."

"You must come again, soon, as they only sing for about five weeks."

Isobel said, "I must. Oh! I must. It was so enchanting and I will remember this night forever." They all returned to the house to prepare for the journey back to Tillingthorpe.

After they had said goodbye to Mr. and Mrs. Howard, Lance, Richard, Mrs. Langthorne and Isobel all climbed into the Armstrong Siddely car, Isobel and her mother in the back, Richard and Lance in the front with Richard driving. The journey passed pleasantly and on arrival at the post office, Richard collected their cases while Lance assisted them to alight. Turning to Mrs. Langthorne, Lance said, "I do most earnestly hope that you will come again and you know that my father will give you no peace until you agree to show him the secret room and the cupboard where the loot was hidden." To Isobel, he said, "I will show you my own secret place, which only Richard and I share, so you see you must come soon." They agreed they would love to come and would write to Mr. and Mrs. Howard to thank them for their kind hospitality.

While everybody was deeply engrossed in the activities at the post office, one, Peregrine Devereaux, had been making frequent visits to Cock-a-Dobbie cottage undetected by the inhabitants of Tillingthorpe. This blissful state of affairs would sadly not continue. The presence of Peregrine's racing green Alvis car near the cottage was eventually be spotted by the all-seeing eyes of at least one of the village gossips, who were still waiting for just such an opportunity to lay the blame for Kate Farrel's illegitimate son on the shoulders of the hitherto unknown, guilty man. The fact that Peregrine loved Kate would not mitigate the offence by one iota. However, we will leave this clandestine love affair and not divulge their secret passion to another living soul.

On the Saturday morning, a week after their visit to Cornwall Court, Isobel and her mother went to Oxford to confer with the estate agent and the architect. On the way they stopped at a small café to take coffee; but more important, to observe the levels of trade. A pleasant surprise awaited them, as although it was situated at the end of a long drive and well off the road it was packed and consequently Isobel and her mother had to share a table with a couple of elderly American tourists.

At eleven they presented themselves at the agents chambers. They were informed that the refitting of the kitchen would cost one thousand five hundred pounds, the installation of the type of seating specified by Isobel would cost rather more; two thousand pounds. The fitted carpet another five hundred pounds, making a grand total of four thousand pounds. The lease had ten years to run and would be a further one thousand pounds, with an annual rental of two hundred pounds. The rates would be fifty pounds per annum.

Mrs. Langthorne and her daughter requested another week to make a final decision and proceeded to consult the architect whose chambers were a little down the High. The architect showed them the plans of the layout. Both the ladies expressed their admiration for the attractive design. The architect, who looked more like a bishop, with his bald head encircled by thick grey hair, volunteered the opinion that such an establishment was needed and could not fail. He added, with a smile, "If you decide to proceed, I will be your first customer." They thanked him for these words of encouragement and promised to give their final word a week later.

They made an appointment with the bank manager to seek financial advice on the Tuesday morning.

On the return journey, Isobel was silent and thoughtful; but strangely, her mother was very buoyant and confident about the idea but kept her thoughts to herself, to be disclosed at a more opportune moment. Each was aware of the other's contemplations, but said nothing.

On arrival at the post office, Mrs. Langthorne prepared a light meal. They were having a cup of tea and the apprehensive Isobel admitted her doubts and misgivings to her mother. To Isobel's astonishment, her mother replied,

"I do not share your pessimism, in fact quite the contrary, I believe it will be a raging success. The only problem will be, who will run it: you can't." Isobel looked at her mother with admiration for her positive attitude. In previous plans, it had been Isobel who had displayed the exuberant enthusiasm for the venture and her mother who had expressed doubts; now the shoe was on the other foot.

"Do you really believe that the idea will be a success?"

"I am full of confidence!" Mrs. Langthorne asserted.

This conversation was interrupted by the persistent ringing of the phone. Isobel went into the post office to take the call. It was the curate, Andrew Gilbert, requesting permission to call on the Sunday at two o'clock as he had something to tell them. Isobel said, "By all means; is your news good or sad?"

"You shall judge for yourself," Andrew Gilbert replied.

"Then you will be very welcome," Isobel confirmed. The curate thanked her profusely and said he looked forward to seeing them again and hoped that they were both well. Isobel assured him both she and her mother always enjoyed good health.

Isobel returned to her mother who had overheard the phone conversation and resumed the discussion interrupted by the phone call. Isobel suggested that Jane should be consulted about the project and offered the post of manageress of the coffee shop; also to invoke her aid to find a replacement for her in the shop. After all these reassurances and solving of problems, they fell to wondering about the curate's visit on the following day, Sunday.

Chapter 15

On the Sunday the curate arrived, dressed as he was that day when he came to the Dower House. They greeted him warmly and when he was settled and at ease, he told them that, after much heart-searching, he had decided to relinquish his original plans to make a career in the church, and he had made up his mind to enter Sandhurst to train for a commission in the King's Royal Rifle Corps. After twelve months with the regiment, he would apply for secondment to the Ghurkas as he had been informed that after one year with the Ghurkas he would be promoted to first lieutenant. His parents had agreed to continue his allowance, so, with his army pay, he would be quite well off.

Mrs. Langthorne said she was sure he would be far happier in the army and his life henceforth would become one great big adventure. Isobel wished to know all the details of his uniform and a brief history of the regiment. Andrew could describe the uniform in detail but did not, as yet, know much about the regiment's history. He did know, however, that their headquarters were at Winchester.

The curate then told the ladies how surprised and puzzled he had been by the reaction of the Reverend Copplethwaite to his decision to quit the ministry and take up a new life in the army.

"In what way?" enquired Mrs. Langthorne.

"Well, he has always given me the impression that he found my presence irksome, and has never missed an opportunity to administer a stinging rebuke or crush me with a sarcastic retort. Yet, when I told him at dinner, he looked very sad and disappointed and said he would miss me. Had I given the matter the consideration such a momentous change of career warranted?"

The old boy had really thrown him off balance. "I am sure he was sincere and I am equally sure he will miss you as Isobel and I will miss you," Mrs. Langthorne added. The young man felt quite touched by these remarks, secretly hoping that this lovely young woman would miss him the most.

On the Monday evening, Isobel was to receive an unusual gift from Nathanael Martindale, the shepherd, (Caleb's grandson). They had closed for the day and were listening to the news on the wireless after tea when they heard a loud knock on the back door. Isobel rose to answer; opened the door and saw the shepherd standing there with something rolled up in a sack. "Do come in, Mr. Martindale," she invited. Nathanael had met Isobel several times when he purchased postal orders for his football coupon.

Isobel led the way into the warm kitchen and introduced her mother who offered the shepherd a cup of tea, which he gladly accepted. Laying his straw hat on the floor he sat down on a wheel-back kitchen chair and said to Isobel, "My dog, Nell, had a litter of pups about eight weeks ago and I thought you might like one." Nathanael unrolled the sack and a tiny ball of fur emerged which he handed to Isobel. Isobel's eyes shone with surprise and delight as she took this tiny puppy and put its soft warm fur up to her cheek.

"She's so beautiful," cried Isobel, "I love her already."

The puppy's markings were exactly like those of her grandmother; with the white tip of her tail clearly marked. Her body colouring was nondescript at this stage of the puppy's life but the colouring would become richer as she matured. Every young girl needs something or someone to love that is her very own. The puppy could not have come into Isobel's life at a more appropriate time.

"How much shall I give you, Mr. Martindale, for the puppy?"

"Oh, no. I don't want anything for her, she's a present from me." Isobel had soon learned that these men were very proud and possessed independent spirits, so she just thanked him again and promised to take great care of her.

The shepherd was, like his grandfather, a big man and as he left he warned Isobel that the puppy would give her a few sleepless nights and then settle in, but, he told her, she must be kept warm at all times and she liked company.

This tiny creature would enrich Isobel's life in simple but important ways. She would get to know many more people in the village when she took her new canine companion for walks; that was something to enjoy and look forward to. Isobel's mother was very surprised by the way her daughter coped with the small pools of water and tiny mounds on the flags in the kitchen every morning; but Isobel was well aware that it was only a temporary chore and when the puppy outgrew these weaknesses, she would sleep in a basket at the foot of Isobel's bed. But the immediate concern was to find a name for this new addition to the Langthorne household.

Monday morning arrived and reminded them both of more important matters to be dealt with and the two Langthornes could not be certain that Jane would agree to their plans for the coffee shop. When Jane arrived for work they took her into the cosy kitchen and without preamble launched into details of their plans to open the coffee shop with her as manageress. They advised her to think carefully and consult her parents before committing herself. They would pay her ten pounds a week plus one shilling in the pound commission. It was estimated that commission, calculated on the assumption of takings of a minimum of twenty-five pounds a day, would enhance her wages by another seven pounds ten shillings, making a total of twelve pounds ten shillings a week. A considerable level of remuneration in the early thirties.

The Langthornes were not surprised that Jane did not appear too enthusiastic about the idea of leaving the post office where she was very happy. They convinced her they would not be offended if she refused to accept and her present job would always be secure regardless of a refusal. It was concluded that she would ask her parents' opinion, and tell them on Tuesday morning. They advised Jane they would take her to see the project and where she would be working, if acceptable.

All this excitement did not divert Jane's attention from the puppy held by Isobel. She took the tiny collie from Isobel, put the soft bundle of fur to her cheek saying, "What a pretty little dog," and with a tinge of envy said, "Where did you get her?" Isobel explained she was a present from Mr. Martindale, the shepherd. "I could nurse her all day," Jane exclaimed, "but you have given me much to think about and I must start work."

That evening Isobel chose the name of Tess for her little dog.

The following morning, mother and daughter rose early and anxiously awaited the arrival of Jane, hoping that she would say yes to their proposals. Jane arrived and, to the Langthorne's relief, appeared to be her normal cheery self. She was promptly invited into the kitchen where Jane picked up Isobel's puppy, placed it in her lap, stroking it while she spoke. "I have spoken to my mum and dad about your offer, and, although my mum is not so keen, my dad is; in fact, he said that the money you have offered means I will be earning more money than the bailiff. That is exciting."

This morning was the day they had an appointment with the bank manager so it would mean the shop and post office would have to be closed for the day as they were taking Jane with them. They arrived at the bank at ten forty-five, and leaving Jane in the car, they entered the oak doors, announced their arrival to one of the clerks and waited to be called. After a brief wait they were ushered into the manager's office.

Mrs. Langthorne suggested that one half of the initial expenditure: two thousand and twenty pounds, should be disposed of by diverting this amount from her capital. The manager was a very shrewd man and advised his clients conscientiously.

He stated that this would not be a good business tactic, and advised borrowing the whole amount at 6%. They were already getting 5% on their capital, so they would only be paying virtually 1% for the loan and their money would continue to earn interest. Mrs. Langthorne readily appreciated the wisdom in this advice and requested that he expedite all the arrangements. As bank managers are notoriously busy men, they shook hands, thanked him for all the valuable help he had proffered and returned to Jane who was waiting for their return in the car.

She was pleased to see the satisfaction so plainly visible on their faces. Jane was requested to accompany them to the estate agent, who would be instructed to proceed with all necessary formalities to effect a completion of the tenancy agreement and allow Jane to see where she would work.

The estate agent escorted the three ladies to the premises, unlocked the street door and all ascended the wide staircase. Mrs. Langthorne and Isobel keenly scanned Jane's face to capture her first reaction, which would, undoubtedly, signal a yea or nay to their proposal for her to manage the coffee shop. Jane's face lit up as her eyes took in the impressive chamber with its ornate and historic embellishments.

Isobel stepped to her side and explained the eighteenth century layout of the wooden, canopied settles which faced each other over a small oak table. Jane's female faculty of a vivid imagination could see the gentlemen in their satin knee breeches and beautiful coloured full-skirted coats. The foam of lace at their throats and the Small-Swords dangling at their sides.

Jane turned to Mrs. Langthorne saying, "I think I shall like it here." Isobel and her mother gave sighs of relief, for it was absolutely vital that someone honest and intelligent should be in sole charge of the venture, which, if mismanaged, could end in total disaster. Isobel informed Jane that it was planned to engage two other young girls to assist her.

All made their way back to the car to make the return journey to Tillingthorpe. Two of the women felt a glow of satisfaction at the smooth progress of events; the third experienced the mixed feelings of excitement, leavened with apprehension and self-doubt.

Mrs. Langthorne, who was sitting in the back with Jane, took Jane's hand in hers and thanked her for agreeing to help them. Jane, in future years, would have cause to give fate her heartfelt thanks for this opportunity. The reader will recall that when Jane took the post in the village shop, it was predicted that it would set in motion a train of events which would lead her to the man who would become her husband, with whom she would spend many, many happy years.

On arrival at the post office, Isobel rushed into the house to see if her puppy was alright. They had been away for nearly four hours and she was, naturally, anxious that her latest and much loved acquisition had come to no harm.

Tess had been left in a wooden orange box, snuggled up to a hot water bottle wrapped in an old woollen jumper. She was fast asleep but awoke immediately her hypersensitive sense of smell detected the presence of her mistress. After ensuring that Tess was none the worse for their temporary neglect, Isobel assisted her mother in preparing a meal for the three of them.

Jane was now regarded as a member of their small family and indeed had made a great contribution to the healing processes that followed that never-to-be-forgotten tragedy in India. Further assistance from Jane was still needed. Who would succeed her when she left the post office to take up her duties as manageress of the coffee shop? This problem needed to be discussed without too much delay, and what better time than the present?

After dinner, they all conferred to solve this last serious problem, and it was more of a problem because Jane had fitted in so well and set such a high standard; equally important was the happy atmosphere she had created from the day that she had stepped through the door. Isobel had taken on a new lease of life and glowed with a new-found contentment. All this might be adversely affected when Jane departed to Oxford. These uncomfortable thoughts troubled Mrs. Langthorne more than she revealed to Isobel, for she was well aware of the tremendous improvement in her daughter which had coincided with the advent of Jane, who was truly a loveable personality.

Jane was sure that she could find someone of a happy disposition and also honest. Afterwards, Mrs. Langthorne murmured in Jane's ear, "Someone youthful and vibrant like yourself, for she must not only fit in, but be a companion to my daughter." Jane thought that she would find another girl whom they would like within the next two weeks.

At the weekend, they had a phone call from Lance's father who said he would be visiting the Beldrakes and would like to call on them on the way back. "You did promise to show me the highwayman's lair, remember?" he reminded them, banteringly. Mr. Howard arrived about three o'clock and was welcomed by Mrs. Langthorne. She invited him into the sitting room where she had tea and cakes laid out on a silver tray. After he was comfortably seated, Mrs. Langthorne called Isobel who was in the garden playing with her puppy.

"Isobel," she called, "Mr. Howard has come to see us." Isobel ceased her romps with Tess and hurried to greet their guest. She wore a black cashmere jumper, a red velvet skirt, and buckled shoes. As she stood with Tess cradled beneath her left arm and framed by the ancient oak door frame, Mr. Howard thought she looked like a Victorian painting come to life. How beautiful she was.

Isobel moved towards him, shook hands, enquired after his health and then added, "How is your son, Lance?" Angels sang in Mr. Howard's heart. He recalled the blush that had suffused her cheeks when he promised that if she ever got married she should wear the family coronet and now she was asking about his son, the apple of his eye. Oh! Truly things looked promising.

He pleased her by enquiring where she had got the puppy and Isobel, always ready to talk about her – at present – most treasured possession, gazed into the big man's face and told him all about the unexpected visit of Mr. Martindale, the shepherd, and the furry bundle that he had carried, rolled in a corn sack. He listened intently, studying the artless, childlike innocence reflected in her dark eyes with their long curling lashes.

After tea, Mr. Howard looked at his watch and said, "I must be getting along, but not before you show me where the jewels were found and the secret chamber."

Isobel showed him the twin cupboards and the secret panel in the back where the jewels had been hidden. She picked up a torch and Mrs. Langthorne and Mr. Howard followed her to the green gate into the concealed passage between the walls. Lance had told his father about the cleverly fashioned bolt mechanism which opened the door and Mr. Howard was just as intrigued by it. Isobel opened the door and lit their path with her torch; they passed through the second door and descended the stone steps into the secret chamber.

"Mind your head," she cautioned Mr. Howard, "The arch is very low." He looked around the chamber and marvelled at its sinister history. Isobel invited him to stand with her on the hearth to look up the chimney to observe the cunningly hidden escape hatch. Like his son, he was fascinated by what he saw and seemed loth to leave the room which, Mrs. Langthorne pointed out, was beneath the larder.

"How extraordinary," he commented. "Villains they may have been, but what fiendishly clever villains: in a way, I admire them." They ascended the steps and walked along the passage into the bright sunlight where Mr. Howard carefully examined both sides of the double wall expressing surprise that it had remained undiscovered for such a long time.

They all walked round to the front of the house where they bid Mr. Howard goodbye after charging him with a goodwill message to his family. Mrs. Langthorne and Isobel waved to him until the car was out of sight.

Mr. Howard was a very happy man as he drove home to Cornwall Court that day. He was now fairly certain that Isobel had more than a passing interest in his son, and his wife was convinced that their son was deeply in love with Isobel. So far so good. The thought that this beautiful young woman would one day be his son's bride and eventually mistress of Cornwall Court was all that he could desire.

Mr. Howard had also another snippet of information to impart to his wife in the privacy of their bedroom; young Beldrake was Isobel's cousin. She would like that. He was also fairly sure that even his adopted son, Richard, was not aware of this relationship.

Chapter 16

A week later, Jane informed Mrs. Langthorne and her daughter that she might have found a suitable girl to take her place: Mary Griffin. Jane and Mary had been at school together and Jane held her in high regard.

Mary worked at Steeple Ashton Manor as personal maid to Lady Lucia Heatherington and was not happy in this post. Lady Lucia was a querulous and very demanding woman, not at all considerate of servants' feelings or their need to have time off. She would be compelled to give one month's notice, as per her terms of employment, but this circumstance would not create any difficulties as the project in Oxford would not be ready for another three months.

Jane was in correspondence with Mary, and, when convenient, it was arranged for Jane and Isobel to pick her up on her day off, bring her over to the post office to meet the Langthornes and accept or reject their offer of employment. On the Thursday of the second week, Jane informed Mrs. Langthorne that Mary had agreed with this plan and that she was looking forward to the trip.

Mary was the daughter of Reg and Helen Griffin who ran a smallholding of fifty acres, two miles from Tillingthorpe, devoted mainly to the production of porker pigs of two score pounds in weight. These porkers were sold off as stores in Abingdon Market. Reg also kept two pedigree Jersey cows that provided cream which his wife made into butter. The hundred Rhode Island Red poultry produced a steady stream of large brown speckled eggs. These eggs, together with the butter, were sold from a stall in the market every week. Altogether, Reg and his wife made a comfortable living.

Mary, their daughter, had long fair hair down to her waist; this was plaited and coiled on her head like the fashion sported by Swiss girls. She was about five feet nine inches in height, with blue eyes and a fair complexion. She was the same age as Jane. Although not as extrovert as Jane, Mary was a happy girl with a ready smile and highly intelligent. In her own mind, Jane was certain that her friend would fit in very well at the post office.

Ten days later, Jane told Isobel that Mary would expect them at two on Saturday and would be waiting at the gate of the Manor. Mary had the rest of the weekend off, returning to the Manor on Sunday evening.

Everything was proceeding smoothly according to plan, to the utter satisfaction of Jane.

The appointed Saturday arrived and Isobel, accompanied by Jane, set off for the rendezvous ten miles distant. They sighted Mary standing by the gate of the manor staring expectantly in the direction from which Isobel and Jane would approach. The car came to a halt and both Isobel and Jane alighted to engage in the formality of introductions. This necessary function disposed of, they all entered the car to make the return journey. Jane had already given her friend a thorough briefing concerning the Langthornes in her letter so Mary felt quite at ease.

Mrs. Langthorne was waiting to welcome Mary Griffin and would ensure that she was not inhibited by a formal atmosphere in a strange house. While Isobel went into the garden to play with Tess, her mother prepared tea.

Jane took Mary into the shop and explained the simple duties expected of her and pointed out the price tags she had devised, aided by her father. Jane had purchased some small open topped brass frames from the Woolworth's store in Oxford. These were nailed to the shelves underneath the goods. Gardener's labels were then cut to size and slid into them after the price had been inscribed. All the various utensils hanging from the ceiling were priced with small sticky labels. Mary was also instructed in the operation of the wooden till with its price recording paper roll. Mary assured Jane that she would have no difficulty in complying with any of the tasks so described.

They returned to the kitchen and after tea Jane showed her the cupboard where the jewels were found and then conducted her to the secret chamber. Mary was quite thrilled by her visit and would look forward to starting her new job.

Isobel took Mary home and met her parents who were truly pleased that their daughter was coming home to live, especially as Isobel would fetch their daughter in the mornings and bring her home at night. Mary would also dine with her employers at midday and would therefore not need sandwiches.

The month passed swiftly, not least because they had received a visit from the Oxford Antiquarian Society who requested permission to take photographs of the small cupboard and the secret chamber. When Isobel informed them that she now held the lease on their old meeting room in the High in Oxford, they became quite excited,

"What a strange coincidence," they cried. "How very, very odd. We feel so gratified that the Society has links with you and your house even if they are but tenuous."

After viewing the house and taking numerous photographs, they departed, chattering like a gaggle of geese. They promised the Langthornes that they would consult their many reference books in the headquarters' library which, they assured Isobel, would yield further information on the infamous Robert Noakes.

Isobel and her mother were enveloped in a great wave of satisfaction as the machinery of fate - which governs all our destinies - was operating with well-oiled smoothness in their favour. Now they must contain their impatience until the agent in Oxford informed them that all renovations were complete.

The dog, Tess, was now three months old and a round leather collar (always round for dogs with long fur) and a thin lead had been purchased for her. Isobel and Tess would explore the village together, enabling Tess to become accustomed to the many strange sights and interesting smells.

When dogs are taken for a walk and make frequent stops to sniff the ground or clumps of grass, that is like handing a human being a good book to read. All those smells are catalogued and categorised in the canine brain in preparation for future reference. It is alleged also, that the hearing of a sheep-dog bitch is so acute that they can hear the click of a gate one and a half miles away.

As they skipped through the village, they would pause to talk to people working in their gardens and often received, most gratefully, bunches of flowers which would make their rooms even prettier.

On one occasion Hilda Humphrey emerged from the side door of The Red Lion and invited Isobel to come in. Isobel was introduced to her husband, Joshua, who was pleased to see this young woman, about whom he had heard so much from his wife during supper time conversations. He was also pleased to learn that, for once, Hilda had not indulged in her customary exaggerations, when describing people. That night Joshua would tell his good friend, the blacksmith, about this encounter with the new postmistress.

Hilda showed Isobel round the pub and gave a running commentary on the various animals and birds high up on the walls in their glass cases. The young girl was intrigued by the dark passages which zigzagged with their nooks and crannies throughout the pub. After accepting a glass of real lemon drink, she took her leave after thanking Hilda for showing her their home.

After Isobel had departed, Hilda marched into the bar parlour and, with arms akimbo, demanded to know what Joshua had thought of the postmistress.

"A real lady and no mistake. A bootiful young woman and no swank!" Joshua retorted.

That evening in the bar Joshua stared Bill Copeland in the eye after he had downed his first mug of ale and enquired laconically, "Have you seen the new postmistress, Bill?" The blacksmith removed his pipe from his mouth and gave Joshua a long, suspicious look. Had his old friend been working out in the sun too long? Maybe he was light-headed through drinking his own ale. What a daft question.

"Why do you ask?" he enquired.

"She came in here today and Hilda showed her round," Joshua continued. "She's a real lady. No airs and graces." Bill was not interested in female postmistresses nor any female for that matter. His wife had been demanding a new cooking range, hinting that the new Aga oil burning range would be very suitable, and this woman Joshua was talking about was to blame. No, the smith could not care less about this woman who was causing so much trouble in his marriage.

When Isobel returned from these local expeditions, her mother noted the radiant exhilaration illuminating her daughter's flushed face.

The weather was oppressively hot and both had learned the wisdom imparted to them by Martha, the lowering of the milk can into the cold water of the well to prevent the milk going sour. One morning, Isobel noted that the windlass was in urgent need of repair and decided that on Wednesday morning, when the business was very quiet, she would take Tess for a walk to the forge to ask Mr. Copeland to repair it. Leaving Jane in charge on the Wednesday morning, Isobel set off to invoke the aid of the mighty smith.

Isobel, with Tess, made her way to the forge which was located on the edge of the village; Tess leaping up and biting the slack in the lead. Tess was getting stronger day by day, but still retained her nondescript coloured fur of a dirty fawn, flecked with black. She was very frightened by the fountain of popping sparks that flew from this strange fire set in the middle of a table. Tess put her tail between her back legs and whined with fear prompting Isobel to pick her up protectively.

The smith was thrusting a strip of iron into the heart of the fire while his mate, his striker, operated the large bellows standing in a roomy alcove at the side of the forge. A stout wooden handle, about four feet long, protruded from the top of the bellows which was in the firm grasp of the smith's assistant, Frank Burrows. Frank made frantic signals to the smith to indicate the presence of a stranger. Bill looked over his shoulder to espy the cause of the agitation in his assistant's gesticulations. The thought flashed into the smith's brain that it must be serious, because he had never seen his mate behave so strangely in the twenty years that they had worked together in the confined spaces of the Tillingthorpe smithy. The smith mopped his brow with a cloth tucked into his apron for that very purpose.

His mate ceased his vigorous operation of the bellows as Bill walked towards Isobel with, "Can I help you, ma'am?"

Isobel smiled and said, "I am sure you can, but it will only be a small job."

"No matter," responded the smith, "Every mickle makes a muckle; its all grist to the mill, as they say." Isobel gazed up into the face of this bulky muscular giant and explained that the windlass on their well was in urgent need of repair and would he be so kind as to come and look at it. He would come and look at it the very next day he assured her. "Would half-past seven in the morning be too early?"

"It is a trifle. Could you make it half past eight?" Isobel enquired.

"Eight-thirty it is, then," Bill agreed.

Bill then looked down at Tess, as the Gods looked down from Mount Olympus. "A pretty little dog you have there, ma'am."

"Yes, Mr. Martindale, the shepherd, gave her to me."

"Ah. yes," quoth the smith. "I know Nathanael very well, in fact I have known him since he was a boy and I knew his grandfather, Caleb, very well. Right then, ma'am, I'll see you in the morning, eight-thirty sharp."

"Yes. I must get back to my work in the post office." Then, laying her small white hand on his enormous hairy forearm, Isobel said, "By the way, my name is Isobel; do address me as such, not ma'am, please."

The smith glanced at Frank and beamed with pleasure at this invitation to address this handsome young woman as a friend. "Just as you wish, ma— Isobel," he corrected. "I will like that, and a very pretty name it is, if I may say so." Bill walked with Isobel on to the road, bade her goodbye and returned to the ancient craft of blacksmithing, with a thoughtful look of exultation on his face.

The next morning, as the church clock struck the half hour, the smith knocked on the back door of the shop, to be greeted by Isobel with, "Good morning, Mr. Copeland, please come in, my mother would like to meet you."

The smith removed his cap, crouched down to enter the door with only a bare inch to clear his broad shoulders. Mrs. Langthorne was an inch shorter than Isobel and found it necessary to tilt her head back to look the smith in the eye. "How do you do, Mr. Copeland. My daughter has told me all about her visit to your forge. Have you time for a mug of fresh coffee or are you in great haste?" The smith assured her he had 'all the time in the world'.

"Please sit down, Mr. Copeland, and drink your coffee in comfort." The smith sat down in the same wheelback chair used by the shepherd when he delivered the puppy. Isobel watched, apprehensively, as the smith lowered his vast bulk on to the fragile looking chair and wondered if it would collapse.

Isobel thought it might be an opportune moment to mention her pony, who might need a new set of shoes. The mention of her pony and a new set of shoes kindled a light in the smith's eyes. "You couldn't do better than to bring her to me, Isobel," he said. "She'll be in good hands. I've shod shires, cobs, polo ponies and thoroughbreds," he assured her, "and I am a member of the Master Farriers Association." He rose to his feet and reminded Isobel about the windlass on the well and stated he must be getting back to the forge or Frank would think he had fallen down it.

Wait till he told his friend Joshua. "I was saying to my friend, Isobel - you know, Joshua - the postmistress, this morning, etc.!" That should put Joshua in his place and not before time, for the smith had noticed that the innkeeper had become a trifle uppity of late, aggressive in fact and such an attitude was not seemly; not if you wanted to keep your regulars.

At the end of his working day, the smith plodded into his cottage, situated slightly to the rear but attached to the smithy, where his wife, Lucy, had prepared a meal of four large thick slices of home-cured ham, five tomatoes, two whole cos lettuce, homemade pickle and four thick slices of home-baked bread, spread lavishly with the purest of butter. Lucy would ensure that Bill was fed well, as she had been somewhat anxious concerning the number of stamps on his insurance cards. She knew that she was a good wife, not that Bill was always mindful of her wifely virtues and that the time was coming when she would remind him once again that he had taken the best years of her life and might even threaten him with a legal separation: that should bring him to heel. These modern flibbertigibbets of girls simply did not know how to feed a man. In fact, the smith had often remarked about this serious shortcoming of the modern girls.

Big men, especially smiths, needed a lot of sustenance; that is, if they were to achieve their allotted three score years and ten, as promised in the Good Book, and thus die in their beds as all law abiding citizens should strive to do.

However, the smith was obviously in good humour tonight, if the half-smile on his ruddy face was anything to go by.

"Lucy," he said, in the solemn tones of a judge about to pass sentence, "Lucy, what was that you were saying about a new cooker? I've been thinking: we could not afford an Aga cooker, but you can have one of them newfangled ranges with the hot water tank on one side with the brass tap. I think you'd like that." The blacksmith's wife eyed her husband suspiciously.

Bill never drank in the daytime, perhaps this was the first sign of a brainstorm. You could never tell with a man of his age and temper. Lucy continued to stare at the smith and decided that caution must prevail. "Let me think about it, Bill, tomorrow," she replied.

The smith donned his hat and set forth to The Red Lion. As soon as the blacksmith set foot in the bar, Joshua noticed the crafty glitter in his old friend's eyes and felt a little uneasy. Not only that, the smith had a strange expression on his face; the sort of look of 'I've put one over on you and you don't know about it' look. Joshua 'boxed clever', as they say, and gave no sign that he had noticed.

The smith was gazing into his half-empty beer mug wondering how he could broach the subject of Isobel's visit to the forge. Finally he decided how he would open the conversation. "I had my friend, Isobel, in to see me at the forge, today, Josh. I don't suppose you would know her; she's the new postmistress, you know?" Joshua glared at the smith. What was the man talking about; had the man become unhinged? He knew, full well, that Joshua knew the postmistress. Had he not told Bill only the previous night how Isobel had been in his house and how Hilda had introduced him to her. Either the smith was suffering from that terrible disease, amnesia, which makes a man's hair fall out until he is as bald as a coot; it was either that or loss of memory. It could be that the smith had suffered a blow on the head from his striker's hammer which had left him mentally deranged. Another thing, why had Bill Copeland called him Josh? His anger now turned to sorrow that such a fine man could come to such a sorry end.

That night, after closing time, Joshua did not appear to be his normal self. Something was troubling him and Hilda knew it. After all, every woman knows her man better than he knows himself. Joshua stared into his mug of cocoa and was plainly engrossed in his own serious thoughts. Hilda knew any woman worth her salt can get the upper hand of a husband by simply playing a waiting game. After a protracted silence, Joshua looked at his wife and enquired, "Have you seen the smith's wife, lately?"

"Of course: I saw her this morning in the post office," she retorted. A long pause.

"Did she seem concerned about Bill's health?"

"No. Why should she, the great lummox is as strong as an ox?" Joshua lapsed into silence but was not a happy man.

The next morning, Joshua's wife met the smith's wife in the shop and greeted her with, "My Joshua thinks your Bill is not in good health. Are you feeding him right, Lucy?"

"Funny you should say that, Hilda," the smith's wife countered, "My Bill said last night he was worried about Joshua's health as he had been acting queerly, recently, and wondered if the innkeeper's wife was giving her husband the support a man has a right to expect from his wife."

Hilda Humphrey took umbrage at this implied slight on her wifely prowess and retaliated thus, "My man always goes to work with a good lining in his belly and has a comfortable feather bed to lie on at night with me to keep him company. Joshua is a very contented man, unlike some I could name!" And as she made her exit called, "not so very far from here." Such is the making of family feuds.

The curiosity of the older members of the Tillingthorpe community was still rife and they were most perplexed by the comings and goings of so many total strangers, some of them over seven feet tall.

One evening, Dusty Miller entered The Red Lion looking very smug. Dusty was in sole charge of all the threshing tackle on the estate. He was, also, one of those old fashioned pipe smokers who always smoked a pipe with a tiny silver lid hinged to the bowl. The Millers were the village bee keepers and when Dusty Miller's father died in 1931, aged ninety-two, Dusty dutifully observed the tradition of 'telling the bees'. Thursday at six, Dusty proceeded down the long garden to the two hives; tapping softly on the side he informed the residents that the master had passed away that very morning at four o'clock. Failure to carry out this ritual would cause the bees to take umbrage, abandon the hives, and to swarm in someone else's garden to be scooped up and accommodated in a brand new hive with its strange smells. But Dusty was determined that he had a duty to his recently departed father and also to the bees. Townsfolk would deride and sneer at such revelations, but wiser souls, in any village, would solemnly assure these doubting Thomases that these functions were absolutely necessary.

Dusty ordered his usual: a pint of dark, and laid on the bar counter an opened Woodbine cigarette packet with a car registration number written on it. He placed the scrap of paper on the counter with the air of a man who has just trumped the winning trick in the village whist drive to win the first prize of a cockerel and a voucher for five shillings.

"There it is!" he cried. "That's the answer!" All crowded round, the better to see this magic answer to the mysterious activities at the post office. "I shall give that to my brother-in-law, Wilf, and he will soon trace the owner of that car."

This plan was doomed to failure, as Wilf did not have access to records in head office; but ignorance is bliss, or so it is said. The request was duly conveyed to Wilf through the chain of in-laws. He was not at all cooperative: quite the contrary. Wilf was very angry at this stupid request which indicated how ignorant they were of the complicated and important duties of all A.A. scouts. His wife, Daisy, who should have known better, was the victim of Wilf's disgruntled tirade and, as a result, she threatened to leave him. This stung Wilf into replying that her blankety, blank, blank relations were trying to break up his marriage.

The chain of in-law communication system was once again invoked to convey the message back to Tillingthorpe, and in particular one Dusty Miller, that the brother-in-law, a certain Wilf Tulley, could not and would not help to find the car of the registration number stated on the cigarette packet. Didn't they understand he saw millions of cars every day and it would be like 'looking for a needle in a haystack'? Furthermore, he would be obliged if all concerned would stop messing him about and interfering with his married life. After receiving this blunt message, Dusty Miller was forced to concede that his well intentioned suggestion to throw some light on the mysterious activities at the post office had not worked.

The strained relations between the blacksmith and the innkeeper and the crestfallen Dusty Miller ensured that the wave of inquisitiveness about the Langthornes subsided.

Dusty Miller's wife's brother-in-law, Wilf Tulley, had served throughout the Great War as a dispatch rider and had been fortunate in obtaining a post as an A.A. scout based in Oxford. He was a man of gaunt appearance; emaciated would not be an exaggeration. His wife, Daisy, felt that he 'showed her up' as she was a very good cook and fed her husband well. He, being as thin as a lath, attracted such comments from vindictive neighbours as, 'that man is not getting enough to eat'. That was a bare-faced lie and they knew it. Daisy was an old-fashioned girl and was well aware that if you wanted to keep a man, you had to send him off to work with a warm lining in his stomach. Otherwise, you could lose him to pneumonia and funerals didn't come cheap: and another thing; he was not insured.

Daisy gave Wilf plenty of good solid food; Irish stew with suet dumplings, steak and kidney pie, Lancashire hot-pot, suet roll with pieces of rasher bacon, jam roly-poly, and pancakes on Shrove Tuesday. Yes, her Wilf was well taken care of, that is why, when her old crow of a mother-in-law called and abused Daisy's hospitality with remarks like,

"I hope you are looking after my boy, Daisy, he is very thin and pale," or, "You know when my Wilf married you he left a good home," Daisy resented these innuendoes. All the while these arrows of spite were flying through the highly charged atmosphere, she would peer intently into her daughter-in-law's face looking for the tell-tale reddening of the cheeks: an infallible indicator of a guilty woman. The old crow, as Daisy had named her – some years ago – with her drooping eyelids, reminded Daisy of a vulture waiting for some unfortunate wounded beast to expire.

Wilf, Daisy's husband, was, – in a peculiar way – a most interesting character. He believed, and had been brought up to believe, by a mother with religious mania, that all the working class had their own particular cross to bear. She often quoted that passage from the Bible where it states that: 'To him that hath much shall be given. From him that hath not, even that which he hath, shall be taken from him'.

The essence of Wilf's own heavy burden was encapsulated in the A.A. Handbook as issued to members only. It stated, categorically that gratuities were not to be given to A.A. Scouts after they had rendered certain services. Wilf regarded this as a pernicious system. He did not know what the word meant but he had once heard a trade union official say that, "This pernicious exploitation of the working class must cease." Wilf claimed that if this perk was denied the scouts, it would be a grave injustice as many people relied on their perks. After all, as he would often say, "There's no taste in nuffink!" Even his wife, Daisy, always gave a tip to the coal man, providing, of course, that he slipped in an extra bag and didn't write on the bill.

The reader may not know of this custom, but when scouts failed to salute members, that member was advised to enquire the reason. He would then be warned of roadworks, diversions and even police speed traps.

When this frequent and onerous duty fell upon Wilf's shoulders he would approach the motorist and presenting the side of his face to the driver and by a strange convulsive contortion transfer his mouth from its normal position in the front of his head to the side of his face, much like the mouth of many species of flat fish. The startled member would then hear this strange human creature, with a mouth of a plaice, croak hoarsely into his ear that a police speed trap was in operation on the Kidlington road. Wilf had once explained the reason for this strange behaviour was to prevent non-members gaining access to information that was for members' ears only. Wilf had noted that when he was giving information to members, non-members would stop their cars opposite to him, wind down their window and try to hear information which they were not entitled to hear.

Chapter 17

Meanwhile, Isobel and her mother proceeded about their daily lives blissfully unaware of the turbulent effect which their presence was having upon the worthy inhabitants of the ancient village of Tillingthorpe. They had received a letter from the architect that the requested installations and renovations would be completed in approximately six weeks' time.

This gave the Langthornes an opportunity to recruit two sixteen or seventeen year old girls to help Jane and measure them for the early eighteenth century costumes they would wear. These would consist of a red flannel petticoat and a long skirt which would be caught up at the front to expose the petticoat, fitted with two deep pockets. The bodice would be tight-fitting and laced. A white blouse would be worn underneath. Each girl would wear a different coloured skirt: blue, green and saffron. Buckled shoes would be worn. All the girls would wear a four inch wide chatelaine round their waist, made in a chain-linked style. A bunch of false keys, a captive order pad and pencil would dangle at their side from a two foot chain. A small round flat lace cap on the crown of their head would complete the costume. Jane loved the idea and felt it would attract custom.

The Oxford Labour Exchange was visited to request assistance in finding two girls of good figure with attractive personalities.

They then returned to Tillingthorpe, where they found the curate sitting in the shop talking to Jane. He had come to tell them that he was leaving the rectory that weekend to return home for two weeks' holiday. Mrs. Langthorne invited him into their private quarters so that he could enlighten them of all his plans for the future. He would, after two weeks, report to Sandhurst Royal Military Academy and would, after passing out, be posted to the King's Royal Rifle Corps. With their approval, he would like to write to them occasionally. Approval was enthusiastically given. His training would take nine months, abbreviated from the two years which it used to take some years previously. Andrew Gilbert would be sorry to leave the village but not the rectory.

Mrs. Langthorne and Isobel assured him - that in their opinion - he was doing the right thing and his life in the army would be a great deal more fulfilling than a career in the church. For example, he would know the comradeship of other lively young men and in the process would make friendships that would last all his life.

A message had been received from Akbar advising Isobel that her pony had arrived and was now conforming to a six month quarantine law. Akbar groomed her every day and kept up a routine of exercise to prevent the mare from becoming bored and lethargic. Isobel wrote back and promised to come to see Akbar and her precious gift from the Maharajah. Money was also enclosed to dispose of any expenses Akbar might incur. Isobel included her phone number and requested Akbar to call her.

On the Friday evening, the Langthornes had a phone call from the vicar inviting them to dinner to say goodbye to the curate. The invitation was gladly accepted. They had already purchased a parting gift for Mr. Gilbert; a gentleman's toilet kit in a pigskin case. The late Colonel Langthorne had had one exactly like it.

The two ladies arrived punctually at eight-thirty and were welcomed by the curate as the vicar was on the phone completing arrangements for the funeral on the Wednesday of Amos Atkinson who was ninety-three years of age and being born in the year 1840 could remember when stage coaches were a familiar sight. He also recalled the highwayman, Robert Noakes, as his grandfather was a contemporary of this villain.

The dinner passed pleasantly, with the vicar embarrassing the curate with his fulsome praise of how Mr. Gilbert would be sadly missed in the parish and at his table. They all drank a toast to the curate's future in his army career. The ladies gave him their gift, kissed him on the cheek and urged him to keep in touch. They also thanked the vicar for his hospitality and departed.

A lull in Isobel's burgeoning business venture gave her more time to exercise Tess and to explore more of the village; the more she walked around, the more she loved it. It was truly most picturesque and the maintenance of the cottage by the Beldrakes gave it an air of neatness. She also met and made so many new friends: Mrs. Wilkinson, who was eighty-three years old and lived at the Homestead; Fred Hallett, whose grandfather had taken part in the Charge of the Light Brigade in the Crimean War, and who still grew all his own vegetables in a large garden at the back of the cottage where not a weed could be seen; old Mrs. Green who had once been a parlour maid in royal service and her son Carlo Green who was a gardener at the Big House; Tom Gilles who ran a flourishing dairy farm and many others, and when invited in, Isobel gazed around in wide-eyed wonder that so many knick knacks and so much highly polished furniture could be crowded into such a small space.

Some of these treasured possessions had poignant associations, a keepsake from a soldier who died several thousands of miles from home and loved ones. A bundle of picture postcards sent from many foreign lands. Curiously, Isobel noted that every home, without exception, had two large portraits of a handsome man, frequently wearing a scarlet tunic, paired with another portrait of a beautiful young woman.

Isobel would sit for hours as the inhabitants regaled her with stories of their lives and a youth spent in an idyllic unspoiled countryside, which, for too many years, concealed severe hardship, misery, repression and sometimes brutality. This happy mode of life, triggered by a mind-numbing tragedy, was also the result of Isobel's inspired idea conceived in the most unlikely circumstances. Even Mrs. Langthorne, who believed that she would never recover from her bereavement, could often be heard singing as she went about her work.

The Labour Exchange, in Oxford, had rung through to say they could put forward six girls whom they believed would meet the Langthorne's specified qualifications. The post office was closed all day on Wednesday as Jane was invited to meet these young women who would be required to work harmoniously with her in the coffee shop. All were smiling, happy, young girls. Two were accepted and the others persuaded to leave their names and addresses as it was highly probable they would be offered a post in the near future.

The two girls, Susan and Rachel, together with Jane, were taken to a dressmaker in Oxford: a Miss Stokes, who had the brilliant idea of hiring a costume, as described, from a firm of theatrical costumiers. She would measure Jane, who would wear it in a dress rehearsal. If Jane liked it, they would order the three costumes.

Three days later, they had the call that a suitable costume had been hired and if they would make a visit on Saturday afternoon. Miss Stokes was awaiting them in her workroom with a costume draped over the back of a chair. Jane swiftly changed into the dress to cries of delight from the Langthornes. Isobel's mother hugged Jane and said how lovely she looked, and did she like it?

"I love it!" replied Jane. Such unanimous approval clinched the order for three costumes.

They returned to Tillingthorpe on a crest of euphoria and over tea discussed this most satisfactory day of decision making. There was still one other outstanding matter to be dealt with: a large advertisement in *The Oxford Herald*, accompanied by a write-up stating the object was to fill a need for professional men to bring clients to tie up deals and partake of refreshment in a tranquil atmosphere.

On the Sunday morning, the secretary of the Antiquarian Society phoned to enquire if it would be convenient to call on the Langthornes in the evening, as they had information about the highwayman. Copies of all their research would be given to Mrs. Langthorne. She wished to know how many gentlemen would be coming. "Only myself," he responded. He would be very welcome and they would eagerly await him. In due course the secretary arrived at seven to be greeted by Isobel who conducted him into the sitting room.

Without further preamble, he opened his briefcase and withdrew a sheaf of papers. The first paper described how Robert Noakes operated for five years, before being apprehended, on the Oxford to Bath, Oxford to Reading, and Oxford to Gloucester roads.

He was found sitting in The Bear Inn in Cheltenham disguised as a clergyman. Although he was booted and spurred and had a fine blood horse tethered outside, equipped with saddle holsters containing a brace of pistols ready primed, he declared that he was the Reverend Bartholomew Virgil Anthony Burgoyne, M.A. D.D. (Cantab.)

He presented the officer of the Red Coats with his card with a low bow, taking a delicate pinch of snuff while he coolly watched the officer scrutinise the ornate card, embellished with the coat of arms of the Archbishop of Canterbury. Seeing the hesitancy in the officer's manner, he informed the Red Coat that he was carrying secret state papers to the Bishop of Gloucester who would hold anyone – regardless of rank – to account if they dared to impede the progress of his lordship's personal messenger. "Where are these secret papers?" demanded the officer. Noakes reached into his full-skirted riding coat and produced a roll of parchment bearing the seal of the Archbishop of Canterbury. The officer made his apologies to this reverend gentleman and wished him a safe journey.

Then, if the officer had not been extremely alert, the rogue would have escaped, but as the highwayman mounted his restive horse, his lace cravat gaped revealing a livid scar on the base of his neck. This identified him as Robert Noakes, the highwayman. The officer barked an order to the Red Coats to shoot the horse. Noakes immediately dismounted and gave himself up.

The other two papers were a full transcript of Robert Noakes' trial and subsequent hanging.

After sentence had been passed, he addressed the court as follows: "I have relieved the rich of the heavy burden of carrying so much gold on their persons. I have relieved the poor of the even greater burden of poverty."

The horse that carried him so faithfully was never found. The horse on which he was arrested was hired from a livery stable. It was truly a noble act to throw away his last slender chance of freedom to save the horse's life.

Robert Noakes was a tall man, all of six feet, and of athletic physique. All Tillingthorpe men were tall: it must have been something in the local soil that stimulated the pituitary gland.

Many fine ladies and gentlemen crowded the court at Reading Assizes. Many were not involved, some had been called as witnesses.

Robert Noakes was a handsome and proud man who walked with just a slight swing of the shoulders as all superbly fit and confident men do. The expensive Toledo rapier which swung and bumped against his tight doeskin breeches was always close to hand to defend his person and honour. The rapier was one of the fruits of his calling. The elaborate steel basket hilt was richly engraved. The pommel of the hilt was set with a large amethyst. The scabbard was decorated with several heavy silver ferrules. The rapier was fitted with the finest of Toledo blades. A Spanish Grandee had been relieved of this highly prized possession during his journey to Bristol docks to embark on a ship sailing for Spain.

THE HIGHWAYMAN

BY ALFRED NOYES

The wind was a torrent of darkness among the gusty trees,
The moon was a ghostly galleon tossed upon cloudy seas.
The road was a ribbon of moonlight over the purple moor,
And the highwayman came riding – riding – riding –
The highwayman came riding, up to the old inn door.

* * *

He'd a French cocked-hat on his forehead, a bunch of lace at his chin,
A coat of the claret velvet, and breeches of brown doeskin.
They fitted with never a wrinkle. His boots were up to the thigh.
And he rode with a jewelled twinkle, his pistol butts a-twinkle,
His rapier hilt a-twinkle, under the jewelled sky.

* * *

Over the cobbles he clattered and clashed in the dark inn yard.
He tapped with his whip on the shutters, but all was locked and
barred.
He whistled a tune to the window, but who should be waiting
there
But the landlord's black-eyed daughter, Bess, the landlord's
daughter,
Plaiting a dark red love-knot into her long black hair.

* * *

And dark in the dark old inn yard a stable-wicket creaked
Where Tim the ostler listened. His face was white and peaked.
His eyes were hollows of madness, his hair like mouldy hay,
But he loved the landlord's daughter, the landlord's red-lipped
daughter
Dumb as a dog he listened, and he heard the robber say –

* * *

"One kiss, my bonny sweetheart, I'm after a prize tonight,
But I shall be back with the yellow gold before the morning light;
Yet, if they press me sharply, and harry me through the day,
Then look for me by moonlight, watch for me by moonlight,
I'll come to thee by moonlight, though hell should bar the way."

* * *

He rose upright in the stirrups. He scarce could reach her hand,
But she loosened her hair in the casement. His face burnt like a
brand
As the black cascade of perfume came tumbling over his breast
And he kissed its waves in the moonlight, (Oh, sweet black waves
in the moonlight!)
Then he tugged at his rein in the moonlight and galloped away to
the west.

* * *

He did not come in the dawning. He did not come at noon;
And out o' the tawny sunset, before the rise o' the moon,
When the road was a gypsy's ribbon, looping the purple moor,
A red coat troop came marching – marching – marching –
King George's men came marching, up to the old inn door.

* * *

They said no word to the landlord. They drank his ale instead.
But they gagged his daughter, and bound her to the foot of her
narrow bed.
Two of them knelt at her casement, with muskets at their side!
There was death at every window; and hell at one dark window;
For Bess could see, through her casement the road that he would
ride.

* * *

They had tied her up to attention, with many a sniggering jest,
They had bound a musket beside her, with the muzzle beneath her
breast!
"Now, keep good watch!" and they kissed her.
She heard the dead man say –
"Look for me by moonlight; watch for me by moonlight;
I'll come to thee by moonlight, though hell should bar the way!"

* * *

She twisted her hands behind her; but all the knots held good!
She writhed her hands till her fingers were wet with sweat or
blood!
They stretched and strained in the darkness, and the hours crawled
by like years,
Till, now, on the stroke of midnight, cold on the stroke of
midnight.
The tip of one finger touched it. The trigger at least was hers!

* * *

The tip of one finger touched it. She strove no more for the rest.

Up, she stood up to attention, with the muzzle beneath her breast.
She would not risk their hearing; she would not strive again;
For the road lay bare in the moonlight; blank and bare in the
moonlight;
And the blood of her veins in the moonlight, throbbed to her
love's refrain.

* * *

Tlot-tlot; tlot-tlot! Had they heard it? The horse-hoofs ringing
clear;
Tlot-tlot, tlot-tlot, in the distance! Were they deaf that they did not
hear?
Down the ribbon of moonlight, over the brow of the hill,
The highwayman came riding, riding, riding!
The Red Coats looked to their priming! She stood up, straight and
still.

* * *

Tlot-tlot, in the frosty silence! Tlot-tlot, in the echoing night!
Nearer he came and nearer. Her face was like a light.
Her eyes grew wide for a moment; she drew one last deep breath,
Then her finger moved in the moonlight, her musket shattered the
moonlight,
Shattered her breast in the moonlight and warned him - with her
death.

* * *

He turned. He spurred to the west; he did not know who stood
Bowed, with her head o'er the musket, drenched with her own red
blood!
Not till the dawn he heard it, and his face grew grey to hear
How Bess, the landlord's daughter, the landlord's black-eyed
daughter,
Had watched for her love in the moonlight, and died in the
darkness there.

* * *

Back, he spurred like a madman, shouting a curse to the sky,
With the white road smoking behind him and his rapier brandished

high.
Blood-red were his spurs i' the golden noon; wine-red was his
velvet coat;
When they shot him down on the highway, down like a dog on the
highway,
And he lay in his blood on the highway, with the bunch of lace at
his throat.

* * *

And still of a winter's night, they say, when the wind is in the
trees,
When the moon is a ghostly galleon tossed upon cloudy seas,
When the road is a ribbon of moonlight over the purple moor,
A highwayman comes riding – riding – riding –
A highwayman comes riding, up to the old inn door.

* * *

Over the cobbles he clatters and clangs in the dark inn yard.
And he taps with his whip on the shutters, but all is locked and
barred.
He whistles a tune to the window, and who should be waiting there
But the landlord's black-eyed daughter,
Bess, the landlord's daughter,
Plaiting a dark red love-knot into her long black hair.

* * *

As the ladies were called to testify against the rogue who had so cruelly robbed them, only one, a scrawny hatchet faced shrewish dowager, identified the highwayman as the villain who had robbed – at pistol point – both her and her portly husband. All the rest gazed into the bold twinkly blue eyes of Robert Noakes and said, somewhat breathlessly, "This is not the man!" or "I have never seen this man before!" Even one gentleman stared at Robert and wondered, with admiration, how this man, facing such a grisly end, could be so calm and composed. Although the gentleman had lost his gold watch in an encounter with the highwayman and did recognise him, he responded to the query, "Is this the man who robbed you and your fellow travellers while travelling on the Oxford to Bath turnpike?" with a firm, "No my lord."

All this history of Robert Noakes dispelled from Isobel's mind any revulsion she had previously felt when showing people the secret chamber beneath their larder.

The secretary of the Antiquarian Society thanked them for the interest the Langthornes had displayed in the researches of the Society and made his departure. The Langthornes reciprocated by giving his members permission to examine the chamber any time they wished.

Chapter 18

Monday, Tuesday, Wednesday and Thursday were busy days in the shop and post office. The evenings were spent going for walks with Tess and Isobel was delighted when her mother expressed a desire to accompany them. Mrs. Langthorne had seen nothing of the village and its surrounding countryside. Her daughter pointed out the cottages she had visited and told her mother all about the interesting people who lived in them. They admired the pretty gardens and resolved to plant a climbing rose at the front of the shop and post office.

One evening, after their walk – now a part of their daily routine – a phone call was received from Akbar seeking permission to call on them to make his report. Isobel was overjoyed to hear the faithful Akbar's voice and informed him she would make all arrangements for his journey and instructed him to await a call from her. After enquiring about his health and the pony, she rang off and told her mother, with considerable excitement, of Akbar's pending visit and invited her assistance in making arrangements to ensure a safe and comfortable journey for their eagerly awaited friend.

Isobel decided that she would call Richard for advice and help. Richard thought for a brief moment and said, "Let me ring you back; I have an idea."

An hour later, Richard called back and said, "This is clearly a case where 'the mountain must go to Mahomet,' so I have conferred with Lance and he has made this suggestion: we will ring up and make a reservation at the Haymarket Theatre for four to see Agatha Christie's play. We will see Akbar the following morning, hear his report, and, if permitted by the authorities, inspect your pony. We will then all go for lunch at a restaurant. Afterwards, we will all spend the night at the Howard's town house. If you wish to bring Akbar back with you, there will be plenty of room in the car. Isobel old girl, talk it over with your mother and ring me back."

Isobel thought it was a most exciting idea and immediately sought her mother's acquiescence. Mrs. Langthorne had made a decision, some time previously, that the day of mourning must be terminated as she was positive that the late colonel would not wish them to be unhappy. She therefore instructed her daughter to thank Richard and his step-brother Lance for their generous and excellent solution to the problem. Isobel rang Richard, conveyed their appreciation and told him how excited she felt at the prospect of a visit to London.

"Right then, old girl, we will pick you up at nine-thirty next Saturday morning." Isobel simply could not contain her eagerness for time to fly until that wonderful adventure materialised. Now the tempo of life for the Langthornes began to speed up.

A call was received from the architect saying that all was now ready for their inspection at the coffee shop. An early visit would be much appreciated. They decided to leave Jane and Mary in charge and make a flying visit to see the new installations and arrange for a confectioner to supply them daily with fresh brown and white bread and an extensive selection of cream cakes and pastries. All sorts of ingredients would be required; ham, lettuce, eggs, cress, cheese, tomatoes, cucumbers, etc., and arrangements would be necessary for a supplier.

In due course, they arrived at the architect's chambers and met the partner who had promised to be their first customer. The old, bishop-like gentleman took a bundle of keys from a wall cupboard and conducted them to the coffee shop a few paces down the High. They ascended the stairs and the architect opened the door; Isobel gasped at the transformation which had been wrought by the craftsmen. "Like it?" the old gentleman enquired.

"I am enchanted by it; it far exceeds anything I anticipated!" cried Isobel.

The architect had been born, reared and educated in Oxford and could advise them about their needs for bread and cakes, etc., by recommending an old established confectioner. The other requirements would present no problems. If the architect kept his promise to patronise their coffee shop, he would never be asked to pay. A ploy that would pay off handsomely in the future as he knew most of the people they would look to for patronage.

After thanking him warmly for all his very valuable help, they departed to call on the dressmaker, Miss Stokes, to check the progress of her work. Two dresses were almost completed and the third would not be ready for another ten days. The ladies returned to Tillingthorpe, delighted by all that they had seen.

When Isobel described the coffee shop to Jane, the young girl expressed her eagerness to start her new job at the earliest possible moment. It must be revealed that Jane's eagerness was tinged with expectations of all those handsome young undergraduates she would meet in her new job as manageress of the finest coffee shop in Oxford.

That evening, as Isobel and her mother took Tess for a walk, Isobel turned to her mother saying,

"Do you know, when the architect opened the door, I could imagine, so vividly, all the gentlemen in their beautiful early eighteenth century costumes, sipping their coffee or chocolate and ogling the serving girls; especially if one gentleman was Samuel Pepys!"

All these romantic reflections were interrupted by Mrs. Wilson calling to them to come and meet Bert Wilson, her husband, the wheelwright. They crossed over and after admiring her front garden were ushered into the cottage. Bert, sitting in his wooden armchair, was perusing the 'For Sale' columns in *The Berkshire Chronicle*. Bert rose to his feet and surveyed these two ladies of whom he had heard so much, and who had been the subject of so much heated discussion in The Red Lion. He thought what pleasant, unassuming folk they were and pondered all the lurid rumours circulating about them for so long. In future, any loose-tongued gossip would certainly be made aware of his disapproval of such far-fetched and exaggerated stories.

There, true to Isobel's previous observations, were the two photographs. One of Violet Wilson as a fine young woman, and the other of her husband, Bert, in a scarlet tunic.

"May I enquire, Mr. Wilson, the name of your regiment?" asked Mrs. Langthorne, "Only we are army people."

"I served in the Royal Berkshire, ma'am," he replied, "along with Joshua. In fact, I was with him when he got wounded at Passchendaele."

"It must have been quite horrific." Mrs. Langthorne exclaimed.

"Yes; we try to forget it, but that is not easy," replied Bert.

Bert changed the subject of conversation by enquiring about the hidden cache of jewels and told them that his great-grandfather grew up with Robert Noakes and knew him well. The Langthornes were intrigued by this revelation of yet another link with the gallant and incredibly brave rogue.

The more Isobel learned, the more real he became and that night, for the second time, she dreamed about him once more. She heard that gentle tap, tap of his whip on her window. Had he not promised 'I'll come to thee by moonlight. Look for me by moonlight'? Isobel sat up in her bed, only half-awake, to hear her mother tapping on her door, calling, "Isobel, are you alright, it's time to get up." At breakfast that morning, Mrs. Langthorne looked at her daughter curiously and asked, "Were you having a bad dream when I came to call you? You were crying out in your sleep."

Isobel blushed and said, "I really cannot remember."

The next few days passed without incident and the big adventure of the trip to London would become reality on the next day, Saturday. At nine thirty, as arranged, the Howard's large Daimler limousine drew up outside the post office with one of the footmen acting as chauffeur. It was a very large vehicle, specially built by Hoopers of London, the world famous coach builders, who also coach built the royal limousines. You will never see an advertisement issued by this company. They trade by reputation only. They do not need to advertise. The car was luxurious in the extreme, being upholstered in cream suede leather. It would seat five adults in comfort, plus driver and footman.

Richard entered the house and reminded the ladies that they would need a small case for an overnight stay. Even Mrs. Langthorne, normally very controlled and dignified, succumbed to the air of excitement.

The journey passed off smoothly, with one stop for lunch. They arrived at the house overlooking the Thames at Twickenham, and quickly refreshing themselves, proceeded to the National Gallery in Trafalgar Square. From there to the Victoria and Albert Museum by taxi to make the trip more fulfilling for Isobel. Then it was back to the house at Twickenham for dinner.

After being refreshed, they all set off for the Haymarket Theatre where Lance had reserved a private box. Richard adroitly arranged for Lance and Isobel to sit together, while he sat with Mrs. Langthorne and engaged her in conversation leaving Lance and Isobel to get to know each other. Isobel was ecstatically happy; she had seen many wonderful treasures this day and was now sitting in close proximity to her very own personal giant in the romantic and intimate darkness of this historic theatre. Occasionally she looked up into those wide-set, deep grey eyes and just for a fleeting moment they both saw what they wanted to see: the dawning of love.

On the Sunday morning, they all drove to the quarantine stables to meet Akbar. He was wearing the undress uniform of his regiment. He saluted Richard, unaware that he had resigned his commission. Mrs. Langthorne and her daughter greeted him warmly and wished to know if he was in comfortable quarters and whether he was being well looked after. Akbar reassured them on all counts and was patently delighted to see them. Memories, both painful and nostalgic, were aroused by the sight of this man who had served them so loyally. Even Richard was similarly affected and felt a sharp pang of regret that he was no longer a member of the famous Bengal Lancers.

Akbar conducted them to the loose box where Bahadra was stabled. The mare recognised Isobel at once and rubbed her velvet muzzle against her to identify her scent. While this affectionate reunion was taking place, Richard examined the pony's legs and found them to be perfectly healthy. Mrs. Langthorne wanted Akbar to return with them, but he pointed out that the quarantine period had another two weeks to run and he could not leave Bahadra unguarded.

Lance, who had been watching closely this reunion of old friends, turned to Isobel and said,

"Where will you keep your Arab horse when you get her back to Tillingthorpe?"

Isobel's brow creased into a worried frown and said, "Do you know Lance, until you mentioned it, that had not entered my head and it is so important."

"Well," Lance continued, "What better place than the stables at the Court?"

Isobel looked at her mother who exclaimed, "How generous of you, Lance, you are truly a 'friend in need'!"

"That's settled then," and turning to Akbar, he informed him that when he gave the word they would send a horse box to transport him and the mare to the stables at Cornwall Court. Shaking hands with Akbar, Lance surreptitiously passed a ten pound note into the Bengali's hand. As they made their goodbyes, Isobel hugged Akbar and thanked him for looking after Bahadra assuring him he could stay with them at Tillingthorpe as long as he wished. Watched by Akbar, they departed for their long journey home.

On arrival at Tillingthorpe, they all entered the cottage to enable Mrs. Langthorne and Isobel to thank them for their organisation of such an entertaining weekend which would linger in their minds for many a year. Mother and daughter retired to bed, exhausted by this unanticipated adventure.

Chapter 19

It was now the month of July and all the hard work of the past eighteen months had given them a nice home and financial security. They were indeed riding on the crest of a wave of successful business ventures. Mrs. Langthorne often recalled that day in India when Isobel returned from her ride, with what appeared to be an outrageous and risky idea, to give them a home and income. Thank God she had agreed to let Isobel have complete freedom to pursue what she considered to be a mad-cap proposal.

Her daughter was not preoccupied with such mundane cogitations for Isobel was in love, and as all women would know, Lance was in love with her. She sensed it in the box at the theatre when their eyes met and held in the spell of the unspoken word.

On Wednesday, Miss Stokes rang to say the third costume was ready and awaited collection at their convenience. Isobel immediately rang the confectioners to order the cakes, and various grocers and greengrocers to deliver their goods at eight a.m. on Monday.

They would go to Oxford and deliver the costumes to their new assistants. Isobel would take Sarah over on Monday morning to supervise the frantic preparation of sandwiches and the brewing of coffee. The next three days would be fraught with tension, as they all awaited the critical 'do or die' phase of this ambitious venture.

On Sunday night, Mrs. Langthorne and her daughter slept fitfully, as apprehension flitted in and out of their minds like some tantalising will-o'-the-wisp. They were both glad to rise at six-thirty and prayed that all would go well.

Isobel picked up Jane at seven. Jane was quite untroubled by the fears that bedevilled the Langthornes. In response to Isobel's query, "How do you feel, Jane?" she replied, "Fine. Looking forward to it." After dropping Jane at the coffee shop, Isobel returned to her own duties at the post office assisted by her new girl.

The morning came and went and at three o'clock, Isobel could contain her acute anxiety no longer and rang Jane. After a long lapse of time, which to Isobel seemed an eternity, Jane answered and on learning that the call was from Isobel said,

"I can't stop, Isobel, we are packed out. Tell you later." and rang off. Isobel rushed up to Mary and to the astonishment of the several customers, hugged her fiercely, then hurried into the sitting room to her mother to tell her the exciting news.

That evening, Isobel closed the post office sharply at five o'clock and dashed over to Jane at the coffee shop. They had just closed. The three girls were exceedingly tired but all very happy and told Isobel they had six pounds to share in tips on the very first day. As they were going home, Jane told Isobel in most determined tones that they must have more help and proposed at least one of the other four girls be employed straight away even before her costume was ready. Isobel readily agreed and expressed her relief that trade on the first day had exceeded all expectations. She also informed Jane of the considerable financial investment that they had made and their consequent anxiety.

It was mutually agreed between Isobel and her mother that Jane should be given complete control without any interference.

That evening, Mrs. Langthorne expressed her astonishment that her original fears that their lives in a village would be terribly boring had proved so inaccurate. Indeed, their lives had become so full of exciting activity, with so much social life, that it was sometimes difficult to establish priorities and at the same time not offend their many kind and generous friends.

The attention of the few inquisitive villagers was now focused on the comings and goings at Kate Farrel's cottage and furthermore, a very pretty ring had been observed on Kate's engagement finger and the green Alvis Car was now parked right outside Cock-a-Dobbie cottage.

The time had now arrived when the expert advice and support of Mr. Pringle regarding certain proposed changes in the staffing of

Tillingthorpe Post Office would be required. Anticipating a hardening of Mr. Archibald Pringle's attitude to any change of staff in that nationwide service of His Majesty's Royal Mail, it was decided that the issue was so important that all influence available must be marshalled, to counter any resistance to the replacement of Isobel as the incumbent postmistress, even though such tactics were abhorrent to well-bred ladies. But desperate circumstances call for desperate measures.

On Tuesday morning – Monday is always a bad time to request favours – Isobel rang Mr. Pringle to ask if it would be convenient for him to make another visit to Tillingthorpe in the next few days, as they were in urgent need of advice, which only someone with his personal expertise and knowledge of 'the service' could proffer. Had Mr. Pringle been a bird, he would have preened himself with utter satisfaction at this request from someone whom he regarded as his star pupil, a pupil who would (with his help) go far in the service.

"May I enquire the nature of your problem, Miss Langthorne?" he said. His suspicions were also aroused by this unexpected appeal for help.

"It is a matter which also involves my mother and I would therefore prefer not to discuss it over the phone."

"I will come on Wednesday afternoon, will that suit you?"

"Admirably," replied Isobel, "That is always our quietest period."

Mr. Pringle replaced the phone with a thoughtful gleam in his eyes. He sensed that this would be an occasion where all his diplomatic cunning would be called upon to preserve his authority and dignity. Reminding himself of his seniority in 'the service' and the fact that he was the son-in-law of the postmaster of Oxford restored his uncharacteristic flutter of an emotion akin to panic, to his normal unctuous self.

On the Wednesday, as arranged, Mr. Pringle presented himself at the post office and was welcomed by Isobel, who immediately ushered him into the sitting room where her mother awaited his arrival. Mr. Pringle never drank coffee, always tea; he had once read that coffee grains solidified into stones in the kidneys and were the direct cause of 'Bright's disease'. Another thing; if he contracted some terrible disease it might mean the closure of Cowley Post Office. He shuddered at the thought of such a disastrous eventuality.

He beamed at Mrs. Langthorne who enquired if he was in good health and hoped that his dear wife was now showing signs of recovery from the shock of losing her little dog, Toto. She plied him with cream cakes and tea, saying, "Please do not feel you have to rush back, Mr. Pringle, as Isobel will take you back in the car. We are in urgent need of your advice. Advice which we believe only someone of your status and experience in 'the service' can provide."

Mr. Pringle felt a warm glow of satisfaction at this recognition of his expertise in the labyrinthine rules and regulations of 'the service'. "Anything, my dear lady. I am at your service."

"My daughter has, with your considerable help, held the position of sub-postmistress of Tillingthorpe and now wishes to make certain changes which necessitates your approval." Mr. Pringle was extremely gratified that Mrs. Langthorne had used the prefix sub. Such acknowledgements were highly commendable, unlike some sub-postmasters he knew, who got ideas above their station and regularly referred to themselves as postmasters. That was until he reminded them that these assumptions were a serious breach of regulations.

"Now, dear lady, how may Pringle be of service to you, and be assured that no problem in 'the service' is insoluble to a civil servant with my experience. Did I ever tell you it is now forty years since I started at Cowley as a telegram boy?" Mrs. Langthorne assured him that he had never imparted these details of his loyal service in the Post Office. However, she then related the problem that troubled them to him.

Her daughter would like to enjoy more leisure time and to achieve this would desire to engage another officially trained person of more mature years. This could only be possible with his help and official approval. He would readily understand that as they were merely tenants it was necessary to obtain the sanction of such changes from her nephew. Now it was Mr. Pringle's turn to be perplexed. "Nephew, nephew?" he repeated, "But I thought Viscount Beldrake owned the property." Nephew, nephew, had he or had he not heard the word nephew?

"Yes," Mrs. Langthorne replied, "He is Isobel's cousin - did you not know?"

The blood rushed to Mr. Pringle's head; he was a drowning man and there were no straws to clutch at. He was brought back to reality by the sound of Mrs. Langthorne's voice saying,
"Are you all right, Mr. Pringle?" She was bending over him staring anxiously at his face which had been almost purple and was now grey. She hastily placed a large brandy in his hand which he swallowed in one life saving gulp, much as a gourmet swallows an oyster.

"So, all this time I have - unwittingly - been dealing with members of the aristocracy!" gurgled Mr. Pringle.

"Oh, no! Isobel and I do not see ourselves as such. We are simply two ordinary people who have been exceedingly grateful for all the practical assistance and advice you have given in such generous measure. You must regard us as your friends." All these words appeared to emanate and echo from a long dark tunnel. The brandy had now entered the blood-stream and dispelled the unbridled overpowering sense of utter helplessness.

Mr. Pringle had now regained his normal pallor together with a modicum of self control and addressed Mrs. Langthorne as ma'am. "Quite frankly I do not foresee any obstacles to your request, but I think it would help me if your daughter put it in writing which I will stamp urgent. Leave it with me and I will fill in the appropriate forms as soon as I get back to Cowley."

Mrs. Langthorne called her daughter to take Mr. Pringle home. During the journey, Mr. Pringle began to realise that, in spite of the shock to his nervous system so recently inflicted, all was not lost, as of today he too had friends in high places. This thought being digested led to a more mellow frame of mind and he began to tell Isobel that as his petition to the highest authority in 'the service' for suitable forms for notification of Bubonic Plague (Black Death) to be supplied to all offices, had not received the endorsement it warranted, he had written to the Ministry of Health who had replied in more favourable terms and thanked him for drawing their attention to this grave oversight. Isobel expressed her whole-hearted support for Mr. Pringle's persistent efforts to secure these vital forms.

When they arrived at the seat of Mr. Pringle's power, he paused before leaving the car, turned to Isobel saying, "When you have found a suitable replacement to your good self, let me know and I will make all the necessary arrangements." Isobel reciprocated by conveying the wishes of her mother and herself that Mr. Pringle would not neglect to come and see them whenever his numerous and onerous responsibilities permitted. Mr. Pringle patted Isobel's hand and said, "My dear lady, I shall be honoured to accept your kind invitation and rest assured that if ever Pringle can be of service, well, the phone is at your elbow."

Isobel returned to Tillingthorpe relieved and pleased that she would now have more free time to expand her new business interests and, what was equally important, spend more time with her mother.

During their evening walks with Tess, they had become acquainted with many more of the inhabitants of Tillingthorpe and indeed had been invited into their homes. Mrs. Langthorne and her daughter were discussing the urgent requirement for a new assistant in the post office when Mrs. Langthorne recalled a spinster lady whom they had met on one of their first walks round the village with Tess.

Emily Haynes, for that was her name, had told them that she had worked as a clerk in an auctioneer's office in Witney. Emily had been engaged to Fred Flowers, a footman at the Big House before he had enlisted in the army and had been posted to the Enniskillen Fusiliers. Sadly, this regiment formed part of the 29th. Division which was so horrendously decimated at the Battle of Mons and Fred died in an heroic advance on the German trenches. Fred was one of the men a German General described as 'lions led by donkeys'. Emily had never found another sweetheart. She lived with her grandfather near the forge and they often heard the ring of sledge on anvil.

When her mother suggested this lady, Isobel remarked, "What a splendid idea, shall we invite her round for tea to ask her if she will consider the post." That evening, they called on Emily to invite her to take tea with them on Sunday. Needless to say, Emily was flabbergasted to hear the proposition and invited them to come in.

Emily's grandfather was a fine looking man, as upright as a pine tree, he was born in 1870 at the time of the Franco-Prussian War. Having been born in the village he was related to many of the families and could tell much about life when he was a young man. He described how he and others were paid one farthing a sheaf to sickle corn from six a.m. to six p.m. "Had he ever heard of the highwayman, Robert Noakes?"

"Yes," he replied, "My mother often spoke of him."

After a glass of homemade cowslip wine, the Langthornes continued their walk, much to the relief of Tess who always wanted to be up and doing, for was she not a working dog? Tess was now six months old, but still very leggy and had not shed her puppy coat, however, she was already showing signs of her illustrious sheep-dog ancestry, necessitating a firm grip on the lead when crossing a field containing sheep. Tess instinctively knew that she ought to be guarding, driving or herding them.

When they were sitting in their cottage, after the evening walk, Mrs. Langthorne exclaimed, "You know, Isobel, our lives have proceeded so smoothly and we have enjoyed so much good fortune that sometimes I am reminded of a previous experience when our happiness and security were so tragically and cruelly terminated."

Isobel retorted, "I have no such worries, mother, because I believe daddy is watching over us."

"You could well be right," her mother responded, "I do most fervently hope that you are."

On the Sunday, Emily Haynes called and was warmly welcomed. After tea, Emily expressed a desire to see the secret room, so Isobel picked up a torch and took her into the underground chamber. Emily, like everyone else, marvelled at the ingenious escape hatch. "I wonder what he was really like?" Emily mused aloud.

"From all I have read and been told, a loveable rogue!" Isobel opined.

The two returned to Mrs. Langthorne who was listening to Albert Sandler in the Palm Court Hotel orchestra. "Well, what did you think of our secret room?" she enquired of Emily.

"Strange, very strange; I could almost feel the highwayman's presence."

"Several other people have expressed the same sensation." Mrs. Langthorne rejoined.

After a certain amount of general gossip Isobel's mother asked Emily if she would consider their proposal that she should take over the post office from Isobel. Emily requested time to think it over and to confer with her grandfather and then, as an afterthought, said,
"What wages would you pay?"

Mrs. Langthorne replied, "What is your present salary?"
"Four pounds a week," Emily disclosed.
"We will pay you six pounds a week, to be reviewed each year."
"That would really make me three pounds a week better off as it costs me one pound a week in bus fares."

"Well, take a week to think it over, and remember, if you should reject the offer we will not be offended in the least. Think only of what is best for you." Emily returned home and promised to let them know within ten days.

Chapter 20

In the middle of the week, a call from Akbar informed Isobel that her pony had been released from quarantine and he would now await the horse box as planned. Isobel promised to call him back. She then rang Lance and passed on Akbar's message. "What about this weekend?" he suggested.

"Perfect," Isobel replied.

"Are you engaged at this time?"

"No."

"Well, why don't you and your mother come over for a couple of days; it will give you an opportunity to ride your pony."

"If you are sure that your parents will not object; we do not wish to impose on you or your family."

"That's settled then. I will pick you up at two. All right?"

"You are very kind to us Lance. I must confess I am longing to ride Bahadra. Thank you so much."

On Saturday morning, the horse box was despatched to pick up the pony and Akbar. Isobel suddenly realised she would not be able to pick up Jane at the coffee shop and hastily phoned Jane and instructed her to take a taxi and pay from the petty cash.

Mrs. Langthorne told Isobel that there was a problem which had to be dealt with urgently: accommodation for Akbar at Cornwall Court and his meals, as he would not eat English food. The advice and help of Richard would have to be enlisted. A phone call was made at once. When this dilemma was explained to Richard, he said,

"Don't worry, the problem is not as great as you imagine. Leave it to me."

Isobel eagerly awaited the hour when she would be reunited with Bahadra and the prospect of riding - perhaps with Lance - round the beautiful park land surrounding the Court.

Mrs. Langthorne was well aware of Isobel's feelings for Lance and was convinced her late husband, the colonel, would have fully approved of a match between his beloved daughter and this highly eligible young man of such magnificent physique.

At a quarter to the hour Lance arrived at the post office and was met by Mrs. Langthorne who conducted him into the sitting room. She regarded this young giant, as her daughter called him, with a twinkle in her eyes.
"Our small cottage does not accommodate you very well!"

Lance grinned and said, "I am quite happy here, it has a mellow and friendly atmosphere." With a mischievous gleam in his eyes he added, "You and Isobel could, if you so desired, move into the Court. There is plenty of room: half of the house is never used."

"I will not take that remark seriously," retorted Mrs. Langthorne, "For we are quite happy here, you know, and Isobel has so many friends in the village, in fact, everyone loves her."

Isobel appeared wearing a white cotton shirt blouse, a red skirt and a green silk scarf round her neck worn in the fashion of a cowboy. Lance looked appreciatively at the young woman, standing in the doorway holding a small case and said, "I hope you have remembered to pack your riding clothes."

Isobel put her hand to her mouth and blurted out, "I quite forgot!" Dashing back upstairs to remedy this oversight she called, "I won't be long." She soon reappeared carrying a larger case which Lance took from her and placed it in the car.

"Aren't you taking your little dog?" he queried.

"No," replied Isobel, "Mary is looking after her."

The twenty mile journey to Cornwall Court soon passed. Lance drove straight to the stables where Richard and Akbar were awaiting their arrival. While Akbar led Lance and Isobel into the stable, Richard took Mrs. Langthorne on one side and explained the arrangements for Akbar. He would be accommodated in a tiny flat over the coach house. The cook would make special meals for him which the kitchen maid would deliver to the flat. Then they joined Isobel and Lance in the stable.

"What do you think of the mare?" enquired Mrs. Langthorne of Lance.

"She is of the finest quality and beautiful with it, and absolutely fit, thanks to Akbar," he commented. Isobel was enquiring of Akbar if he was fully comfortable with the arrangements made for him; he confirmed he was very happy and the cook made him an excellent lunch when he arrived at noon.

They all returned to the car and Lance drove them to the house where they retired to the drawing room for tea where Mrs. Howard awaited them. The talk was mainly of Richard's forthcoming wedding, two weeks hence. After tea, Mrs. Langthorne and her daughter rested in their room before preparing to dress for dinner.

Isobel selected a dark navy blue dress of a heavy artificial silk material (Celanese), much in vogue in the early thirties. Six inches above the hemline a two inch band of lime green, surmounted by a band of scarlet encircled the dress. This decoration was repeated on the Peter Pan collar; the waist was gathered by a narrow black belt. The dress extended four inches below her knee. Isobel's hair was restrained only at the side of the face by two half-inch scarlet ribbons to expose the emerald dropper earrings to match the large emerald pendant from the highwayman's hoard. Her mother wore a simple pale blue gown with a sapphire pendant.

At dinner, Richard had given instructions that his adoptive brother, Lance, and Isobel would be placed next to each other,

The two girls had gone to Spain for a month and Mr. Howard was away in Norfolk for important consultations with his farm accountant and would not return till the following Tuesday.

Lance was of quiet disposition, but never dull and was always happy to listen to his brother's witty and lively conversation at table; it also permitted him to enjoy Isobel's presence at his side to the full. Isobel was a very feminine person, with an instinct to choose clothes of style and colour which never failed to accentuate her natural and stunning beauty.

After dinner, Richard excused himself to make a long phone call to his fiancée. Lance and Isobel adjourned to the music room where she played Chopin and Mozart to him. Lance sat in an armchair facing Isobel, savouring to the full the romantic atmosphere of the magnificent music room enhanced by this glorious creature whom he was confident would, one day, play that same instrument in that same chamber, as his wife.

While the young ones were thus preoccupied, Mrs. Langthorne and Mrs. Howard were seated in the huge book-lined library where Mrs. Langthorne told her hostess of their life in India and of its tragic and mysterious termination. Mrs. Howard expressed her heartfelt sympathy and guided the conversation on to a less mournful topic. She then astonished Isobel's mother by saying, "I think my son, Lance, is in love with your daughter, Isobel."

Mrs. Langthorne was thrown off-balance by this sudden and unexpected pronouncement and was not a little embarrassed by this forthright statement of fact. "I believe my daughter is also in love with your son." After a momentary pause added, "Does this assumption worry you?"

"Not at all, my husband and I would be so happy for them; in fact, he has already told your daughter that he will insist on her wearing the family coronet when she becomes a bride."

"Would you object if we kept this conversation secret?" asked Mrs. Langthorne. "Just between ourselves, for Isobel has not revealed her feelings to me, although I believe our mutual speculations may have some substance." Mrs. Langthorne felt a strong sense of relief and gratitude that Lance's mother had brought the matter into the open and given her approval.

They both joined Lance and Isobel in the music room where Isobel was playing Chopin's *Moonlight Sonata* to her spellbound audience of one.

After partaking of a cup of Ovaltine prior to retiring to bed, Isobel announced that she and Lance would rise early to go riding in the park.

At seven in the morning, Isobel made her way to a side entrance in the west wing where Lance was waiting. Together they walked to the stables to find Akbar. He was walking Isobel's mare and a bay gelding for Lance.

The young couple made a pleasing sight as they rode off side by side. Lance showed her the spectacular displays of rhododendrons and azaleas. At the lake, they dismounted to watch the graceful swans gliding on the mirrored water with their tiny brood of cygnets on their backs. The noisy flock of wild duck taxied and splashed towards them clamouring for bread. Isobel looked up at Lance saying, "Isn't it all just perfect: like the Garden of Eden. I could so easily imagine we were the only two people left on earth."

Lance smiled, his dark grey eyes gazing into his companion's dark brown velvety eyes and said, "On reflection, I do not think that would be the perfect world you imagine. For example, if you and I were the only two humans left, you would not have your mother, I would not have my family and the insatiable longing to see these near and dear ones would be painfully intolerable! No," he continued, "I believe that true happiness may only be enjoyed via the process of making other people happy."

Isobel was quite impressed with this glimpse into her companion's inner self. Laying her hand on Lance's sleeve, she exclaimed, "What a profound philosopher you are, Lance! I will always remember this moment."

They remounted and set off for another of Lance's favourite haunts; a woodland ride through a long avenue of wild cherry trees. The mossy carpet underfoot rendered their progress so silent that many wild creatures were thus unaware of their presence. Suddenly, Lance laid a restraining hand on Bahadra's bridle and whispered, "Look; a fox." Isobel looked in the direction indicated to see a vixen and three cubs at the entrance to an earth. The two riders remained silent and immobile watching the vigorous antics of the cubs under the alert supervision of their mother. After a few minutes, the vixen caught the scent of the intruders and bustled her boisterous offspring into the safe concealment of her lair.

"Wasn't that a pretty sight?" Isobel cried.

"Yes," Lance responded, "When I was a boy I would come here and lure foxes to within a few feet of me."

"How?" Isobel queried.

"With a wooden gadget like a whistle," Lance replied. "By the way, you should see these woods in bluebell time; they are an unbroken mass of colour, as far as the eye can see."

"Well, that will be something I shall look forward to very much, providing, of course, you invite me."

"Isobel, you are welcome to come to Cornwall Court as frequently as you wish. My parents love to see you here!"

Then, in a fit of uncharacteristic boldness Isobel said, "But would you want me to come, Lance?"

"Certainly, but I suspect you may know the answer to your own question," he said with eyes atwinkle.

They rode back to the stables to find Akbar sitting on a mounting stone waiting to receive the horses back into his care. Lance paused to question the Indian as to his welfare. "Are you quite comfortable? Is the food to your liking? Remember, Akbar, you are quite free to go anywhere in the house or park that you feel inclined. Why not take my horse and explore the park?"

"Thank you, Sahib, I would like that very much."

Lance then escorted Isobel back to the house for a hearty breakfast. He was, as we have said, a big man, all of twelve and a half stone and needed a lot of sustenance.

After breakfast, Lance initiated Isobel into the game of croquet, which served to wile away the time before lunch. Following lunch, Lance and Isobel sat in the library. Lance selected a beautiful volume depicting uniforms of the Indian army in full colour. They sat closely at a table staring down at the illustrations. Lance was extremely aware of this rare opportunity to enjoy a modicum of intimacy with the one woman whom he adored. He could smell her perfume of Bean Flower and knew that this fragrance would linger in his sense of nostalgia to the day he died. Prompted by the pictures which aroused such poignant and happy memories, Isobel told Lance about her life in India as the daughter of a colonel in the Bengal Lancers and the tragic event which destroyed their lives. Lance took her small white hand saying, "My family love you and – if you will permit them – they will try to dispel the hideous memories of that awful night."

Then, returning the book to the shelf, he fetched a heavy Victorian photograph album with a strong brass clasp from another table. When he turned the thick leaves to reveal the old photographs of members of his family, Isobel was fascinated by the clothes worn by the ladies with their high-necked blouses and cameo brooches. As the pages displayed more recent members of the Howard family, Isobel's interest livened. Lance found a picture of Richard at the age of twelve mounted on his pony. Further on, the two boys at prep school. Isobel paused to give this photograph her undivided scrutiny and Lance felt this was an opportune moment to explain his relationship to Richard; telling her that although they were not brothers of the same blood, they were nevertheless exceedingly close and their lives had been closely intertwined from the age of three.

The turning of the pages then depicted one of Lance at Eton at the age of sixteen. Isobel looked long and hard at this portrayal of the young man, now seated beside her, and turning to him said, "I would have recognised you without hesitation, you have changed so little."

"Oh, thank you, Isobel, for warming the cockles of the heart of an old man of twenty-four summers." The next photograph to intrigue Isobel was one of Lance with his grandmother, Eliza Coleman. It was the occasion of her seventy-sixth birthday. "She was a lovely old lady, she always smelled of fresh picked lavender. I was the main beneficiary under the terms of her will. That is why I bear her name and the reason that my surname is different to other members of my family."

"How interesting," Isobel asserted, "I must confess, I have always been curious about this anomaly."

"Yes, when she died, I was very upset, for she was such a happy, lively person. However, life must go on," Lance averred, "but I will never forget her; in fact that would not be possible now that her name is irrevocably joined to mine," he concluded.

The afternoon had passed even more pleasantly than the morning and both these young people felt that from today, their relationship would become even closer.

At dinner, it was proposed by Mrs. Howard that the Langthornes should stay over the Sunday night and allow Lance to run them back to Tillingthorpe early on Monday morning.

After dinner, Mrs. Howard, Lance, Mrs. Langthorne and Isobel played Gin Rummy in the drawing room. When an hour of this diversion had passed, Lance played records of light opera and Gilbert and Sullivan on a splendid Marconi radiogram. Lance listened to his favourite selections with a thoughtful look on his face and intermittently made interjections into the conversation which permitted a glance at Isobel, in an effort to make conjectures as to what her thoughts were about the day's events. He hoped it would not be too long before she made another visit. Maybe for a whole week.

Early on Monday morning, they set off on the journey home after Mrs. Langthorne had made arrangements with Lance for Akbar to stay another week. It would then be necessary to confer with Richard about Akbar's return to India and the regiment of which he was still a serving trooper. He was only here by permission of Major, now Colonel, Mackenzie, who had been more than generous in allowing Akbar to stay so long and any further delay would cause the new colonel considerable embarrassment. It was a serious problem which should have been dealt with earlier and Mrs. Langthorne was beginning to feel guilty that she had not acted before. Richard's knowledge of army regulations must be enlisted as the more Mrs. Langthorne thought about Akbar, the more worried she became.

On the Monday evening, she rang Richard, apologising profusely for imposing yet again on his kindness, and conveyed her dilemma to him. There was a long silence eliciting her anxious, "Are you there, Richard?"

"Sorry," he responded, "I was lost in thought. Off the cuff, this is what I think may be a tentative answer but it will need Lance's full co-operation. We could – if Akbar agrees – refund his pay to the army (about twenty-five pounds) and then buy him out of the regiment providing Lance will employ him as a groom, but even then there will be a lot of loose ends to tie up: work permit, etc. Mrs. Langthorne, I will call you back after I have conferred with Lance; for it is, as you so rightly assume, a very urgent matter."

Mrs. Langthorne reiterated her grateful thanks, "How would Isobel and I have coped without all the vital assistance you have so unstintingly extended to us."

"Don't worry," Richard retorted, "I like to help and another thing the colonel would have wanted me to take care of you both. Once a Bengal Lancer, always a Bengal Lancer! Just leave it with me." Mrs.

Langthorne thanked God for a friend of Richard's calibre and felt much relieved.

That evening, she briefed her daughter concerning her phone conversation with Richard. Isobel agreed that they must be guided and advised by Richard at all times.

During their evening walk, they called on Emily Haynes to enquire if she had made a decision to take the appointment they offered. They were pleased to be told that she had given her notice to leave and would be ready to start one week from that Monday. Once again, fate had smiled on them making Isobel's young life more congenial.

Chapter 21

On Tuesday, Richard called on them to enlighten them concerning the plan to resolve the problems referred to by Mrs. Langthorne. Akbar had been approached and thoroughly briefed. It appeared that he was a widower, with one son who had a good position on the Indian railway. He would, he said, be honoured to serve the two sahibs. He would be paid three pounds a week plus his food and clothing. He was warned that the English climate was very different from that of India but he assured them that he was a very fit man and the climate would not be a hardship. "What about the regiment?" Richard asked. A sadness clouded Akbar's face; yes, he would miss the Lancers and the break would be painful, but he must think about his old age, also the generous wages and conditions offered. Sahibs were very different from the ten shillings a week paid to a Bengal Lancer.

"Another thing," said Akbar, "I will be on call to the Missy Memsahib." It was explained to Akbar that he must return to India to take his discharge from the army, but his return fare would be paid.

In the meantime, Richard would write to Colonel Mackenzie requesting permission to buy Akbar's release. All these procedures would take about six months to complete and must be instigated without further delay, which meant that Akbar would return as soon as a passage could be arranged. After talking about his forthcoming wedding now one week away, Isobel and her mother thanked Richard and kissed him goodbye.

During the next few days, the carrier, Albert Dodson, delivered a large crate containing the portrait of the late Colonel Langthorne. Its delivery had been delayed for three weeks, because the address had been defaced. Bribed with a plate of sandwiches and a mug of tea, Albert Dodson offered to open it for them. The ladies gratefully agreed, after insisting that he partake of the refreshments which they had provided.

When the painting was exposed in all its glory, Albert gasped, "Strewth! Who's that?"

"My late husband, Colonel Langthorne of the Bengal Lancers," Mrs. Langthorne responded.

Albert stared at the picture and added, "A big man, a fine man."

"We like to think so," Isobel and her mother murmured.

A place on the end wall of the sitting room had long been prepared to receive the colonel's portrait and Albert easily lifted the heavy picture in its ornate gilt frame on to the hooks. The trio stood back to admire this fine likeness of the colonel. "He looks good up there, don't he," Albert said, with some satisfaction, for had he not delivered it and hung it?

"Well, if you ladies don't mind, I'll be getting along, a lot of folk waiting. I've got a crate of pullets for old Mrs. Courtney and a roll of stair carpet for Alice Rogers."

Albert Dodson resumed his delivery rounds and ruminated on what his wife would think when he told her that the ladies who ran the Tillingthorpe Post Office were the wife and daughter of a colonel of the Bengal Lancers, and a fine looking man to boot.

It was now the second week in July and the days were hot and humid and the two ladies looked forward to their walk in the cool of the evening. During one such stroll, Isobel confided to her mother that she thought that she might be in love with Lance. Her mother concealed her surprise at this sudden bout of frankness and retorted, "I believe you are."

Now it was Isobel's turn to be surprised. "Do you think daddy would approve of Lance?"

"I am certain," replied her mother.

In one more week, Isobel would be free of the shackles of the post office and thus able to maintain more frequent visits to Oxford, where the thriving coffee shop takings were averaging £250 per week leaving a clear profit margin of £7,500 per annum.

The Langthornes were now financially secure and could lead a fuller, if more relaxed, mode of life. Jane was also a beneficiary in her new role as manageress of the business and had moved to Oxford into lodgings.

Chapter 22

As we predicted in an earlier chapter, Jane's employment in Tillingthorpe shop would be the precursor to other events instrumental in bringing romance and ultimately marriage into her life. Jane was being courted by a young undergraduate of Jesus College. He was studying Classics, prior to taking the law. Douglas Beadle was the son of the solicitor, Beadle, the senior partner of Beadle, Beadle and Sons, who were, incidentally, the solicitors of the Reverend Sebastian Erasmus Copplethwaite. Douglas was a regular at the coffee shop and, like all undergraduates, a high spirited young man who had been awarded a Blue as captain of the Varsity rugby team.

Already, the indefatigable Isobel was dreaming of a new business venture, but more of that anon.

A letter had arrived from Andrew Gilbert, the ex-curate, who was now at Sandhurst, and who was by all accounts relishing army life to the full. He hoped that Mrs. Langthorne and her daughter would come to the Passing Out Parade in a few months time. He would like them to know that, as Mrs. Langthorne had foreseen, he had made many good friends and received several invitations to visit their homes. Isobel's mother wisely decided that she, not her daughter, would respond to Andrew's letter.

On Monday, Emily Haynes reported for her new duties in the post office and as Mr. Pringle would not arrive until three, Isobel was able to give her a lot of advice. Emily was fully experienced in office routine and readily absorbed this brief period of instruction.

Although Isobel and her mother led such busy lives, they still met their old friends almost daily and considered it both prudent and enjoyable to sustain contact with their many customers, most of whom were known by name to Isobel. The shop and post office maintained their cheerful happy atmosphere where the old folk would confide their problems to Isobel. The smith's wife had now patched up her differences with Joshua's wife and peace reigned at their frequent meetings in the shop.

The building of the village hall was making rapid progress. It would cost £1,500. The erection of a War Memorial of Portland Stone had been entrusted to Eli Marriot, the village mason, who had quoted a figure of £850. The sale of the jewels had raised one hundred and twenty thousand pounds. After the following amounts had been paid:

£1,500	Village Hall
£850	War Memorial
£200	Apprentice
£200	Two Mates
£400	Martha Howkins
TOTAL	£3,150

this left a balance of £116,850

Viscount Beldrake requested the inhabitants of Tillingthorpe to appoint a committee, comprising twenty-one representatives, to decide how to spend this money in order to benefit every member of the village. They were summoned to the Big House to assemble in the ballroom, where the Viscount made a proposal which they could veto or modify on a vote. He made this suggestion. The £16,850 should be invested to provide coal and blankets at Christmas to the poor and elderly in perpetuity with the residue of £100,000 to be invested to provide scholarships or apprenticeships to any third generation resident of Tillingthorpe. "In short," said the Viscount, "It would be a trust fund from which every man, woman and child of the village could benefit!" He warned them that the whole scheme would have to be given full legal status and would necessitate expensive legal advice.

After a lengthy discussion, it was decided to take a postal vote from all the inhabitants. The form would simply state: 'Do you accept this Plan: YES or NO'. Should it be unanimously rejected, they would have to hold another meeting at the Big House to discuss an alternative. To everyone's surprise, only twenty people dissented and it was therefore agreed that the whole matter should be left to Viscount Beldrake and his legal advisers. All the regulars at The Red Lion gave the idea their full approval and were mutually agreed that only an educated man could have thought of it.

The last Saturday in July was Richard's wedding day and a whole first class carriage had been reserved on the ten-forty Oxford to London train. This was essential to accommodate all the Howard family and all the servants, including Akbar, who was resplendent in the undress uniform of the Bengal Lancers. The wedding was to be held in Westminster Abbey, followed by a reception in the Savoy Hotel. Lance would naturally be his brother's best man. Isobel and her mother would be fetched by the footman driving the Armstrong. The entire party would then be taken by coach to Oxford station to begin the train journey to London.

The cook had been instructed to sit next to Akbar to ensure that his sensitivities were not offended by food which was taboo to a Muslim.

The wedding was a grand affair in the setting of the historic abbey. After the traditional speeches, Lance, as best man, read out the numerous telegrams conveying the good wishes of the many friends of both bride and groom. Lance deliberately kept a cablegram from India until last. It stated, 'With good wishes for your future health and happiness, from all ranks of the Bengal Lancers.'

After a honeymoon in Barbados, they would return to a lovely old manor house standing in eight hundred and fifty acres, ten miles from Cheltenham and fifteen miles from Cornwall Court. It was a wedding present from Mr. and Mrs. Howard to their adopted son, Richard. Richard would also continue to receive two thousand pounds a year from a trust fund which Mr. Howard had set up on his fourteenth birthday.

After the wedding, preparations were made for everyone to return to Cornwall Court. Mrs. Langthorne and her daughter kissed the bride then hugged and kissed Richard, wishing them every happiness and a safe journey.

On arrival at Cornwall Court, Isobel and her mother said *au revoir* to the Howards while Lance instructed the coach driver to take the two ladies home to Tillingthorpe. Lance told Mrs. Langthorne that, sometime in the near future, he would be in the vicinity of

Tillingthorpe on business for his father and would like to call on them. "Anytime, Lance, you know you will always be welcome." Isobel and her mother re-entered the coach to be whisked back to the village. During the trip they animatedly discussed the day's events covering all facets of the ceremony from the bride's gown to her relations and friends.

After tea they drove down to Mary Griffin's home to fetch Tess and learn of any untoward happenings. Mrs. Griffin told them her daughter was out exercising Tess and would they come in and await her return. Mrs. Griffin told the Langthornes that her daughter was very happy to be home every night and away from her demanding, querulous, previous employer. Mrs. Langthorne assured Mrs. Griffin that they considered themselves very lucky to have the services of pretty, happy Mary.

They had not been waiting long when Mary appeared glowing and breathless from her boisterous romps with Tess. Mary said everything had gone without a hitch in their brief absence; she also asserted that she had kept Tess amused. Tess was now eight months old and beginning her first moult. She was also losing that leggy look that seems so prevalent in Collies in their transition from puppyhood to maturity. The ladies took their leave of the Griffins and drove back home with a parting, "See you on Monday."

One week after the wedding, Lance called at the post office to advise them that on the eve of the wedding, Richard had acquainted him of the arrangements for Akbar to return to his regiment. He would write to the colonel from their hotel to furnish him with all the relevant details. A passage had been booked for Akbar on a passenger ship sailing from Tilbury on the fifteenth of August. Akbar would report to the colonel and make a formal application to purchase his discharge from the army. Mother and daughter expressed their profound gratitude to Lance for relieving them of this onerous responsibility. Before taking his departure, Lance conveyed an invitation to them both from his sisters to spend the last week in August at the Court.

Mrs. Langthorne's intuitive sensitivities told her that this was a time when her presence would be superfluous. She thanked Lance for the invitation, telling him that it would not be possible for them both to be away from the post office for a whole week, but that it would do Isobel good to enjoy the companionship of his sisters who were girls of her own age. When Lance rose to go, he shook hands with Isobel's mother, lightly squeezing her hand twice in quick succession, signalling, 'You and I know you know.' Turning to Isobel, he said, "I will pick you up in three weeks time, at the usual time, two thirty, if that's all right with you."

Isobel walked with Lance to the car saying, "Tell Margaret and Christal I am looking forward to my holiday with them."

"What about me?" Lance quipped with a cheeky grin.

"I may spare you a few hours," retorted Isobel archly, "That is, on condition that you keep your promise to show me over the house."

"Well, that will take at least six hours so I will settle for that," he smiled and then took off.

Life in the post office pursued its normal course, coloured by the gossip mulled over by the daily incursions of the older female members of the village fraternity. Several visits to the coffee shop also helped to pass the time away for Isobel. During one of these visits, Jane informed Isobel that her boyfriend had told her that there was an urgent need for a café where undergraduates could obtain a satisfying meal at an economic price. Isobel promised to talk this over with Jane after her holiday at Cornwall Court at the end of August.

On the fourteenth of August, Mrs. Langthorne and Isobel accompanied Akbar to London where they had three reservations for the night at a modest hotel. In the morning, the three made their way to the docks where Akbar would embark on the first stage of his return to India. Isobel and her mother insisted on boarding the ship to inspect the second class private cabin which they had reserved for Akbar. Having satisfied their concern for his comfort, Mrs. Langthorne handed Akbar an envelope containing one hundred pound notes. After assuring him that all would be well, they bid him farewell and returned to Tillingthorpe.

Their evening walks had now assumed a greater significance, for these regular evening strolls had brought them many new friends which further enriched their sense of belonging to the village community. Although they had a special place in their hearts for the old age pensioners, many of whom Isobel knew by name, they were also often invited – by proud young mothers – to inspect the most recent arrivals in Tillingthorpe. One young mother placed her six-month old baby girl in Isobel's arms. This was Isobel's very first experience of nursing a baby, albeit someone else's. It was a moment that would linger in her memory.

In the week, they had a visit from the vicar who had called ostensibly to request their presence at dinner on the following Thursday. He was enjoying a week's sabbatical, thanks to the good offices of his friend, the Reverend Felix Chambers, Esquire, who had promised to take over his parochial duties for one week. Furthermore, if they would consent to be his guests for one whole day, he would enjoy showing them round some of the more interesting colleges in Oxford. Mrs. Langthorne and Isobel enthusiastically accepted both invitations.

Over a cup of coffee, the ladies told the vicar of the interest displayed by the Antiquarian Society. They also gave him the literature given to them by the Society which he might care to take away to peruse at his leisure.

Their trips to Oxford were now becoming more frequent, and it was recalled by Mrs. Langthorne that in spite of their numerous visits, they had never called on their predecessor, Martha, nor fulfilled the promise they had made when taking over the post office to invite her to spend a week with them. They would rectify this oversight after they had disposed of their social commitments to the vicar.

On Thursday evening, they drove to the rectory where the Reverend Copplethwaite was waiting, as on previous visits, standing in the porch. When he moved to meet them as they alighted from their car, the vicar's expression revealed his unmitigated pleasure at the prospect of a pleasant evening spent with such charming company. "So pleased you could come," he said as he ushered them into his sitting room.

Over dinner, he referred to the curate's decision to resign from the church to enter the army. Then to their astonishment, added, "I miss the young rascal very much and in retrospect I feel that I was a little hard on the boy. However, he apparently bears me no ill will because I have received a long letter from him; I was quite touched." After dinner, the vicar rang for coffee to be served in the sitting room.

Once they were all comfortably seated, the reverend gentleman spoke of the highwayman, Robert Noakes, and the crucifix which Viscount Beldrake had generously presented to him. "It was an exceedingly valuable artefact and I have since discovered that it concealed an extraordinary secret weapon." Rising from his chair he crossed the room to his desk, opening a small drawer he took out the cross on its gold chain, he went on to describe how, one evening, he noted that the top of the crucifix appeared to be parting from the main vertical of the cross. He gently pulled on it and was flabbergasted to see a four inch blade emerge. The blade bore an inscription as follows: *THE SWORD OF THE SPIRIT*.

The vicar's guests were keenly interested by this remarkable novelty and enquired if he had informed Viscount Beldrake of his discovery. "Yes," he replied, "He was quite intrigued and I have promised to allow him to inspect it." Replacing the small dagger in its gold scabbard, the vicar expressed the opinion that it was of Italian origin and probably the property of a visiting senior ecclesiastical dignitary. "Perhaps an envoy of the Pope; but that is something we shall never know," he concluded.

As the vicar assisted the ladies with their coats, he thanked them warmly for a most enjoyable evening. After reminding Isobel and her mother that he would pick them up at nine, he assured them that they would enjoy the visit to the colleges which were not only beautiful, architecturally, but every block of stone was a silent testament of their historic and noble foundations.

The next morning, Isobel and her mother left Mary and Emily in charge and set off to the city, driven and escorted by the Reverend Copplethwaite, for a day which the ladies contemplated with eager anticipation.

After an hour's visit to Christchurch where the vicar excelled himself as a guide to historic buildings, Isobel turned to the vicar and said, "Mother and I would like you to be our guest for coffee and sandwiches. We also have something to show you."

This suggestion aroused the vicar's curiosity. "How can I resist such an invitation?" Isobel had taken the precaution of ringing Jane to reserve a cubicle.

When they were seated the vicar gazed about him with avid interest. He particularly studied the ceiling with a scholarly scrutiny and could identify the heads of all the kings and queens who had founded the various colleges. Mrs. Langthorne told him it was once the meeting hall of the Oxford Antiquarian Society and was now leased by her and her daughter who had designed the interior. To describe the vicar's reaction to this information would be quite impossible. He was utterly dumbfounded and responded with exclamations such as, "Amazing! I must confess I am very surprised; but I do congratulate you both on your courage and enterprising spirit. In all my three years at Magdalen College during which I spent many hours exploring the city, I had no idea that this magnificent room existed and neither was I aware that the Antiquarian Society was active here." The vicar had been surprised, but it was a most enjoyable experience for him and these two ladies had proved to be stimulating companions. Never again, he promised himself, would he be astounded by his new friends.

After a conducted tour of Christchurch, New College and Magdalen, which many people regard as the most beautiful, it was time to return home. During the drive, Isobel, her mother and the vicar discussed the fine old buildings and their unique history. They complimented the reverend gentleman on his encyclopaedic knowledge of the university and hoped that he would permit them to enjoy his company on future expeditions. "This would be a privilege and an honour and give me infinite pleasure," he asserted. As they arrived at Tillingthorpe, they thanked him warmly for a happy and most enjoyable day. It was an outing which they would always remember. The vicar returned to his house a happy and contented man.

Mrs. Langthorne was anxious to dispose of one last social duty; an invitation to Martha to spend a week with them. After this last obligation had been fulfilled, Isobel and her mother could rest prior to her holiday.

Mrs. Langthorne was determined that her daughter should look her best when she arrived at Cornwall Court for she knew just as surely as if Lance had told her, that he would propose to Isobel during that week. She was equally certain that when her daughter returned to Tillingthorpe, it would be as Lance's fiancée. The intuitive powers of all women should never, ever be treated lightly.

Chapter 23

On the Wednesday afternoon Mr. Pringle rang to inform them, that, thanks to his personal intervention, all formalities had been expedited and head office had now confirmed the appointment of Miss Emily Haynes as a sub-postmistress.

"Were you aware that this young woman had spent fifteen years of her life in her previous post?" Mr. Pringle enquired. Mrs. Langthorne confessed she was quite ignorant of these facts. "Such a pity," Mr. Pringle retorted, "Miss Haynes had squandered many years of a life that could – in the 'service' – have given her considerable amount of seniority and may even have given her postmistress status. No good crying over spilt milk," he exclaimed. "We all make errors of judgement, although I must say I have, so far, avoided such pitfalls." He rang off after Mrs. Langthorne had urged him to come and see them whenever pressures of his vital responsibilities allowed.

On one of their infrequent visits to Oxford, they called on Martha whose appearance was much enhanced now that she had relinquished the business and post office. She was overjoyed to see them and over a cup of tea, arrangements were concluded to fetch her the ensuing weekend.

On the Friday they called at the coffee shop, but the girls were so busy that they could not spare a single moment to talk to Mrs. Langthorne and her daughter. The place hummed with the chatter of many tourists, mostly American with some French and a few Germans. The ladies were somewhat bewildered by the rampant success of this other business and departed to another less spectacular establishment for light refreshments prior to calling to pick up Martha. They found her waiting outside her sister's cottage standing by her new suitcases. She entered the car with all the eagerness of a child about to embark on a Sunday school outing. During the journey they asked Martha if she had heard about the discoveries of the secret chamber and the cache of jewels.

"Yes," Martha replied, "An article had appeared in *The Oxford Herald.*" She was very surprised but recalled that when she was a young girl, about ten years of age, her grandmother had told her the story of the Noakes brothers and how rumours had been rife in the village for many years concerning their activities. The fact that the brothers were never short of money only served to fuel the gossip in The Red Lion.

Martha became visibly excited as they approached Tillingthorpe and she recognised the homes of women she had grown up with; women with whom she had played hopscotch in the playground of the village school. Some of her teachers: Miss Green, Mrs. Davies and Mr. Rouse, the stern but kindly headmaster, now lay at peace in the churchyard awaiting the Resurrection and a summons, Martha believed, 'as sure as God made little apples' would come for certain. Martha would remember, for the rest of her life, that night that God had spoken to her as clearly as she heard the ringing of the church bell every Sunday morning and evening.

As Isobel and her mother showed the old lady round the cottage Martha was wide-eyed at the transformation of the familiar surroundings where she had raised two sons and experienced the awful trauma of widowhood. Isobel then invited Martha to peer into the small cupboards each side of the inglenook. "To think that all those years when my life was such a hard struggle, a vast fortune was hidden a few inches from me."

Throughout the week, Martha visited her old customers who regaled her with all the gossip of events which had come and gone since she had departed from Tillingthorpe. Martha felt a slight twinge of envy as she listened to all the exciting news, not all of it referred to the Langthornes. Kate Farrel would now figure prominently in their close surveillance of events now unfolding at Cock-a-Dobbie cottage. The father of Timothy was no longer Martha's personal and exclusive knowledge. It was now plainly obvious to all the village that the father was Peregrine Albert Rudolf Devereaux. Better informed people were saying, quite openly, that Peregrine was now preparing to wed Kate in the village church, if you please. Martha was shocked that an unmarried mother should be allowed to marry in their church.

It was also rumoured that this had been made possible by the application of the 'old pals act' as the servants at the rectory could testify. The Reverend Devereaux had been to dinner several times and snippets of the conversation at dinner had been duly noted by the maid.

"You will observe the traditional reading of the banns, Sebastian, old boy."

"The full service will be adhered to, but," the Reverend Sebastian Erasmus Copplethwaite interjected, "The bride must not wear white; only a simple frock of any other colour." The Reverend Devereaux expressed his grateful appreciation of the favour his old friend had bestowed upon him and his errant son. "You know, I am sure, how headstrong the modern generation are, Sebastian, old boy." The Reverend Copplethwaite, thinking of the arrogant, obstreperous young curates he had suffered over the years, hastily assured his ecclesiastical friend that he knew only too well. After dinner, the Reverend Devereaux returned to his parish duties in Wantage, well satisfied that through the loyalty of his old colleague, an ungodly registry office wedding had been averted.

Martha really enjoyed her week's holiday in her old haunts and the attitude of her successors had made her welcome and she had been treated as an equal. When the time came for her to return home, she felt pangs of doubt that in leaving her native village she may have made an error of judgement.

Isobel was preparing for her invitation to Cornwall Court for a holiday which would produce developments that would decide the course of her future destiny, happiness and security. Lance appeared at one thirty, forty-five minutes earlier than arranged, inducing Isobel to retreat to her bedroom as Lance called, "Plenty of time Isobel; no hurry. Take your time."

Taking Mrs. Langthorne's hand in his, Lance lowered his voice and said, "I am going to burden you with a secret that only you and I will share; that is for another few days. I intend, with your permission, to ask your daughter to marry me. Would you object?"

Mrs. Langthorne looked at the young gentleman and their eyes met expressing the unreserved trust of two people who had great respect for each other. "Lance, I have known for some considerable time that my daughter is deeply in love with you, although, I hasten to add, she has not mentioned it to me. Mothers of daughters know these things instinctively, Lance. As for my objections, I have none; for I know my daughter's life will be in safe, loving hands. Isobel will be a very lucky girl to have the love of a man such as yourself." She rose from her chair, shook hands with him saying, "I know you will both be very happy." Lance bent down and kissed his future mother-in-law on the cheek.

To break the tension she knew Lance felt, she drew his attention to the full length portrait of her late husband, Colonel Langthorne, in full dress uniform of the Bengal Lancers. "He is a fine looking man," Lance murmured, "and what a splendid uniform."

"Yes. He adored Isobel, who will probably tell you, at an appropriate moment, of his tragic and premature death." Lance did not disclose that Richard had previously enlightened him concerning the dreadful circumstances which had precipitated the Langthornes return to England.

Isobel now appeared with one of her cases and was in the act of returning to her room for the other. She was wearing her Donegal tweed suit and looked radiant at the prospect of many pleasant hours of companionship with her beloved giant. Lance placed the cases in the boot and returned to the sitting room where Isobel was expressing her concern at leaving her mother alone in the house for a whole week. "Do not worry yourself, child. Mary is going to stay here while you are away. She will also take care of Tess."

"Why not come with us," Lance urged.

"No, it would not be advisable to leave the house for one week; it would not be fair to the girls," Mrs. Langthorne retorted. Isobel kissed her mother and promised to phone every day. Her mother accompanied them to the car and waved until they were out of sight.

As she walked into the post office Mrs. Langthorne felt an indescribable sense of joy and contentment. Her heart swelled with pride as she stood before her husband's portrait and told him that his adored daughter's happiness and security were now ensured. The colonel's wife often talked to the picture when she felt that events in their lives warranted his approval. She was always very careful to indulge in this ritual when alone, for any third person would consider this behaviour peculiar and eccentric. No one else could ever give the comfort which she derived from this simple intimacy.

The weekend passed swiftly for Mrs. Langthorne. The evening walks continued around the village and Tess did not appear to be pining for Isobel. Indeed, she displayed as much joyful exuberance towards Mary as she had for her mistress, and always slept at the foot of her bed on a protective rug; a privilege not conceded by Isobel who confined Tess to a dog basket. During the regular walks, many people spoke to Mary as she too had made many new friends through her work in the shop. Thus the days and nights passed pleasantly for Mrs. Langthorne, and Mary's youthful company, although she was not as vivacious as Jane, was nevertheless a delightful and pretty companion.

Isobel phoned her mother every day, as she had promised, and appeared to be enjoying her holiday. She had been shopping with Lance's two sisters in Oxford and Isobel had taken them to her coffee shop. They were enchanted with the layout of canopied seats in that historic chamber with its oak panelling and richly ornate ceiling. "Very romantic," was the sisters' verdict. When they were told that Isobel and her mother owned it they were dumbfounded. After they had recovered from this amazing revelation, the sisters unequivocally congratulated Isobel for this daring adventure.

Chapter 24

Every day Isobel and Lance went riding together. On one of these rides, he showed her his long promised secret place where only Richard and he had ever been. Lance tethered the horses at the foot of a grassy hill. Hand in hand, they ascended the short steep hill together. Concealed in thick rhododendron bushes was a tiny log hut with an oak bench seat. From the open front, a wide panoramic view unfolded of rolling farmland where cattle and sheep grazed.

"Isn't that simply breathtaking?" Isobel exclaimed.

Lance heartily agreed and informed her that all the land, as far as the eye could see, belonged to the Howard estate. Lance then told her, that when Richard and he were boys, the estate workers built the hut for them and no one else knew of its existence.

"Not even your family?" Isobel enquired.

"Not even my family," Lance echoed. "Only myself and Richard and now you. It is now necessary," he said, with eyes atwinkle, "for you to place your hand on your heart and swear that you will never divulge the whereabouts of our secret hideaway!"

Isobel placed her small hand on her breast and said solemnly, "I swear that I will never divulge the whereabouts of the secret hideaway." Lance leaned towards her and gently kissed her on the lips. Hand in hand, they retraced their steps to where the horses were tethered and rode back to the stables.

They unsaddled and gave their horses a quick brush down with a body brush. Lance gave each one a measure of crushed oats and racked up with hay.

After dinner, when the ladies had retired to the drawing room, Lance told his father that he wished to speak with him and his mother in private, at their earliest convenience. "What better time than now?" his father replied, "I will request your mother to join us in the library at once."

"Please be discreet!" Lance added. Lance made his way to the library and awaited their arrival. When they were all seated, Lance informed them that before Isobel returned home, he intended to ask her to marry him, but he also realised that this serious step could not take place without their blessing and approval.

Mr. Howard leapt from his chair, shook his son's hand, congratulated him and said, "We are so pleased for you, old chap: your mother and I have been hoping that this announcement would not be long delayed."

His mother hugged him and added her congratulations saying, "I am so glad that you have made this decision: Isobel will make a good wife and what is also important, is that Isobel will integrate with the family perfectly."

Lance then produced the ring he had ordered from Garrards of London, the royal jewellers. It was a Burma ruby - all the finest rubies are mined in Burma - cut in the shape of a heart, surrounded by ten diamonds. Lance handed it to his mother enquiring, "Do you like it, mother?"

"It is truly beautiful and so unusual; you have displayed excellent taste, my son. Isobel will be enchanted with it. When will you propose to her?"

"On Thursday evening, after dinner," Lance replied. His father was filling three glasses with port to toast the health and happiness of his beloved son and the girl he would hope to make his bride.

The next day Isobel asked Lance to take her into Oxford as she wanted to show him something. Lance said, "That reminds me, I must find my sisters to ask if they would like to come with us to see the D'Oyly Carte Opera Company perform Gilbert and Sullivan's *The Mikado*. If they agree, I can reserve a box while we are there." They set off to find the girls; no easy task in that great house, and finally found them talking to the gardener in one of the glass houses. They enthusiastically concurred and asked Isobel if she had ever seen it; when she replied that she had never seen any of the Gilbert and Sullivan productions, they assured her that she would enjoy it as it was the most colourful of all the light operas. Lance turned to Isobel saying, "That's settled then, we'll get going."

In Oxford, Lance took Isobel to Magdalen College. She did not spoil his pleasure by telling him that the vicar had already shown them round this most attractive of all the colleges. To Lance's amazement and pleasure the porter recognised him, causing them to pause in the ancient entrance to exchange greetings. "Wasn't that extraordinary?" Isobel exclaimed, "after all those years he recognised you without a moment's hesitation."

"Only three years," Lance corrected.

Afterwards, they made their way to the coffee shop where they sat closely together in the privacy of the cubicle. It was a rare occasion when there was a lull in the flow of customers. Jane came forward to serve them, looking very attractive in her eighteenth century costume. She exchanged a few words with Isobel intimating that everything was under control. Turning to her companion, Isobel invited his opinion of the layout. "Very novel, very unusual," he said.

"I designed it!" Isobel informed him with a sense of pride, "and it belongs to mummy and me. We are equal partners."

"Well, well, well!" Lance exclaimed, "You're quite a little tycoon, aren't you?" Isobel laughed as she told him that the enterprise was born of dire necessity to obtain for two vulnerable ladies independence of others. Lance was full of admiration for their resourcefulness and pondered the circumstances so fleetingly referred to. He regarded it as a brilliant idea and it also indicated another facet of this young woman's character.

After saying goodbye to Jane, they drove back to Cornwall Court as they would need to take possession of their reservation in the New

Theatre by seven thirty. It was now three and they would have a light meal with Margaret and Christal at six.

They all spent a most enjoyable evening at the Theatre and motored home. They arrived home at eleven fifteen, and after a glass of milk and a biscuit, they all dispersed to their rooms.

On the Thursday morning, Lance took Isobel on the long promised tour of the house. It was truly a most impressive building, packed with gleaming antique furniture, art treasures and fine pictures. Isobel was intrigued by the Long Gallery which gave a fine southerly view of the park with the lake in the distance.

"This is known to the servants as the Lady Gallery. As you will see, the whole wall on one side is filled with portraits of ladies of the Howard family. Some are very beautiful and this one is my favourite. It depicted a young girl of the seventeenth century in a striking dark red gown. Her dark hair framed a pale, pensive face, accentuated by the thoughtful expression in her dark eyes. The Gallery was one hundred and eighty feet long and served to provide exercise during inclement weather. Isobel gazed up in awe at these lovely women of the Howard family who were chatelaines of Cornwall Court from 1400 to 1880.

Lance looked at his watch, saying, "Dear me, how time has flown; we will be late for lunch, we must hurry or mother will rebuke us. If you are still interested to see more, we will resume our tour this afternoon."

"Oh, indeed yes, Lance!" cried Isobel, "I want to see it all and you have given me an experience of stepping back in time. I love every minute."

After lunch they resumed their wanderings round this historic mansion and ended it in the Great Hall, the oldest part of the house, with its magnificent oak staircase. The main lower oak newel supported a carving of St. George and facing him on the opposite support a fierce looking dragon. At intervals up the banister rail were carved effigies of men at arms. Some depicted in armour, some bowmen, pikemen, some halberdiers. They had been added at various periods and gleamed with the polishing of many generations of loyal retainers. The staircase was ten feet wide and divided at the top into two landings. Two suits of armour guarded the head of the stairs, their gauntlets resting on drawn swords.

The walls of the hall were covered in all types of weapons, from swords and daggers to muskets, all arranged in patterns. Isobel gazed up and around her, overawed by the atmosphere of the Great Hall and its display of weapons and wondered at the tales they could tell if endowed with the faculty of speech. All had spilled blood on the battlefields which figure so prominently throughout English history. Isobel was so carried away by her imagination that she had become oblivious of Lance standing a few feet from her. He laid his hand on her shoulder saying, "Come back, Isobel, you are lost."

She started, smiled up at him and said, "I was, I was, Lance."

"Well that's where we came in! What shall we do now?" enquired Lance.

"But where do you live, Lance?" Isobel wanted to know. "I have seen where Margaret and Christal live, but not where you live."

Lance said, "I am afraid there is little to see in comparison to the impressive rooms that you have already seen; but just to complete the tour, I will show you." He led her through the intricate maze of rooms, chambers and corridors to an almost hidden corner of the main body of the house, opened double mahogany doors giving access to a short passage. Lance threw open a single door at the end and said, "This is it."

The room was about twenty feet by fifteen feet. On the walls were two landscapes by Herring senior, some watercolours by his sister, a few groups of Eton boys, some of his college and a photograph of Lance and Richard together.

An iron hospital-type bed, a tallboy and a wardrobe completed the furnishings. Isobel looked around wide-eyed with astonishment at the spartan room. Lance leaned in the open doorway saying, with a grin, "I told you there was nothing to see."

Isobel walked across to the bed and pressed on the mattress, then sat on it, saying with a grimace, "It's hard!" Then, the tour completed, they made their way to the drawing room where they would have tea.

On the Thursday evening, after dinner, Lance invited Isobel to stroll outside, warning, "You will require a wrap of some kind as the evenings become chilly at this time of the year."

Isobel was wearing a royal blue velvet dress with long sleeves. Throwing a large cashmere shawl over her shoulders she announced, "I'm ready, where shall we go?" Slipping her hand into Lance's arm they set off. Emerging from the south door, they walked a short distance through the avenue of chestnut trees. Turning sharp left between them, they came to a good old fashioned stile. Isobel perched on the top rail with Lance standing beside her. The enormous harvest moon hung low in the sky at thirty degrees. Why the moon at this time is so large and so near is one of natures mysteries; and why is it usually honey-coloured, so unlike the hunters' moon in October which is cold, bright and pale?

As he looked at Isobel, Lance was startled to see that the back of her head was in direct line with the centre of the Moon, which appeared to encircle her head like a halo. She looked like a medieval painting of the Madonna. He took her hand and said quietly, "You are very beautiful, Isobel." Isobel remained silent staring back at Lance with her large dark trusting eyes. A powerful aura of mystery enveloped this young woman casting its spell on her companion. Lance reminded Isobel of that May morning in the post office when their eyes first met and told her that on that day, he had fallen deeply in love with her and had hoped that one day she would agree to marry him.

"Will you marry me, Isobel, and allow me to look after you for the rest of your life?" Isobel entwined her slim white arms around his neck telling of her efforts to find him. Efforts which failed until a benevolent Fate intervened and led her to him.

"I will marry you, Lance and I love you with all my heart." They kissed a lingering kiss; not a lustful kiss; simply an intimate sealing of their troth.

Lance then said, "I do hope you will not condemn me as presumptuous but I have bought you a ring. I resolved to follow the Howard motto, 'Fortune Favours the Audacious'. However, if you do not like it, Garrards have agreed to change it for something you may care to select yourself." Lance then groped in his pocket extracting a small ring case. He opened it to reveal the ring with the heart-shaped ruby surrounded by diamonds, which reflected the moonlight in a hundred sparkling colours.

"It's beautiful, Lance," Isobel exclaimed, "Please put it on my finger." She extended her small white finger. It fitted perfectly. They kissed and returned to the house where Lance's parents waited expectantly.

Mrs. Howard had wisely requested her daughters to remain with her and her husband in the music room as there was a possibility that they would all hear Lance and Isobel make a very important announcement. "Are they getting engaged?" chorused the sisters.

"Maybe," Mr. Howard responded, "but please do not sit here all agog at what you may or may not hear. Just be preoccupied and nonchalant or you will embarrass them both."

In due course, Lance and Isobel appeared after enquiring of the butler the whereabouts of Lance's parents. Margaret was playing the piano, their mother chatting to Christal and Mr. Howard reading *The Field* magazine. As Lance and Isobel entered the room, Margaret continued to play and Mr. Howard appeared to be engrossed in his magazine. Mrs. Howard looked up and Christal enquired, "Where have you two been? You look very happy!"

"We are happy," Lance responded, "and with good reason. I am now able to reveal that Isobel and I are engaged. A few minutes ago she promised to be my wife and that is why we are so happy."

Mrs. Howard rose from her chair, hugged her future daughter-in-law saying, "Welcome to our small family."

Mr. Howard enveloped her slender form in a bear-like hug, kissed the top of her head and murmured, "I have been hoping for this for a very long time." The girls then embraced Isobel, kissed her on the cheek telling her that their brother was a very lucky man. Then they all warmly congratulated Lance and drank a toast to this young, radiant, and ecstatically happy couple.

The following day, Friday, Christal was excitedly talking of wedding plans and wondering who would design and make Isobel's wedding gown. But sinister events would occur before that happy day would become reality. The long dark shadow of the evil Sabridin was yet to darken and menace their lives once again. This time, however, Isobel and her mother would have powerful protectors.

The week had passed all too swiftly, for in two days time, Isobel would return home to her mother, who had already been informed of the wonderful news of the formal betrothal of her daughter to Lance.

Mrs. Langthorne decided that the Reverend Sebastian Erasmus Copplethwaite should be the first person in Tillingthorpe to learn of this momentous announcement, not only out of respect for the old gentleman, but he would be asked to marry the happy couple in his own church. When the vicar received this important news, his reaction was of profound surprise as he did not know the Howards of Cornwall Court; they were well out of his parochial orbit.

Isobel returned home to a rapturous welcome from her mother and Tess. Mrs. Langthorne quickly perceived that behind the joyous, rapturous demeanour a subtle change was manifest in her daughter. She had left home for her holiday a young beautiful girl; she was now transformed into a glowing, lovely, but mature, young woman.

Mrs. Langthorne congratulated Lance telling him that after Isobel had retired to bed she would face her husband's portrait and tell the colonel that his adored Isobel was now in the safe loving hands of a fine young gentleman.

"That is my secret, Lance and I do beg you not to think me to be an eccentric old woman."

Chapter 25

The following day, Isobel had much to tell her mother; how warmly the Howards had welcomed her into their family and described all the day's events which had collectively contributed so much to a holiday that would never be forgotten. A holiday during which Lance had proposed to her; a holiday that would remain in her memory with a freshness and clarity to the day she died. It is a human experience known as nostalgia.

After lengthy discussions with her mother about the arrangements for the wedding, Isobel decided that she would like to be married during the month of May of the ensuing year. This was mutually accepted as a most suitable time, for there would be much to think about, much to organise. Mother and daughter wisely concluded that all this sudden excitement was a trifle overwhelming and deemed it wise to concentrate their minds on their normal hum-drum routine.

A welcome distraction was provided by news of Kate Farrel's imminent wedding in the parish church of St. Botolph's. The Langthornes intended to support Kate with their presence at the ceremony, a week hence. Isobel knew Kate quite well and had enjoyed many conversations with her in the post office. In fact, Isobel hoped that she could persuade Kate to design and to make her wedding dress. It must be remembered that Kate Farrel was not only an expert needlewoman, but was also very artistic.

A trip to Oxford was arranged to ensure that the girls were still able to cope with the frenetic pressures imposed by the constant but welcome flow of patrons to the coffee shop. The girls were so busy that it would have been unkind to add to their burden. Isobel hastily scribbled a note requesting Jane to phone at her convenience to make a note of any urgent problems. That evening, Mrs. Langthorne put it to Isobel that it might be a good idea to deliver Kate Farrel's wedding present - a bone china tea service - early one evening, after ascertaining the visit would not incommode Kate, nor embarrass her or themselves.

One afternoon, Kate came into the shop to purchase certain items for Timothy's tea. Isobel immediately invited Kate into their private quarters enquiring if she had a few moments to hear a favour desired of her. Kate's understandable curiosity evoked an affirmative response. Isobel being a forthright and volatile young woman put the question without a shred of procrastination. "Next year I am to be married," Isobel announced to Kate, "and I would like you to design and make my wedding gown. We will, of course, pay you handsomely and I would be eternally grateful if you say yes."

Kate gulped with astonishment at, not one, but two startling and totally unexpected revelations. Kate had never seen Isobel with a gentleman. After she had recovered her composure, Kate asked them to leave her decision until after her wedding. The Langthornes thought it an opportune moment to ask Kate if it would be alright to call on her the next evening as they had something for her and to inform her that they would attend her wedding service. The young woman's eyes moistened with emotion as she told them she would greatly appreciate their presence as it was possible that, apart from her future father-in-law, they would be the only members of the congregation. "Your visit will be convenient the very next night."

Kate returned home deep in thought, wondering who Isobel's fiancé was and also reflected, with gratitude, on their promise to attend her wedding. Many folk would be surprised by the number of people who would be present in church to witness Kate's wedding. Most of them – regrettably – to satisfy their curiosity concerning her bridegroom.

Early the next evening, Isobel and her mother called on Kate Farrel to deliver the promised gift. They were met at the door by Kate's son, Timothy, and invited to enter. They smiled at this handsome youth who had been the subject of almost perpetual conjecture and gossip. Kate received the gift with obvious pleasure and opened it without further preamble. It consisted of a full tea service decorated with a motif of woodland violets. The large teapot was particularly elegant and Kate was delighted and deeply touched by this generous gift.

Timothy was now nearly sixteen years of age and beginning – very naturally – to notice girls in a new light. He looked admiringly at Isobel and wondered if she would fall in love with him. He asked Isobel about the treasure and the secret chamber saying he would love to see it. Isobel replied, "Why not come with us and see it now."

"Could I, Mum?" he asked.

"Yes, provided you do not make a nuisance of yourself." Isobel handed Tess's lead to Timothy and thanked Kate who showed them out and watched as the three wended their way home.

When Kate's son saw the splendid painting of the colonel he turned to Isobel saying, "Who is that soldier?" Isobel looked at the portrait, wistfully, informing Timothy that the gentleman portrayed was her late father. "I would like to join the army, but my mum won't let me."

Isobel showed the boy where the jewels had been discovered by the young apprentice. He peered long and hard into the dark interior of the small cupboard until Isobel said, "Come, Timothy, and I will show you the secret chamber." Together they went to the concealed entrance, passing, as Isobel pointed out, between the walls, and descended into the chamber. Timothy's eyes were as round as saucers as he gazed around the dark room illuminated by Isobel's torch.

When shown the cavernous chimney with its footholds, he said, "I would love to climb up to the escape hatch."

"We can't return you to your mother looking like a sweep!" Isobel demurred leading the way back up the steps. Timothy returned to his mother to tell her about the secret underground room and how he had seen a large picture of Isobel's dad.

Lance was now a frequent visitor to the post office, occasionally staying for two nights. During one of these brief visits, the Reverend Copplethwaite called and was introduced to Lance. He promptly invited them all to dinner, taking an instant liking to this tall young man with the twinkly grey eyes.

Chapter 26

In September, a letter arrived from Andrew Gilbert containing two tickets for the Passing Out Parade on the fifteenth of September. In the letter, the young man wrote that he was looking forward to meeting Isobel and her mother and hoped that they would be able to attend the Passing Out Ball to be held in the academy gymnasium.

Mrs. Langthorne could sense that this young man might be harbouring a deep affection for her daughter and to avoid hurting this sensitive young cadet even more deeply, she must write accepting the invitation and simultaneously break the news of Isobel's engagement to permit him to meet them with the composure of old friends other than a young man whose secret aspirations, involving her daughter, could never materialise.

Meanwhile, the new village memorial hall had been completed. The foundation stone had been laid by the youngest apprentice with the builder who had built it, and thus his name of Frederick Fairbrother had been carved into a block of Portland stone by Eli Marriot for future generations to read and identify with. The official opening ceremony was performed by Viscount Beldrake. The unveiling of the other war memorial would take place in a ceremony on November the eleventh.

The blacksmith, Bill Copeland, had been approached by an official from the Witney orphanage to enquire if the smith would accept a fourteen-year-old boy into his home as an apprentice. The smith mopped his brow and face with the cloth tucked into his apron and stared at the caller thoughtfully. The official, who was no mean student of human nature, added with consummate timing, "You would, of course, be reimbursed for his keep, plus five pounds for his Binding Indentures."

Peering intently into the official's face Bill enquired, "How much?"

"Three pounds a week," was the brisk reply.

"Leave it with me," said Bill, leading him into his cottage. "If the wife says yes, its OK with me, but she will say yea or nay, and that's the end on it, mind."

Mrs. Copeland was in the act of making a fig pudding and was somewhat taken aback by this sudden invasion of a stranger, and by what Bill was doing away from the forge. He had never, to her knowledge, been a lazy man, although he had been a trifle contrary of late. Lucy was a very shrewd woman and quickly foresaw the accruing advantages of an apprentice. There was the three pounds a week, for example, and if Bill failed to acquire the requisite number of stamps on his insurance cards by dying prematurely, the apprentice would, as he got older, represent further security for her.

"What do you think of the idea?" queried Lucy of Bill.

"Well, I'm agreeable if you are, but we would want to see the lad first," Bill replied.

"That will be no problem," the official assured them. "I will bring him over on Monday; he will, of course, be on probation for six months so if he does not fit in, he will return to the orphanage." Lucy visibly shuddered at the mention of orphanage. Lucy could recall the days of the grim workhouses scattered throughout the land.

On Monday the man from the orphanage arrived at ten, with a young, sturdy, rosy-cheeked boy of fourteen. Lucy displayed no emotion as she eyed the boy with a shrewd look of appraisal. Inwardly she liked what she saw and at heart was a kindly motherly soul. Bill and Lucy had never had children, but neither had there been any recriminations in spite of Bill's longing for a son who would ultimately take over the forge. Bill obviously liked the boy and it was mutually agreed they would take the orphan on trial.

Bill was an ardent believer in the old saying, 'Start as you mean to go on'; he looked the new apprentice straight in the eyes and said, "We'll give you a good home, boy, and I'll teach you the oldest craft in the world, blacksmithing, but if you are cheeky or don't do as you're told, you will get a clip round the ear. Every village has its ne'er-do-wells and I warn you if you run wild and keep bad company, you will be in serious trouble."

"Do you accept these terms, lad?" enquired the smith.

"Yes, sir," the small, apprehensive boy replied.

"That's settled, then. Now we'll sign the documents."

"Not yet," interjected the official. "After the probationary period."

The new addition to the Copeland family was the illegitimate son of a farmer's son and a young dairy maid, who had sadly died giving birth. Her name was Ruth Robinson and before she died, she had chosen the names of Robert Arthur for her son. The poor law infirmary had duly had him baptised in these names.

Bill returned to his forge a happy man; he felt instinctively that they had done the right thing and what was more, he now had a son. Frank Burrows looked up from the fire, where he was busily placing more coke, to see the smith reappear with a look on his face which Frank had never seen before. "Frank," the smith said, "The wife and me have adopted a young apprentice and we will have to be careful about swearing in front of the boy; I don't want him learning bad habits." Frank received this warning with his usual phlegmatic philosophical air of resignation so typical in men who had survived that hellish war.

After the smith had returned to his labour, his wife turned her attention to her new charge, instructing him to follow her upstairs. She opened a door into a small bedroom at the back of the cottage. It looked out on to lush meadowland and trees. The youth's eyes lit up with joy as he gazed out on this green vista, so different from the harsh brick walls of the orphanage. The room contained a small iron bed, a chest of drawers, with a mirror and a chair. A small bedside rug was placed on the lino covered floor. "Unpack your things," Lucy ordered, "Come down and I will give you something to eat."

The young boy looked round his bedroom. It was his, he said to himself, for the first time in his life that he had a room of his very own. He paused to look at the idyllic scene from his window and descended the dark stairs with a door at the bottom giving access to the dining room. The smith's wife had placed a large cup of tea on the table at the side of a plate supporting a huge wedge of homemade fruit cake.

Before Robert was permitted to sit down to this tempting repast, he was ushered into the kitchen where he was ordered to wash his hands thoroughly and dry them on a roller towel secured to the back of the door. Robert was also told that he would take two baths a week and if he had trouble with his feet, he would wash them every night. Robert hastily assured the smith's wife he did not suffer in this way and at the orphanage had been forced to bathe every day. "Sit down, lad, and eat, it's a long time until dinner." Although the boy was hungry, Lucy noted, with satisfaction, he had impeccable table manners. When Lucy's furry cat leapt on to his lap, his youthful face lit up with delight. That was a good sign, Lucy thought, as the cat usually bolted when strangers called.

The next morning, Lucy would take Robert into Witney to buy suitable working clothes for him, as the following day the new apprentice would be required to start work at the forge.

In the mysterious and so far unexplained ways of village life, the news of the adoption spread like fire through a stubble field and in so doing aroused feelings of envy in other childless couples: Joshua's wife for one. The focal point of the village had now shifted from the Langthornes to the smithy, and the smith could not understand why so many people with dogs were walking past his forge. All were trying to steal a glimpse of the Copeland's new adopted son. Every night, after closing time, Joshua was interrogated by his wife to discover if the smith had said anything. "No," the innkeeper asserted, "the old fool just stands there with a silly smirk on his face saying nothing."

This latest and unusual occurrence in Tillingthorpe had diverted attention from Kate Farrel's wedding in two days time but would, no doubt, return to favour after Kate had departed for a honeymoon touring Devon and Cornwall.

At two on Thursday Isobel and her mother walked to the church to support Kate when she walked down the aisle at two-thirty to take her place at the side of her beloved Peregrine. The Langthornes were astounded to see that a congregation of at least fifty had already assembled. The ancient church had a large three manual organ, thanks to the beneficence of the late grandfather of Viscount Beldrake, who was an accomplished musician and had been known to play it when the resident organist was sick. The organist on this happy day had come from Wantage. He was a close friend of Peregrine's family and was determined to make up for the absence of bridesmaids and a beautiful white veiled bride. He decided that, when he received the signal, he would pull out all the stops and make the old church tremble to the sound of Mendelssohn's 'Wedding March.' The signal was given.

The Langthornes turned to watch a radiant Kate make her entry on the arm of her father. She wore a cool green frock, white shoes and a wide brimmed white hat. Round her neck was a chain bearing a heavy gold crucifix; the bridegroom's present. Timothy, her son, did not attend. Timothy loved his mother and was very proud of her, because she was to him the prettiest woman in the village.

Chapter 27

Three months had elapsed since the smith and his wife had accepted young Robert into their home. One night, he opened the door to the staircase to go to bed, and suddenly he hesitated with his hand still grasping the thumb latch and said, with a disconcerting candour so often displayed by children, "I never had a mum or dad; I don't know why," he added with a puzzled expression in his eyes. A long silence ensued, "Would you mind if I called you mum and dad?"

Standing there, he looked like Cupid asking his mother, Venus, if he could go out to play. Butterflies fluttered in Lucy Copeland's stomach as she rose from her chair and clasped him to her ample bosom. "Robert, I know that you did not come from inside my body, but I really do feel that I am your mother." The smith tapped his pipe out on the fire grate with such force that the bowl snapped from its stem. He stared at the damage ruefully, took out a large red, white spotted handkerchief and blew his nose with exaggerated vigour.

"We'd like that, wouldn't we, Lucy. Yes, wed really like that, Robert."

"We'll start tomorrow, then," the smith said, "and we'll look after you and love you until the day we die. That's it, then, that's settled, then, and I am glad you asked, young fella-me-lad." The boy retired to bed.

The smith looked at his wife who said, "You're a good man, Bill Copeland, even if you did fob me off with a second-rate cooking range."

In the morning, the smith wrote out the bill for the repairs to the windlass on the Langthorne's well. It stated: 'To one new spindle and fitting of same, one pound twelve shillings and sixpence. Pay at your convenience.'

The smith had to explain to his striker, Frank Burrows, the new arrangements of the previous evening. This was a necessary precaution, as if the boy called him 'Dad' just as Frank was raising the sledge to strike the white hot steel, it could cause him to miss and hit Bill's hand.

Bill handed his brand new son the envelope and directed him to the post office. Isobel knew all about Robert, as those who worked in a village post office were more cognisant with all the goings on than anybody else. She noticed, that when this small boy entered, he removed his cap. Robert handed her the envelope containing the bill and made to leave until she checked him with a "Don't go, young man." Isobel opened the envelope and placed the indicated amount inside. Taking a handful of Bluebird toffees from a jar, she put them in a bag and handed them to Robert who was preoccupied with his inspection of all around him.

His blue eyes met Isobel's as he said, "Thank you, ma'am" She watched him go. She now regarded children in a different light and was much more sensitive to them.

Robert returned to the forge and waited until the smith pushed the iron back into the fire and heaped the hot coke over it. Robert handed the envelope and the bag of toffees to the smith. "What's this?" the smith enquired of Robert.

"The lady at the post office sent them," he replied.

The smith opened the small paper bag perceiving the contents and said, "These are for you, son," and handed them back. The new apprentice handed one to Frank and then one to the smith.

On the fourteenth of September, the Langthornes travelled to Camberley in Surrey where they had reservations at the Cambridge Hotel. The following morning they were unable to pick out Andrew Gilbert from the precise ranks of the cadets on parade. After the adjutant had ridden his horse up the steps of the academy, signalling the end of the ceremony, close friends and relatives were permitted to enter the main hall and the room adjacent where many photographs and trophies bedecked the walls. On small tables several large Victorian albums were on display.

Isobel and her mother stood at the entrance, eagerly awaiting the young man whom they had known as the parish curate and who was now a soldier. They did not have long to wait, but they would not have easily recognised the cadet who now stood before them. He had grown a little taller and was definitely a lot broader. He also oozed the confidence engendered in those men by their rigorous physical and mental training.

Andrew, accompanied by his parents, greeted Isobel and her mother warmly and immediately introduced his father and mother. Mrs. Gilbert looked at the young girl with keen interest and could readily understand why her son was so fascinated by her. Andrew congratulated Isobel on her recent engagement, displaying admirable self-control to the relief of Mrs. Langthorne who was only too well aware of the hurt and disappointment contained within his heart.

He showed them round the academy and its beautiful extensive grounds, also the two large lakes used by flocks of cruising swans and a variety of wild life.

Mrs. Langthorne and her daughter invited Andrew and his parents to join them for dinner at their hotel. "Will you be coming to the Ball?" he enquired wistfully.

Mrs. Langthorne gently explained to him their newly opened business ventures and of the consequent absorption of their free time. "However, you will now get six weeks leave before joining your regiment so do please come and stay with us."

Isobel also added her own words of consolation by saying, "You must never lose touch with us, Andrew, because I have come to regard you as a brother."

The Langthornes rose early the day after the parade to catch the half-hourly train service to London; from there they would travel to Oxford, the train making only two stops, Reading and Didcot. During the journey, Mrs. Langthorne's thoughts were tinged with sadness for the young, manly and now dashing, officer who had harboured such strong romantic feelings for her daughter.

At the end of September, Isobel recalled Jane's comments concerning a need for a café where undergraduates could obtain a good substantial meal at a moderate price. This would not be a simple straightforward enterprise like the coffee shop. After prolonged discussion, it was decided to seek the practical aid and advice of an experienced cook. This idea would require considerable planning and a lot of research. It was, therefore, left in abeyance until after Christmas, now three months away.

Such was the prosperity of the Langthornes, that all the money which they had borrowed had now been repaid. The tourist season in Oxford was now over and contrary to all expectations, the coffee shop continued to thrive and Jane had felt it expedient to engage another girl. The coffee shop, together with the Tillingthorpe shop and the post office now gave the Langthornes a very substantial income.

Isobel's mother often thought back to that day in India when her daughter had returned from her exhilarating ride and propounded her scheme to provide them with a home and income. Never in their wildest dreams could they have envisaged the exceedingly fruitful results. Not only were they materially rewarded, but life in Tillingthorpe had also brought much happiness.

Mrs. Langthorne recalled that had they not petitioned the aid of her nephew, Viscount Beldrake, Isobel would never have met Lance. Sometimes she wondered if fate – as some people thought – really did map out our lives at birth.

Chapter 28

The inhabitants of Tillingthorpe were now thinking of preparations for Christmas. North-easterly winds had produced early morning frosts and flurries of snow during the day. At night, the curtained windows emitted the soft romantic glow of oil lamps.

For the vicar, this was a very busy time of the year with carol services and, most important of all, the midnight service on Christmas Eve.

In the smithy, one half of the large wooden doors was closed with the fierce coke fire spewing sparks like a miniature volcano. A strange atmosphere of cosiness and shelter was conveyed to the casual observer, accentuated by the fire's illumination of the ruddy faces of the two men and the young boy. The young apprentice had now been promoted to the task of operating the bellows, although it was necessary for him to stand on a box to reach the long wooden lever. After one year, he would be expected to make his own tools, tongs, hammers, and so on. These operations were a very sound basis for the developing skills which would take seven years of Robert's life before he became a fully competent blacksmith.

The Langthornes would spend the Christmas at Cornwall Court and Isobel was, naturally, excitedly looking forward to the visit.

The Red Lion was still the hub of village life. Members of the thriving Slate Club were, without exception, all Joshua's regulars. Coach trips and raffles were also organised within the ancient and hospitable walls of the pub.

Two weeks before Christmas, Isobel and her mother were preoccupied with the seasonal obligation of writing and posting Christmas cards. Presents had been purchased and neatly wrapped and were now stored in a cupboard under the stairs. Mary had, enthusiastically, agreed to look after Tess who was now resplendent in her winter coat and exactly like her grandmother, Nell, Calebs dog.

A week before Christmas, Lance fetched his fiancée and her mother to spend the holiday at Cornwall Court. Christmas was always an enjoyable season for the Howards.

A firm of contractors were engaged to erect a long table in the Great Hall. A catering company took over the kitchen to prepare the Christmas dinner in order to free the servants. The Howards, guests, and servants would sit down together, in keeping with a tradition established two centuries ago.

The Hall was lavishly decorated with holly and ivy by the gardeners who would light the two huge log fires at eight. At the foot of the grand staircase, a tall Christmas tree had been placed in a barrel. It had been decorated by the maids aided by the footmen, who had all displayed their artistic appreciation with spectacular effect. All the presents were arranged around the tree.

On Christmas Eve, the park was covered in a two inch blanket of snow. In olden times, the Howards retained their personal priest but now the ancient church, with its many ornate tombs of past Howards, was, sadly, only used on special occasions: weddings, funerals, baptisms, and other important occasions. The whole household attended the midnight service on Christmas Eve, conducted by a vicar from the village of Stoneyford which belonged to the estate. As the church was only two fields away from the house, everyone walked in procession, headed by Mr. and Mrs. Howard.

The church was illuminated by oil lamps and candles, but was not heated. Consequently, all were dressed in warm clothing and found the walk most exhilarating. Isobel wore a seal-skin fur coat with a hood lined with white rabbit fur. The hood was thrown back as she wore a soft wool tam-o'-shanter hat. Lance stole fleeting glimpses at the glowing face of his lovely companion and thought what a lucky and happy man he was. His beautiful butterfly had at last been captured in his poised net.

The chattering voices of the party echoed across the snow covered fields and all would remember these magic hours. Isobel clutched the arm of her handsome fiancé, her eyes alight with excitement and love.

After the service, they all assembled in the library for hot drinks before going to their respective rooms. It was truly a happy Christmas Eve and the old mansion provided an almost holy atmosphere. Before parting, Isobel and Lance took advantage of their brief moment of privacy in the long corridor to hold each other close in a long sweet lingering kiss.

While the gentry were celebrating Christmas, the humbler folk of Tillingthorpe were also ensuring that they too would not allow this season of the year to pass without their traditional, albeit more modest, observance. The parish church was packed for the midnight service to the gratification of the vicar, who reflected that many of them had been married and baptised by him in that same church, Christmas was a sad and lonely time for him and he was, therefore, grateful that his parishioners had provided him with a welcome preoccupation by their attendance at this most important event in the ecclesiastical calendar.

Joshua and Hilda at The Red Lion would also enjoy a much needed and well-deserved respite from their hectic labours. Timothy Farrel now enjoyed his first Christmas with his father and perhaps his last in Cock-a-Dobbie cottage. The smith and his wife, Lucy, would know a unique happiness this day with their newly acquired son, Robert. After ascertaining that Robert was Church of England, they all walked to church for the Christmas morning service. The vicar observed their presence with much satisfaction and pleasure for Bill had a fine baritone voice and would, therefore, give body to the sometimes reedy vocal efforts of his elderly congregation, during the singing of the much loved old and favourite carols. Mary Griffin was also there with her parents and looking forward to taking Tess for a walk after the service. Tess was now more attached to Mary than to Isobel.

Mary dreamed – as all young girls do – of acquiring a sweetheart, but there were few boys of her age in the village and none of them appealed to her. Mary was a pretty, sensitive girl, and was very rigid in her expectations of a boy she would like to court and one day marry. Her old friend, Jane, at the coffee shop, now that she had found a beau was, when work permitted, looking for a suitable young man as her special friend.

The spring ploughing and harrowing was now in progress in the fields of Tillingthorpe. The blackthorn blossom - that first harbinger of spring - was now visible on the hedgerows.

Chapter 29

Christmas was but a memory and little girls wheeled their doll's prams through the village to show off their new dolls to anyone who evinced the slightest interest. These were the days when little girls, in their divine innocence, could roam freely to play around the meadows and woods of their village, safe from marauding perverts who were non-existent in those law-abiding days.

The Langthornes pursued their daily routine which included an investigation into Jane's idea for another café where undergraduates could obtain wholesome, satisfying meals at modest prices.

The Red Lion still hummed and buzzed like the proverbial bee hive.

Timber Woods' business was prospering and it had been necessary to employ a fully experienced undertaker to cope with the older inhabitants who had exceeded their allotted span of three score years and ten and had wearily departed from this mortal life. These sad occasions never failed to touch Timber's heart; they had been living links with the glorious history of England's Victorian era.

The smith had now received a visit from an official from the orphanage, bearing the forms of final adoption. He put the questions to Robert, "Are you happy here? Are you being well-fed and clothed? Are you being looked after properly?"

Robert responded to these inquisitorial probings with emphatic affirmatives on all counts. "Yes, sir." he replied to every query.

"Now, Mr. Copeland, are you and your spouse willing to take this boy as your legally adopted son?"

"Most certainly," the smith and his wife chorused. "He is our son and we love him as such and one day he will inherit this forge and cottage," the smith continued. The forge and attached cottage was one of a very few freehold properties in Tillingthorpe. It had been a gift to Bill's grandfather from the Beldrakes. During the Zulu War Bill's grandfather had carried the badly wounded Viscount Beldrake to safety during a fierce stage of the battle when the English positions had been overrun.

Chapter 30

Sinister events threatened the bucolic and tranquil scene of Tillingthorpe, events which would strike terror into the Langthornes household and would transport Isobel back to India into the clutches of the villainous and evil Sabridin.

Very few cars were ever seen in Tillingthorpe apart from trades vehicles and yet no one appeared to be aware of a black saloon car containing two men and a woman, who occupied the rear seat, in the vicinity of the post office. At six in the evening, the unlit roads in the village were very dark and presented ideal conditions for evildoers to wreak their nefarious activities on any unsuspecting prey. Fate always seems to favour those of criminal intent to the detriment of the innocent and law-abiding, and so it was in this case.

Isobel was normally accompanied by her mother when walking the dog, but on this night, her mother had an important letter to write and thus Isobel was quite alone in the deserted village street. Tess was running free, nose to the ground reading all those interesting scents, some now familiar, some strange, to be carefully stored in her memory to be identified on some future expedition.

This was the opportunity that the sinister agents of Sabridin had been waiting for during the two weeks of their surveillance of the daily routines followed by the Langthornes. One man and the woman alighted from the car and bundled Isobel into the rear seat where the woman pressed a chloroform-soaked pad over her nose.

The car moved silently away from the scene of the abduction and sped towards the main Witney road. After travelling approximately a mile, they turned into a minor road known as the Newnham Turn where a large furniture removal van was parked, with the tail board down. The car was driven skilfully up this ramp into its spacious interior and the tail board was hastily raised and bolted. The kidnappers then drove to a warehouse on the outskirts of Oxford.

Isobel was now removed from the car and placed on a divan, still unconscious. Another van was loaded with furniture and such was the fiendish thoroughness of these miscreants, that gardening tools were neatly lashed together and placed in the rear of the van. A cat basket with a live cat in it was placed where it would be immediately seen should the load be examined.

After a quick meal of sandwiches and coffee eaten by her abductors, Isobel was transferred to a secret compartment behind the driver's cab. The compartment was of spacious size easily accommodating Isobel and the woman accomplice, who had been a nurse in a famous mental hospital.

The whole operation, so swiftly executed, had only taken an hour and a half, and the criminals were now on their way to Bristol where a fast motor yacht, chartered by Sabridin, awaited delivery of their precious cargo.

Back at the post office, Mrs. Langthorne heard Tess frantically scratching at the door. When she opened it Tess jumped up and down barking furiously, running a few yards then back to Mrs. Langthorne, saying in her limited powers of canine communication, "Follow me," which Isobel's mother had the good sense to do. Tess took her to the spot where her daughter was forced into the car, and ran about in circles with her nose to the ground. It was now terrifyingly obvious that something terrible had happened to Isobel.

Never in her whole life had Mrs. Langthorne felt such utter helplessness, which in turn, generated a paralysing sense of panic. Through this fog of indecision, Mrs. Langthorne knew that she must summon up all her reserves of physical and mental strength if she was to prevail over the forces of evil which once before had well-nigh destroyed both her and her daughter. She must return home, pull herself together and decide where she could turn for help which would be swift and positive.

In spite of the distance, all her instincts impelled her to ring Lance. A phone call to Cornwall Court revealed that he was not available but Mr. Howard was; would she like to speak with him? After a brief pause, Mrs. Langthorne confirmed that as it was a matter of extreme urgency she would speak to him and was put through without further delay.

Mr. Howard could sense that something dreadful must have happened and took the call at once. After Mrs. Langthorne had choked out the word Isobel, Mr. Howard said, "I am on my way."

He ordered his car and drove at break-neck speed to Tillingthorpe Post Office where he found a distraught Mrs. Langthorne who blurted out, "Isobel has disappeared."

Mr. Howard was stunned by this startling assertion and said,

"Sit down, my dear, and tell me as calmly as you are able, exactly what happened?" Mrs. Langthorne then explained that her daughter had gone for a short walk with her dog and failed to return. She also described Tess's agitated behaviour. Mr. Howard thought for a few minutes and rang the Oxford police, requesting that a senior officer be sent over immediately to investigate a very serious crime.

An inspector arrived after a lapse of an hour; a delay which exacerbated the impatience and anxiety Mrs. Langthorne suffered. Mr. Howard explained to the inspector the vague details available concerning the disappearance of his son's fiancée. The inspector said,

"It is quite obvious that this young lady has been abducted by persons unknown." After a brief questioning of Mrs. Langthorne, he turned to Mr. Howard saying, "I feel it prudent to observe a discreet silence as a blaze of publicity may panic the perpetrators and imperil this young lady's life. If we suppress all reference to this incident the criminals may be lulled into a false sense of security and give us an opportunity to make up some of the time that we have lost." He assured Mr. Howard and Isobel's mother that an immediate warning would be flashed to all ports and customs, plus an investigation into all strangers observed in the area over the preceding six weeks. The inspector added there was a remote possibility that the kidnappers might, in the next few days, demand a ransom. If this occurred, he must be informed without a moment's delay. The inspector took his departure after reiterating his promise to put his most competent C.I.D. officers on the case that very night.

When Mr. Howard and Mrs. Langthorne were alone, he exhorted her to return with him to Cornwall Court; an offer which Isobel's mother declined. Mr. Howard insisted, however, on remaining with her until long past midnight, and discussed the problem of keeping the abduction secret. For example, if Lance came to the post office to stay, the curiosity of the girls would be aroused and both agreed with the inspector that secrecy was absolutely imperative.

Mr. Howard phoned his son, Lance, and requested him to remain available as he would make a full report of the night's events when he returned.

Meanwhile, the base, sinister agents of the cunning Sabridin had carried the drugged Isobel on to the waiting motor yacht. The crew, three rascally Frenchmen, had let it be known around the docks they were awaiting a wealthy client whose hobby was big game fishing and their destination was Cornwall. The men who had delivered Isobel on to the yacht had already been paid off. The yacht headed straight out to sea into international waters. They would rendezvous with another agent south of Roscoff where the three men would be paid off with a dire warning of what would happen to them if they talked to the police.

Isobel was now transferred to a Rolls Royce limousine on the third stage of the journey to Marseilles where a state room had been reserved on a small cruise ship, which catered for tourists. The head steward had been generously tipped and informed that the young lady had been very ill and must not be disturbed. She was, the escorting nurse informed him, returning to India to rejoin her father, a colonel in the Indian army.

It must be remembered that Isobel had been in a drugged stupor for twenty-four hours and had been kept alive by glasses of milk or coffee which she drank mechanically without recognition of her surroundings.

Once possession of the state room had been accomplished, Isobel was permitted to regain consciousness and was offered a nicely served meal. She looked about her, utterly bewildered, and enquired of the nurse now in full uniform, "Where am I?"

The unscrupulous attendant replied, "You have been very ill and are on your way to recuperate at the house of an old friend of your late father."

"What old friend?" Isobel demanded.

"I do not know his name; I was only engaged to take care of you on the journey," the nurse responded. "When we reach Calcutta, I will be discharged," she added. "I live in Berkshire, England," Isobel persisted. "How did I get here?" Her custodian shrugged her shoulders and remained silent.

Isobel had recovered sufficiently to understand that she had been brought there against her will. She sat down to eat the meal laid before her in the knowledge that food would help her to recover from her severely debilitated condition. The next day, the captive felt a lot stronger and her brain was rapidly recovering from the highly potent drugs administered in the past forty-eight hours. All her early spartan training now began to assert itself and she could think more clearly, more lucidly and made a decision to remain dignified and aloof from this woman who was patently a renegade from her profession and a traitor to an honourable vocation.

"I would like some books to be brought to me," Isobel requested. "If I am to remain in enforced confinement I need something to relieve the mind-numbing tedium which I will suffer in this prison for the next three weeks."

Few people of Isobel's age could have survived the trauma of this nightmare experience, but it has already been revealed that Isobel was both resourceful and of very strong character. She would inform this ogre that she had exceedingly powerful, wealthy friends and relations not only in England but also in India. The nurse, who was also her gaoler, was visibly affected by this intelligence and Isobel, discerning this reaction, followed up this powerful sally by informing her that these friends, who included her fiancé and a colonel in the Bengal

Lancers, would never, never cease their efforts to bring the perpetrators of this criminal act – which incurred the severest penalties – to justice; even if it took years.

The nurse quailed at the mention of a fiancé and the colonel of the Bengal Lancers and now realised that she was deeply involved in an illegal and criminal conspiracy from which she could not extricate herself. The contemptible ogre turned deathly pale and lapsed into a long silence. Somehow she had to escape from her obligations, but how, was a serious problem, as she would not be paid the five hundred pounds until she delivered her charge to Sabridin's agent in Calcutta, and furthermore, she was mindful of the threat to cut her throat if she ever divulged the smallest details of the operation to any third party.

After hours of deep thought, she decided she must display a more respectful demeanour towards her prisoner and at the same time rigidly adhere to her instructions until she had concluded her commission and drew her considerable fee. She would then return to England where she would assume a false name and secure a post in another mental hospital. If she was ever caught she would plead complete ignorance of the illegality of the engagement.

After a boring voyage incarcerated in the state cabin they disembarked after Isobel had been stupefied once again with a mild drug. Sabridin's cousin and major-domo of his house in the hills ushered them through customs and presented a forged passport for his captive, explaining that Isobel was the daughter of a colonel in the Indian Army and was rejoining him after a prolonged illness. After parting with her charge, the nurse hastily returned to the ship having warned Sabridin's cousin of Isobel's family connections.

Ali Suleiman Mahomet was a worried man as he helped Isobel into the magnificent Rolls Royce. He had, in earlier years, served five years in an Indian prison for abducting children to be trained in Sabridin's carpet factory and was, therefore, keenly anxious not to repeat this very unpleasant experience. He cursed his imbecile cousin for implicating him in yet another illicit escapade which could result in him serving not five but ten years and that was a very high price to pay for the comfort and security he enjoyed as his cousin's steward. He must give this unwilling and latest involvement in his master's nefarious schemes a great deal of thought. He must, somehow, devise ways and means of disassociating himself from this seizing of an English memsahib which would surely incur the wrath of not one but four very powerful bodies; the Indian police, the Indian government, the Indian army, and the prisoner's own wealthy and highly influential relations and friends.

The major-domo shuddered at the mere thought of what these, unquestionably revengeful people could do to not only him and his stupid cousin but everybody in the house. He knew full well that the Indian police would arrest everyone, innocent or guilty. During the long dusty drive, he sat next to the driver, his head slumped on his chest, wrestling with the most dangerous problem in his whole life.

By the time they had reached their destination, he had formulated a plan to save himself from his bullying master's perilous imbecilic indiscretions. If his job in Sabridin's house meant a precarious life, constantly on the edge of a long spell in prison, he would gladly relinquish it for a humbler post, without this awful, perpetual anxiety and fear. He had a strong feeling that his master's conduct could even result in both their deaths.

Chapter 31

Back in England, the police had drawn a blank and it seemed that Isobel had completely vanished.

A week later, a letter arrived at the post office bearing an Indian postmark and was addressed to Mrs. Langthorne. It was from a firm of solicitors, known as Prakash & Patel, who practised in Calcutta. It tersely stated that as the late Colonel Langthorne had failed to repay the loan of fifty thousand pounds on the agreed date of September the twentieth, 1932, the terms of the contract, drawn up by them between his excellency Prince Sabridin Abdul Suliman, must now be implemented. As an honourable English gentlewoman they were sure she would raise no obstacles to the redemption of the security given by her late husband, Colonel Langthorne. A copy of the original agreement was enclosed for her perusal and retention.

Mrs. Langthorne was deathly pale as she read the contract and saw the unmistakable signature of her late beloved husband appended at the bottom. It had been signed in the presence of two witnesses. While she could not deny the evidence of her own eyes, she was equally convinced that her husband could never be guilty of such a base act.

The contract clearly stated that should the loan not be repaid on the specified date, the colonel would consent to an arranged marriage under Muslim law between his daughter, Isobel Langthorne, and their client, Prince Sabridin.

A black mist swam before the acutely distressed widow's eyes as she lurched towards the phone to call Lance, her only hope of support in her terrible dilemma. When the call came, Lance and his father and mother were in the library discussing the advisability of engaging the services of a private detective agency. Mrs. Langthorne was greatly relieved to hear the comforting voice of Lance who assured her he and his father would be with her in one hour.

While awaiting their arrival Mrs. Langthorne sat down to rescrutinise the dreadful document and in particular, the colonel's signature.

The two gentlemen arrived as they promised within the hour and Mrs. Langthorne handed the menacing letter to Mr. Howard. He read every word and extracting a small magnifying glass from his waistcoat pocket peered intently at the colonel's signature. He stared thoughtfully at the infamous document, replaced the magnifying glass in his pocket and addressed the words of comfort that Mrs. Langthorne was longing to hear. "This signature is a forgery and I feel convinced that we will have proof of my opinion before this day is over." Turning to Lance he said, "This letter is the breakthrough we have all been praying for. We now know where Isobel is; that is the most vital evidence of all. We also know, that if my suspicions are verified, this document can easily be invalidated in the Indian High Court." Turning to Mrs. Langthorne, he laid a comforting hand upon her shoulder saying, "Now all our worries are over and I would lay a thousand pounds to nothing that Isobel will be back in Tillingthorpe within four weeks."

It was decided that the police should not be informed of this most recent development, and also that all the Langthornes staff should be left with the impression that Isobel was on holiday at Cornwall Court. Mr. Howard said, "Come, Lance, we have work to do." They both bade Mrs. Langthorne *au revoir* and begged her not to worry as everything would be alright and promised to phone immediately they had checked the colonel's signature.

The Howards drove to Balliol College, Oxford, where an old friend of Mr. Howard, senior, was head of the Biochemistry Laboratory. After the customary exchange of pleasantries, Mr. Howard produced the alleged contract, requesting the professor to subject the offending signature to his most powerful microscope. The professor crossed to a bench, supporting an array of binocular microscopes. He slid the signature under the lens and after no more than ten seconds had elapsed, he turned to the two Howards and enquired, "What do you wish to know about it?"

"We would like to know if you could tell us if you suspect that it might be a forgery."

"It is a forgery," the Professor replied. "This signature has been traced. Look for yourself," he invited.

"Adjust this knurled screw to focus it to your eyes; now, do you see those tiny grooves where the forger has failed to follow the tracing precisely."

"Yes, I certainly do," exclaimed Mr. Howard in jubilant tones. "That's good enough for me; that's all the proof we need. Come, Lance, see for yourself, old chap." Lance peered through the lens and saw clearly the tiny grooves referred to by the professor. Mr. Howard thanked his old friend effusively for his invaluable assistance.

Father and son departed post haste to Tillingthorpe, where a very tense and anxious lady awaited the news she prayed to God they would bring. They arrived at the post office and without further ado, imparted the proof that the husband she had loved and cherished had been basely maligned and impugned. To a brave woman, who had endured so much, this was the straw that broke the proverbial camel's back and for the first time in her life Mrs. Langthorne lost her dignified self-control and collapsed in a deluge of tears.

Mr. Howard quickly poured her a glass of brandy and ordered Lance to make tea for them all. Over tea, they were all in a happy mood because Lance's fathers confident optimism proved infectious as he reassured them that Isobel would soon be back home, little the worse for her adventure.

After further discussion, it was agreed that Lance, Richard and Mr. Howard would charter a De Havilland plane and as soon as they could get authorisation, they would fly to Calcutta and pick up Akbar who would have a shrewd idea where Sabridin's minions had incarcerated Isobel.

Lance was a man of few words and was not given to bluster or indulging in empty threats, but inside, he was smouldering with fury and was more than physically capable of breaking Sabridin's vile neck like a dry stick.

After pulling a few convenient strings, the small party were on their way to release Lance's beloved fiancée from the dastardly villains who had dared to lay their filthy hands on this pure young woman who had once been the darling of the famous Bengal Lancers regiment. After two stops for refuelling at Brindisi and Karachi, they arrived at their hotel.

While all this feverish activity was in progress, Isobel had arrived at Sabridin's Palace perched on the slope of a steep hill clothed in rhododendrons. It was surrounded by high walls, with one entrance sealed by massive wrought iron gates. These gates were guarded, day and night, by armed guards.

Sabridin lived in regal splendour and it was rumoured that he had a large harem concealed in a separate wing with the traditional courtyard, lily pond and fountains.

Isobel was conducted to a spacious room, with bathroom and toilet adjoining. It was furnished luxuriously in the western style. Isobel was greatly relieved to see the well-fitted bathroom and used this welcome facility at once, as she had not bathed since she was captured. A young Anglo-Indian girl was appointed as her personal maid. She removed Isobel's clothing to be laundered and pressed, leaving an Indian sari for her to wear while this process was completed. After a refreshing bath, a meal was served of cold chicken and salad. These necessities gave Isobel new strength and a new confidence.

That evening, the maid whispered that a plan had been devised to assist Isobel in escaping and that she would be kept informed.

The next day, Isobel received a visit from Sabridin's steward who enquired if she was comfortable. Isobel sensed that this man was merely a pawn in the execution of the abduction plot, and it might be to her advantage to treat him as she had always treated servants in her father's household; with courtesy and kindness. Her dignified bearing and total lack of fear he found acutely disconcerting and this impelled him to pose the question, "Are you not afraid?"

"Afraid?" Isobel countered. "Why should I be afraid? Abduction is a very serious crime, even in India and right at this very moment, four very powerful men are in India and will effect my release within three days. My fiancée, my future father-in-law, who is an exceedingly wealthy and influential gentleman and my future brother-in-law, who was, until recently, an officer in the Bengal Lancers Regiment, of which my late father was colonel-in-chief. They will be accompanied by my late father's servant who is a subadar in the same regiment, who will guide them to this house."

The steward was now visibly disturbed by this enlightenment and decided, there and then, to set in motion his plan for self-survival. It was as he had feared: his stupid irresponsible cousin had involved him in a criminal conspiracy regarding this beautiful English woman and never once had he referred to her identity, nor the fact her father had been the commanding officer of the Bengal Lancers. He must act immediately if he was to avoid spending the rest of his life in the harsh foetid stinking environment of an Indian prison. He would order the chauffeur to take him into Calcutta, ostensibly to visit Sabridin's solicitors. Once there, he would warn them of all the facts; he would then leave by a rear entrance, go to the police station and turn informer. This would, at least, ensure a light sentence for himself.

While Isobel had been taken to Sabridin's Palace, Sabridin was over a thousand miles away in Bombay, visiting his carpet factories. He was in a very self-satisfied frame of mind; after all, in less than one month, he would marry the most beautiful woman in all India. The ceremony would be conducted with all the binding rites of Islamic law. That night he smoked his hookah pipe and sipped sweet strong coffee. He contemplated his future life, when he would show off his beautiful wife to all his visiting business friends, who would doubtless, be consumed with envy. What a pretty name she had: Isobel, he ruminated, so pretty.

She would wear the richest of silk saris, the finest of jewels would adorn her lovely form. It is often said that, 'Where ignorance is bliss, 'tis folly to be wise'. Never was this more applicable than in reference to Sabridin, for the next day, Nemesis would avenge her father's death and indirectly that of his bosom friend, the Maharajah of Bahadra.

Sabridin retired to bed a happy man; truly Allah was great and a curse on all infidels.

The next morning, he rose early to inspect his most important carpet factory and then he would travel back to his home to make plans for his wedding day. Sabridin always carried an ebony walking stick with a large solid silver knob. It was, in reality, a sword stick. It had a triangular blade forged to a long needle point; a fearsome weapon in the hands of an assassin. A twist-and-pull bayonet joint concealed by a silver band permitted the blade to be withdrawn swiftly. On this most fateful morning he swung the stick with an air of gay abandon.

Chapter 32

Sabridin entered the office where his manager was poring over his production records. He looked at his master with a flicker of alarm in his eyes. "Sahib," he said, "I have serious matters to report to you. Last night, two of our best workers absconded; one was our head trainer and the other our most experienced checker." The boys were thirteen and twelve years of age respectively, and both had been kidnapped from villages in Pakistan.

Sabridin flew into a blind rage, so typical of people who sniff heroin. He belaboured his unfortunate manager across his shoulders with his ebony stick. The manager, Ramada Savaundra Singh, a Hindu, was so deeply affronted and humiliated that he drew his dagger, concealed in his clothing, and savagely retaliated in a frenzy of stabbing. Sabridin fell to the ground in a pool of blood, his body irrigated by five deep stab wounds.

Ramada was now deeply shocked and terrified of discovery. He dragged the body into a small room at the rear of his office, closed and locked the door. He sat down and smoked a cigarette while deciding what to do. The office was apart from the main building and luckily there were no witnesses. Also, his master was an extremely secretive man and thus no one could be sure of his whereabouts at any given time. After a few minutes of intense thought, he had a plan of action. After the child slaves were asleep and under lock and key, he would drag the body out, load it into his car and drive out fifty miles and bury the corpse somewhere off the beaten track. Returning to his office he would thoroughly remove all traces of bloodstains, drive home and have a meal.

The next morning, he reported for work at his customary hour of seven. When the boys were assembled, he addressed them, saying that his master was displeased with the output and angry with the two boys who had absconded the night before; they would be recaptured and severely whipped, he assured them.

Ramada Savaundra Singh reversed his decision to run away because he was an intelligent man and realised that the police would immediately associate the disappearance of Sabridin with him. He would become the prime suspect and the Indian police were only too ready to arrest and jail on the qualification of suspicion. When the police called to interview him, as they surely would, he would tell them that Sabridin had been very angry when told that two of his boys had absconded and he would replace them at a later date as he had to return home at once. He would rigidly adhere to this story and ask their advice about the running of the factory.

Chapter 33

The rescue party, namely the two Howards and Richard had picked up Akbar from the barracks, whose eyes glowed with the ferocity of a tiger when told that his beloved mistress had been kidnapped by Sabridin. Akbar told them, "I know exactly where she has been taken to, but we must lose no time." Arming himself with a scimitar, a service pistol and rifle, they set off for the foothills of Darjeeling where Sabridin's palace was located. It was one hundred and fifty miles from Calcutta.

After a bumpy three hour journey, they arrived at their destination to find the impressive residence deserted, the wrought iron gates swinging open. Akbar, with scimitar in one hand and pistol in the other entered the house cautiously. It was as silent as the grave, totally deserted. Isobel, knowing they would come, had pinned her small lace-trimmed monogrammed handkerchief to a satin cushion. A further meticulous search of the house confirmed that no one remained.

Akbar led them to the guard house where he found blood spots on the flags; at least one of the guards had been shot, he concluded. They now searched the extensive garden and discovered a gardener cowering behind a growth of shrubs. Akbar drew his stave and gave him three smart blows saying, "Speak, dog, where is my mistress, the beautiful English memsahib?"

The terrified gardener replied, "I do not know, excellency, I only know that the police came here, shot one of the guards who had refused to open the gate and arrested every one in the house including all the servants."

The four men realised that they must visit the local police station and make their presence known. The quaking gardener directed them to the town of Patna and informed them that he had recognised one of the constables.

A discussion took place between the rescue party who assumed that Isobel was now in safe hands, and as they had driven one hundred and fifty miles and Patna was another fifty miles away, they should search the house for refreshments to sustain them. Akbar was despatched to locate the kitchen, where he found an abundance of food, much of it stored in ice containers immersed in a series of shallow wells to keep it fresh. Akbar, assisted by Richard, served cool drinks of orange and lemon, followed by biscuits and cheese, with all kinds of fruit for dessert. This meal was hastily consumed as all were anxious to resume the journey.

When they arrived at Patna, after another bone-jarring drive, Akbar enquired where the police station was to be found. On arrival Akbar introduced his companions and described the reason for their visit. They were promptly ushered into an inner office where they found Isobel and her maid sitting on cane chairs with a smiling police superintendent sitting at his desk. A joyous reunion took place from which the faithful Akbar was not excluded, but received with equal warmth.

Isobel swiftly briefed them concerning all she remembered from the night of the abduction. The police officer listened intently to all she had to say and cautiously requested that they remain available for another week to complete his enquiries.

Isobel desperately required a change of clothes and whispered this urgent need to Mr. Howard who, turning to the police officer, enquired if there was a train service between Patna and Calcutta. The officer informed him there was, but only three trains a day; they ran at four hour intervals. It was agreed they would all return to Calcutta where there was an excellent hotel, and travel back to Patna as required. Akbar would drive the hired car back accompanied by Richard.

It was also remembered that Isobel's mother must be informed by cablegram at the first available opportunity. On arrival in Calcutta, they checked in to a hotel where, after baths and an appetising meal served by liveried servants, they summoned a taxi instructing the driver to take them to the post office. A Cablegram was duly dispatched to Mrs. Langthorne; it stated simply:

ISOBEL, WELL, SAFE AND UNHARMED.

Richard rejoined them at eight, in time for dinner, after a dusty, exhausting journey. Akbar had returned to his barracks and was, no doubt, similarly refreshed.

The next morning Isobel and her maid set off escorted by Lance and his father on a shopping expedition. Mr. Howard had, very wisely, brought plenty of cash and told Isobel, very quietly, to buy whatever she needed, reminding her she would need a small suitcase for the journey home. He handed Isobel an envelope containing two hundred pounds which she blushingly accepted.

Entering the shop which displayed a wide variety of western clothes, Isobel chose strictly those of a utilitarian type; linen skirts, cotton shirt blouses, and so on, plus some exquisite hand-made silk lingerie, and a three-quarter length coat in black woollen material with a round astrakhan collar, which was fastened by silken cord toggles. This addition to her temporary wardrobe would be welcome on the return flight. The maid, who was still wearing a sari, was also provided with several items of western clothing. A medium size suitcase completed Isobel's purchases.

Lance and his father were awaiting them, sitting on a seat overlooking a small colourful garden. Neither Mr. Howard nor his son had ever been to India and were enthralled by the ever changing kaleidoscope of humanity streaming past their incredulous gaze. They all returned to their hotel to allow Isobel to change in time for lunch.

During coffee, they discussed the desirability of informing the superintendent of police at Oxford, who had been the first person to be called the night of Isobel's abduction. Lance vehemently expressed the opinion that he should be informed without further procrastination as it was still of the utmost urgency that he continue his efforts to apprehend the villainous rascals who had initiated the original seizure of Isobel.

A second visit was made to the post office and a second cablegram despatched, which stated:

ISOBEL LANGTHORNE FOUND UNHARMED IN INDIA STOP A FULL REPORT WILL BE GIVEN WHEN WE RETURN. STOP. (SIGNED) HOWARD.

A phone call to the police at Patna informed them of their place of residence and telephone number.

Chapter 34

Richard thoroughly enjoyed a visit to his former comrades in the regiment, although the visit was primarily to seek an audience with the commanding officer, Colonel Mackenzie. The colonel greeted him warmly and after enquiring how he liked civilian life and the welfare of his predecessor's wife and daughter, Richard informed him that Isobel had been kidnapped on the orders of Sabridin. He was happy to report that she had been rescued unharmed and was at that very moment staying at a hotel in Calcutta.

The colonel recoiled in his chair with blank astonishment and when Richard handed the forged contract sent to Mrs. Langthorne by Sabridin's lawyers for his perusal, he was even more astounded.

After reading and rereading the document, he looked at Richard saying, "Has this cunning fellow been arrested?"

"No," Richard replied. "Regrettably, he has apparently disappeared without trace."

"Well that's one mystery solved that has plagued me ever since Langthorne's death." The colonel then showed Richard the desk calendar displaying the date ringed in red ink: the twentieth of September, 1932, which he had never changed and was exactly as Colonel Langthorne had left it. "I have wracked my brains, many times, to discover the significance of this date which is also ringed in red in his personal diary. I wonder why the poor fellow felt the need to borrow such a large sum, and why of all people from a villainous character like Sabridin?"

The colonel asked Richard if he thought that Isobel would be distressed by a visit to her old home, as he would like to invite them all to dinner. Richard gladly accepted, assuring the colonel that Isobel would welcome an opportunity to convey her personal thanks to him for his generous help in the past. Also, he continued, it would be a rare and unexpected pleasure to present his adoptive father and brother to the regiment. The next night was designated as the most suitable.

Richard, realising Isobel would need to buy a new dress, hastened back to the hotel. Richard's fears, that Isobel might feel a modicum of distress when introduced back into an environment where a certain tragic event had made an indelible mark on her mind, were soon dispelled as he saw her joyous reaction to the invitation, and the prospect of a reunion with the young officers who had pandered so cheerfully to her every whim. Richard reminded Isobel that, although they had not brought dinner jackets, she would definitely need a suitable dress.

Turning to her fiancé Isobel said, "Could you loan me some money? I will pay you back when we get home, but it must be a loan as it would not be proper for you to buy my clothes," she smiled. Lance handed Isobel his wallet and urged her to take whatever she needed. The next morning, she explored the shops to purchase a dark red velvet gown. Only one shop stocked this material, but to her great disappointment, there were no dresses. Seeing the unhappiness reflected in her face, the owners of the shop consoled the beautiful memsahib by suggesting that they could make the dress in time, providing she chose a suitable design. Isobel was full of gratitude for this kindly offer and explained she would like a tight fitting bodice, which exposed her shoulders, with a full skirt down to her shoes. Measurements were swiftly taken and Isobel was asked to come back at six o'clock when it would be ready. At six, Isobel returned with her maid and anxiously hoped that the dress would fit.

The proprietors with their assistants, all in their colourful saris, flitted around her like gorgeous butterflies round a flower. It fitted to perfection, the bodice, being a trifle tight, showed off Isobel's youthful figure. Isobel was an affectionate personality and in her innocence impulsive with it, thus in her gratitude she hugged each of the women in turn, who displayed their surprise and pleasure in radiant flashing smiles. Such appreciation had never been expressed so delightfully in their shop by the patrons before. They would not forget this beautiful English memsahib.

Mr. Howard and his two sons had made themselves as presentable as circumstances permitted. All three men wore drill tunics and trousers. Isobel looked stunning in her dark red velvet dress with a white rose in her hair, which shone with much brushing by her maid.

On the way to the officer's mess, Isobel expressed her anxiety concerning the maid's future once they had taken their departure. She told them of the plan conceived by this maid to aid her escape from Sabridin's house. She could not, therefore, just abandon her. It was decided to have a full discussion with this young girl the following day and the subject was dropped until some positive action could be taken.

They arrived at Colonel Mackenzie's house at seven thirty-five in the evening. Isobel looked around at the familiar rooms which had once been her home, and remarked to Richard how strange she felt to be back in a house which she had never expected to see again. "You must never look back, old girl, only to the future life that you will enjoy as mistress of Cornwall Court."

The colonel conducted his guests to the mess for drinks before dinner, where Isobel was greeted warmly by the officers who had once been a part of her every day life. Lance and his father looked round the unfamiliar room with much interest, mingled with curiosity, as this is where their adopted son and brother, respectively, had spent several exciting years of his life as a young cavalry officer. Many trophies for polo, shooting, cricket and tennis gleamed in their glass cabinets; all impressive works of the Indian silversmiths.

As the colonel moved to his place at the long table, bedecked with the finest regimental silver, he signalled to his guests to sit near him. Richard remained standing and when the usual hubbub subsided, he addressed his apologies to the assembled officers for he, his father and brother, Lance, in failing to honour mess regulations to appear in more formal attire. "We left England in considerable haste, on a very important mission, and never expected to have the pleasure of dining in the officer's mess of the finest cavalry regiment in India." This announcement was greeted with a murmur of approval from around the table. All eyes were on Isobel and most of them had known her when she was the colonel's daughter.

After dinner, when the port was served, Mr. Howard intimated that any of Richard's brother officers, who might be taking their precious leave in England, would be welcome to spend a few days at Cornwall Court, should they feel disposed to do so. Richard and Isobel made their farewells and hoped that an opportunity would present itself for another reunion in the years to come and reminded all of Mr. Howard's invitation.

Back in the colonel's house, they discussed the events surrounding Isobel's abduction, but certain aspects of Colonel Langthorne's death were discreetly omitted. At midnight, they took their leave of Colonel Mackenzie thanking him for the hospitality accorded them by he and his officers. Isobel had the last word by imploring him to come to her wedding in May. He embraced her and promised he would make strenuous efforts to accept; then exhorting her to convey his good wishes and compliments to her mother, kissed her goodbye. As they waited for the colonel's chauffeur, Mr. Howard gazed up into the night sky and remarked how beautiful and awe inspiring it was.

Chapter 35

Isobel rose late, as her experiences over the past week were now beginning to take their toll of her reserves of nervous energy.

Mr. Howard was on the phone to the chief of police at Patna enquiring if any developments had occurred in their pursuit of Sabridin. The officer informed him that Sabridin's grave had been discovered by shepherds, approximately sixty miles north-west of Bombay and Ramada Savaundra Singh had confessed to his murder. Ramada, the police officer added, was a very stubborn man but had finally succumbed to long and intensive interrogation. Mr. Howard could well imagine what that statement implied and muttered, "Poor devil."

"Will you require our presence at Patna as witnesses?" Mr. Howard enquired.

"No," the police officer replied, "We have the evidence of Sabridin's steward corroborating the abduction and Ramada's confession is all we require. A verdict of guilty is more or less a foregone conclusion."

"What will happen to Ramada?" Mr. Howard persisted.

"As you are aware, murder, as in your own country, is a capital offence; he will, therefore, be hanged." Mr. Howard shuddered at the thought of this awful mode of terminating the life of a fellow human being and concluded the conversation by thanking the police superintendent for his efficiency and courtesy and rang off. He put the phone down with a thoughtful expression on his face.

Ramada might have been guilty of murder, but he had also removed an evil man who could have been a constant threat to his future daughter-in-law. That night at dinner, he broached the subject of Ramada to his two sons, Lance and Richard. He stated that he would like their views on his thoughts that morning after his conversation with the police at Patna. He reminded them that Ramada had rendered them all a great service when he had murdered Sabridin, not least because Isobel could once more resume her carefree life without the menace of Sabridin in the background. Mr. Howard paused as his two sons urged him to proceed. "Well, I can't help thinking of that poor wretch, Ramada, sitting in Patna gaol."

"You want us to help him?" Lance interjected.

"Yes," his father responded.

"What do you have in mind?" his sons chorused.

"The briefing of a good lawyer," he exclaimed.

"Good," Lance agreed, "Let's do it tomorrow."

On the morrow they enquired of the hotelier where they could obtain the services of a good criminal lawyer. He mentioned a name and after consulting the telephone directory gave them the address. They summoned a taxi and ordered the driver to proceed to the address given. The driver drew up outside a large white house. The very English looking brass plate indicated that these were the chambers of Ram Singh Mahara, B.A. (Oxon.). A servant admitted them to a cool waiting room. After no more than ten minutes, an Indian gentleman appeared, wearing a perfectly cut English suit, his head bound neatly in the traditional turban. He invited them to enter his consulting room, furnished with good, solid-looking furniture. Lance said, "I see you went to Oxford. May I ask which particular college you attended?"

"Brasenose," the lawyer replied. "I enjoyed every minute of my stay and made many lasting friendships. I must confess I missed my polo. But you, sir, you went to Oxford?"

"Yes." Lance replied, "I went to Magdalen."

"Well, well, what a small world it is and what brings you to my chambers, gentlemen?"

Mr. Howard briefed him fully concerning all the bizarre events of the preceding seven days. He also explained that it was now imperative that they all returned home, but before doing so, he would like to retain his services to defend the unfortunate Ramada Savaundra Singh now languishing in Patna Prison. "Now," Mr. Howard continued, "We would like to dispose of your fees before our departure; thus I must now pose the two questions. A) Will you accept the defending brief? And B) What will be your total fee?"

After a superficial appraisal of the case, the lawyer said, "I must warn you that it will not be an easy task for this is India, not England, and the evidence is so strong against Ramada that I cannot promise to secure an acquittal, but I can only try for a prison sentence. As for your second question, my fee would be one thousand rupees, adjustable either way." Lance wrote a cheque for five hundred rupees and Mr. Howard handed him a cheque for another five hundred rupees. They shook hands with the lawyer, thanking him profusely for accepting the brief and said goodbye.

They returned to the hotel and after dinner, Mr. Howard expressed his anxiety to return to England as there were commitments which had been left in abeyance too long, and also living in austere conditions that he found somewhat inconvenient. Therefore, turning to Lance's fiancée, he raised the last outstanding problem: what to do about her temporary maid, acquired as a result of such nerve-wracking and painful events. "We can't take her with us, because I doubt if she has a passport."

"Well," Isobel responded, "I do not require a maid but we might be able to find her a job among the married couples of the regiment."

"But you will need a maid after we're married," exclaimed Lance.

"Since I left India, I have managed without one," Isobel replied. "Nevertheless, she is very proficient, intelligent and brightly cheerful and I would like to help her. After all, she had plans to help me escape and that alone is something for us all to be grateful for; she could have lost her life had events turned against me." Lance, ever the practical one of the three gentlemen, proposed that the young lady in question should be sent for to ascertain what she would like to do.

"I will fetch her," Isobel exclaimed, and rising from her chair hurried to her room. "Janet, I want you to come to meet my friends, who are at this moment, trying to decide how they can help and reward you for all the support you gave me in a very dangerous situation." Taking her by the hand, Isobel led her to where her companions awaited them.

All three men rose from their seats: Isobel then introduced Janet. After these formalities, Mr. Howard addressed this young woman, saying, "Now, my dear, how may we help you; tell us something of your background." Janet was about five feet eight inches tall, with dark, wavy auburn hair gathered at the nape of her neck by a tortoiseshell slide.

"My name is Janet MacDonald. I am eighteen years of age. My father was a corporal in the Royal Horse Artillery. He was killed during his service on the north-west Frontier. My mother sold me to Sabridin when I was sixteen years of age. Indian men regard women with auburn hair as a prized possession. That's exactly what I became, a chattel of Sabridin. Luckily, he already had two very beautiful Indian wives of high caste. They excluded me from his presence, which means that I became a slave to these two women."

Lance had already decided that this young girl would make an excellent companion for his future wife and he would, therefore, pay all her expenses to return to England. As she sat there in her Indian sari and slippers, the three gentlemen thought what an incongruous spectacle to see this attractive young girl dressed in Indian attire speaking flawless English. "Now tell us how we can help you," Mr. Howard enquired, adding, "Do you have an English passport?" Janet affirmed that she did not.

Lance, turning to his father, begged to be excused for interrupting, and said, "I will pay for Janet to come back to England." Turning to Janet he said, "These last few hectic days you have been acting as maid to my fiancée. Would you care to continue in that capacity until you return to England? Once you are home, you can make a final decision as to what you would like to do with your future life." Janet, realising that she was in a precarious position without money or a job, seized this opportunity to return to England with alacrity, gratitude shining in her tawny eyes.

After she had retired, it was decided that Mr. Howard would take Janet into Calcutta the following day to visit the British Embassy to obtain a passport. He anticipated some difficulties as she would also need to produce her birth certificate, which she did not possess. On arrival at the Embassy, Mr. Howard introduced himself and gave his home address, Cornwall Court. He was immensely relieved the lack of a birth certificate was not an insurmountable problem because army records were meticulously accurate and comprehensive. The assistant disappeared into another room and after a brief absence returned carrying a sheet of paper. He asked Janet her full name. "Janet Flora MacDonald," she replied.

"And your father's name?"

"Donald Glenveagan MacDonald."

"And your mother's name?"

"Shari Mohammet Ranji," she asserted.

The junior diplomat smiled and said, "There is one more simple formality to complete the application: a photograph. If you leave this office, turn left and then right, you will find several studios where you will obtain the regulation size."

While Mr. Howard was thus engaged, Richard rang Colonel Mackenzie concerning Akbar's discharge from the army. The colonel promised that he would expedite the application, but that it would not be confirmed for another month. Richard tendered his thanks, reminding his former commanding officer that Isobel would be keenly disappointed should he not be able to attend her wedding in approximately ten weeks' time.

Lance had not been idle while his father and brother were so preoccupied. He had visited the booking office of British Imperial Airways to make five reservations on the ten o'clock in the morning flight to England. They had now been absent from home for nearly two weeks and were very naturally looking forward to the hour when they would be reunited with their families.

The conversation round the dinner table would not be dull and Lance's sisters would listen avidly to a detailed account of their adventures, wishing at the same time that they could have shared in these incredible experiences so reminiscent of a novel by the famous female Edwardian novelist, Maud Diver.

The flight home was, thankfully, uneventful with Isobel spending most of the journey fast asleep leaning on her fiancé's broad shoulders. They arrived at London on a cool showery morning all saying how good it was to be back in England. Such was their eagerness to be home, that after negotiating customs they crossed to Paddington where they caught the fast train to Oxford. From thence they would all proceed to Cornwall Court and once there, would arrange for Mrs. Langthorne to be fetched.

Arriving at Cornwall Court at four o'clock to an animated reception, all expressed their immediate desire to immerse themselves in a deep hot bath and to don a change of clothing. Isobel, accompanied by her maid, was conducted to the large room occupied by Mrs. Langthorne and her daughter on a previous visit.

The intrepid adventurers were now fully refreshed and gathered in the library to brief their eager audience, who simply refused to wait for a full account from the day they left England to execute the rescue mission. Isobel's newly acquired maid, Janet Flora MacDonald, declined the invitation to dine with the family and elected to remain in her room. When Mrs. Howard was informed she promptly gave orders for a tray of food to be served for her.

Mr. Howard had dispatched a car to fetch Isobel's mother, who doubtless, would be longing to be reunited with her daughter after the acute anxiety and fear she had endured over the past two weeks.

When the butler announced her arrival and showed her into the drawing room, Isobel leapt to her feet, begged to be excused and hurried to meet her mother. The mother inspected her daughter, looking for signs of severe physical and mental stress, but was astonished to see Isobel looking confident and very fit. On the other hand, Isobel was shocked to perceive the signs of profound and protracted suffering so deeply etched on her mother's countenance. After a while, they were joined by the family who felt shocked also by the appearance of Isobel's mother. Granville dispensed brandy all round, at the request of Mr. Howard and all were grateful for this thoughtful act.

It was decided that Isobel and her mother, accompanied by Janet MacDonald, would return to Tillingthorpe that evening escorted by Lance and Richard.

Even the robust Mr. Howard was now feeling somewhat fatigued and looking forward to a good night's sleep in his own bed.

In their home at the post office there were four bedrooms, so Isobel's new maid could be easily accommodated, and the Langthornes could, with their substantial income – now enhanced by the coffee shop – well afford to pay her wages.

Tess gave them all a joyous, if frantic reception. Mrs. Langthorne made coffee while Isobel thanked her escort for all they had accomplished to restore her to her mother. She added, "You know, I was so certain that you would find me that never for one moment did I experience the slightest twinge of apprehension; and good has emerged from this unpleasant adventure. Sabridin is no longer a threat to me or any other unfortunate person who might attract his evil covetous ambitions."

The two gentlemen kissed Isobel and her mother goodbye, Lance assuring them he would be back soon. After Lance and Richard had departed, Isobel and her mother talked long into the night until sheer exhaustion forced them to bed.

Chapter 36

The next ten weeks would be fraught with activity, and many family conferences would be necessary to complete all the vital preparations to ensure that the forthcoming wedding proceeded smoothly, to guarantee the happy couple's big day would not be marred by petty upsets.

Mr. and Mrs. Howard had already offered to provide the reception at Cornwall Court; this would relieve Isobel and her mother of the worry and tensions generated by these occasions. Lance would arrange all the transport. This would leave the Langthornes to concentrate on Isobels wedding dress and the invitations.

That indispensable latter-day Solomon, the Reverend Copplethwaite, who would perform the ceremony in his church, would once again be begged to render his aid in finding four little girls from the village to support the bride on this glorious day. A day the children of Tillingthorpe would tell their children about.

Viscount Beldrake had gladly consented to give the bride away.

All the inhabitants of Tillingthorpe would be invited, plus, of course, the tenants of the Howard estate.

Two marquees had been ordered from Selfridges of London and a firm of caterers in Oxford would arrange a lavish running buffet. The family would sit down to a reception in the house. Coaches would be provided to transport the villagers and tenants. The celebrations would end at ten, with a splendid fireworks display staged by the famous makers Brocks. A strong contingent of police from Oxford would be despatched to patrol the grounds and park.

Mr. Howard, now completely recovered from his gruelling ten days in India, had spoken to the superintendent of police in Oxford

and given him a brief account of all that had transpired, promising a detailed report after his son's wedding.

Mrs. Langthorne had received a letter from Colonel Mackenzie, informing her that he would be coming to the wedding and he would be granted three months' leave. The colonel had good cause to rejoice on Isobel's wedding day, for he too would find romance and eventually a wife to bring his bachelorhood to a pleasant end. That, however, must be left locked in Dame Fate's locker, to be brought out only when she deemed the day and the precise hour had come.

A visit to Cock-a-Dobbie Cottage relieved Isobel of a great anxiety when Kate Devereaux revealed that, far from forgetting her promise, she had prepared two designs of wedding dresses, one in a medieval style and one of a crinoline type, which instantly appealed to Isobel. They then discussed the elaborations.

The main part of the dress would consist of ivory satin and the overlay on the skirt, Indian white silk. The neckline would be heart shaped, edged with guipure lace of small roses. It would have a plain close fitting bodice with the waistline curved to heart shape, outlined with rosebuds. The front and back panels would be in plain ivory satin in the crinoline mode, with fullness at the sides and back. The overlay on the skirt, of Indian white silk, would be draped to the sides. It would be scalloped with lace edging and delicately embroidered at intervals with roses. The long sleeves of ivory satin were to be slightly puffed at the shoulder. The whole concoction was to convey a magical picture of an enchanting princess. White satin shoes would complete the ensemble. Finally the coronet, that Mr. Howard had desired Isobel to wear at her wedding, would adorn her head like a crown.

Isobel returned home with the sketches to seek her mother's opinion of her choice. Mrs. Langthorne unhesitatingly agreed with Isobel's selection and reminded her daughter that there must be several women in the village more than capable of assisting Kate with the sewing.

Chapter 37

English villages do not pivot on any one person or family, so life goes on as it has done for centuries, with every man, woman and child contributing to the fabric of life's tapestry.

The blacksmith's adopted son, Robert, was now fifteen years old, and life with the Copelands went from strength to strength. He was happy and content and glowed with good health. As Lucy would say, "We have 'done him right'!"

Timothy was also thriving as an apprentice with Timber Woods and both he and his wife regarded him as a son.

Joshua and Hilda had even discussed adoption; for as Joshua had been reminded by his wife, they must have someone to take over The Red Lion and look after them in their old age. The innkeeper promptly told his beloved Hilda that he could look after himself and her if need be, but the pub and the licence were another matter. That was important he agreed and he promised to give the idea some thought. He would discuss the pros and cons with his old friend, the smith, who had knowledge of these matters.

Joshua spoke to Bill that night. Bill glowed with pleasure as his wisdom and advice were sought by his lifelong friend. After Bill had downed his first pint, he said,

"Joshua, old son, you couldn't do better. Our lad has changed our lives; we've got someone to live for, someone to work for and I'll tell you, Joshua, Lucy has never been so content. She's a different woman, and another thing, Robert will take over the forge when I retire and that is a very comforting thought, Joshua. Yes, you go ahead, you can't go wrong; I recommend adoption."

After closing time, Joshua sat down to his supper deep in thought; he was mulling over all that the smith had said. "Something on your mind, Joshua?" Hilda queried.

"Yes," he replied, "I have been talking to Bill about adopting a boy, like he and Lucy did."

Hilda's body perceptibly stiffened, her eyes became alert as her primitive maternal instincts welled up inside her. "Adoption?" Hilda repeated quietly.

"Yes, like you were saying the other day. Bill thinks it's a good idea; couldn't go wrong, he says."

Hilda stared at her husband for a brief moment and said, "Let's do something tomorrow, Joshua, no point in putting it off. Let's ring up the orphanage and ask if someone can call soon." Hilda was anxious to act before Joshua could have second thoughts.

"Alright," he agreed, "but before we do, are you sure you can cope with a child; remember it will mean a lot of hard work for you."

"Yes, yes," Hilda exclaimed vehemently, "That will not bother me one jot." The following morning, Hilda rang the orphanage who took all their particulars and promised to call on the Thursday.

While the Humphreys were deeply engrossed in their adoption plans, Isobel was making a list of guests to be invited to her wedding. There would not be many invitation cards, because the inhabitants of Tillingthorpe had been invited *en bloc*. Viscount Beldrake would give her away. There remained only his sister, Phillipa Sylvia Beldrake, Mr. Pringle and Colonel Mackenzie. The Howard girls had told Isobel and her mother that they would design and despatch all the invitation cards, which would relieve the Langthornes of a great deal of worry.

Four little girls from the village had been chosen by the vicar to be bridesmaids and had been measured by Kate Devereaux for their dresses. Intense disappointment would be felt by the children who had not been selected. The stonemason's twins, Rose and Dorothy Marriot, aged twelve years, Mary Griffin's younger sister, Lily, and Hilda Humphrey's niece, Rachel Evans, both aged ten years, completed the bride's retinue.

They would wear miniature crinoline dresses. The twins would be the colour of bluebells and the other two primrose yellow. The design to be very simple. The heart-shaped neckline would be embroidered with pink rosebuds and the two flounces round the skirt thickly embroidered with forget-me-nots. They would all wear heart shaped gold lockets; a present from the bridegroom. On their heads would be circlets of orange blossom. The bridesmaids would carry small posies of white roses. The bride's bouquet would comprise white roses and lily of the valley. The present from Lance to Isobel was a large oval gold locket in three sections. The centre held a portrait of Isobel in one side. On the back of this section was a portrait of Lance. The two outer compartments would contain portraits of Isobel's mother and father. All were painted by Italian artists in oils on ivory ovals. On the front were the intertwined initials of Lance and Isobel. On the back were the arms of the Howards in enamel. Isobel gave Lance gold cufflinks, with the arms of the Howards in coloured enamel.

Only close friends and family would sit down to the reception in the Great Hall of the house.

Chapter 38

All the excitement of this once in a lifetime event must not divert us from the more mundane, but no less vital aspects of life in Tillingthorpe. In 1935, the English landscape had not yet been ravaged by the predatorial developers and the short-sighted destroyers of the hedgerows which conserve the soil, shelter the stock and also provide a haven for weasels, stoats, shrews, field mice and many birds. The raucous, reeking tractor, although more common, had not yet eliminated the shire horse, and thus, the picturesque, nostalgic sight of teams ploughing the stubble could still be seen.

Children would make their way to the stream, near the village, armed with glass jam jars fitted, by their mothers, with cleverly contrived handles made of cord. With their white nets secured to the end of long canes, and twittering like small flocks of sparrows, they would follow the footpath across the meadow to the stream. No ghastly, evil perverts lurked in the bushes waiting to destroy their carefree childhood innocence or worse, to snuff out their unfulfilled life. They would return home in triumph to display their catch of sticklebacks or perhaps a newt to their parents.

Hilda had spent all her time brushing and polishing every room in the inn in preparation for the visit of the official from the orphanage, and every night said a little prayer that the official would view their case favourably. He arrived, as promised, on the Thursday and after a few customary questions, requested Joshua's wife to show him around their home. After satisfying himself that it conformed to the stringent standards imposed by the home, he promised to call on them on the following Thursday, exactly one week hence. He would then tell them more about the conditions of adoption and the boy whom they proposed. Joshua seized this opportunity to tell him they would prefer a boy, as they hoped that, one day, he would inherit the pub, which had such historic connections with his family dating back one hundred and fifty years. The gentleman appeared to be impressed with this piece of family history and was shown out by Hilda.

Mrs. Langthorne always remarked that Tillingthorpe in the spring was the epitome of all that was English. In May, it was Isobel's birthday, and on the twentieth – her wedding day – she would be twenty-one years of age. The hawthorn would be spreading its almond-like perfume and the several lilac and laburnum trees in the village would be in full bloom. Isobel's mother prayed that the sun would shine for her daughter's wedding; that would make everything just perfect.

Two fittings had been made for the dress and Kate, aided by another woman, was now putting the finishing touches to a spectacular bridal gown which would bring gasps of delight from the congregation.

The large Norman church had been built by Roger de Caen who had been a favourite of Richard the First, who had endowed him with vast estates. He had fought in the Crusades and like many of his compatriots, he had erected the church as a thanksgiving to God for his safe deliverance from the wars.

It had a wide centre aisle with two rows of pews to the right and left. Massive Norman arches divided the centre of the church from the other wings of flanking pews. The nail-studded door was sheltered by a porch, fitted with oak bench seats. On a wooden noticeboard were pinned parochial notices with two rotas of cleaning duties and flower arranging. The flagstones were deeply worn into a wide groove by many, many generations of parishioners, not all of whom were devout Christians. They attended merely because they were afraid of incurring the wrath of not only the Lord of the Manor, but also for fear of the vicar, who would condemn them to eternal damnation. In those days of superstition and ignorance, this was a threat not to be taken lightly.

To the right of the door a tomb – known as a table top tomb – contained the mortal remains of one Hubert Beldrake who died, according to the legend carved on the slab of marble, in the year 1468 of colic. To the left of the door, at the foot of the belfry, a most ornate canopied alabaster tomb supported the recumbent effigies of Lord Beldrake and his lady in full Elizabethan dress, who were laid to rest in the year 1540. Several other Beldrakes occupied the mortuary vaults beneath the centre aisle.

On the walls were several plaques, memorials to military officers who had faithfully served king or queen and country in far-flung foreign lands.

The tomb of Roger de Caen was located near the first step to Heaven, adjacent to the altar. The benefactors of this magnificent church felt that Roger was entitled to be first in the queue when the trumpets sounded the Resurrection. His recumbent figure dressed in chain mail, his crossed legs proclaiming to all the world that he fought valiantly against the heathen in the Crusades. His foot rested on a small stone lion.

This then was the ancient inspiring setting for Isobel's marriage to Lance.

All the invitation cards had now been despatched; they were of simple design. The arms of the Langthornes and the Howards were displayed at the top of a single gold-edged card, the words couched in copperplate writing, requested the honour of the recipient's presence at the forthcoming wedding.

Isobel would have one more fitting for her gown then spend her last few days at Cornwall Court as a spinster lady.

Joshua's wife had received a visit from the orphanage official, who fully briefed them on the conditions and terms of remuneration.

Hilda assured him that the money was not important but, given the opportunity, they would love and cherish any suitable boy entrusted to them. The gentleman from the home replied, "We have chosen a young boy of twelve years of age. We have deliberated in protracted consultations to find a youth who could be trusted to fit into the environment of licensed premises. As I told you on my previous visit, it is contrary to the policy of the adoption committee to place boys in households where they may be exposed to temptation." Joshua hastily retorted, a trifle belligerently, that they ran a highly respected public house and in any case, the boy would not be permitted to enter the public areas. The official replied,

"Please do not take umbrage, Mr. Humphrey, but we do have to be extremely careful, for I can tell you that not all of the boys are little angels! Now," he proceeded, "the boy that we have in mind was a foundling; his name is Nicholas Carol and, if I may make a suggestion, should you be completely satisfied, you could, at some later date, have his name changed by deed poll to Nicholas Carol Humphrey." Joshua thought that was a capital idea and could visualise the name over the door:

LICENSEE, NICHOLAS HUMPHREY.

That really warmed the cockles of Joshua's heart.

"If the boy was a foundling, how do you know his name?" Hilda demanded.

"He was found by some carol singers one Christmas Eve, hence the name of Nicholas, who is, as you know, the patron saint of Christmas, and the name Carol: well that is obvious."

Joshua and Hilda bade the official goodbye and called, "We'll see you on Wednesday morning, then, that's our quietest day."

In Oxford, contrary to all their fears, the coffee shop continued to thrive and Jane had announced her engagement, but Oxford did not have a monopoly of romance, for Timothy now did all his mother's shopping and his mother – shrewd in the ways of the world – knew exactly why her son was always so ready to cope with a chore he had previously executed so grudgingly. He was in love with Mary Griffin and the young sweethearts were often observed strolling hand in hand through the meadows when Mary took Tess for exercise.

Hilda was counting the hours to Wednesday morning when, if all went well, their humdrum lives would assume a new significance, a new purpose. Even Joshua had a new light in his eyes and often wondered what the boy would be like. Joshua prayed that they would be as lucky as the smith and his wife had been. Hilda, his wife, looked so radiant in anticipation that Joshua thought how pretty she was and felt it necessary to warn her of disappointment.

The man from the orphanage was, as the orphans were constantly exhorted to be, punctual. Hilda surveyed the youth standing at the gentleman's elbow, looking for any signs of abnormalities, cross eyes, bow legs, curvature of the spine, and so on. The boy stared back at Hilda with his large brown eyes, uncowed by her scrutiny. Hilda Humphrey was impressed by what she saw and smiled at him.

While his wife was satisfying herself concerning the youth's physical attributes, Joshua was judging his character and no man was more qualified to make that vital judgement than a man who has lived with and fought with men of all types in the appalling conditions of trench warfare. Joshua knew that here was a boy they could trust and love. His face broke into a broad smile, as the sun breaks through a black raincloud, piercing the woods and trees with sunbeams like the thrusts of a rapier in the hands of a master swordsman.

The young boy smiled back, and man and wife knew their mutual happiness had been sealed by that fleeting illumination of the face of their son, for that was how they would always regard him. "Well, boy, what do you have to say, do you think you could be happy with us?"

"Yes, sir," the boy responded with surprising alacrity. Hilda, with her womanly powers of intuition, had already decided she would give this orphan a good home and lots of love.

The official then reminded all three that there would be a six month probationary period, which would permit any one of them to withdraw. During this six months, they would be paid three pounds a week. After a 'see you all in six months time', the man from the orphanage returned to his duties and to many other deserving children whom he hoped would be as fortunate.

Hilda summoned Nicholas to show him his room. All the rooms in The Red Lion were large and this particular room quite overwhelmed the small boy. To him, it was as large as the dormitory that he had shared with ten other boys. It was situated at the rear of the house and looked over the courtyard with its two tall walnut trees. A view of the downs was also visible in the distance. A double bed was placed at one end, covered by a colourful patchwork quilt. A large mahogany wardrobe at the other end was complemented by a dressing table near one of the two windows.

Nicholas gazed round, with eyes like saucers, and turning to Hilda said,

"I have always slept by myself in a little iron bed, never with other people in a big bed." Hilda laughed and assured him that only he would occupy the double bed and indeed the room was his very own. She opened the wardrobe and withdrew two drawers in the dressing table which would be more than sufficient to accommodate his few possessions. A few hunting prints adorned the walls. The boy opened his small case containing two rough towels, a bar of hard soap, a comb and a spare shirt and placed them in the open drawers, placing a small night-shirt on top. Hilda then took him by the hand along the landing and showed him where she and her husband slept, just so that he would know where to come if he became scared in the night.

Hilda knew enough about small boys to know that they were always hungry. Ordering him to wash his hands, she placed a glass of milk and a wedge of homemade cake before him. Leaving Hilda to fuss over her new charge, like a hen with a newly hatched chick, we shall return to the star of the forthcoming wedding.

At that precise moment, Isobel was being dressed in all her bridal glory in the dress created by her friend, Kate. The kitchen table had been pushed aside to make room for the voluminous gown. The critical eye of Kate surveyed the bridal gown, searching for the smallest flaws and could find none. Kate and her helper were more than pleased with their handiwork and rapturously acclaimed how beautiful Isobel looked. The dress was carefully removed and placed into a capacious box acquired for the purpose. It would then be taken to the rectory and placed under lock and key. Kate would dress Isobel for her wedding day and travel to the church with the bride.

The appointed day, now only two weeks away: Thursday, had been carefully chosen to permit the maximum amount of privacy. Another weekend at Cornwall Court would allow Isobel to finalise all arrangements with her fiancé and his family and to rest, away from the hubbub of the post office.

A word must now be devoted to the worthy Mr. Pringle who has figured so prominently in the Langthornes lives. At Isobel's wish an invitation had been sent to him and moreover he would be one of the chosen few to sit down at the reception in the Great Hall.

When Mr. Pringle received the envelope containing the invitation, he peered at the neat unfamiliar handwriting of Margaret Howard and once again, the magnifying glass was extricated from the drawer in his desk and the postmark, the stamp, and every letter of the address was intensely scrutinised. He selected a knife from the drawer and cautiously opened the envelope. He gingerly withdrew the card embossed with its coats of arms and read the gold copperplate writing, requesting the honour of Mr. and Mrs. Pringle's presence at the forthcoming wedding of Miss Isobel Langthorne, only daughter of Mrs. and the late Colonel Langthorne.

The blood rushed to Mr. Pringle's brain turning his normally pallid face a curious colour that may only be described as puce. He felt faint and staggering to a cupboard, groped into its depths to locate a bottle of brandy, hidden away behind stacks of forms for Wireless Licences, Gun Licences, Dog Licences and his pride and joy, Notification of Bubonic Plague forms. His shaking hands located the life saving bottle and removing the cork, he imbibed a prodigious gulp. The fiery liquor calmed his palpitating heart and returning to his desk, he grasped the magnifying glass to confirm the message that he and his wife were invited to the church and afterwards to the reception in the Great Hall of Cornwall Court. Tickets would, in due course, be despatched.

Mr. Pringle was now calm but very elated; he decided this was the opportunity to take his bumptious father-in-law down a peg or two. For years, he had suffered the lash of contempt wielded, so unfairly, by his superior and he would strike while the iron was hot so to speak.

Donning his grey trilby hat he made his way to the bus stop to catch the vehicle which would speed him on his way to confront his tormentor in his own den.

On arrival at his superior's office, he knocked, not timidly, as was his wont heretofore, but with a thunderous assault on the mahogany door, which had guarded the inner sanctum of many Oxford postmasters since the days of good Queen Victoria. Mr. Pringle's new-found boldness was rewarded with a polite, "Come in," instead of the usual throaty roar of a lion disturbed from his slumber in the heat of the day.

"Pringle," he barked, "Why are you absent from your office and don't give me any of your usual half baked reasons. Speak, man, don't just stand there."

Mr. Pringle stood his ground, for did he not have friends in high places who would swiftly come to his aid. "Sir," he uttered with a deadly calm, "On May the twentieth I shall require to be relieved of my duties for one clear day, in other words I shall require you to furnish me with a relief."

The postmaster ran a loosening finger round his stiff collar which had suddenly become very tight. He had never seen his subordinate so cocky and instead of proceeding with caution, he decided that this jack-a-napes must be put in his place once and for all.

"No!" he roared, "It is not convenient and if I have any more of this intolerable insolence, I shall put in an adverse report about you to Head Office."

"With respect, sir, I think that it would be most unwise for you to adopt such a cavalier attitude to my request." Pringle was mad, he'd always been a bit 'doolally', but he would go along with the imbecile.

"For what reason?" he snapped. Mr. Pringle slowly withdrew the invitation card and placed it on his superior's desk.

"That is one reason," he stated in the same menacing tones. The senior postmaster snatched it up, and read it. While he was thus engaged, Pringle moved in for the kill, saying, "These people are friends of mine and the lady's cousin is Viscount Beldrake who will give her away." Pringle relishing every minute of the situation proceeded, saying, "That same gentleman is a personal friend of Sir Arbuthnot Hickingbotham who, as you are well aware, is the Postmaster General." The senior postmaster of Oxford slumped over his desk, a beaten man; the proverbial pricked balloon. Pringle silently withdrew, very satisfied with his sweet revenge, after all those years of humiliating brow-beating.

Mr. Pringle returned home, head held high; he was a changed man. Entering his office, he opened the safe and extracted an envelope containing one hundred pounds. He took out fifty, went into his private quarters, and handed them to his wife with a demand that she visit Oxford to purchase a suitable dress, hat and shoes as they had been invited to a society wedding. "Where?" she queried.

"Never mind where," he replied testily, "They are friends of mine." Mabel said no more and promised to do as he said.

Chapter 39

Joshua Humphrey left his customers as often as he dared to share with his wife the joys of parenthood. The boy had settled in better than expected and he appeared to be enjoying his new home. One evening, he was leaning forward in his chair with a skein of wool looped over his outstretched hands, helping Hilda to roll it into a ball. Suddenly he looked into her face and said,

"Did the House Father tell you that I was a foundling?" While the startled Hilda pondered a suitable reply, Nicholas continued to enlighten her, telling her that he was found in a cardboard box by carol singers one Christmas Eve.

The nonplussed Hilda countered, "How do you know that, Nicholas?"

"The other boys told me," he asserted.

"That was a very long time ago, Nicholas." Then, swiftly changing the subject she asked, "Do you like it here?"

"Oh, yes," he replied enthusiastically.

"You know, of course, that you can always change your mind within the six months," she reminded him.

"I won't change my mind," he assured her, then after they had resumed the wool winding operation he said, "Do you like me and will you tell the House Father, when he comes, that you want to keep me."

"Most certainly," Hilda assured him, "It would break our hearts if you left us."

"I'm glad!" he said, with a trace of relief in his voice.

When he first came, Joshua feared that he might not sleep well in such strange surroundings, but his wife knew that their adopted son had no such problems as when she entered his bedroom to call him at seven thirty, he was curled up in a deep sleep like a hibernating dormouse.

On Monday morning, Hilda would take him to enrol in the village school. Joshua and his wife were very anxious about how he would be received and treated by the other children and decided to seek the counsel of the headmaster, who was duly requested to call one evening.

He called the next night and after a brief discussion, he was able to allay their fears as he was now forewarned and would also be forearmed. Joshua was very relieved by the headmaster's assurances as Nicholas would be the only boy in the school who was adopted.

Isobel had now rejoined her mother at the post office, who was pleased to see that the excitement and tension in her daughter had evaporated and had been displaced by a calm happiness. Meetings with the vicar had discussed the necessity of tickets for the church ceremony. The vicar was certain that tickets would have to be issued and that a police presence would be desirable. Although only a few places would be required by the Langthornes side, Lance's relatives and friends would be numerous. Lists would have to be compiled and Isobel would ring Mrs. Howard at Cornwall Court to ask if they would provide such a list.

The few remaining days of Isobel's spinsterhood were passing swiftly and she was looking forward to being a good wife to Lance, to loving him and sharing all his joys and sorrows wherever and whenever they might be. She truly believed that fate had directed him that never-to-be-forgotten May morning.

Mrs. Langthorne insisted on her daughter retiring to bed early. She wisely knew that the forthcoming ceremony would impose severe strains on her.

On Wednesday evening, Lance and his brother, Richard, his best man, called at the rectory to place the coronet in the vicar's safe. They then returned to Cornwall Court, avoiding the post office.

Kate had stayed at the rectory overnight, to be on hand to prepare Isobel for the wedding at two o'clock.

The coffee shop would be closed all day to permit the girls to attend. The post office would also be closed.

Nathanael Martindale had been persuaded to take Isobel's car to pick up Mr. and Mrs. Pringle.

Chapter 40

Now the stage was set for the big day, not only for Isobel, but for the whole village. That memorable day, Tillingthorpe was permeated by an atmosphere of happy expectancy, and all those who could be spared from their duties would see the lady from the post office in all her glory as a bride. There was also great excitement in the homes of the little bridesmaids, who too would share the glories of that glorious day, and possibly, evoke as much admiration as the bride from the assembled witnesses.

Isobel, at the insistence of her mother, had eaten a hearty breakfast, and she was now on her way to the rectory, where Kate awaited her. Isobel was given a small glass of brandy to calm the butterflies that flutter in the tummy of every bride.

The church was rapidly filling up; the guests were directed to their allotted places by Martindale, the shepherd, and the smith. They were both big men and their presence alone would serve as a deterrent to those inclined to be obstreperous, and it must be said that not all were satisfied with the arrangements.

The Red Lion was closed all day for the first time in its history. The landlord and his lady had already claimed their privileged seats and Hilda was looking round, wondering about the identity of the assembled gentry.

It was already common knowledge that Viscount Beldrake would give the bride away to the waiting bridegroom. Viscount Beldrake would drop Mrs. Langthorne off at the Lych Gate on his way to pick up Isobel.

At one forty-five precisely, Lance and his best man arrived at the Lych Gate and walked over the red carpet, laid from the gate to the church porch to ensure that Isobel would not stumble, causing the priceless coronet to fall from her head.

Colonel Mackenzie would be waiting to escort Mrs. Langthorne into the church.

The bride would travel in the Rolls with Viscount Beldrake, attended by Kate who sat next to the chauffeur.

The bridesmaids were, at this very moment, on their way to the church. A crowd of villagers lined the edge of the path from the Lych Gate to the porch. The four little girls, who would provide the bride's retinue, had been deposited at the gate and prepared to walk the fifty yards to await the arrival of the bride. With consummate timing, the bride had now arrived and was making her way on the arm of her cousin between the ranks of spectators. There were many audible gasps from the bystanders at the sheer splendour of this vision of beauty. The coronet reflected a thousand scintillating colours. The cloud of white which enveloped the bride in an almost ethereal aura of virginal white accentuated her startling loveliness. Isobel gazed about her, radiantly happy, smiling at the many friends who had come to see her and her alone.

The cluster of bridesmaids in the porch were restless and when they sighted the bride, they began to chatter like a flock of blue-tits, transmitting a warning to the congregation that the bride was about to join them. A few adjustments were made by Kate to the bridal gown, followed by a quick check on the diminutive bridesmaids who were also given their final instructions.

The Viscount was garbed in the same fashion as the waiting groom and his brother, the best man; grey morning coat and striped trousers and all carried grey silk top hats. The gentlemen wore lilac coloured cravats.

The organist, who had played at Kate's wedding, responded to the appropriate signal and broke into the majestic strains of Mendelssohn's 'Wedding March'. The whole assembly made a half-turn to stare, almost in awe, at the small procession approaching the waiting bridegroom. Many sharp intakes of breath could be heard in that throng of people who had come to witness the joining of two people, they knew and loved, in holy wedlock.

The little girls wore mother nature's colours of bluebell blue and primrose yellow as proudly as any strutting herald in his richly emblazoned tabard at a Garter ceremony.

Mr. and Mrs. Howard with their two daughters watched this breath-taking spectacle. Different emotions were reflected in their faces: in the girls total admiration; in Mrs. Howard pride, mingled with complete happiness; but Mr. Howard's face beamed with sheer unadulterated delight. He was a proud man that, while he watched, his thoughts reached back to that day when he had placed the coronet on Isobel's head.

Lance and Richard watched as Isobel drew near; a smile wreathed Lance's expression of adoration, but Richard's mind was in turmoil. Memories of that night in India, of Isobel's ball, the bringing together of the two people he loved most, the night that the regiment learned of their colonel's mysterious death. It all seemed so long ago.

Kate took her place at the end of the front pew reserved for her.

Only one hymn was sung, 'The voice that breathed o'er Eden.'

The vicar was a man of common sense and would not waste time on personal foibles as many parsons do, to satisfy their own preoccupation with ritual. As the vicar proclaimed them man and wife, Kate stepped forward to raise the bride's veil to permit Isobel to slightly tilt her head and present the cupid's bow of her full lips to allow her husband to seal their marriage with the traditional kiss.

After the customary formalities of signing the register had been completed, they returned to the altar to reform the wedding procession and make their exit to the sound of Mendelssohn's 'Spring Song', played by the organist who had certainly excelled himself this happy day.

The bells crashed out a joyous peal as the new bride and groom stepped into the bright sunlight to be greeted by the waiting onlookers.

A photographer had been invited from *The Oxford Herald* in addition to a private photographer.

The smith and Nathanael, the shepherd, reminded people of the village that coaches were waiting to transport them to Cornwall Court, where they would be entertained with a running buffet, housed in a marquee. One marquee had been reserved for them and the other for the estate tenants and workers only. They followed this information with the warning that anyone misbehaving would be evicted from the park.

All the guests close to the two families sat down to a wedding breakfast in the Great Hall: smoked salmon pinwheels, shrimp tartlets, caviar on crisp biscuits, pâté whirls, asparagus rolls, meringues, strawberries and cream. The traditional three tier wedding cake occupied its favoured position at the head of the long table. After the customary speeches, the reading of the many goodwill telegrams, and the cutting of the cake with Mr. Howard's sword, the bridal couple circulated among the guests, and our worthy Mr. Pringle and his lady were not overlooked.

Indeed, Mrs. Pringle was quite overawed by the presence of so many grand people, and when Isobel introduced them to Lance she spontaneously gave a deep curtsey. Things would never be the same again and she realised that her husband must be regarded with the respect due to a man with such aristocratic friends. Even the visits to the Dog Cemetery would be less frequent to permit a full exploitation of this never-to-be-forgotten experience on those occasions when she would entertain the wives of the two senior postmen, whom she had always regarded as her social inferiors. She would, henceforth, address her husband as Mr. Pringle not Archie as was her previous wont.

It should be remembered that Dame Fate would smile on Colonel Mackenzie this day, and so she had guilefully cast her spell and placed the sister of Viscount Beldrake next to him. The Honourable Phillipa Sylvia Beldrake was thirty years of age; a personal assistant in the Foreign Office and had, luckily for the colonel, never married, although she was a very attractive lady. The colonel quickly discovered they had several common interests, light classical music, fly fishing on a good clean trout stream and, naturally, horses. They chatted animatedly throughout the reception and he used the opportunity to inform her that he was on three months leave from his regiment in India. He also said he would be spending a part of his leave at the post office in Tillingthorpe, to enable him to clear up certain matters concerning Mrs. Langthorne's late husband's death.

At the bottom end of the table, our worthy Pringle and his good lady had already drunk in all the atmosphere of the historic Great Hall perfumed by masses of flowers. He felt a warm glow of satisfaction and marvelled that his sub-postmistress would one day be mistress of this great house.

The villagers of Tillingthorpe also stared in awe at the mansion which was the home of the husband of the young girl who had come to their village surrounded by so much conjecture and mystery.

The honeymoon would be spent in Italy, where Lance had rented a villa in Tuscany, complete with servants, for three months.

Isobel's going away outfit was a tailored plum-coloured costume, the jacket having wide lapels. This was worn with a cream silk blouse. At the front and rear of the skirt, two box pleats lined with Cambridge blue gaped as she walked. Isobel wore her new wedding ring and her engagement ring, together with her Rolex wristwatch.

The occupants of the two marquees emerged to wish the happy couple Godspeed. The important guests assembled on the terrace and waved their goodbyes as the Rolls whisked Lance and his new bride away. All would remember this day as one of the outstanding events of their lives.

After the fireworks display, the villagers of Tillingthorpe and the tenants and estate workers were ferried back to their respective homes.

Colonel Mackenzie bade *au revoir* to the Howards and escorted Isobel's mother back to the post office where he would be her guest for the ensuing three days.

Chapter 41

On the Sunday evening, Mr. Howard called a family meeting to resolve the problem of how their new daughter-in-law would address him and his wife. Pater and mater were suggested, but as Isobel was such an affectionate personality, papa and mama should be adopted. Mr. Howard thought that a discreet approach should be made to their son to request him to make a tactful sounding of Isobel's choice. All this must be left in abeyance for at least the next three months, when Lance and his wife would take up residence in a four bedroomed farmhouse on the estate.

The village of Tillingthorpe would talk of the day that they attended the wedding of their village postmistress in the years to come, an event so spectacular that it would never be repeated.

The years were quietly slipping away and Robert, the smith's adopted son, was sixteen years of age and was now being instructed in the skills of making his own tongs, flatters, hammers, and so on. His leisure time he spent riding his New Forest pony around the local countryside. The smith and his wife, Lucy, bought him the pony for his sixteenth birthday as they regarded bicycles as very dangerous. He would also go fishing; he was, in modern parlance, a loner, but also a bright and happy boy.

The lad adopted by the innkeeper and his wife now attended the village school and was doing so well that the headmaster proposed preparing him for a scholarship to Abingdon Grammar School. The Humphreys adored their son and were very proud when the headmaster spoke in such glowing terms of his progress.

Mrs. Langthorne was glad of the colonel's company; it relieved the heartache that she felt in Isobel's absence. The colonel would, after the weekend, go to spend a month with his mother, the daughter of a Scottish marquis. In her widowhood, she had struggled to keep the two thousand acre estate intact for the day when her son would retire from the army, in five years time. During the last month of his leave, he hoped to spend some time with the Honourable Phillipa Beldrake.

Akbar had been unable to attend Isobel's wedding because his discharge papers had not been finalised, but nevertheless, he would bring her a wedding present; a beautifully carved figure of a Bengal Lancer painted in all the authentic colours.

Isobel's Anglo-Indian maid, Janet, accompanied her on her honeymoon and in time became a close companion.

Chapter 42

'Time and Tide wait for no Man' and Tillingthorpe, in the year 1938, was still unaffected by what the modern attitudes describe as progress, which shrewder souls regarded as another name for legalised vandalism. The population had increased, but not enough to warrant the building of new houses. Apart from this, Tillingthorpe was still much as the Langthornes had first seen it in 1933.

Older members of the village, who were now in their early fifties, scanned the headlines of their morning papers apprehensively.

This man, Adolf Hitler, who was he, and where had he come from, and why was he allowed to flout the Versailles Treaty with such impunity? These men knew all about the futility of war, but all agreed that he had to be stopped. They also felt the heart-chilling blast of reality with the realisation that it would be their sons who would have to do the stopping. Would yet another German General refer to the British soldiers as 'lions led by donkeys' and if so, at what cost?

While the journalists and correspondents ruminated on the probability of war, the vicar, Sebastian Erasmus Copplethwaite, was a frequent visitor at the post office and sadly noted a subtle deterioration in Mrs. Langthorne's levels of vitality; she, at times, looked very, very tired. Such was the old gentleman's concern that he decided that it would be prudent if he called on her daughter to inform her of his observations and fears.

It must be borne in mind that our heroine had now been married for three years and was the mother of a little boy named Richard, and a little girl named Sarah Victoria. When the vicar enlightened Isobel of his fears for her mother's health, she thanked him for his kind concern and informed him that she would insist that her mother came to live with them and added, "You know that you are always welcome to visit us."

Problems usually produce other problems and the future of the post office and the coffee shop were not least of the ensuing difficulties.

After lengthy discussions involving Isobel's mother and Lance, it was arranged that Mrs. Langthorne would move in with her daughter on a permanent basis. The tenancy of the post office - with Viscount Beldrake's acquiescence - would be transferred to Mary Griffin, who was now engaged to Timothy, with the proviso that Emily Haynes should be assured of her position as postmistress as long as she desired and a pension fund set up for her. The coffee shop in Oxford should be made over to Jane Turner and her three assistants as equal partners. Mrs. Langthorne would retain a quarter share which would expire with her death. The existing furnishings of the cottage would be shared between Mary Griffin and Emily Haynes.

Isobel had given Tess to Mary when she got married. The young girl and the dog were a familiar sight in the village and occasionally Mary would take Tess for a walk up to Glebe Down to see Nathanael Martindale. These trips were pure delight to Tess, as the shepherd would allow her to run with Nell who would demonstrate to her the art of herding sheep, giving Tess an admonishing nip when she became too boisterous.

The smith still made his nightly visits to The Red Lion where the two old friends would express their mutual fears for their much loved adopted sons should war be declared.

"You know, Joshua, and I know", the smith averred, "that wars are fought to keep the rich richer and the poor poorer, and it's the working class who make all the sacrifices. No, Joshua, if I can keep my lad out of it I will, and I hope you'll do the same."

In the spring of 1939, the paper headlines were openly predicting that war was now inevitable and the government began to call up reserves. The dogs of war had slipped their leash and running with rabid ferocity across the whole of Europe.

In Britain, young men and women rallied to their county regimental standards, and would, in the fullness of time, add to the battle honours embroidered on the colours. Thousands would be killed, even young women manning the ack-ack batteries around cities, or driving buses and ambulances at the height of the Blitz. The British race would not yield to tyrants.

The parents of young men of military age in the village were now feeling deeply apprehensive; many of them could vividly remember the war which had been supposed to have been the war that would end all wars.

Andrew Gilbert who had been, in his younger days, curate to the Reverend Copplethwaite, was now a captain in the Ghurkha Rifles. He had married the sister of a fellow cadet with whom he had become close friends at Sandhurst.

Timothy Devereaux and Mary Griffin, realising that Timothy would be called up, wisely elected to request the vicar to call the Banns and made immediate preparations to marry them. The vicar was a man of the old school and regarded all his flock with a strong paternalistic attitude and if anything pleased him more than a baptism it was, without doubt, a full-blown wedding. Mary made a delightful and pretty bride, with her long fair hair and cornflower blue eyes, and when she walked down the centre aisle on the arm of Timothy, all agreed that they made a handsome couple. A honeymoon could wait they said, as the prospect of being together in their own snug cottage would more than compensate them for this small sacrifice.

The German hordes had already marched into the Sudetenland and were now flooding into Czechoslovakia and Hungary. A final ultimatum had been presented to Hitler that an invasion of Poland would be followed by a declaration of war.

The smith had received a visit from an official of the Ministry of Supply informing him that he, his premises, and his two assistants, would be requisitioned under the Emergency Powers Act. He would be given contracts to forge components for submarines and surface ships. All materials would be provided. The mighty smith was a trifle overawed by the man from the Ministry and so shocked, that he called a halt to all operations in the forge and ordered Frank, his striker, and the boy to follow him into the house.

Hilda was astounded by this unprecedented mass invasion of her kitchen. Before she could raise any objections, the smith told his spouse of the visit of the official and reminded her that a mug of tea and a piece of cake would not come amiss while he gave her further details. After the smith's inner man had been refuelled, Hilda, whose brain had been working at treble its normal speed, enquired what he meant by reserved occupation.

"Well, Robert won't be called up," he replied. Hilda breathed a silent prayer of thanks, for she still had vivid memories of those years when Bill was away during the Great War, when the sight of a telegraph boy in the village would strike cold, stark terror into the hearts of any of the folk who saw him. They would watch his progress through the village with a kind of hypnotic stare, breathing a great sigh of relief when he passed their cottage. This relief was followed by a flood of sympathy for the unfortunate recipient of the missive contained in the belt pouch worn by the youthful bearer of such dreadful tidings, a message which would inform a woman that she was now a widow and that her children no longer had a father. The pink form would simply state that, 'The Secretary of State regrets to inform you that your husband/son has been killed in action', or perhaps, even worse, that he had died of wounds. The mute proof of these awful experiences was inscribed on the war memorial near the church.

In 1943, Timothy Devereaux and Nicholas Humphrey joined the Royal Air Force. After nine months' intensive training, Timothy was posted to the Photographic Reconnaissance Unit at Benson as a sergeant pilot, flying Mosquitos. Nicholas, who had received a better education, was posted to North Africa as a pilot officer, flying Hurricanes.

Lance's brother, Richard, had joined The Queen's Hussars and became a tank commander, being glad to return to a life that he preferred and knew so well as a soldier. Richard's natural father was, at the time of his death, a major in the Indian army. All Richard's forebears had been military men; his grandfather had been a major general in the Queen's Bays.

Lance, his brother, joined his father's old regiment the Grenadier Guards. While Richard trained for the second front, Lance fought in the North Africa Campaign against the famous and gallant German General Rommel.

The good folk of Tillingthorpe settled down with the resilience which is such an inherent characteristic of the people described by Winston Churchill as 'This Island Race'. To suffer and endure.

Akbar, who had served and protected his beloved mistress for so many faithful years, caught pneumonia and died. He was cremated and his ashes were lodged at the mosque in Woking, where the Imam promised to return them to Akbar's native India, after the war. The ashes would be buried in the Military Cemetery in Calcutta.

A stone bearing the legend,

Here lie the remains of a proud Bengal Lancer.

This stone was erected on the orders of Isobel Howard-Coleman,
whom he served and guarded with such
devotion and loyalty from
1930 - 1943.

While the war developed to a hellish crescendo, the people of Tillingthorpe village went about their normal lives comparatively untouched by the events suffered by the cities. For example, most of the cottages still had a pigsty in the garden and weaner pigs – in spite of stringent controls imposed by the Ministry of Food – suddenly and miraculously appeared as residents in these sties. Also, most acquired a few poultry. Many of the local farmers made their own butter and thus with fresh eggs, and occasionally a leg of pork, plus a plentiful supply of potatoes, no one went hungry in Tillingthorpe. The villagers were merely reacting as their forebears had done for centuries; in an emergency, they would close ranks and defend their own.

Lance survived the African Campaign winning the M.C. and D.S.O. at Tobruk and after a brief rest in Cairo, he was to be embroiled in the invasion of Italy. He often received letters from Richard, who was patently in an ebullient mood and enjoying his return to army life to the full. Young men like Richard had built the British Empire and their deeds of valour on battlefields, all over the world, have been recorded in their thousands. But most of all, Lance enjoyed his letters from his beloved Isobel who wrote twice a week. Her letters gave him a detailed report of the children, taking care to include snapshots of them. She had already sent him a leather photograph holder, containing large studio portraits of Sarah and Richard. Every night, in the privacy of his small tent, he would take them out and wonder if he would ever see his lovely wife and children again.

We, who are privy to Fate's plans for him, know that the reunion he craved would materialise in the not too distant future. He would be restored to his family, albeit a trifle the worse for wear.

Mrs. Howard wrote regularly once a week to her sons and prayed every night that they would return to her.

The Eighth army, elated with victory over the formidable Rommel, were poised like a falcon, who has sighted the quarry, and crouches before launching himself into space. In the initial assault at Salerno, Lance was rendered *hors de combat* by a mortar shell which killed one grenadier, shattered Lance's ankle, and laid his face open in a grisly wound extending from his right ear to the corner of his mouth.

Captain Lance Howard-Coleman M.C. D.S.O. Grenadier Guards, would take no further part in the war, and would, by the grace of God, be returned to the arms of his family and the tranquillity of his home, deep in the heart of the English countryside.

While he rested in the peace and security of his home, he enjoyed a visit from his brother, Richard, who was making the most of his two weeks' leave before D Day, when he would take part in the spear-head of the final thrust to destroy the Nazi war machines.

The two men spent most of the time riding and fishing together. They were, unconsciously, reliving their boyhood and Lance would, in the years ahead, recall this period with intense nostalgia and infinite sadness.

The children of the brothers, Richard's twins, together with Lance's children, were having the time of their lives, being utterly spoiled by their adoring grandparents.

One morning, during their rides, Richard turned to his brother, Lance, and said earnestly, "If anything should happen to me and I fail to come home, will you look after my wife and the twins for me?"

"My dear chap," Lance responded, "Nothing like that will happen and you may rest assured, if it did, your request would take precedence over all other duties, so do put such depressing thoughts and apprehensions from your mind." Then to drive away such morose contemplations, he said, "Come, Richard, I will race you to our seat on the hill."

It is said that God's greatest gift to mankind is the inability to foresee the future; and so it would prove to be.

Chapter 43

Richard's two weeks leave passed all too quickly and when he departed he left a cloud of foreboding over his family, especially his sisters, Margaret and Christal, who wondered if they would ever see him again.

The last night at dinner, Richard was his normal entertaining self but Lance was in a thoughtful mood. In the morning, they rose early as Lance was to drive his brother to Oxford station where they would say their final goodbyes. Mercifully, the train arrived promptly and the brothers gripped hands in a sad farewell. Lance watched the train until it disappeared from sight. He felt the need to be alone, somewhere quiet, and drove back into the city, parked his car, and made his way to gardens at the back of Magdalen College where he sat down to compose his troubled thoughts. With a troubled mind and sad heart, he finally made his way back to Cornwall Court and resolved to hide his feelings from his family and above all from Lydia, his brother's wife.

It had been arranged that, for the duration of the war, Isobel and Richard's wife, Lydia, together with their children, would all live at Cornwall Court. Mrs. Howard, in her infinite wisdom, believed that if the unthinkable became reality and one of those dreaded pink envelopes arrived announcing that either or both of her beloved sons had fallen in battle never to return - as thousands of gallant British men had over the centuries - it would be prudent to receive the dreadful news in the security of their home, where all would give their support to a loved one who would be stricken with a grief which would never abate.

Richard had survived the Normandy invasion and enjoyed many miraculous escapes, as the armoured division, in which he served as a tank commander, swept across Europe in a triumphant conquering cavalcade. They were advancing across lush meadowland on the German border, which Intelligence had informed the major in command of the squadron, had been cleared of all resistance. Richard was standing in the turret of his tank, feeling a sense of euphoria at the uneventful advance, when he was struck by a bullet fired by an S.S. sniper. Ironically, the bullet missed and struck the tank on Richard's right flank, ricocheted off, passing through his head killing him instantly.

So, the Angel of Death was on her way to Cornwall Court.

Sam Woodcock, the postman, had served in the first Great War and knew all about the terse pink forms which would inform the recipient that their own private little world had come to an end. Sam handed the telegram to Granville, the butler, with the warning words, "You know, and I know what's in this, so be careful." Granville did know and discreetly decided that he would hand it to Mr. Howard rather than Richard's wife, to whom it was addressed. Granville located Mr. Howard in his study, immediately stating his misgivings. Mr. Howard knew the dreaded news referred to his son, Richard. He requested Granville to summon the family - excluding the children - to the library.

When they were all assembled, Mr. Howard addressed them thus. Turning to his daughter-in-law Lydia, he said,

"My dear, this message was addressed to you, but as it affects all the family I have taken the liberty of reading it to save you the shock of opening it when you were alone." He took the telegram from his pocket and read the following message:

The Secretary of State regrets to inform you that your husband, Captain Richard Billingham, has been killed in action.

The reaction of the family to this cataclysmic news was nil; they were a group of people who, an observer would have thought, had been turned to stone. All had the fixed frozen expression so typical of those who have sustained a shock so mind-numbing that the ensuing paralysis leaves the victim unable to express any emotion or to speak. After quite ten minutes had elapsed, Isobel threw her arms around Richard's widow to give the consolation that only physical contact can bring.

Mr. Howard rose to his feet and requested Granville to serve brandy all round. He swallowed his in one gulp and was relieved to feel the fiery golden liquid relaxing the taut muscles of his throat. He said, "We will never, never, forget Richard and it will take years for us all to come to terms with a grievous loss which affects us all in equal measure. I do not believe that my son would want our future to be blighted by his gallant departure from this mortal life. I now suggest that we all meet again at lunch." The small sad gathering were glad of the opportunity to be alone with their own personal heartbreak.

In the evening, Mr. Howard summoned Lance to his study to discuss the painful decision involved in bringing Richard back or leaving him to be ultimately laid to rest in a Military Cemetery where he would be among his comrades. They decided that after an interval of one week they would have another family conference and allow Lydia, Richard's widow, to make the final decision. Ten days later, all mutually agreed that Richard should be left where he had fallen. Every year, they would all make the pilgrimage to lay a poppy wreath on his grave.

Mrs. Howard agreed to inform Richard's children that their father had made the supreme sacrifice and although he could not return he would live on in the hearts and minds of all who had loved him so dearly.

Chapter 44

In the midst of so much grief and tragedy, seemingly callous decisions have to be made to continue life's normal routine, and the heartache would eventually give way to a suppressed, but ever present sadness. We must, therefore, turn once again to the proud, independent folk of Tillingthorpe.

The husbands and wives lived a natural life untrammelled by the complexities of modern philosophies. Had one questioned the women of the village about their lack of equality, they would have faced the questioner with an uncomprehending stare. There were no inequalities; for were they not man and wife joined in holy matrimony in the parish church? They knew, but never gave it a moment's thought, that they relied on each other for their very existence.

The men of Tillingthorpe loved and respected their wives and were well aware that a good wife was vital to their survival; they would often refer to their wife as a 'pearl beyond price'. It must be remembered that Social Services were non-existent in those hard times. When one of them died, the other soon followed; some say of a broken heart.

Many of the Tillingthorpe women, alarmed by the decline in post-war morals, now hoped that women would be persuaded to return to the mode of life that Nature intended. Many women would pray that, for the sake of all humanity, they would, once again, don the mantle of virtue and modesty and compel men to accord them the respect and protection that is an inborn right of all women.

Does the female of the species really scorn the God-given role as supporter and maker of men? A truly feminine woman is a beautiful and joyous creature to behold. Was it Shelley or Keats who proclaimed the immortal words that 'a thing of beauty is a joy for ever? Lastly some readers would have the temerity to remind all women that Mother Nature had imbued them with a grave and vital responsibility, for deep within their bodies lies the mould which will ensure the continuity of the human race whom we are taught is fashioned in the image of God.

Well, dear friends, before we say a sad farewell to the ancient village of Tillingthorpe, let us take one last peep into the lives of the villagers who - unlike the stereo types of a modern world - were fascinating and sometimes amusing characters in their own right.

Our heroine, Isobel, had a daughter who promised to be as beautiful as her mother; also a son named Richard, who would be a sad reminder of his much loved namesake. He would grow up as closely to his cousin, Lance, as his father and his Uncle Richard had been. The two boys would spend most of their lives at Cornwall Court attending the same prep school and afterwards go to Eton together. Their boyhood would be spent riding, fishing, shooting; and in the course of time they would be shown the secret hideaway.

The smith had become rich through government contracts, but he would return to his pre-war mode of life with his adopted son, Robert, who was now courting Sally Lovelace of Highfield Farm.

Timber Woods had also become rich in the same way as the smith, and had now planned to launch out into shop fittings, for which there was considerable demand. Timothy was now a full partner and turned his back on flying with no regrets, pleased to return to the freedom of civilian life.

After the war, Andrew Gilbert, who it will be remembered, turned his back on the church for a career in the military, was so deeply disturbed by his appalling experiences in Burma, that, with the help of the Reverend Copplethwaite, he was granted the living of Tillingthorpe and now lived in the rectory; the vicar retained a suite of rooms, but lived with Andrew, his wife and two young daughters.

The Reverend Sebastian Erasmus Copplethwaite spent much of his time as a guest of Lance and Isobel, who were touched by his devotion to Mrs. Langthorne. On fine days, he would push her wheelchair on to the terrace and talk or read to her.

The village shop had increased its trade fourfold, permitting Timothy's wife, Mary, to employ another girl. Emily Haynes had retired as postmistress and lived alone now that her grandfather had passed on.

Joshua and his wife, Hilda, were overjoyed to get their adopted son, Nicholas, back from South Africa, where he had been drafted to operate as a flying instructor. Nicholas was a very astute young man and while away in the war, had formulated ambitious plans for The Red Lion. He hoped to buy the freehold from the Beldrakes. He would refurbish the inn, taking care to leave its quaint interior and mellow exterior intact. He was well aware of the opportunities to take advantage of the increasing car ownership which would bring trade for his scheme to introduce traditional English food in the restaurant, which would be established in one of the many unused rooms on the ground floor. The large open fire grate and the massive oak beams in the ceiling would make a congenial and rustic environment for the patrons.

When Joshua and Hilda retired, the licence was transferred to their son, Nicholas; the narrow board over the door proclaiming to all who entered that the licensee was one, Nicholas Humphrey. Joshua would often look up to read the inscription with pride and some relief that the name board would not, as he had once feared, display a name other than his own.

Bert Wilson, the wheelwright, had not enjoyed the prosperity of his old friends and the declining demands for his ancient craft were now virtually non-existent, but like his stalwart forebears, he was not a man to sit down wringing his hands in a welter of anguish and self pity. He now produced quarter size models of haywains and tipper carts for museums, and in the process, enjoyed a comfortable living for himself and his wife, Violet.

Our good ladies, who played such a prominent role in the opening chapters and gave spice to our story, were now vigorously campaigning to raise funds to keep the church of St. Botolph's in good repair; after all, the Norman church was inextricably interwoven in the lives of the inhabitants of Tillingthorpe since shortly after the conquest of 1066. It had more than earned its right to a few more centuries of existence.

Viscount Beldrake served in the famous Royal Berkshire Regiment throughout the war as liaison officer to General Eisenhower. He had travelled extensively in Europe before the war and had a unique expertise in reading contour maps. He was also fluent in French with a smattering of German. He would emerge from the conflict unscathed and marry Christal Howard.

Colonel Mackenzie married Viscount Beldrake's sister, the Honourable Phillipa Sylvia Beldrake, after a whirlwind courtship, and shortly afterwards retired to his small estate in Scotland where he supplemented his army pension by entertaining paying guests for salmon fishing and deer stalking.

Margaret Howard, the most talented of Lance's two sisters, married a member of an impoverished land-owning family and was devoted to her adoring husband.

Nathanael Martindale took over as bailiff on the Beldrake estate as Septimus Reeve had retired. Food production was of paramount importance and some people in government were mindful of the profoundly wise utterance of Napoleon who once remarked that 'an army marches on its stomach'. Nathanael chose a girl from the Women's Land army to train as a shepherdess. He provided her with a dog, one of Nell's descendants, instructing her in the commands which would enable her to communicate with the dog, who, Nathanael assured her, would know more about herding sheep than she would ever learn.

Our Mr. Pringle, who was so proud of his friends in high places, covered himself with glory during the solitary bombing raid on the works at Cowley. As Senior A.R.P. Warden, he crawled into the twisted iron work and fallen masonry, to lead a doctor to a badly injured casualty, knowing that they could be crushed to death at any moment. When he was summoned to Buckingham Palace to receive the George Medal from the King, an equerry read out the citation as follows:

Archibald Pringle, Esquire,
on the night of the 22nd. October, 1941, displayed courage of the highest order in that he did, without regard for his own life, enter the piles of masonry to guide a doctor to a severely injured casualty.

Mrs. Pringle now realised that she was indeed fortunate to possess a husband who not only had friends in high places - whom she had seen with her own eyes - but also had been decorated for bravery by King George the sixth.

True to her promise, Isobel phoned Sotheby's to call and discuss the valuation and sale of the ring. The chief auctioneer, in charge of jewellery, was very impressed with the quality of the ruby, but also agreed with Mr. Howard's opinion that the ring had important historical associations. He was a very astute man and decided to invite the opinion of a famous Indian archaeologist who promptly identified it as the ring depicted on the finger of Genghis Khan in certain mosaics and wall paintings in the Northern Province.

It was subsequently sold to the Indian Ambassador in London for fifteen thousand pounds. This money was transferred to an investment account at compound interest for ten years and would, thereafter, be set up as a trust fund to supplement the small pension paid to troopers and non-commissioned ranks of the Bengal Lancers.

We must not turn away without recalling Tess, the granddaughter of Caleb's dog Nell, who the reader may remember was buried up on Glebe Down. She no longer slept on Mary's bed, but in a basket at the foot of the bed, as Timothy had now returned to his young wife and would naturally sleep in his rightful place at Mary's side.

Well, my dear friends, we have been permitted to share the joys and sorrows of the good folk of Tillingthorpe. In peace and war we have been privy to their hopes, fears and doubts. The quaint attitudes and mode of expression have made us laugh, but to me they are the 'salt of the earth'.

I walked slowly down the lane with a heavy heart and as I came to the bend in the road, I turned to feast my eyes, for the last time, on the village of Tillingthorpe and its sturdy Norman church, whose tower had provided one of the hundreds of beacons warning the inhabitants of England of the approaching Armada from Spain.